"The sailing passages bring forth the power and agility of the
Baltimore privateers and the bold confidence of their handlers.
Captain Tom Boyle had to be a master of sailing to elude the
Royal Navy, so effective at privateering that England put a
price on his head. *Banners* is a vividly imagined exploration of
early American nationhood."

Captain Jan C. Miles

Master, the Pride of Baltimore II

Banners
by Diane Carey

© Copyright 2014 Diane Carey

ISBN 978-1-938467-95-0

Published by
◤ köehlerbooks ™

210 60th Street
Virginia Beach, VA 23451
212-574-7939
www.koehlerbooks.com

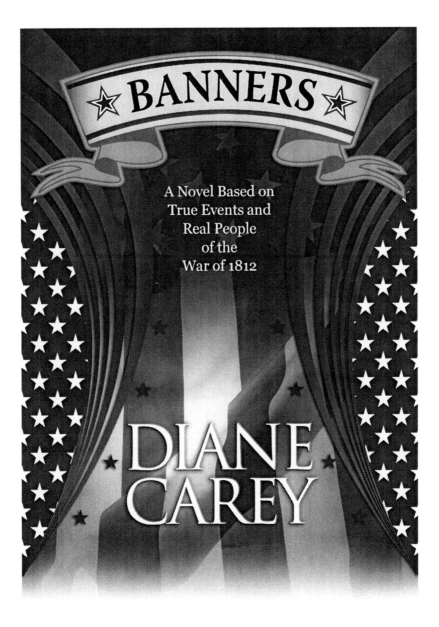

☆ BANNERS ☆

A Novel Based on
True Events and
Real People
of the
War of 1812

DIANE
CAREY

VIRGINIA BEACH
CAPE CHARLES

Revere not this bit of cloth, but revere its message.

Protect not its fibers, but its foresight.

Live not in its shadow, but in its gleam.

1811

EMISSARY OF PRINCES IMMEMORIAL

The West Indies

"SIR, CAN YOU SEE?"

The sky had died. Caped in fog, the Brig *Helen* scratched through paraffin seas. Not a wave cut across her bow. The water was glass. The world colorless.

A young commander trembled inside his Royal Navy jacket as if he were wearing a ghost's coat. He yearned to brush the wrinkles from his woolen sleeves, but such a gesture would communicate his doubts to the crew. They were watching him. These were baneful days.

"Can you see?" his first mate called.

The young commander had no answer, and could not see.

The fog had the character of metal shavings, gray, coarse and moving, twisting like an animal, and high, perhaps three hundred feet high, unnavigable except by instinct and a few tricks of the trade. All hands were to quarters, and the larboard rail was lined with men, crouching, hunched, squinting into the fog, listening, yet there was no human sound. There was only the soft flap of the English Royal Standard high overhead, starved for breeze, and the moan of leather fittings where the yards met the masts. The order of the hour was silence, the silence of a prowling hunter. James E. Gordon of His Majesty's Royal Navy blinked up at the standard, high on the main t'gallant masthead, displaying the distinguished lineage of this ship, but he could not divine more than a soggy streak of red, white, and blue, as if the great flag had been reduced to a hem. All that the flag declared was lost to the flat air and fog.

Pressing both hands to the moist wood of the larboard rail, he leaned out over the water. He squinted at an imaginary horizon and canted his head. If he could not see, he would at least listen. He pressed his hollow belly against the rail and damned the fog. *Let me see.*

As if he had not heard his first lieutenant's question, he spoke to the waxy sea. "The lawless American. I smell his boiling blood."

A shipmaster of the Navy should be able to turn a back on his crew, but such luxury was not afforded Gordon. On the open ocean, each man's life depended upon the next, and all knew it. Collusion offered no gain when the seas rolled and the spray bit. But this was not the open ocean. This was the West Indies, where island shores romanced conspiracy, where even Gordon's salt-crusted first lieutenant became shifty and muttering.

Creases bracketed young Gordon's mouth, creases which had not been there when he first took the *Helen*'s deck four months ago. His thick Black Irish hair, his mother's pride, had gone dull and gritty. Drawn back in a queue that fell stiff and filthy between his shoulder blades, it was bound by a red velvet ribbon she had given him when he attained his first command. Blessed be that she could not see him here. Lady Gordon would unsettle at her son's condition. He thought of her, sitting in the family country house in Ireland, tutoring him and his brothers to keep the King's English and avoid an Irish accent, the irony of which was lost on her young Jamie as he rode his pony across the jeweled hills, falling in love with the land and even some of the people.

Damn the fog ... I don't like fog.

Gordon squinted at the bowsprit and scouted the water. There was forward progress, but only the kind that comes from current and possibly a knot of wind or less. From here on the quarterdeck, aft of everything, the best way to sense faint movement was to project his gaze forward, all the way to the sprit, and beyond to the jib-boom spearing outward before the vessel like a giant insect's feeler. The jib-boom carried the headsails well out over the water, a dynamic sight which today was veiled by mist. He shifted his eyes slightly to starboard of the foremast, let them fall out of focus, and waited to see whether the bowsprit would come to meet his line of sight, showing there was some movement.

Befallen by a sudden foulness in the air, Gordon choked and brought a hand to his mouth. Speaking into his palm, he rasped, "Moycroft, please God that's not our bilge ..."

First Officer Angus Moycroft's cheeks puffed out as he stifled his own gagging. Up and down the larboard rail the crewmen balked and grimaced. To their credit, only a few small chokes caused any disruption to the order of silence. Moycroft somehow managed to lean closer to Gordon without coming too near. "Came when the breeze shifted, sir," he whispered, gazing up at the weather gauge, which ruffled without enthusiasm on the mizzen topmast. "Southeast by east now."

Gordon's stomach crumpled. "More like south by sick house."

"Might be a dead whale floating by, sir."

"I think he vomited before he died." Nauseated, Gordon turned from the odor as if it wouldn't follow him. As he turned, four men crowding the quarterdeck ladder abruptly ceased shifting about and stood perfectly still, staring up at him. Two jumps away.

Breaking his own order, he sharply said, "Moycroft, what are those men doing abaft of the main? I have my pistol!"

His voice cracked. They hadn't possessed sufficient drinking water in a month. Even the green horror in the scuttlebutts had been niggardly rationed. The moment he gave that rationing order, he began seriously fearing for his life. Nine days now. Most of his crew believed Gordon lingered on the quarterdeck because of command devotion or superhuman will, but like clairvoyance he possessed neither. Exhaustion ruined the youth in his eyes. Distrust had soured his heart.

Moycroft scowled and, uncharacteristically, did not respond. Was his annoyance for the hellish stink or for Gordon's comment about the pistol? The archetypical first officer was devoid of personality and impervious to insult, concerned only with the ship, mindless of any human being on earth including himself, and utterly humorless. He could sleep in the fighting tops if he slept at all, had more oakum in his veins than blood, and his feet had spent more days with decks under them than solid ground. He had no finesse, no subtlety, was unburdened by devotion, and boggled by his young commander's intuitions.

"Forward of the main, you cockroaches, if you've no duty here." Moycroft spoke quietly, but with a snap of his fingers. "Give the command some breathing room!"

Moycroft's tone pretended that Gordon had nothing to fear from him, which was not true. The stocky, muscular mate had been a professional boxer on Liverpool's smarmy docks. Moycroft had no memory of mother's knee, hearth, or home. It's as if he were dropped at the age of four aboard a ship, with a bucket in his little puffy hands. To him, there was no earth, no street, home port, or bed. He had never slept upon a mattress. Only hammocks. He enjoyed more real power aboard than Gordon, who with his aristocratic past had no such leavening upon which to call. But for the loaded pistol stuck in his belt and the tattered gold braid upon his shoulder, he held little influence over this crew. They had their secret code of action—*never let him go unobserved.*

Would the mood improve if he bribed them? Promised them shore leave on some fruitful island, in spite of the risk? A few days of relief—

No. That was William Bligh's mistake. The taste of forbidden fruit.

The breeze was barely firm enough to push the brig forward, but she was indeed moving. Two knots, perhaps three with a good pinch of the wheel. Enough to maneuver, to hunt. The smallest two-master in the Royal Navy, the *Helen* was fit for these shallow Caribbean waters, with a draft at the sternpost of only six feet. She could skulk into narrow coves and scratch over the eternal sandbars, yet she could turn a fair broadside of six-pounder guns on pirates or blockade-runners. If she could find them.

This single ship was the entire blockade in these waters,

the lone presence of the English blockade, and Gordon was her brain. With her two good masts and her shallow draft, she was the guardian of the Indies. The deckhands were her arms and legs, the officers her pumping heart. Together they should be one body, but Gordon simply could not trust them. He had failed to divine whom among them he could depend upon, and thus ultimately he trusted none. Those islands beyond the cinder-gray fog, those tropical beaches bowered by fruit trees, those jungle ponds of fresh water beckoned too temptingly the scrawny, ill-fed, sick, and parched men aboard a British ship in these terrible times. He both feared and pitied them. They had little reason to care about their mission here. Even the willing ones were ill, sluggish at best. How many had cousins in the United States and saw no reason to wrangle with the outlaw nation? They could easily mutiny, become pirates or privateers, and cast their lot with the lawless for better food and higher pay. After the *Bounty*, all captains slept with one eye open. If Gordon and his fellow commanders did not hold the barrier high, history would record in its diary the year 1810 as the ruinous and unstopped Age of Napoleon.

But those pages were not yet struck to paper. The hand of history was stayed, and waiting.

A flicker in the fog jolted him. He blinked. Had he seen a brief brown slash with a wink of yellow?

"I see it!" he rasped. "Starboard, Ramsay!"

Three steps away on the raised quarterdeck, fifteen-year-old helmsman Isaac Ramsay flinched like a bird and cranked the stiff wheel over.

"Repeat your order, Ramsay," Moycroft said with irritation.

"St-starboard, aye." Ramsay put his foot on a pin to press the wheel over.

Nothing happened. The wheel was over, but nothing changed. Gordon squinted forward again to see if there was movement.

Aware of the deck beneath his feet, he felt no movement to the side ... only a wobble of impending change. Too slow.

"Chills the blood," Moycroft commented. "The Yank's handier in these daft airs."

Gordon bristled beneath his coat. The American ship was made of oak and fittings and line, same as any ship, but disappeared as if made of vapor. A wink, and fog again. He had heard of these birdlike Baltimore rigs, but he had never seen one.

This had been going on for nine hours. With the American near enough to hear, to spit upon, he had not seen his enemy yet. They had spied bits of the American ship four times, but only in flashes—a wink of sail, a swinging gaff, a shrouded phantom, a murmur on the water. Only the configuration of the islands and sandbars had prevented the American from simply sliding away in her chosen direction, forcing the cat-and-mouse operation to maneuver through known and charted thoroughfares.

But even that would end. The islands would give way to the open sea, and Americans' favor would be lost.

Gordon parted his lips to speak his thoughts, but drew back. Better not confide too much to too many, a difficult style for a young officer who had not long ago been a privileged but timid boy. Command had aged him, set him apart. Stress and starvation made his men unscrupulous. For weakness of the flesh, he could not blame them, but was not a man measured by more hallowed things?

Holding his eyes out of focus made him dizzy. He grasped a deadeye for support. The heavily tarred shroud cables shot upward from his hand to support the main mast. In days gone by, those shrouds had been so numerous as to earn their name by blurring the view of a ship's mast. Today they were stronger and fewer, but still carried their cryptic name. Gordon looked up at them as if beseeching their counsel, but the shrouds pierced the cottony fog and disappeared even before he could see the futtocks at the topmast fittings. Linked by the ratlines spaced just far enough above each other to allow a man to take a step up, the shrouds seemed like a ladder to the heavens beckoning Gordon to simply climb them out of all this.

He squinted into the fog, forward, but could barely see the *Helen*'s bowsprit or her headsails, great fifty-foot sickles of canvas licking at meager airs. The sails were no more than ghosts.

There was commotion at the lookout. The crew pushed off the larboard rail and pattered athwartships on their leathery feet to the starboard side, as if the deck had tipped and rolled them there like marbles.

"What's this?" Gordon demanded. No one responded. Only

then did he realize his own order was keeping him ignorant. None dared answer him.

Moycroft clambered down and plowed forward, elbowing through the filthy knot of men, met the lookout and engaged in a confusion of pointing and whispering. After a moment, he came scurrying back to Gordon. "Something afloat, sir, fine on the starboard bow. Coming right for us."

"Is it the dead whale?" Gordon leaned over the rail, almost unbalancing himself. Something in the water.

He strained to make out a sodden shape moving slowly toward him, scratching along the ship's planks. He heard the bump on the ship's hull before he saw a mass come scratching along the tumblehome, a sodden bundle the color of wheat.

Young Ramsay craned over the wheel spokes. "Maybe it's a horse carcass! There's the hoodoo in these waters! Maybe it won't have a head!"

Moycroft already had the boathook off-board, poking toward the mass.

Gordon parted his dry lips. "Well?"

"A bale of cotton, sir," Moycroft struggled to remain quiet, and to keep from splashing or knocking the side of the ship with the boathook.

Slowly sinking, the mass dragged on the boathook so heavily that two other men came to help Moycroft hold it.

"Cotton ..." Gordon pondered. "How long would it take seawater to saturate a mass that size?"

"No idea, sir."

"Have you no estimate, Moycroft?"

"Eh ... maybe a quarter-hour, sir?"

The guess was not much help.

"Seems he jettisoned his cargo," Moycroft quickly added, covering the fact that he had provided a useless answer to an impossible question.

Gordon fidgeted and scratched his sweaty cheek. "Why would he do that in a cloaking fog?"

Again having no answer, this time Moycroft said nothing.

Gordon turned to Ramsay. "What is the projected course back from that bale?"

The helmsman blinked, confused, then said, "North by

northeast, sir."

"Take that course."

The bowsprit dipped, very slightly. The deck went down, perhaps two inches under his left foot, rose under his right in a rocking motion. He flexed his knees and waited to feel another clue.

A brief *boomph* erupted from somewhere in the fog—a sound recognized by every man aboard. Gordon flinched, waiting for the shock of a musket ball between his shoulder blades. He heard only a brief echo of the sound they'd just heard.

"Firing on us!" Moycroft spat in the direction of the gunshot. "They're due north!"

Caught up in the action, Ramsay began to turn the wheel.

Once Gordon realized that he had not yet been assassinated, he quickly said, "No, belay that!"

"But that was a gunshot, sir!" Moycroft said. "We should adjust toward it!"

"Didn't you listen?"

"But the direction ..."

Gordon held up a hand, feeling for a breeze. The direction. The direction—

"Turn the ship," he began, and paused to think. "Turn the ship ... northeast."

"Sir? That shot—"

"Do it or I'll nail your toes to the garboard strake!"

Moycroft nodded at Ramsay, who then hauled the huge wooden tiller against the current running beneath the keel.

"The sound was wrong," Gordon uttered. "And there was no splash. It was no long gun, no carronade—"

"A swivel gun?" Moycroft asked.

Gordon made a short nod. "One bale does not make a cargo and one shot is no broadside. Turn the ship northeast, quickly!"

Moycroft glanced at Gordon uneasily and finally spoke down to the sailing master. "Trim for this course."

"Trim for northeast, aye," the sailing master called back.

"Keep your voices down." Gordon leaned over the rail and cupped a hand to his ear, facing due west.

The sailing master cast him a squinty glare, then turned to the sail handlers and somehow shouted without shouting.

"Hands to braces, boys!"

Deckhands scrambled to the belaying pins where the braces and sheets were made off. The ship had no need to tack about, but only to adjust her heading, thus the men on the working braces and sheets on each of *Helen*'s two masts hauled in and the men on the opposite braces and sheets eased out their lines, each man eying the sail for which he was responsible. Each of the dirty yellowed square sails took four men, two on braces and two on sheets, pivoting the yards around till the wind was behind the sail, when the sailing master gave a "That's well!"

Once the *Helen*'s sails were braced to the new course, the ship seemed to know what Gordon was after and made a noble bob forward.

"Do as I say with precision," he murmured to Moycroft. "No responses to orders. This is an inexact science ..."

Moycroft frowned and looked down from the quarterdeck to the crew. "Stand by your positions. Keep quiet. 'Vast responding. Send the word forward."

Perplexed, the word of stand-by and silence murmured its way to the bow. The unexpected result was that all the men turned, even while manning their lines, canted their ears and eyes to their captain, the unsure young officer pretending omniscience.

With some effort he managed to separate the creak of his own ship's spars and the flap of her sails from other sounds out on the ocean ... the rumble of other voices, the snap of other commands, the click of a block as a sheet was drawn inward, out there, somewhere, on the water.

"Better east," he snapped.

"Better—" Ramsay clamped his mouth shut, recalling a bit late the command for no responses.

The ship reacted poorly in the soft water and swiveled against the current, which flooded around some island behind them that they could not see, and changed the course of the water's flow. Gordon continued listening and a moment later said, "East by north."

And half a minute later—

The bow bobbed like a cobra's head. Every few seconds he whispered a new correction, hoping his ears were not as exhausted as the rest of his body. The putrid odor continued to puff across the deck with every faltering bit of breeze that ruffled the fog, overlying the pervasive scent of oiled hemp and tar that floated along with every ship everywhere. Each ship carried its own scent, personal to her own cargo, her captain's whims of construction and maintenance, and any new science that came along.

"Sir, we're moving away from them, is my reckoning," Moycroft attempted. "The sound was over there."

"As was the course of the cotton," Ramsay agreed.

Gordon's eyes shifted, but he continued to scan the fog and ignored the men's challenge. Was Ramsay helping him discover their enemy or diminishing him in Moycroft's eyes?

His legs throbbed against the rail with sheer tension. He leaned so far out that Moycroft or Ramsay might easily knock him overboard and be done with him once and for all.

When they did not take their advantage, he thought them cowards, for he knew their wishes. Once a man knows his own wishes—

"There!" The cry bolted from his throat.

He saw only a sliver of the American ship's stern, low to the water's surface. Then the fog parted better and he saw a confident hand on the slackened main sheet. One man in particular turned fully to Gordon and the two looked in raw awareness at each other. Envy flared up in Gordon's chest that the other captain could stand with his helmsman behind him without fearing having his brains bashed out.

The American captain was dark-haired too, but his hair was brown while Gordon's was nearly black. He wore tidy whiskers down the sides of his face to the level of his mouth, as if to frame his commands when he spoke. Otherwise he was clean-shaven and rosy-cheeked, wearing a clean white shirt, a black day coat, and an impertinent neckerchief of Brittany blue.

The stealthy American smiled at Gordon, wickedly, as might a leprechaun about to hide gold.

Balls of fog rolled between them and the American ship disappeared again. Gordon pressed his legs against the rail as if to push the *Helen* onward. "Larboard better."

"Larboard better, sir."

He hated Ramsay's voice. If only he could take the wheel himself!

"Adjust the trim as needed, Mr. Moycroft. Go ahead and shout."

Moycroft shot him an ugly glance. "Brace to this course!"

Amidships, the sailing master called back, "Brace over, aye!"

Gordon sensed the sloop's turning, but with the fog obscuring his view of the bow he could no more than assume the movement. He also sensed the men's irritation at his strange commands.

A nervous flutter ran around the wall of his stomach. He was going on instinct and a guess, walking on the edge between the respect of his men and their ridicule. From morning to morning, he never knew which would play out the day.

As if they had floated through a doorway, the wall of mist thinned quite suddenly. Now the fog was only a sheet of gauze between Gordon and the world. He could make out the deck of the American ship.

"There you are," he murmured. "*There* you are ..."

Thicker fog still hovered over the American's topmasts and sails, but he could see the American captain standing on his afterdeck as if deliberately striking a storied pose for Gordon's torment.

"Strike, I tell you!" Gordon shouted at the American captain, but his words were snatched away by a short gust of breeze.

The other captain raised his hand to wave at the British pursuers.

No, not a wave. The American lost his balance, wobbled, nearly fell overboard of his own stern. His smile disappeared. Two men snatched out and caught him back from where he seemed to hover above the water, and the Yankee ship broke into chaos.

"What's happening to'm?" Ramsay uttered.

Shouts came now from the American ship, muffled orders and responses, confused, angry, frantic. Fog clouded the view again, then again thinned enough for Gordon to see the schooner's captain was bent at the waste over the port rail, peering down into the water. Reflection? Sharks?

Yes—the sky was changing. He had no need for a barometer

to know the weather was turning squally. This air made no secrets.

He could see the American ship from stern to midships now,
and his own vessel to the tip of the sprit and the all the way up
the masts to the fore t'gallant.

"Sandbar!" Moycroft choked. "By the king, they're stuck!"

And that was the only fate that could put this moment into
the hands of the British. Both gratified and petrified, Gordon
watched the Americans and they watched him. Suddenly enough
sun burned through to see the ring of brownish tint in the water
just under the American ship, and the bluer water around that,
as if the sea bottom had put up a thumb to hold the Americans
in place.

"Moycroft, brace over and trice up," Gordon said quickly.

Moycroft whirled around and shouted, "Braces and clews!
Dump the jibs!"

The crew scrambled like bees with a purpose. Men ran to
the foredeck and unmade the jib sheets. Immediately the giant
triangular headsails spilled their air and began whipping like
angry horses. The men held those sheets, but did not pass the
jibs to the other side, letting them instead flap in protest.

"Trice the courses!" Moycroft shouted. But the sailing master and his hands had already figured out that the ship was to
be stopped of her forward way and they were ready. The outside
bottom points of the lower square sails crawled upward, letting
the sails dump air and hang instead like laundry. The *Helen* was
a quick ship and hard to stop, but with her sails like this she
suddenly washed to a near-stop and bobbed slowly, abeam of
the Americans.

"Keep us a half-cable's length away from them," Gordon
said. "Ready a boat."

"I'm sure we can draw up close, sir, if that sandbar's shaped
right."

"Half a length!" Gordon snapped.

Moycroft hesitated, then gave the only acceptable response.
"Aye, sir. If they choose to fire?"

"Would you fire on a Royal Navy brig while you're ground-
ed?"

Moycroft fell silent. His giant single eyebrow went up on

both ends.

Gordon croaked, "Give me the half-length while we still have a mist about us. Keep them under our starboard guns. Keep the gun crews very visible."

"Aye, sir. Hands to the starboard guns!"

As Moycroft began barking orders, Gordon shivered with relief that he wasn't compelled to entertain questions, thanks to Royal Navy protocol. The men might wonder why he would not come alongside the Americans, where the size of the frigate alone would inflict intimidation, but he was not obliged to tell them.

Now as the fog grew still thinner, out on the water they could see a little dory boat with a swivel gun mounted upon its bow, from which obviously the bale of cotton had been jettisoned. So there was the attempted trick. James Gordon's stomach hardened at the lack of congratulations from his own men. There was no cheer of victory, no word of good work from his officers. He had just performed a miracle of instinct, turning away from the obvious direction of the gunshot and the drift of the cotton bale, and he had won.

He shook off the insult of silence.

Was half a cable's length enough? Would three hundred feet blur the frayed splices, the shabby lines, the scratched chainwales, the halfpenny repairs, the hollow-cheeked crew or their diminished numbers? Nine more dead since Sunday.

"Mr. Moycroft, be wary." Gordon turned at random to one of the nearest midshipman who lingered on the main deck. "Mr. Hennessy, you will accompany me. As soon as we're aboard, find the manifest. I want to know what she's carrying besides cotton."

"Yes, sir. Might be cotton alone, sir."

"Why do you think so?"

"Grain, lumber, wood or ironwares would ride her lower in the water."

"Just find the manifest. And keep away from me."

He put his hand upon his pistol. Andrew Hennessy, younger by three years and twice heavier than Gordon, could easily knock his commanding officer over the side and claim an accident. All the men would see, of course, but who would defend Gordon?

The American pirates were aground on a sandbar, and within a few minutes four men were rowing Lieutenant Gordon in his gig toward the American ship.

Gordon wished he could do the rowing rather than just sit. The American captain hadn't made a mistake—Gordon might've felt better if he had. The sandbar had been hidden by the fog. Now he could see it, a sugary tan smudge in the pearly water. For the first time he got a good look at the notorious Yankee rig, that infamous Baltimore design whose most prominent characteristic was the rake of her masts. The two giant timbers seemed too tall for the low-lying yellow hull, and were stepped at such a tilt that they seemed to be blown backward.

The American vessel's hull was narrow and sharp. Her bowsprit made a natural extension of the shearline, as if the ship were a swordsman's arm and the sprit his rapier. The schooner's huge trapezoid sails were strung between horizontal spars running fore and aft. Enormous blades of headsails speared one over the other well out over the water, larger than the frigate's headsails and more sharply cut. High in the sky flew a triangular topsail on the foretopmast, probably used to pivot the schooner in light following airs. Aft, the main boom extended far out over the water, carrying the sail plan beyond the ship's stern. Her captain snapped orders to tune the rig in a way that might press the ship off the sandbar. He'd still bear off if he could, Royal guns or not. He was still trying to get away.

Better take care of that.

Gordon cupped his hand to his mouth. "Spill air, captain, or I shall order a broadside!"

The American captain's blue eyes met Gordon's brown ones. After a moment's consideration, the other man waved a hand at his own crew without speaking a single word.

The American crew reluctantly eased their sheets. Blocks and sheaves clattered softly as they fell to the deck. The booms and gaffs floated out over the water in relaxed posture. The sails gave up their air, which poured out across Gordon's face like a bad woman's breath. The schooner made a slight moan as strain fell away, then relaxed and accepted her predicament on the sandbar, under the muzzles of *Helen*'s guns.

Was there no one whose counsel he could trust? There were

four other men in this boat, yet he dared not but sit in the stern rather than move forward to meet his foe and put his back to his own men. Strange to think ... in moments he would be aboard the American ship and be safer there than aboard his own brig.

Only when the gig bumped the schooner's yellow tumble-home did he stand and allow himself a moment with his men behind him. He scanned the hull—no name board, no identification but the United States' ensign quietly flicking on the stern. The defiant Stars and Stripes made big motions in the heavy air, not hanging, but not exactly flying.

That flag. That sassy flag.

He looked between the gig and the schooner into the crystal water, down at the brown water where the sandy bottom held the American keel between its fingers. He knew the sight of pure fortune—nothing else could have given him this prize.

Taking his life in his hands for the tenth time today, he put his foot over the *Helen*'s rail and climbed over the side.

The Americans

THE SCHOONER'S VARNISHED RAIL was cool to his touch as James Gordon pulled himself aboard. He tottered briefly in imbalance, then clumsily discovered the fir deck. Everyone was watching him. Every man on two ships.

The silent and quick Hennessy arrived immediately and thumped down the nearest companionway as if he knew his way around. Despite his bulk, the midshipman was light on his toes and comfortable in the cramped quarters of a ship. The two of them stood now on the deck of the Yankee schooner, before an audience of rebels, scoundrels and deserters.

Gordon scanned the American crew. Their cheeks were rosy, their eyes free of jaundice, their lips moist and hair clean. There was not a hint of scurvy. How boastful, in its way. There were all manner of men here, with a harmony of skills that came from willing participation. Their faces spoke of a dozen ethnic roots—German, Swedish, Dutch, French, Celtic, Negro, and of course English.

And there was the captain, mere steps from Gordon. The blue neckerchief flipped against his neatly whiskered jaw.

"Welcome aboard," the captain said. His voice was intellectual, his diction commendable, his accent decidedly Northern.

Suddenly Gordon felt hot inside his wool jacket. The tropical sun disclosed itself through the dispersing fog and beat upon his shoulders. God, but these latitudes were despicable. Not only must their siren call threaten his command, but he must sweat in his uniform. The indignity.

He drew a breath to clear his head.

"I am Lieutenant James Edgar Gordon of His Majesty's Royal Navy. You are defying the Crown's legitimate wartime blockade of hostile ports."

Dry throat.

The American captain said nothing.

Gordon ignored the slight. "I almost didn't find you, Captain. Your distraction nearly worked."

"Distraction?"

"You have no yawl boat aboard. Your boat is out there, in the water somewhere, dumping flotsam and firing a signal gun, pretending to be big. You are an intriguer, sir."

Hennessy thumped up from the aft hatch and handed Gordon a clutch of papers in a leather pouch. Gordon opened it and rifled the papers. It was the cargo manifest.

"The *Comet*," he began slowly. "And it seems you're carrying dangerous cargo."

In an oddly friendly manner, the American asked, "Are you endangered by baled cotton?"

The schooner's crew broke into laughter at Gordon's expense.

His dry lips pulled at each other. "Cotton, for wadding to tamp into French guns."

"Perhaps, if we were carrying saltpetre or gunpowder. Cotton is not contraband, Mr. Gordon. Would you deny natural trade with our island neighbors?"

"There is a blockade of America, sir. There is war."

"America is not at war, sir."

"What difference does America make to the world?"

Gordon did not dare look up from the papers in his hands. The men were all looking at him, but for different reasons.

The other captain asked, "Is Britain so uncivilized as to deny us a means of prosperity?"

"Britain civilized the seas, Captain," Gordon quickly corrected. "If not for us, there would be no trade at all. Pirates would roam unchecked. You Americans stomp and whine, all the while making profits upon the waters. Who patrolled those waters and spilled the blood and cleared out the pirates—"

"Britain has been stifling our commerce since 1787, Lieutenant," the captain said. "The sea is the common highway of all nations. The United States have the right to free trade."

Gordon looked up from the manifests. "Is that how you justify smuggling?"

"What do you expect when Britain blockades our waters?"

"People cannot be controlled on land," Gordon said. "The sea is the key to the land. We know we must control it."

"You've never respected our victory in the War of Independence."

Gordon drove away the humor. "What is there about it to respect?"

The American captain's eyes flickered like water. Something about all this was entertaining to him. For a moment the two men seemed almost to be seated over lamb and crumpets, discussing politics before a crackling fire.

Silence fell between them. Gordon sensed he'd stepped over an invisible line. The American captain had no need to argue this point, for the answer shone in every face among his crew. There was no shame among them, but only freshening defiance. Gordon understood that he would be in peril here too, were it not for the captain's restraint.

The physical condition of the Americans made him nervous. Bronzed and well-fed, these men glowed with a tale of short supply lines and friendly ports. Americans were welcomed in these barbarous Caribbe colonies for daring to trade right through the British restrictions. Only a few days of sailing would bring them to ports along the American eastern coast, while Gordon and his crew were months from succor.

He saw resistance in their eyes. They knew why he was here. He could seize the schooner. He could, but Parliament did not want such obvious problems with the United States. If he seized the ship and the act was deemed unjustified, the gesture could backfire. No, he would do something else. Something more precedented.

And that captain ... he was a medley. Gordon sensed the light of hazard in the other man's eyes. This man reveled in riding the dark horse.

Unsettled, Gordon searched for a good voice. This next duty was distasteful and he was not of a mind to enjoy it, yet desperation drove him on.

"It befalls me," he began, "to remove English sailors from American ships and call them to duty in the Royal Navy against the forces of Napoleon Bonaparte on the European continent. Ye who will be chosen, rejoice in your being relieved of this vulgar service under that ridiculous ensign."

He cast a gesture at the stern, where the flag of the young United States snapped its hem at the sandbar.

But for hardened glares and knotted fists, the American crewmen were laudably restrained. To these men the prospect of changing service was sour. The Royal Navy remained the strongest, most far-reaching naval force in history, the quintessence of dominion, pride of the Empire, yet none of these men wanted part of it. How had the Crown's supreme force come to such poor repute? The Royal Navy, famed since antiquity, reviled by this rabble?

Yet they all wanted a life at sea. All were here voluntarily.

"We have no English sailors here," their captain said. For the first time there was true acrimony in the American's voice. The blue neckerchief fluttered as if he had a pet bird.

At least Gordon had prepared for this moment. "America has eighty thousand seamen. One quarter of them are, in fact, British. Most are deserters, greedy for the better pay in the American merchant trade. A British citizen aboard your ship is considered contraband, the same is if you were carrying gunpowder to Napoleon. Will you tell me this schooner is exempt from such a population? That your ship alone has avoided boarding a single English seaman?"

A pause, then the captain insisted, "All here are American citizens."

"Your country allows any foreigner to become American after only five years of residency and a few paltry requirements. Being 'American' means nothing more than that. You are a nation of knaves and deserters."

The captain was clearly livid now. His restraint was admirable, given that his eyes were hot enough to broil cod.

Gordon had to move, had to get away from him. He found his feet and walked forward along the line of Americans. He found a blue-eyed red-haired man with pale skin and blond eyebrows, and noted that the man was a few inches shorter than most of the others.

"What is your name?"

"Bristow."

"An English name."

The American captain protested, "English names are common in the United States. You know that."

"Ironic, for so ungoverned a people. Mr. Hennessy, take custody of this deserter."

"I'm not English, sir," Bristow insisted. "I'm from Connecticut!"

Gordon challenged, "What is your given name?"

The man shifted a glance to his captain. Finding no alternative there, he furnished, "Ian."

"Ian Bristow. English with Scottish influence."

"Mr. Gordon," their captain interrupted, "half of all Americans are of English descent. If that is your criterion, then take us all."

Under the muskets of the Royal Marines and the frigate's heavy guns, the American could be only a barrister, not a soldier, and he did it well. Gordon felt his face turn hot, his lips pale. How many could be seized without causing an international incident? Two? Three?

Having no response, Gordon faced the man named Bristow and played his best card. Feeling as if his shoulders were too narrow, he squared and looked him in the eye. "Tell me on your word of honor that you were not born on British soil."

Bristow turned purple in the face and neck. He struggled, his mouth twisting. Several times he glanced at his captain. In the end, truth choked him silent and he bitterly lowered his eyes to the deck.

Gordon felt justified and deeply threatened. He raised his voice so all could hear, and hoped it would not crack.

"Ian Bristow, you were born under the protection of the Crown. For the rest of your life you have certain specific rights. To say, 'I am a British citizen' carries privilege around the globe. Wherever you are in the world, we will protect you and you have reciprocal obligations. Anyone born under the Crown has a duty to the Crown. England did not ask for war with Napoleon, but we have it. Escaping to another country does not get you out of it. Only in our hour of need do we call upon you to fulfill your duty. Be glad you're not a recaptured deserter, else you would be hanged."

"A net gain of zero," the other captain commented drably, in a voice just barely to be heard—but to be heard for certain.

Gordon stiffened his lips and jaw, lest the insult show to have stung him. He looked at the captain. "God will settle the score, sir, not you."

While he had reason to be angry, the America smirked and his blue eyes twinkled. "Watch me."

Those boiling eyes were hard to meet. The Yankee men grumbled with satisfaction.

Gordon spoke up quickly to kill it. "There is another Briton aboard."

The American captain's demeanor shifted slightly. "Only one more?"

Around them the thirty-odd men in the crew watched tensely. Which of them would be next impressed into the British ship's crew? How random was Gordon's logic? He had chosen a man because of his hair, his name, and his stature, knowing that Americans tended to be a few inches taller than most Britons because of the abundance and variety of foodstuffs on their continent. Bristow had no trace of Britain in his speech, yet had all but admitted his British birth. The truth had been teased out. Would fortune favor Gordon a second time?

Over the water, from only three hundred feet, his own crew watched, waited. Many of them had also been pressed, some from other ships, some from the docks, some from the streets while going about their business. He had neither a willing crew nor a loyal one, and they all spied the glitter of islands with fruit and fresh water. Danger lurked on all fronts in these waters.

Danger, and a pestilential smell he choked when a breeze brought the putrid odor to him again. He cupped his hand over his nose, relieved to see the other men also gag and grimace. Was it coming from an island? A flock of dead waterfowl, perhaps? A slaughterhouse?

No. As before, it came from the open sea to the south.

His eyes began to water. His stomach rolled. Had it not been a gesture of weakness, he might've clutched this main halyard to steady himself.

"Dead whale," he postulated, just to hear a voice, and to sound wise and experienced.

"Whale?" The American captain squinted at the sea. "Mr. Gordon, that is a slave ship."

Gordon looked up. The captain only gazed out over the misty water.

Hennessy, Bristow, the American crew, the Britons in the boat—all now gazed out at the horizon, taking through their nostrils information to startle their souls. It was the odor of life, of death, in chains. Urine, defecation, vomit, and corpse rot.

They saw nothing but the gray ocean. A moment later, to their ears came a single strain, the thin distant cry of a human soul in torment.

Then the sea went silent again. The wind changed. The odor of pitiable humanity faded as if caught back by a giant hand that meant to hide it.

Gordon looked at the men who had a moment ago seemed so strong, so harsh, and discovered a flock of soggy-eyed boys, many holding their noses.

Feeling as if he were about to explode, Gordon stepped to the nearest reasonable candidate, an ordinary-looking fellow with hair as black as Gordon's and a complexion as fair. If he could not look in a crystal ball, he would look in a mirror.

"You appear Irish to me," he said. "What is your name?"

The man uttered a most piteous, "*Oh, no.*"

The sincerity caused Gordon to hesitate, then suddenly to shake off his hesitation. Weakness shown here and now before Hennessy and the Americans could be fatal later.

"Your name," he insisted.

"Moore."

"Was it O'More before you changed it?"

"Please," the man quietly implored. Immediately he clamped his lips, torn between his fate aboard the Royal Navy ship and the plain fact that were he rejected, another of his shipmates would pay the price.

"Where were you born?" Gordon asked.

Moore glanced at his own captain. "Don't rightly know that

... never knew the mother."

"Yet your accent is English, is it not?"

In desperation, Moore stammered, "Gloucester, Massachusetts, sir! Not England. Please—"

"Hennessy, this one as well, if you will." Gordon backed up almost to the rail. "You two men are British. Your king needs you and you will go."

The other men around Moore gave him silent hands in comfort for his obvious misery. Wisely, Hennessy pulled the man away before their sympathy turned to resolve.

"Wait!" the American captain interrupted. "Wait, I beg you." His tone was different, even conciliatory as he stepped toward Gordon. "I'm sure you've made an error. Moore here has recently become the father of twins. His wife failed to survive, leaving a daughter of eleven years to raise the infants. If he disappears into the Royal Navy—"

"Am I to falter before this dirge?" Gordon challenged. "Of years absent and babes orphaned?"

"Not at all, but ... you do want to get your ship back to open water."

Gordon stared at him. How could he know—?

The other captain was scouring him with a special glare, adding factors in his head that others could not cipher. The tilt of an eyebrow. The dip of a shoulder. Gauging Gordon's nerve as if this were a game of poker.

The American tucked his chin a bit. *You're lost. Let us parlay.*

Gordon, humiliated, despised the American captain in that moment. Could all the other Americans see what was going on?

The American captain saw in Gordon's face that his hook had been taken. He dropped his defiance and spoke man to man, in a plea for decency and lenience. "I'm certain you know twins are rarely born to Englishmen with American wives."

For a fleeting moment they understood each other. As a thread through a needle, empathy stole into James Gordon. He thought of his own mother.

"Especially Englishmen with eleven-year-old daughters, I suppose," he said.

Damn. His humanity was showing. So was his mistake.

Trembling, Moore whispered, "Thank you, sir, thank you, thank you—"

"Shut up!" Gordon understood now the true nature of the man's fear of impressment. This was not cowardice. "Then who is the other deserter aboard?" he asked. Now that he had declared a goal of pressing two men, he could not back down.

The captain scanned his crew. His gaze settled upon a blond-haired young man in a tweed touring-cap, no taller than Gordon. He had a thin beard running like a pen line around his cheeks and an admirable physique, with a chest hard as rock pressing at his red cotton shirt. The schooner's captain approached this man and for a moment they communed in silence.

The sailor clearly comprehended the captain's wordless plea and digested the implications. An uneasy moment passed as the captain offered his hand to the man and they exchanged a solemnity reserved only to friends. They turned together, side by side, each burying personal anguish. Over those few steps, perhaps three, four, the blond man in the red shirt bravely accepted his sacrifice.

Gordon scowled, knowing he was being made the fool. Dismally he asked, "Your name?"

"Victor Tarkio."

There was no "sir," no "Lieutenant," no recognition of office or respect for the uniform.

A nub formed in Gordon's stomach. "Of the Sussex Tarkios, I suppose."

"Suppose so," Tarkio passively said.

Shoulders knotted with exhaustion, Gordon uttered, "Welcome to the Royal Navy."

He had just taken on another man who would happily kill him.

"From now on, you men will address me as 'sir' or 'Mr. Gordon,'" he instructed.

"Yes, sir," Ian Bristow mumbled.

Tarkio said nothing, but only gripped Gordon by the throat with his glare.

Gordon tried to return the glare without breaking. "Do you know what British Navy discipline is like? I can have the skin flayed from your back for such defiance."

Tarkio nodded now, as if he and Gordon had known each other for years. "Flay away. I'll never say it. You're not my better."

"I am your captain," Gordon snapped.

"I have a captain. You're not his better either."

A rumble of sour approval rolled through the American crew as they stood spread out behind their own commanding officer.

Affected, the American captain had lost his flippancy. Holding back obvious heartache, he extended a hand in silence to the man called Tarkio, who took that hand in both of his. Gordon battled to ignore the pain of devotion in the two men's faces as they looked at each other for probably the last time. The same anguish creased every American face. They were here because they wanted to be here. Not like the *Helen*'s crew, who had been dragged kicking from dark wharves, wrenched from their families, and forced to serve. There was no such warmth in the Royal Navy.

Gordon pretended not to see. "Hennessy, take this man."

Tarkio was hustled over the side into the gig. The American captain seemed to weaken for a moment or two.

As though alone, he murmured, "What will I tell Mary?"

The question hung in the air.

"Now, Captain," Gordon began, but did not finish.

The other man waved some of his men forward, so that he and Gordon might speak more privately. Then he looked out over the water. He spoke without pointing or gesturing.

"Starboard of your ship you can see the prevailing swell. Now look for the counter-swell." He did not point at it.

"I ... see it," Gordon said, a few seconds earlier than actually seeing it.

"It runs through the lee side at a right angle to the main swell."

"Yes ..."

"That is the swell line. You see that island there—"

"Of course."

"The swell running over the top of the oncoming swell is reflected off another island that we can't see. We can tell where it is by the swells. We are between the two. Go east along the counter-swell, follow the water of the deepest blue and you shall find open sea, but not run afoul of coral heads."

Moving away from him sharply, Gordon said, "Very good. Now, you will suffer your flags to be brought to my gig, Captain."

Shocked, the captain raised his voice. "Mr. Gordon, you wouldn't confiscate my flags!"

"What better way to discourage you from engaging in piracy and smuggling than to deprive you of communication? Warn your fellow schooner masters."

Anger ran under Boyle's forced restraint. "You leave us crippled, sir."

But he was honorable in some way, Gordon knew, for the other man did not mention their bargain, or that it was satisfied, or that Gordon was returning favor for injury. Their bargain had been made and was over now. On with business.

"I will send a prize crew to transfer your cargo to our hold," Gordon struggled on. "The reduced weight will free you to ride off this shoal."

The American captain's blue eyes iced over. "You leave us with no revenue from this voyage. Will you also force us to turn back and sail north without ballast?"

Gordon got a feeling it was good luck that he wasn't standing closer. "Take on water, then. Or sand. You schooner men fancy yourselves wizards of the wind. Let your talent be your ballast."

"How shall I appeal this insult?"

"There is no appeal. My judgment is irrevocable."

"Impressment of my crewmen strains the laws between our nations."

"I am enforcing international law, sir!" Gordon snapped as he might to an errant dog. His fears came together into a pique. "Who protects America? You call yourselves 'independent,' but who pays your extortion against pirates in the Bay of Tunis and the Caribbean? The Royal Navy protects you. The Navy of King George III, and no one else. Once again Great Britain stands alone against aggressors and America does nothing to help, but only manipulates the tension. Do you understand what will happen to freedom of the seas if Napoleon conquers Britain? While America whines its ungrateful song, Napoleon will take Russia. He will have the French Navy, the Russian Navy, the Spanish and Dutch Navies, he will regroup, he will blockade, he will aggress, and what will happen to you? Your fledgling United States should stand fast beside the King against this maniac!"

The American captain dropped all pretense of cooperation and proclaimed, "One tyrant is like another."

Gordon stared at him, unable to cloak the fury, the insult boiling in his mind. With a slight shudder, he said, "You *will* be driven down."

The captain's countenance hardened before Gordon's eyes. "Go whistle up a rope."

As his legs quaked with rage at the captain's unthinkable words, Gordon knew he was not hiding his emotions as well as his adversary. He knew it. They both knew it. "If your Congress declares war against Great Britain, who will protect America then?"

With his crew behind him, the schooner man boldly declared, "I will protect it."

"How? You live in a disorderly nation."

"Disorder works in my favor."

The canny response drew bitter laughter from the schooner's crew and diminished Gordon's presence, if not his authority. Gordon couldn't help but feel foolish, whether the law came down on his side or not. He could do nothing but endure the disrespect. He swung a leg over the rail, then paused.

"Who are you, captain, that I might anticipate your legend?"

The American offered only the flick of an eyebrow.

"I'm Thomas Boyle of Baltimore," he said. "Like it or not."

The Road

A LARGE SHOE WITH a lanky leg snaked out of the coach's passenger window. The window, because the doors were bolted shut at the bottoms for the safety of the passengers.

The extended leg jostled in rhythm with the huge nine-seat coach as it bounced and quavered on the washboard-rutted road, as if calling to the wheel it had lost a quarter-mile back.

In front of the huge flat-bottomed coach, four matched horses thundered down the road, spooked to the marrow.

"Ho—wah—whoa—hah!" cried a black boy from the driver's seat. He tried to reach for the reins that had slipped out of his hands, but they were beyond reach, dancing across the rear horses' two rumps.

But that leg, that lanky gray-trousered leg, was almost out the window, and behind the leg, a lawyer.

"Hold tightly!" the lawyer called to the boy.

"I lost the reins!" the boy croaked back. His pitiful voice was torn away by the speed and the clattering of the axles. The corner with no wheel bobbed up and down, every other bob making terrific contact with the road's stony ruts. A long twirl of leather trim that had been ripped from the axle flew along behind.

Trees shot by. Branches clawed at the luggage strapped on top. With every bounce, the four horses panicked and galloped faster. They were used to hauling two or three tons of freight thirty miles a day on the rutted post roads that connected New York to Boston, Baltimore, and Philadelphia, but today the twelve-seat coach carried only seven passengers and the driver, four of whom were children, not enough weight to tire the horses and make them slow down. The riders had been roused by the sharp crack of a wheel hitting a boulder in the road. After that, chaos.

Flecks of foam from the team's flanks splattered the lawyer's plum-colored jacket and the long maple-colored curls which fell almost to his shoulders. He had a narrow face and large thoughtful eyes with lashes like a woman's. There was nothing adventurous about him as he climbed, not gracefully, out the window and somehow found the footboard with that long leg and foot. A shorter man could not have done it. He hadn't believed he could do it himself, but traveling with a woman and her three children, an elderly doctor and two nuns, he was the unfortunate candidate.

There was no sense of heroism. He knew he was no hero. Heroes were anointed by God and certainly would be launched upon their destinies by His voice. The lawyer heard no divine murmur over the rattle of the horses' livery. Not a whisper. Not a burp.

The lawyer's whitened hand reached for the driver's seat. The black boy, one arm linked with the iron structure of the seat, reached for him and caught him by the coat sleeve. This didn't help, but the lawyer politely accepted it without protest.

"Thank you," he struggled.

At a moment when the horse team slowed to go left around a bend, the lawyer flung himself to the driver's seat and somehow twisted onto the leathered plank. For a terrible moment he pivoted on his backside, arms and legs flying upward, and was almost cast off. His stomach went for its own ride.

The last mad seconds were offset by his mind's antics about how God might burp.

"Ho!" he called. How well trained were these four demons?

Three of the horses were tiring, their heads down and gaits flagging. The horse in the left-hand rear position, clearly much younger, tossed its head and screamed in protest. It wanted to run.

The lawyer hooked his bony hand around the iron brace of the seat and reached forward toward the reins with the other hand. The road swam below him. The horses' undulating rumps and flashing hooves made him dizzy.

"Ho, please!" he called.

The horses fought their harnesses and each other, but the three older horses forced the angry young one to slow the pace by half, enough to bring them from a gallop to a fast trot. Still they gulped ground at an alarming pace.

Dust flew into the lawyer's eyes and mouth as he leaned farther forward. His long limbs gave him a chance of actually reaching the reins, if the dancing leather strips did not fall off the backs of the horses. Another inch or two—

And he had one rein in his grip. Instantly he hauled back pressing his heels into the driver's footrest. The four confused horses skidded, bumped each other and shook their halters. The right rear horse dragged the others to a trot as his young partner kicked and whistled in anger. With an exasperated snort, the young horse relented and finally stopped. The horses heaved great sighs and shook the foam off their mouths. Finally, the huge coach settled to a precarious three-wheeled park.

Cheers and applause broke from inside. Heads popped out the bank of windows, and the lawyer noticed as he glanced back that he could identify their various occupations or social standing simply by looking at their hats. No wonder milliners were so successful.

"Dang done it!" the black boy cried. He nodded in triumph and jumped up to check whether any mailbags had broken loose.

"Well," the lawyer responded, "that's a story we can tell later, isn't it?"

The passengers piled out to survey the damage and settle the pounding of their hearts. The three children jumped up and down, calling, "Let's do it again!"

The two nuns laughed, giddy and excited.

"Is everyone all right?" the lawyer asked as he climbed down to the road. "William?"

"No broken bones," the doctor told him while adjusting his spectacles. He turned to the axle where the wheel had fallen off. "Sheared off at the pins. It's the ruddy road."

"The rutty road," the children's mother corrected dryly.

The elder of the two nuns said, "Since the winter melt it's

been like this. Look—the entire wheel is missing!"

"Perhaps we should retrieve it," the younger nun suggested. "I'll be happy to go, Mother."

"We have no tools to repair this damage," Dr. William Beanes said as he fingered the dust from his whiskers and studied the axle.

"Nor the skill, I'm afraid," the lawyer admitted. "Too bad there's not a man around."

The doctor honored him with a charitable laugh.

"Sir, we are in your debt for such a valiant rescue," the children's mother said. Somehow she had one of her widely set eyes on the lawyer and the other on her children, who were running zigzag between trees.

The lawyer nodded, but in a way that dismissed his part. "I merely provided the length of reach. My hand was the Lord's for the moment." His enunciation was paced and perfect. He made only one gesture, putting out a graceful hand to illustrate his point. Troubled, he paused. "I hope that did not sound as if I were complimenting myself ..."

"Each man of pious soul is God's instrument at some time in his life," the elder nun assured.

"Mother?" the young nun called from a bit down the road, where she had wandered to watch the children.

Both the elder nun and the children's mother turned and responded, "Yes?"

Everyone laughed, and the embarrassed young nun corrected, "Mother Annunciata ... will we walk now?"

"As did the blessed savior, sister," the Mother responded.

The children's mother then took charge. "Since we seem destined to walk together, I shall introduce myself. I am Mrs. Burnstock."

"Mother Annunciata and Sister Mary Ellen."

Though they had been in the coach together for an hour, the lawyer noted, they had not introduced themselves, but had simply ridden in polite silence, not expecting to have relationships.

He bowed his head politely to the ladies and with a gesture said, "This is my friend, Dr. William Beanes of Upper Marlboro." He pronounced the name "Banes," as in the old Scottish manner.

Dr. Beanes wagged his walking stick, accepting his own identity.

"Yes, we know Dr. Beanes," Mrs. Burnstock said. "And you, sir?"

At this moment of destiny, the young horse at the lawyer's side snorted, bucked once, and released a splashy stream of urine onto the shoe that had saved the day.

The lawyer, along with everyone else, looked down at this ignoble baptism.

"Key," he muttered. "Francis Scott Key."

—ᘏ—

Francis Key picked his way along the top of one of the huge ruts running lengthwise down the road. Around him, the former passengers of the old coach trod on ruts of their own choosing. He and Hector, the boy driver, each led two of the horses, now unharnessed and loaded with the luggage, mailbags, and the two smallest of Mrs. Burnstock's three young sons. Exhausted, the horses were compliant.

"America is on the cusp of explosive change. Advancements are at work, which will set all our lives afire. The very ground upon which we walk and ride will be transformed. It is before us like a great and wondrous storm. I see it before me every day, in the vision of my mind."

"Like what, Mr. Key?" the young carriage driver asked.

"For one, we are linking the states with a new road. The National Road, it's called."

Francis Key knew he was about to go into the mode of a lawyer before a bench or a minister at a lectern, but could not resist. There were children and nuns about. He would seize this opportunity for his own children, yes? He felt an irresistible desire to entertain everyone during their long trek, as if God himself had placed the responsibility upon his narrow shoulders.

"The United States road will begin in Cumberland and cut through the shortest, straightest navigable route west. The land will be flattened or filled to achieve a five-degree grade in most places. America's first interstate highway!

"An empire cannot survive which cannot communicate," he continued, his voice taking on a tone of wonder. "The Roman system of roads was built for the military, but it linked the farthest spindles of the Empire and made the Holy Land an international crossroads. The United States cover a vast area, bigger than all of Europe. The turnpike will link us together. The West will be accessible to thousands."

"If anyone wants to go there," Dr. Beanes contributed doubtfully.

"You are a splendid orator, Mr. Key," Mrs. Burnstock noted. "You have a lordly voice, and most melodic."

"And so meticulous," the elder nun added. "You make the English language sound like a song."

"My gracious—thank you," Key said humbly. "When I was a boy, my grandmother had me read scripture from the top of the staircase for her guests. I was dressed in a nightshirt and bare feet. She all but put a wire halo on my head and sugar on my cheeks. What a sight I must've been."

Mrs. Blackstock offered a nod of admiration to Key's grandmother. "With such a speaking voice, do you also sing?"

"I attempt to, but the frogs complain."

Dr. Beanes added, "He became a lawyer instead of a minister because the choir booted him."

"Oh, God forbid!" from Sister Annunciata.

"Yes, God forbade his singing anymore."

"It's true," the lawyer said. "I love music. But I can't hold a note."

"That's a polite way to say 'tone deaf.'"

"I'm not tone deaf," Key protested. "I know a tune when I hear it. I just can't carry it very far."

"Who will pay for the new turnpike, Mr. Key?" Hector persisted.

"Oh, it will be the first federally funded highway, bisecting several states. Imagine building a stone-capped turnpike that drains away the rain and snow-melt, navigable in any weather, Estimates say it will cost six thousand dollars per mile."

"Six thousand!" all the women echoed.

"Six thousand!" two of the children cried.

Key smiled. He liked children. "Someday it will lead all the way to St. Louis, Illinois."

"Where is Illinois?" the black boy asked.

"On the other side of Lake Michigan, speaking longitudinally."

By their wordless reactions he inferred they were astounded at the mysterious distance of western lands, of prairies and great rivers called the Ohio and the Mississippi, on the other side of the Allegheny Mountains, through the dark ancient forests where dangers lurked and thieves and murderers sequestered. Such a road would allow the fastest travel ever known on the continent.

He marveled at the engineering and the promise bestowed upon the young United States and felt a nagging fear, which he managed to hide from his company. The nation had only existed a handful of years, the length of his life, and already there was talk of a new war with England. Many parties argued their reasons for conflict, but not one did he find legitimate. Factions argued in the city of Washington, sometimes in his own dining room, and the only point they had in common was the flagrant, arrogant, desire for a fight. The National Road might be destined to remain only a dream, and that crushed him. The nation had come to a turning point, just around the bend from disaster.

"I'd relish the challenge to build such a marvel," he added quietly, "constructing the future—"

"You?" Dr. Beanes scoffed. "You haven't even decided to be an attorney, and you're already one. Now you're a road engineer? Make up that mind of yours."

Key laughed and shrugged at one of his great weaknesses of character.

"I will be an attorney too," Hector proclaimed. "Then I can speak longitudinally."

The adults laughed, and the boy was proud of himself for it.

Mrs. Burnstock asked, "Mr. Key, how will you get home now?"

"I'll hire a horse from the tavern. What about you, madam?"

"I suppose we'll hire a buggy."

"Allow me to pay the fee." To the nuns, Key added, "And for you ladies as well. And, Hector, I shall write a testimonial to your employers that the wheel was at fault and not yourself."

Thank-yous fluttered all around, until Dr. Beanes asked, "What about me? An old physician helpless on the highway?"

"You'll be put to work in a construction gang."

"You're an evil sprout."

"Joy to you, sir."

"Mr. Key," Hector asked, pulling on the lawyer's sleeve, "where should I go to see this National Turnpike?"

Key looked at the black boy and saw the thrill of future accomplishment in Hector's eyes. But for the color of skin, he might as well have been looking into his own eyes. The lawyer gestured with his long hand down at the gluey mud and ruts beneath them.

"Why, young man," he answered, "you're treading on it now."

—⚹—

The tavern at the crossroads butted up to the road without an inch to spare. The old farmhouse-turned-inn had an idyllic setting but was notorious for back-alley dealings. Any man of any description could find a bed, a meal, a smoke and a drink without question, if he had coins.

Key bade farewell to his traveling companions, who quickly melted into the crowded taproom, and though hunger pulled at him he was distracted by a racket of human voices from behind the stable, on the far side of the hen house, in a gated courtyard that had seen better times.

The wooden fence was a bloodless gray, the weatherworn gate stubborn as Francis Key put his shoulder to it. He was six feet tall and the gate a foot taller, high and long, embracing a goodly tract of land, and had for two generations enclosed a modest but infamous sports arena. Outside the gate, giving him a long serious look, more than thirty horses were tethered. Some had saddles, some were barebacked, and at least six were hitched to wagons or buggies.

"Late in the day for a rodeo," he mumbled. The gate wobbled open a few inches. Leading with a shoulder, he attempted to slip his long body through, only to be caught about the chin. A thick smell of human body odor and cigar smoke painted his face. All he could see was a ridge of shoulders and hats. The place was impenetrably crowded with shouting men. The force of bodies bumped the gate, trapping him with one leg and his face in.

"Em ... pardon me ..." he choked. "May I ... enter? Gentlemen? Hello?"

The shouting broke into a single *whoop!* then a bank of cheers and boos. Suddenly the pressure on the gate dissolved and Key tumbled through into a wall of men and went down on one knee.

Several strong hands seized him and hoisted him to his feet, which he got under him with some stumbling.

"Oh," he uttered, peering over the shoulders of others. "A wrestling match."

Lit only by several lanterns and the bright moon, between banks of shouting men of every description, two men dressed in only knee-length breeches were knotted up in a muddy, greasy bundle, so knotted that Key could not tell which arm or leg went with the other. The odor of manly sweat, filth, ale, and whiskey permeated the air. Men shouted encouragements or frantic advice to the competitors, passing money back and forth in pouches or hats.

Key watched briefly, enjoying the quintessential humanity of the spectacle and studying the intensity of the faces around him, trying to remember the manifold expressions to be used in future poems. Then he spied someone he knew—a familiar man across the mud pit from where Key stood.

He pushed forward through the crowd and waved.

"Captain!" he called.

No less than a dozen men turned at the call for a captain. Key berated himself silently for forgetting just how many Americans were sailing men.

Then his target saw him. A bright smile shone around a cigar so aromatic that Key could smell it all the way across the arena. The captain's two fists were full of loaded coin pouches, his white shirt flecked with mud, trousers caked from the knees down.

"Captain Boyle!" he clarified. "I say there, Captain! Tom!"

Tom Boyle squinted into the lantern light, saw the lawyer, and he let out a bellow of joy.

"Well!" He looked around the arena, seeing no way through or around the shouting men. "Stay where you are!"

Key nodded, and wriggled his way back through the crowd to the relative seclusion near the fence. He had to wait only five minutes before one of the wrestlers got the other around the neck, and the strangling fellow surrendered.

The crowd roared. Money flowed back and forth. As if appearing out of a foggy forest, Boyle appeared from the wall of spectators, carrying a flat-brimmed black hat loaded with coins and promissory notes.

"Longshanks! Well met, my friend!"

"Always gambling, aren't you?" Key said. "Billiards, dice, cards, cock fights—"

The captain threw an arm around the taller fellow. "Don't forget the goat races. Life's no good without gambling. Let me see you. Frank, you look like a poached rat! Are you heading for Baltimore?"

"Coming from it. I'm going to Terra Rubra. How are you?"

"Oh, the life of a captain, you know—too much of everything, not enough of anything."

Key smiled at the truth of it. "Are you heading out to sea?"

"Back to Baltimore. I waylaid here for the match. Made few coins to make up for our losses in the West Indies."

"Losses?"

"We ran the blockade with a load of cotton, but a British upstart pinned us on a sandbar. I didn't see the color of the water because of the fog. You should've seen this boy, Frank. Half terrified and completely furious. He barely knew what to do with his own arms and legs. The rascal seized our cargo and all my flags and pennants!"

"Oh, no, Tom!"

"We flopped our way to the port of Charleston, where I left the *Comet* until I can acquire new flags and a new charter. Were you in Baltimore?"

"Yes. I defended a free Negro in a property case."

"Did you prevail?"

"I did. It was a question of easement."

"Let me get a clean shirt and trousers. I'll meet you inside. Find a table by the fire, away from other ears. I have grave news."

—⁓—

The tavern was nothing more than an old farmhouse whose task had been shifted from growing food to serving it. There were three small rooms on the lower level, two with fireplaces, each with tables for guests. Upstairs were four cramped bedrooms for overnight travelers, and in each room a bed that could reasonably sleep three grown men.

But down here, in the foremost parlor to the road, an inviting fire snapped in the fireplace and flushed the aroma of hickory and cedar through the dining rooms, competing with the constant scents of turkey and venison stews from the kitchen. The tables and chairs were all mismatched, creating an informality that worked. On the mantel a phalanx of salt-glaze stoneware stood guard duty. Next to the hearth were a bootjack and a pottery urn holding several umbrellas. Overhead were beefy chestnut beams, hand-hewn and soaked with a hundred years of smoke and stories. The tavern area was actually three rooms, which flowed into each other, converted from the parlor and bedrooms when this had once been a farmhouse.

There were many guests here tonight and almost every table was taken. Across the room, the most interesting view was that of a stout man and a drab woman in travelling clothes, with a model of a ship on the table between them. The man was picking at the tiny ship's rigging while also stirring an aromatic bowl of very hot turkey stew.

In the corner of the next room over, a Negro man played a fiddle, smiling at the guests and playing tunes he knew by heart. He had performed for the guests of this tavern for many years now, by choice, for he was a freed man. He played cheerily, but softly, so folks could hear themselves think and engage in private conversations, and he was known to play special requests.

At a table near the hearth, Frank Key whistled softly to himself and tampered with a little square pencil and a much-scribbled piece of paper. He was barely aware of the whistling, but this was a tune he couldn't get out of his head.

On the table rested his cup of lemonade and a chunk of sugar in a wooden bowl, with a pair of sugar nippers. He liked looking at the sugar, which reflected with particular loveliness the flickering fire, like new snow.

"No whistling," said a voice suddenly behind him. "It's bad luck."

Key looked up at Boyle. "Oh, Tom. Welcome, please. That's

only on ships, isn't it?"

"Right. No whistling on ships." Boyle cuffed him on the shoulder with an easy and lingering hand. "That's 'Anacreon in Heaven.' It's hard to sing."

"That's why I'm whistling. The Anacreontic Society would hang me if I tried to sing it."

"Have you ever been to one of their concerts?"

"Yes, a few. Their tenors enjoy the challenge of 'To Anacreon in Heaven.' Those high, long notes. I once wrote words to it, back in 1805."

"I remember. Stephen Decatur in Tripoli. I liked your words. They made me want to go out and burn something. What are you writing there?"

"A poem for my wife," the lawyer said, "to practice my penmanship. I'm attempting to get every letter of the alphabet into one quatrain."

"You'll succeed if you keep using words like *quatrain*. How is Baltimore's apprentice Shakespeare this night?"

"Oh, no, please," Key protested. "Don't rank me among the literati. I'm merely a rhymester. I compose in haste, simple couplets—"

"You're too humble."

"'It is as if the rose should pluck herself or the ripe plum finger its timid bloom.'"

"Now, see, that was lovely enough."

"That was Keats."

"Oh ... well, yours or his, poetry is in your blood. Go on, admit it."

"There I can't argue. I'm descended from a sixteenth-century poet-laureate to His Majesty King Edward the Fourth."

"Royalty! Well!" Boyle clapped him on the arm, then fingered the purple fabric of the jacket sleeve. "What's on your coat?"

"Oh ... foam from a horse's mouth. I had an adventure."

"Today?"

"The coach team ran amuck. I played a small part in stopping them."

"Mm. Horses. I'd rather saddle a dolphin. At least they're clean. Ale?"

"I prefer wine." With a whisper, Key added, "But not the

wine here. Tea, please."

"And some stew?"

"Yes, please."

"Venison or turkey?"

"Venison, please. But only a small bowl."

"You don't eat enough." The captain left his chair and stepped between two cupboards full of New England redware mugs and bowls and into the kitchen where the tavern keepers and their four daughters cooked day in and day out. *Tavern keeping must be a life of drudgery*, Key thought, but then he remembered that the keepers and the daughters always seemed chipper.

He pondered on God's plans. Was each person born to his place and constructed to be content there? He had been born to a privileged life, but felt no sense that he deserved it above any other countryman. Was he a lawyer or a poet? A road construction superintendent or a plantation squire? Should he join the Army or become a judge? What was his destiny? Should he or God choose?

Who am I?

"What's that face? Having big ideas again?" Boyle had returned with two glazed bowls of steaming venison stew to see Key lost in another tightly woven skein of thoughts.

"Some," Key admitted. "I wouldn't trouble you."

"Yes, you will." Boyle sat down and plucked a clay pipe from a small stone vase of them on the hearth. With nippers sitting next to the vase he clipped a half-inch off the pipe's long stem. "Where's the humidor? Ah—there."

"At least eat before you smoke," Key said.

Boyle smiled. "I like my pleasures stacked tight."

As the venison stew, too hot to eat, steamed passively between them, the captain tamped tobacco into the pipe and lit it with a twig from the fire. The fatherly aroma soon entwined with those of the stew and the fire.

"Your law practice is prosperous, isn't it?" Boyle asked.

"Mmm."

"And by now you must have your new baby?"

Key beamed wistfully. "Yes, my little daughter."

Boyle's eyes twinkled. "You want for nothing, your reputation is sterling, your wife worships you, your children glow, your plantation is abloom and even your slaves adore you, yet you're beset by purple moods. Why do you do that to yourself?"

Embarrassed, Key felt his cheeks flush. "I hadn't meant to be any particular color."

"I'll sit on you till you hatch."

Though he hesitated a moment longer, Key knew he couldn't duck away from Boyle's intuition. Trying not to sound too impassioned, he said, "I've just come from Washington. I'm disturbed that so many representatives are pressuring President Madison to declare on England. I was with him when Henry Clay, Langdon Cheves, John Calhoun and somebody named Grundy visited and shamelessly pushed for war without even waiting for me to take my leave. They're relentless to push us into a war. A *war*, Tom ... as if they don't remember what that means."

"England's blockading us, not the other way around. Cutting off our rights to trade on the high seas; the nation must maintain its independence. That means trade with other nations. There is a global market opening up. What good is it to lathe a table leg or knit a sock in Maryland if we can't ship it to Belgium or Portugal for profit?"

"Profit is not superior to patriotism in my mind."

"Frank," the captain said, "Profit *is* patriotism."

In any conversation it was never long before Boyle's gamesmanship surfaced. He was an anti-idealist of the first order, a hard-boiled entrepreneur by whom every opportunity for wager or challenge was eagerly seized. The only things he protected more fiercely than freedom of trade were his ship and crew.

"But don't you think it's poor sportsmanship," Key asked, "to make war on England in this dark hour? They're fighting for their very survival. It's like casting our lot with Napoleon."

"If the British want to fight for their own survival, let them bring their soldiers back from our western territories and leave the West to us."

"But what is a war really about? Vengeance and conquest?"

"There are other rewards."

"You mean Canada."

Boyle smiled wickedly at the prospect of gamesmanship, which he couldn't pull off all that well, because he really wasn't wicked, and he actually looked appealing when he did that. "Canada will make a good state, I think."

"Oh, not you too ..." Key shook his head as firelight danced on his sand-colored curls. "If we do that, the nation will suffer God's retribution. Such evil will bring divine punishment. Yet I've failed to use my influence to discourage it. I was sitting right there in the same room with the president, yet I said nothing. I hid behind my law practice even as the future of my nation teeters on a needle's point. I'm a coward."

"Don't be a martyr. You might not see so much evil in war if you watched the British seize your crewmen off your own deck."

Key looked up. "Oh, Tom ..."

Boyle nodded. "Lost two men."

"I'm so humbly sorry." And his expression confirmed that he really was. "What were you doing?"

"Smuggling."

"Really ..."

"In their opinion. It's the British who've been stifling commerce, not I, not us. The blockade is their problem, not mine. The water under *my* ship is free water."

He stirred the stew and took a juicy mouthful.

Key watched him, plumbing the captain's expression for wisdom that eluded him. Without much of an appetite, he tapped his spoon absently on the scratched wood of the table. "I pray nightly for wisdom, a sign, but despite my piety I receive no holy guidance. Now we flirt with conflict against the most powerful nation on earth and I have no idea which way to bend."

Boyle frowned. "You wouldn't bend toward Britain, would you?"

"Oh, no," Key replied, "but I am against armed conflict on American soil."

"I'll happily take it to English soil."

They paused as a girl of about twelve years came into the room, retrieved a broom from the corner and shambled out again.

"I was thinking of joining the Army," Key said. "To make some kind of ..."

Boyle let his spoon clack down on the edge of his bowl. "You're no field soldier! You're a squire. A gentleman of letters.

America doesn't need you as a fighter. We need you as a lawyer and a poet."

"What good will that do?" Key asked. "I want a better world, but not this way. I'm a pacifist."

Boyle tapped him on the hand in a light but warning manner. "Pacifists can only exist as long as there are warriors around to defend them."

Poised and quiet, Key knew he was bringing down the mood of what should be a pleasant meeting between friends, but he couldn't help it. Nor could he completely shake the raw truth in the captain's declaration. Boyle was right.

"War is so random," Key said, having no better response. "It starts out one way, then ends some other way that no one anticipated. What if the Canadians fight back? What if they don't want to be a state?"

"The Canadians? Fight?" Boyle offered a laugh of derision.

"Disputes between nations should be solved with diplomacy. With mutual respect."

"Fine. I respect them. What happens when they don't respect me?" When Key again had no answer, Boyle continued. "You don't belong on a battlefield. You're a man of order. The chaos would madden you. The Army has only a few thousand men, the governors won't let their militias cross over state lines, the militia commanders don't support the Army regulars—"

"You're making my points for me, sir."

"Frank, you're too practical to be impetuous," Boyle said. Then he grinned somewhat sheepishly and added, "I suppose the opposite could be said about me."

Key tipped his head very slightly. "Then what can I do?"

"There are other ways you can serve."

"How?"

"Run for office. You're a famous attorney. You had the spunk to defend Aaron Burr when no one else wanted to. Everyone knows you could be elected to Congress any time you please. Senator Francis Key."

"Mmm ..."

"*President* Francis Key!"

"Oh, no!"

"Why not?"

"So distasteful," Key murmured, almost a whispered thought. "I find it odious to aspire to fame and fortune."

"That's because you already have a fortune. Men with money are often quick to dismiss its pursuit."

Key sighed. "You're a fountain of axioms today, aren't you?"

"Little me? You're the president, not I."

"You wouldn't speak like this if you had seen poor Mr. Madison struggling with this very question, with those men biting at him. Party politics is so rancorous, political ambition so crude ... pride is a sin. I can't find it in myself to lust for a title."

"The office seeks the man. You've been positioned by fate, and not to try cases of Negroes' rights in sweltering courtrooms."

"You're not the first to ask," Key told him. "I've been blessed with luxuries which allow me to serve the good of others—"

"I'll make a wager with you that you'll be on the Supreme Court before—"

"Oh, no, no wagers with you! I will not gamble. Not with *you*, certainly!"

The captain's friendly expression flashed wickedly in the firelight as he took a big spoonful of stew. "You have the package for greatness, Frank."

The lawyer troubled over this. "But do I have the will to carry through? That is what makes men great, while I am but a benevolent mediocrity."

With stew in his mouth like a schoolboy, Boyle said, "Well, you can't be a monk like you want. You're too curious."

Key smiled at the captain's conviction about him. Boyle spoke with the quick-time abbreviation of a sailing man who needed to get his point across the first time, much different from Key's slow articulations. While the poetic lawyer cultivated every word, each syllable in each word, and paused to think in the middle of sentences if necessary, the captain spoke his mind confidently and expected instant results.

"Your directness is your competitor's bane, Tom."

"I love my competitors." Under the canopy of dark hair, Boyle's pale blue eyes flashed with the thrill of it all. "I give them suggestions and help them run their businesses so they can challenge me further. They keep me sharp."

The fire crackled loudly as if to punctuate his sentiments. As if in mutual agreement to pause, each revisited his bowl of stew and listened to the fiddler. But Boyle's eye wandered the room, for he was always observing the horizon.

Key noticed. "Something?"

Boyle kept his voice low. "That man over there. He's building a model of a frigate."

"Yes, I saw."

"He's making a mess of it."

Key felt himself smile despite his troubled pattern of thoughts. "What is America to you, Tom? What are we? *Who* are we?"

Boyle's attention returned to see the change in Key's expression. "You're about my age, aren't you? Thirty-three?"

"Yes. Why?"

"You and I were born just as this nation was born around us. Like everything that's worth having, it grew out of bloodshed and trial. Since I was sixteen I've commanded cargo ships. Today I have a partner, own ships and I speculate in real estate. That's America for me. The next ship and what I can earn with her."

"You change ships like trousers," Key said, "and you thrive on dodgery. The only consistent thing about you is that blue neckerchief."

The captain's expression warmed and he laughed. "What is America to you, then?"

"Since I was twelve years old I've believed America is the higher soul of mankind. We stand above bloodline and birthplace. Or we should."

Boyle made a rascally expression. "Tell that to your slaves."

The rebuke opened a whole new door, but Key kicked it closed. "I am not unmoved."

And with that he ended the subject.

Boyle pondered the complex angel across the table. After a moment, he smiled. "You're desperate to make a contribution, aren't you?"

Key shrugged one shoulder—for him an almost wild demonstration. "If fate allows. I shall have to wait and see." Then he shook himself out of his thoughts and asked, "But tell me, was that your grave news?"

"Pardon?"

"You said you had grave news. Was it that your cargo was seized and two men pressed? That's grave enough."

"It should be. Sad to say, there's more to it. One of the men was Victor Tarkio."

"Oh, no ..." Key uttered.

"Even worse," Boyle said, "it was my idea for him to go in the stead of another man. It was a command decision. One of *those*."

For a long moment they were silent. The fiddler played and the murmuring conversations of others at dinner made a pleasant background to their thoughts.

Key felt his brow furrow, no matter how much he tried to control his expression for his friend's sake.

"How will you tell Mary?"

Sailors and Spies

ACROSS THE TAVERN'S FRONT parlor, at a table near the only window, the man with the model ship picked at a length of twine. Outside the window, the night was dark but for a branched cloud that hid the moon, which gave the cloud a ragged gray lining. Through a doorway to another dining room, the man could see one of the tavern keepers' daughters reading a newspaper aloud to the patrons sitting in that room. He wished he could hear the news, but he had to sit here.

"Keep your eyes on your food."

The man spoke without moving his lips.

The hunch-shouldered woman across the table obeyed him scrupulously. "Does you knows that man?"

He stifled a wince at her heavy accent. "I followed him here, didn't I?"

"You said you come to meet me."

"Why would I come to meet *you*?" the man balked. "Eat your food."

Her crocheted bonnet cloaked a mousy knot of hair, its brim falling forward limply to frame a forgettable face and humped nose. Her mother had possessed the same features, but somehow they were packaged differently. The mother, he recalled, had been passably attractive.

Into a spoonful of red bean pie, the woman asked, *"Alors qui l'est? Pourquoi est-il important?"*

"Speak English," the man told her calmly but sternly. "And keep your voice down. That miserable Quebec accent. You should practice to have no accent, as I have none."

The tavern's drowsy atmosphere disguised an undercurrent of hazard. They might as well be standing on a volcano.

"What name for you?" the woman asked. "I call you Yakov or—?"

"I haven't decided. I am a French Jew, but I must be trusted by Americans who are not Jews. Or at least not identified as French or a Jew."

"I dun't like whisker you have."

"It's either the beard or the scars." He tucked his chin, hoping the movement would deplete the firelight's glitter on the silver hairs in his whiskers. "I don't want to be memorable. Which is more likely to be remembered? Whiskers, or half a chin?"

He stopped talking as the man he was watching abruptly rose and went into the kitchen.

"His name is Boyle," the French Jew whispered, toying with the model ship. "Born in Marblehead, '75 or '76. He took to sea at the age of ten, on a ship commanded by his father. No ... yes, by his father. At sixteen he was himself captain of a schooner called *Hester*. He's gained and shed many ships."

"Mays be he was look for right one," the woman said, then she giggled.

"*Maybe*. The word is *maybe*, not *mayzz be*. Save your jokes for your brainless women friends. He lives in Albemarle Street."

"Who?"

"The—*mmm!*" A twist of his mouth brought her attention back to the captain.

"Oh," she said. "I dun't know where is."

"Yes, you do. In Baltimore. The seamstress lives there. That one who repaired the chair covers. He lives kitty-corner from her. His partner is the insurance man Carrere. Boyle is an important figure in Baltimore. A businessman. In 1805 he was in the 51st Baltimore Regiment, but gave it up to take command of the *Comet*. I've heard he speculates in real estate."

"Why you—"

"*Ssst.*" He made a fierce sound with his teeth, to chop her volume down as the man named Boyle came back with two

steaming bowls and joined the tall fellow with the sand-colored
curly hair at the table by the hearth.

The woman tried again. "Why are watch him?"

"I'm watch*ing* him because there are people worth watching.
We don't want to make the wrong kind of history, do we?"

Though he spoke quietly, he was careful not to appear to be
whispering, for that too could draw attention.

The woman moved her caterpillar eyebrows in a shrug, but
kept her shoulders down.

"He's back too soon, you see," the French Jew explained.
"Why does a successful blockade runner come back early and
without a cargo?"

Pausing to turn the ship model around, he pretended to survey the little paper sails and the twine imitating rigging

"He's galled by the takings of men from American ships by
the Royal Navy. It sticks in his craw. The captain will find me in
passionate sympathy with him."

"Why?"

"Idiot, I beg you, *think*." He looked irresistibly at the captain. "I want to influence him."

"Will you introduce?" she asked. "Will you go there?"

"He will come to me."

Her pointy nose wrinkled. "Why he come?"

"Because I'm doing this model wrong."

"How you know ding it wrong?"

"Because I know nothing about ships."

"I thought you did."

"You know I don't."

Feeling himself drawn into a ridiculous argument that could
go for an hour, the Frenchman bottled further talk of the model,
but continued to string the incorrect part of a sail.

"He's glancing this way," the Frenchman uttered. "Don't
look—he'll come soon."

He pulled the model's little anchor on its little anchor string
and draped it over the bowsprit. Even he knew what a bowsprit
was.

Dutifully avoiding a look toward the captain and his companion at the other table, the woman took a mouthful and slop-
pily asked, "Who is pretty one?"

"What? Oh. Handsome, not pretty. Men are handsome." With a cotton napkin he wiped a bean from his beard. "Just a lawyer. Goes around with armloads of law books. He's nobody."

"I like him," she declared. "Him's face ... pretty. Soft eye."

The French Jew made a rude sound through his nose and forced himself to think about something else, something he enjoyed discussing, even though he might as well be in conversation with a goose.

His mind wandered. He smelled the beans and listened to the drone of the girl in the other room reading the news. Something about England. Something about exports. Shoes. Hair combs. Toothbrushes.

"England," he mused. "Monarchies. Corrupt old families, inbred spoiled-brat heirs ... they have no idea what makes a country. A dictator is much better. A dictator must rise through the ranks with no money in his pockets, learn to take orders before he can give them. He would know the face of oppression."

"You mean 'bout 'Nited States?"

Her voice actually startled him. Had he not told her to stop talking?

"Eh? No, certainly not! The United States are nothing. Little bundles of mayhem. What is so noble about breaking the barriers of bloodline? Napoleon has done it already. There must be war between the Americans and Britain. There *must* be! Britain will try to take back this continent, but will fail. America is too weak to wage a good war. They will argue with each other and the states will crack apart."

Pausing for another slurp of bean pie, the French Jew nodded at his own reasoning and agreed with himself. Such exciting thoughts—it was hard to keep his voice down. Such a glory of mischief.

"A dictator is not answerable to the mob. Popular whims mean nothing. This idea of Jefferson's, that rabble can rule themselves—*fft!* A dictator can do what he wants without fear." He waved his spoon. "These Americans, if they knew what was good for them they would ally with France right now, today. I don't know what they think their precarious neutrality is doing for them."

He hunched in his seat, realizing his volume had risen in this one-way conversation, and lowered his voice. Unable to look at his companion's ridiculous face, he gazed at the future in his bean pie.

"In France we are all citizens. Napoleon made us into citizens. Us Jews. He shattered the walls like Alexander, smashed the old kingdoms—everything is new for us and our banking empire. So who cares for the ancient aristocracies? Napoleon has set up what we need and broken down what we don't. Americans make bold talk about freedom while their meals are served by slaves. They want freedom of the seas to bring more slaves. What's down and what's up, they don't know. They don't know ..."

A new aroma flooded the room as one of the owner's other daughters entered with two heaping bowls of something that smelled much better than bean pie and delivered it to a family on the far side of the room.

"But if we are lucky," he went on quietly, "America will keep Britain busy while Napoleon makes our next conquest. When he returns with new land, new wealth, new gold, he will cross the Channel. France will capture the world. Then we will seize this ridiculous continent too."

The woman grinned, baring bean-streaked teeth, and wriggled with joy. "You will name mountain after me, *oui*?"

"What? Yes, why not. Who cares? 'Mount Pdut.'" Regarding her with disgust, he added, "No matter how old you get, you never grow up."

But she was lost in a fantasy, touring in her mind the towns and cities named after her. Pdut, America.

"When he comes to me, you must not speak. Eat your food and crinkle your eyes at him." With a glare from under his coal-smudge brows, he whispered, "And remember ... no mention of the name Rothschild."

"*Non, non, non,*" she muttered, seeming unsure whether she could manage it. "*Non*, Rotshilt, *non*."

"Woman, you are such a—"

A motion caught the corner of his eye, because he had been waiting for it and even had paced out the number of steps needed to cross the room from the hearthside table.

"Now it happens," he murmured. "*Alors* ... here the captain comes."

"Pardon my intrusion ... A model of a frigate, is that?"

"Oh," the bearded man responded, "yes, good sir. A gift for my nephew. He wants to join the Navy."

"Admirable boy. If I may suggest—"

"Is there something wrong with it?"

"You don't mind?"

"Please, not at all."

"Most of your lines are going nowhere."

"Oh ... is that so? Oh, my."

"My name is Captain Boyle, by the way."

"A seaman!"

The captain nodded, trying to add a touch of modesty to the gesture. "May I sit?"

"Be our guest!"

Tom Boyle took a seat upon a three-legged stool and inched up to the table. "So you're visiting the coast? Not from here?"

"We're from the Ohio Valley, but we're living in Baltimore for a time. My name is Yambrick. Samuel Yambrick. This is my niece ... Sophie."

"Ma'am."

The woman said nothing. She made a small grin under the gargoyle of her nose and the tent of her bonnet. Right off Boyle got the idea there was something odd about her, and that she wouldn't say a word no matter how polite he could be. He gave it up immediately.

To the man called Yambrick, he said, "The lines on a ship are like the streets in your town. A ship may have ten miles of running rigging, but every line does only one thing. Once you learn where that *street* goes, then you know it. The starboard mains'l sheet, here, does only one thing—it draws the main this way or lets it out that way. You have it run to a gun truck."

The man frowned over his model. "Probably won't work ..."

"No," Boyle said, trying to be gentle. "And up here, you have the moons'l—the moon sail—you have the sheets and braces tied to each other."

"Please show me, if you will."

Boyle hesitated, then rather eagerly got his sailor's fingers in there to unloop the tiny strings. "The braces turn the yards. Two braces per yard, and two sheets pulling on the lower corners of the sails. Sheets are lines that control the sails."

"Why do they call them that?"

"No idea. On a ship with square sails such as this, the braces and sheets work together to 'brace around' the sails—turn them to catch the wind. Or spill it, depending upon what's happening."

"Why would you spill the wind out?"

"To stop the ship."

"Ah ..."

Boyle leaned back, careful not to take too much charge of the model frigate, and almost forgot he was on a stool instead of a chair. "Go from the largest to the smallest. For instance, the starboard mizzen tops'l brace block. Starboard side, mizzen mast, topsail—"

"I'm lost."

Boyle waved his hand along the side of the model ship. "Did you say you were staying in Baltimore?"

"Renting an apartment in the painted building at the foot of Broadway, yes."

"Neighbors!" Boyle laughed. "I live on Albemarle Street. I'll invite you aboard and give you a tour of the rigging. You'll understand better than on a model."

Yambrick clapped at his victory. "Delight! Now, which ship should I visit, Captain?"

"I'll contact you. I'm talking to an investor about ships to be built in Fell's Point over the next few months."

"And Fell's Point is where?"

"It's where you're living."

"Not really!"

"Really." Boyle made a cursory attempt to meet the eyes of the dowdy woman, just to acknowledge that he wasn't ignoring her in a social situation, but the gesture came to nothing. She did not raise her eyes nor attend their conversation, but simply sucked beans out of her spoon and played with the contents of her bowl. Very well, then ...

Boyle paused, thinking. "You'll have to wait. I just returned from the Bahamas. The ship did not return with me."

"Not a tragedy at sea?"

"Some schedule changes. She's docked on the coast."

"And you have left her to go to your family?"

"Until matters are worked out by the owners."

"Aren't you the owner of your ship?"

"I'm the captain. Most ships are owned by groups of investors who then hire captains."

"Oh, I see." Mr. Yambrick surveyed Boyle with a keen eye. Keener than before. "Tell me, Captain, what is your opinion of the talk of war?"

"Well ..."

"Too personal? I apologize. Some say America shouldn't go to war unless it is invaded. I understand if you are one of them."

"I'm a businessman, Mr. Yambrick, an entrepreneur, as all Americans should be. I'm an American, at liberty to come together to engage in commerce. We must have freedom of trade. For what else did we have a revolution but freedom to meet for the purpose of doing business?"

"Captain, you inspire me," Mr. Yambrick uttered, deeply moved. "The blockade of our waters by the Royal Navy must gall you."

"It does very much. Pardon me, but it occurs that I am ignoring my dinner companion. Good luck with your model. Any sailor can tell you in more detail how to rig it until I can offer you a tour of a ship."

"And American ports are awash with out-of-work sailors. Thank you, Captain Boyle."

"My thanks for your company. Fair weather to you. And you, miss."

—◊—

"Damn the intriguer."

The French Jew pushed the model ship away and returned to his meal, which was now cold and stiff.

"I plumb for information, he cannily gives scant. He sensed something. I must be more clever with him from now on. We will give him one week, then we'll find our way to Fell's Point and once again stumble into Captain Tom Boyle's path."

He paused and looked at Pdut to see whether she was still awake. Her eyes peered back like two black buttons on a dirty white collar.

"And you," he declared. "You were too quiet!"

The Flag Lady

60 ALBEMARLE STREET
BALTIMORE, MARYLAND

"FLAGS ARE THE LANGUAGE of the seas. Mind that our work is important. To be a flag maker, one must command a daunting knowledge of heraldry. Certain colors cannot be placed touching each other. In the language of flag making, blue is called *indigo* or *azure*. Red is *cochineal*, a dye made from the dried bodies of female insects from Mexico that are called cochineal. Blue and red must not ... Caroline, are you paying attention?"

"Mother, I'm historically bored."

"You're always bored. You begin a task already bored. A woman had better learn a skill."

"But I've *heard* all this ..."

"But you haven't *learned* it."

"Yes, yes, yes, yes."

Caroline Pickersgill suffered at her mother's declaration because she had heard it through all of her twelve years. It made no more impression upon her than it had when she was toddling and interested only in chewing a sock.

Mary Pickersgill sighed with a parent's timeless frustration. To her right, Grandmother Rebecca Flower Young tilted her large left ear toward the conversation, but made no comment other than to give her granddaughter a fleeting pinch of her lips.

The group of five women sat in a circle with a large silk standard spread between them, their knees creating bumps in the blue field as they sewed appliqués upon it. Their small parlor and display area here in the front of the house was pleasantly appointed in a working-parlor kind of way, shelved with the family's possessions, but also billowing with the orderly chaos of tools of their trade—skeins of yarn and cordage, tufted pincushions, black irons cast in many sizes and shapes, and mountains of colored fabric folded and stacked on shelves or teetering on the edges of furniture.

"You have no brothers or uncles, nor even any sisters," Mary said to her daughter. "You are my only surviving child. That means you must continue to survive on your own when I and your grandmother are gone."

"I'll have a husband to take care of me," the brown-haired girl told her with teenaged assurance. "My husband will be wealthy and we'll live on a high hill. I'll have children to do chores, and I will keep Grace and Lola with me." She glanced declaratively at the two colored girls in their company. "I'm being courted even now. I'll marry and we'll all be better off for having a man in the family."

Mary noted Caroline's pretentious certainty and said nothing. If Caroline accepted the responsibility of marrying, at least the frivolous girl would have some goal or other in life, for currently she had none. But then, when had there been a twelve-year-old girl with no frivolity?

"Maybe your husband will be a sailor and be gone most of the time," Grace Wisher warned. "A crutch will hold you up, but it will also hold you back. You must resolve to independence, girlie."

Caroline looked down at the part of the blue standard draped across her lap, to which she had been halfheartedly stitching an applique of a gold lion-rampant. "Independence is too much work."

Grandmother Rebecca shook her tiny head. Her voice was weak, cracked, forced, as blanched and fading as the woman herself. "Work is a blessing. You come from a respectable line of flag makers. I made the Grand Union flag for General Washington. He flew it over his garrison headquarters in Cambridge on the first day of 1776. In those days I made drum cases and uniform hats and flags." She looked at Mary. "You were born that year, daughter. When your father went to his reward, I sewed for the military. My brother Benjamin was the Commissary General for—"

Caroline rolled her eyes. "Gran, we *know*—"

"*Sh!*" Mary stung her daughter with that look they both knew. No matter how many times the grandmother wanted to relive her glories, the girls would listen and be amazed. And that was that.

Caroline shrugged. "Good thing that flag was for General Washington himself and not the swampy city. Makes a better story."

The circle of women laughed and forgave her.

"Bless his memory," Gran Rebecca added.

"I thought Betsy Ross made General Washington's flags," the other Negro girl said. Lola was a dutiful servant and cook, and had recognized long ago that she was better off in a household of women, sewing for a living, than many places a slave might be fated to live.

"Betsy Ross wasn't even her name," old Gran declared. "Her name was Elizabeth Ashburn."

Then she dropped her needle. Her two white-knuckled hands flew up like confused birds, flustery at not having a needle and thread in them.

"Don't mind that, Gran!" Grace Wisher flashed her toothy smile, moon-bright against dark brown cheeks, and dived for that trailing yellow thread. "It's right there! I see'r. Ope—slipped again."

While Grace rooted for the impudent needle, Mary settled back to her work.

"Remember, girls," she said, "a woman who acts helpless will be helpless."

As she spoke, a rapping came from the Queen Street door, and she was pretty glad to be interrupted. She would answer herself, since that was the door used by friends or more formal visitors. The side door, on Albemarle, was the business address. Grace usually answered that door.

"Keep working, ladies." Mary squirmed out from under the fabric on her knees, crossed the large-slatted floor into the hallway, turned a shoulder to the business entryway and went to the front door.

The door swung open, and there stood Tom Boyle, unexpected and always welcome. "Oh, Captain, you've returned! Do come in."

Boyle felt gritty and unpresentable. He hadn't even changed clothes yet. Upon greeting his family he had made the quickest polite escape and crossed the filthy street with the kind of hurrying that nobody wants to do. He wrinkled his nose at the odor of the street, grown unfamiliar to him after the fresh sea air. He never quite got used to the nauseating wine of manure and urine ground into a slurry by endless hooves and wagon wheels in this city of forty-six thousand crowded people. Baltimore had become the nation's third largest city, and the port and harbor behind him were the reason.

In these narrow streets, buildings were pressed right up against each other, often sharing walls, and pushed up to the edge of the street. Baltimore was filled with row houses with common walls to make use of the narrow lots, built to three and four stories. The handsome two-story brick house before him was one of the less common harbor homes that stood alone with its own four walls. Like all households, it was crammed with people—families, children, often several generations, relatives or not, young cousins shipped in from farms to learn a city trade or to be educated. These days, three out of four white men could read and write and calculate. Workers, hired hands, boarders, apprentices filled every lodging, changing daily as the population of Baltimore fluxed and grew and ships came in and again sailed out. They slept three and four to a bed, shared meals, and often shared fates. Cooking was almost constant. The average was six souls in each house. No one lived alone—almost like living on a ship.

Boyle shook out of his ruminations as Mary Pickersgill held her dark blue skirts and white petticoat up from the manure and sludge, glancing down now and then to check. This motion caused her dark ringlets to bounce beneath the ruffled brim of her cap.

"Morning, Mary. Might we speak briefly? Out here?"

"Oh, I suppose." Mary pulled the door shut behind her and stepped out, holding her skirts a little higher. "You were expecting to be gone another month, weren't you?"

Boyle couldn't help but smile at Mary's musical voice. The vivacious little woman was a crucible of joy and community spirit in Baltimore, hostess of many parties and lunches, a popular socialite with built-in kindness wrapped around the core of a survivor. She was always smiling, cheery, and had a lilting walk that made her brunette ringlets bounce. Nobody could be too dismal in the presence of those bounces. With her short frame and puffy skirt, chubby cheeks and the little white bonnet on top like a knob, she always reminded him of a ship's bell, quiet and resolute, purposeful, and noisy when necessary.

"I'm sorry to bring distress to your household," he said directly. "Brace yourself, Mary."

She caught herself up and dropped back a step, realizing in her sharp mind the myriad fates that could traffic a merchant ship, much less a ship involved in running the British blockade.

She touched her stout hand to her lips. "Victor ..."

He knew she couldn't be fooled and quickly added, "... but he's not dead."

She said nothing, while her eyes did the questioning.

"A Crown brig caught us in the Caribbe," Boyle explained. "They pressed two men. One was Victor."

"My soul," she whispered. "My soul."

A visible shudder went through her compact body. Boyle waited as the news settled.

After a long moment, Mary asked, "How did it happen?"

"We spent seventeen hours out-maneuvering them in the fog. Winds were very light, which favored us, but the British captain was like a little terrier on my heel. We almost got away, then up came this sand bar and we stuck fast. When he boarded us, he thought our cargo wasn't worth his trouble to justify seizure, so he balanced his books by pressing a couple of men."

"How were they choosing?"

"By names. English names."

"Like Pickersgill," she murmured. "John was from England ... my husband. And now the British may be our enemies once again."

Emotions choked her voice out.

"The British never stopped being our enemies," Boyle told

her, "in their minds, at least. Victor was not originally chosen. You should know that he gave himself in place of a man with several children. Mighty courageous."

"But Tarkio is not an English name. Why would they choose him?"

Boyle, being a captain, immediately plunged into the sad facts.

"I chose him."

—⁂—

The flag maker gazed outward through the buildings and houses, as if looking at the harbor waters, though they were not visible from the corner of Queen and Albemarle.

"The Royal Navy," she quietly said. "We shall never see him again."

Tom Boyle didn't argue or attempt false reassurances. Mary was right.

He gave her time to digest the story. He kept back a few steps, careful of the space between them, resisting the urge to be closer for their moment of mutual grief. On the front stoop this way, such a sight would have been inappropriate and disrespectful to his wife.

"I'm sorry that this should be visited upon you," he said.

"I know you are."

That done, Boyle drew a sailcloth pouch from his jacket pocket. "Here is Victor's pay for the voyage. I know he would want to pay his rent as long as possible. He often spoke of his gladness at adding to your household income."

She looked at the pouch. "Doesn't seem right."

Boyle closed her hand over the pouch. "It's right."

She paused, her kind heart exploring. "Poor man, in the shackles of the British."

He nodded, unable to assure her, to lie to her, that Tarkio would survive the brutal life in the Royal Navy, never mind the war with Napoleon. If anyone could survive, it would be Tarkio, but starvation and scurvy visited even the most hale of men and Boyle had seen the condition of those British sailors on the *Helen*. Their captain too had been gaunt and sick.

"Caroline is very young," he attempted. "There is hope."

"Hope that Victor could return? Of course, you know better. I know what you mean—hope for other suitors for Caroline. A chance for her to marry, more support for our household as we grow older ... I know what you mean. We were just talking about something like that."

She sank into herself a bit. There was no room between the house and the street to pace away, so she only turned away a bit while standing in place. Boyle felt as if he were spying on her.

"I am my mother's only living child," she said quietly. "I don't remember my father. I bore four babies, all girls. Pretty little girls with round faces; three died. My mother was widowed. I am widowed. Now my only living daughter is widowed before even becoming a wife."

As Boyle watched in silence, Mary gave in to a very rare moment of self-pity. All the weight of responsibility seemed to push down her little round shoulders.

"A family of widows."

Mary shook off the pall of the moment and looked at Tom Boyle with clear, determined eyes.

"I will not have a melancholy household," she said. "We will keep up a good spirit before society."

"May I help in any way?"

"You have been my friend unmoved, Captain. When I need your help, be assured I will knock on that door." She nodded at the house across the street.

"And we will answer." He hesitated, trying not to rush her. "Have you a moment for business?"

"Business?"

"The rascal seized my flags. Can you imagine? He might as well have taken my eyes and ears."

For a moment she seemed taken aback, as if he were asking her to pick up her petticoats and chase after a British bandit and reclaim the stolen possessions. Then she said, "Oh, you need *new* flags. A complete set?"

"He left me with a couple of swallowtails and a company ensign, but he seized all my signal flags. I can't send a message but by pigeon or prayer!"

Briefly soul-sick, Mary settled quickly back a bit. "Now, you're not doing this because of Victor ... I don't need that kind of help, Captain."

Boyle raised his hands in a gesture. "No, they really took my flags! I need new ones or I'm as good as aground. Almost the whole country's a sea coast."

As he watched, her round face moved out of heartache to the next thing. "Well, how soon do you need them?"

He sputtered out some vague timetable and she explained that she had some newfangled dyes from India that would make brighter colors. Their conversation was glazed with business, but the undercurrent remained with Victor Tarkio, a dependable renter whose casual between-voyages courtship with Mary's daughter had been succor to the Pickersgill household. Neither spoke of him again, but he was still there.

Boyle always thought of Mary as a pioneer woman without a prairie, with model self-sufficiency and a sighing smile for every hardship, never dispirited for long. She would have done well in the wilderness out West, maybe Kentucky, married to some mountain man who mysteriously vanished or got chewed by a bear. She was the sort of woman every man secretly wanted, buttoned up and patient, devoted to his children, with boundless kindness, and who always bounced back to contentment somehow.

Funny that her daughter had none of those qualities. For a fleeting bad-boy moment, he accidentally thought Victor might be better off with the British.

He shook the naughty thought from his head and remembered that for Mary a future once clear had gone dark.

For him, too. Just over there, spindled with sprits, was Baltimore Harbor, and within it Fell's Point—a sailor's lair if ever one had gurgled up at the water's edge. The place never slept. An anthill of ships and men, lumber and chandleries, rope works and pubs, breweries, brothels and travelers' bedrooms, Fell's Point sizzled round the clock with commerce. That was why Mary was here with her flag-making business, why Boyle lived across the street, neighbored by hundreds more seafarers, looking for their next ships, and the dozens of large and small shops that served them. America had sailors, plenty of them, and sadly sometimes losing a few just didn't matter to the industry. It was a good place for single women to ply almost any trade, and for single men to cobble out the future. Boyle's next venture—or adventure—stood undisclosed for now.

The small woman raised her chin and summoned a stronger voice. "Thank you, Tom, for your candor."

"Be comforted, Mary," he said. "Your sacrifice helped my ship and a houseful of children who might otherwise have suffered without their father."

Mary Pickersgill pursed her lips and let out a long breath to steady herself, and to set her mind on what must come next. She nodded conclusively, setting him free of the burden he had brought to her doorstep.

"Hm," she uttered. "Life is a whirligig."

Free Trade and Sailor's Rights

KINGSTON TOWN, JAMAICA

THE WORLD'S MOST INFAMOUS den of thieves spewed infamous odors long before the lookout shouted, "Land-ho!" Even out at sea on the bejeweled Caribbean, the scents of spiced rum, sun-rotted bananas, coffee, gutter urine, and horse manure swarmed around the ship. These were not the aromas of inviting islands, but the snarling stink of a crowded tropic port. The temptation of fresh limes and fresh water drew generations of British captains to this unfriendly landing, no more any other than the young beleaguered James Gordon and his ship-full of threats.

Worse than approaching, of course, was sitting there made off to a warped skeleton of aging mismatched planks trunneled together into a dock. And the noise—intolerable. Squalling women, shouting street-hustlers, growling slave-drivers, barks and neighs and braying protests from unclean beasts, bosun's mates bellowing up and down the wharf as cargoes were unloaded and others loaded in this horrific, uncivilized place. Through the long weeks defending the blockade of American ports, Gordon had longed for the relief of a landfall. Now he longed for the relief of the open water again as he failed to shield his mind from the savage commerce just outside his open stern ports. He sat in cabin in the only chair aboard the *Helen*, sweltering, filling out the ship's log and trying to pretend he was somewhere else.

"What a hole," he grumbled.

"Talking to yourself?" a voice interrupted. "First sign of lunacy."

"How dare you enter my cabin without knocking," Gordon muttered without raising his head.

Victor Tarkio approached with a tray of food just as smelly as the port outside.

"I enter without knocking every day."

Gordon looked up and watched this creature of America as Tarkio poured the captain's tea and arranged the meal he had brought on a rusty tray. Even deprived of life in the merchant marine, the American still had a bronzed complexion and random yellow streaks in his hair, which otherwise would be not so much lighter than Gordon's. As a sailor, Tarkio wore no hat to blunt the sun's rays as Gordon and the officers always did. He appeared as if he belonged here in this mad tropical nightmare, treading barefoot and unconcerned through these island tracts and eating too much fruit.

"Am I a fool, Tarkio?" Gordon wondered, but it was not a real question.

Tarkio did not look at him, but simply cut the captain's bread as best he could with a dull butter knife. "Dunno. Are you?"

"You have an insubordinate mouth."

"They why'd you ask?"

"You will address me as 'Captain.'"

"I won't. Already told you."

"You've been four months aboard the *Helen* and still you refuse to conform."

"You expected something else?"

"I hate your accent."

"And you so enjoy a good hate."

"You know," Gordon warned, "I've had you flogged. I *can* have you hanged."

"Hang me." The American kept dishing out the fare with a surprisingly delicate touch. "Doesn't make you my better. I can be here four months or four thousand and my captain will still be Tom Boyle. Kill me if you want. Roast and eat me if you want. I'll serve your table and sail your ship for the sakes of the men around me, as most of them were seized same as I and they deserve a right-hearted shipmate who tows his load, but you'll get my respect when you earn it, if you ever do. You want beans, or are you above them too?"

The two had engaged in similar flares for nearly a month, since the day Tarkio had been assigned to bringing breakfast to Gordon's cabin, until last week always under guard of one of the Marines. Such a precaution was ironic, because Gordon didn't trust the Marines any more than he trusted Tarkio. There wasn't room in the cabin for three men anyway, so there had been no point but useless protocol to continuing the Marine guard.

Tarkio and the other impressed men would spend years out of contact with anyone they cherished, away from the splendor of New England's forests and fresh water, and all things of life they had known. They stood a strong chance of never returning, of dying at sea from illness, accident, or enemies. If they ever returned at all, it would be with broken bodies and sick souls. Yet Victor Tarkio had sacrificed himself for his shipmate and three helpless children, to guarantee that pay and fatherhood would continue at another man's house.

Stricken with envy all over again, James Gordon remembered the shrouds of the American schooner and compared the memory to his own command, a tub of rot and leaks, of frayed line spliced and re-spliced, cut and spliced again, of unpainted planks plugging holes in her sides. A sailor's keen eye would note the frays, the sagging sails, yards sawn back to their shortest, the chipped hull-paint and exposed wood, the tattered robands and patched sails. And rot ... red, swollen flakes of dissolving wood poured out of the scuppers like blood every time the deck was washed. He knew the American captain had noticed every deficiency, and Gordon hated him for it. Was this madness? To toil his mind over a man he would never see again?

Gordon had taken the pressed American men aboard his ship without knowing much more than they knew themselves about whether the *Helen* would even survive to return to England for repairs and replenishment. He still didn't know. A Royal Navy vessel had few places to find respite in these western waters. Only the port of Halifax, the Bermuda islands, and these vile Caribbean bedpans were under Crown rule. He had chosen this place in hopes that the stink and the sights of brutality would discourage his crew from wanting to mutiny here or jump ship.

And at sea, of course, he could only pretend that he was in command. In truth, there was no rule. He commanded only through the stubborn will of Moycroft, who harbored no particular loyalties. Neither him nor Gordon nor God nor anyone could be completely in charge. Even the weather had to forgive a great deal day-by-day, and the seas— the ungovernable Atlantic.

Tarkio was not a tall man, yet still stood an inch or two taller than most of the *Helen*'s crew. Unlike them, he was enviably muscled and healthy after a life of corn and venison, bread and potatoes, and an encyclopedia of vegetables which couldn't be stored on a ship, but which poured in an orange and green waterfall from the farms of North America. Americans had so many cabbages, pumpkins, turnips, and squash, and so much fruit, that scurvy was nearly unknown to American sailors. They even had sugar. Wild game flowed from their forests, and cattle farms gave them butter, cheese and beef. Fresh water erupted from every hole punched in the earth. And trees—they had trees by the millions. In England, so many trees had been taken to make ships that there were almost none of any girth left.

"You know why you're bringing my meals?" Gordon asked tonelessly, because that's what was on his mind. He always ate alone. Not even the officers and midshipmen wanted his company, nor he theirs.

"I do," Tarkio answered.

"My steward died of scurvy." Gordon went on despite Tarkio's answer. The sound of his own voice kept him talking. "He died while you were recovering from your first flogging."

"I know."

"Moycroft assigned you to bring my meals because you were healthy and not so inclined to steal food from my tray."

"Yeh."

"The crew is a pack of wild dogs."

"A stout heart here and there. Mr. Moycroft's just taking care of you."

"Moycroft? Moycroft has no heart. He has a bilge pump."

"That's every chief mate."

"Oh?" Gordon looked at him. "What would be your evaluation of 'every chief mate'?"

"A sadistic drone with no personality, no sense of humor,

and no concept of time."

"What gave you this opinion?"

"I worked for the Carrere merchant fleet."

Gordon sat back. "A chief mate?"

"Sometimes."

Fighting a smile because he'd been caught, Gordon leaned forward again and buried his reaction in a spoonful of beans. "One with a heart, I suppose."

"My shipmates are my family, if that's what you mean."

Gordon snorted a response, pretending he had no idea what Tarkio could possibly be talking about, or at least that Tarkio was lying. "I was never a chief mate. My command comes from my birthright."

"What's that mean?"

"It means my grandmother purchased it."

"A bribe, like?"

"A benefit of peerage."

"You a lord?"

"What?"

"Are you a lord?"

"An earl."

Tarkio gave that a moment of thought before going on. "Pa's a coppersmith. He makes kettles and shortbread molds. Ma designs the molds. And stills, we make stills."

"How did you then become a sailor instead of a coppersmith?"

"We make cobblers' nails for sailing shoes, and hoops and rivets for barrels. I did all the deliveries. Made friends at the shipyards. So one day—"

Gordon snapped his fingers. "You see? You Americans pretend to be innocent, but you're making copper nails and hoops! Copper-hooped casks to carry gunpowder, shoes that won't spark! Articles of war! Did you think I wouldn't notice?"

Tarkio shook his head a little and made a sort of smile that should've been insulting. "Copper-nailed shoes and copper-hooped barrels are used in black powder mills," he said. "Powder's used for clearing way for roads and mines. And anybody who works around explosives or sawdust, or even a wheat mill, needs copperwares to keep the sparks down. Don't you know that?"

"You should be a storyteller. Or a mountain climber. Yes, I can see you climbing a mountain."

"Never seen a mountain. Not a real big one, anyway." The American poured a dollop of goat's milk into the cup of tea, milk just brought on board within this hour.

As Tarkio spread the captain's meal on the tiny desktop, Gordon moved the ship's log out of the way to keep it dry. "I've always wanted to climb a mountain. The Alps ... Himalayas... Vesuvius ..."

"Don't know where those be."

"You're uneducated," Gordon snorted.

Tarkio nodded passively.

Irritated, Gordon responded, "I just insulted you. Don't you care? If you don't care about being called ignorant, what could you possibly care about?"

The other man shrugged a shoulder. "I was thinking of marrying. Care about that."

A revelation. Gordon took his teacup and blew across the steaming liquid. "You have a woman?"

"Girl. Too young yet, but in a season or two, might happen. If I stay attractive long enough for her to grow up, that is."

"Oh? How does a man at sea stay attractive with all God's weather and strife constantly upon him?"

Tarkio smiled. "Captain Boyle has a formula."

"Captain Boyle again."

"He's a man of the bigger world, y'see. Never met a man before like him. He keeps us all grinning."

"That's not the role of a captain. What's his formula? Perhaps I shall want to be attractive to a lady some day."

"No reason you can't be."

"Well?"

"Well," Tarkio echoed, "according to Tom, 'An attractive man should smell of bay rum, pipe smoke and freshly sharpened pencils.'"

Then he smiled, remembering better things.

The air in the cabin changed a bit, pushed out by a bit of breeze that carried new scents of nuts, vinegar, and overripe fruit, of sweaty bodies and women rubbed with exotic oils. There was more noise now, new noise, the cries of leashed monkeys and caged birds. New commotion on the docks and in the streets out there reminded Gordon of the dangers in this place, with its habit of too much *bonhomie* and arms too open for deserters.

"Where is this girl?" he asked.

"Baltimore."

"What sort of girl worth marrying comes from that hive?"

"Flag maker's daughter. Young, but fair and sparky. I rent a room in the house, upstairs."

"Rented. Past tense. You're in the Royal Navy now."

"I'll never be in the Royal Navy. I'm a prisoner of war."

"War?"

"Your war with Napoleon."

"But you're an American. You're neutral."

As Tarkio reached around to spread a napkin on Gordon's lap, he had that insulting little non-smile going again.

"If I'm an American," he asked, "what am I doing on this ship?"

"Being impertinent. You're on this ship because you are a British subject who ran to the Americas with the plot to escape your obligation to king and country. Or at least you're replacing a man who did that, something I'll never say outside of this cabin. Britain does not recognize a sailor's right to jump ship and emigrate."

"These are family men," Tarkio pointed out, careful of his tone.

"A quarter of America's sailors are British, and you know it."

"Some were brought to the United States when they were just children."

"Do you think that will keep them safe? Right now the Royal Navy is holding Bonaparte off. Eventually, our army will be smashed and that blood blister will move to the sea. Eventually he will gather enough forces and ordinance that the Navy will no longer be able to stop him and he'll invade England. How long after that do you think it'll take before his gunships darken your harbors?"

Tarkio folded his arms, but not in a hostile way. "Think about this day and night, do you?"

"Look over here." Pleased to be ready with an answer,

though accidentally, Gordon motioned him to the chart table
and the charts and maps upon it. He pointed at the map directly
on top, obviously of Europe and part of Russia, and swept his
finger around a large portion. "Do you see this? This is the land
Bonaparte seized last month. It's twice the size of your entire
nation."

He came back to his desk and once again sat, but did so in a
clumsy way that caused his knee to upset the desk, and the desk
to upset the tray, which upset the teapot.

Gordon jolted when Tarkio suddenly grasped his elbow.
"Get your hand off me!"

Moving with unexpected grace, Tarkio scooped up the teapot and made an arc that magically avoided Gordon's jerking
elbow. "You want to be scalded?"

"Please just put it down and shove off!"

Tarkio backed away, taking the steaming teapot with him,
but his gaze lingered on the captain of this Royal Navy ship as if
he were looking at a lost dog.

He paused a moment. "How old are you?"

Gordon stared back at him. The question hung between
them.

There would be no answer, not today, for a blast of sound
shocked them both and struck away any thoughts—a bellowing
blare, ear-splitting, uninvited, foreign. Gordon had never heard
anything like it and from his expression neither had Tarkio.

Gordon bolted from his chair. "What now!"

But Tarkio was already gone, up the companionway into the
daylight. Gordon broke out of the darkness into blinding sun,
out onto the weather deck. That awful sound came again, along
with a ridiculous jangling of sleigh bells.

Sleigh bells? In Jamaica?

On the shore, just a jump away, a mass of color and savagery
rose before him, higher than the high sides of the ship. Like a fig-
ment of fantasy, the brightly decorated form rolled a giant pink
eye and shook a peacock-feathered head-dress. Painted gaudy
yolk-yellow with *trompe l'oeil* mosaics, the beast could barely be
recognized for what it was. But it knew its own size and pumped
its tree-sized legs and rattled its chains. Wooden cages on the
dock dissolved, freeing wild tropical birds to fly into the rigging

in a panic of colors. The giant shook its face-shield made of layered silver fringe. A long painted trunk twisted in the air before Gordon's face, not four feet away.

One of the terrified marines ended up straddling the ship's rail, his musket flailing uselessly as he tried to balance. Gordon grabbed him by the arm and hauled him back on board.

Two puppeteers, a man with a monkey on a leash, and hucksters cooking in the open streets abandoned their twig shops and scrambled out of the way. Terrified women, with ropy hair tied by strips of bright fabric and big earrings made of salvaged metal, tripped over the wares they had brought to sell.

The *Helen*'s crew panicked. Some tried to climb the shrouds when again the painted monster reared, shook its headdress, rang its bells, rolled its huge pink eye and brayed that abominable noise. On the dock a frantic East Indian man waved a bamboo pole, whacking at the devil and shouting in Hindi. Over the monster's back a calico drapery waved like a flag, and this was where the sleigh bells were, turning an otherwise whimsical sound into something foul.

"Compose yourselves!" Moycroft bellowed. The crew had never seen an elephant before. Even Gordon, a privileged child of the aristocracy, had only seen drawings.

The phantom thudded down to its four feet again, rattling the whole dock. With startling flexibility it turned in the crowded place. The Indian man tried to steer it with the bamboo pole, but the animal flicked its head, caught the man on a tusk and flung him a good twelve feet through the air. He landed on birdcages full of parrots and pelicans. The birds erupted into a wall of wings, then rushed toward the interior of the island. Now the elephant was not only panicked but enraged. It took on a tucked posture and went after its handler.

Dressed in its harlequin decorations, the mad thing went down on its fore knees and crushed the Indian handler under its bent-up trunk. The man tried to cry out, but his ribs and lungs collapsed like paper. The beast was pitiless. Had it had enough of life in chains? Was it somehow humiliated by the farcical costume of feathers and bells? Did it *know*?

The slaughter of the Indian refreshed the chaos. People screamed and ran. The man with the monkey fell off the dock into the water, leaving his monkey to its own resources. Then the elephant saw the monkey.

And the monkey saw the ship's rigging.

Gordon's eyes widened. He saw the elephant's huge pink eye and knew what it was thinking.

"No, no!" he shouted and broke toward the gangway, a massive raft of planks and beams ironically meant for boarding the brig's guns and heavy ordnance. He was about to yell *stop,* but the sound caught in his throat. He might as well have cast a pebble before a landslide. The monster was on him.

—⁀⁀—

The gangway groaned under the four-ton animal, then began to crack. Gordon fell backward and dropped to his rump. Before him the elephant rumbled, snorted, pulled its trunk into that S-formation to begin another murderous attack. All Gordon saw was the silver-fringed face-shield and the peacock headdress. He reached up and received the green painted trunk into his two hands and felt as if he were trying to fend off a mountain. The skin, crusty with dried paint, quivered between his palms, and behind it was the massive skull that would crush him.

An explosion went off above him. He was suddenly covered with blood and bone, flesh, fringe and bells. A peacock feather landed on the back of his right hand.

The elephant's body dropped to the gangway in a solid lump. The gangway cracked, but didn't break. The blocky head landed on the deck between Gordon's knees. He felt suddenly ridiculous. All the noise of moments ago abruptly stopped.

Blood streamed from under the animal's face decoration. It had been shot in the skull. He stared stupidly at the blood that ran down the huge face onto his hands.

Two of the men pulled him out from where he sat cradling the mammoth's head. Before he understood what was happening, he was back on his feet. Around his face a cloud of musket smoke stung his eyes and nostrils.

In a group of marines was Victor Tarkio, holding a smoking weapon. The foolish man had shot the elephant instead of killing Gordon when he had the chance. What a silly ... wasteful fool.

Gordon stared at Tarkio, then at the carcass still shuddering as death overtook it. A heady and offensive stench roused him. The animal's bowels had released their contents all over the gangway and into the already fetid water.

Greasy sweat and the residue of black powder streaked his cheeks. This was no way for a nobleman to look. For a commanding officer ...

Handing the musket back to one of the Marines, Tarkio stepped toward him.

Gordon saw the motion in his periphery and instantly drew away before Tarkio could touch him. *Don't.*

Tarkio paused, one hand partly out.

Gordon reached for his voice, determined that he would make the crew think of Jamaica not as a fertile Utopia, but as hell's butcher-shop.

"Cut it up," he rasped. "Salt and hang the meat. Give the offal to those people out there. I'll take the ivory and one of the feet. Wash this blood away."

How did he sound to them? Commanding? Madcap? Were they trying not to laugh at him?

On thready legs he tried to move toward the stern, back toward his cabin. He would shut the door. Remain alone.

As he was about to step into the companionway, he heard a chittering noise and looked up. There was a monkey sitting on a ratline halfway up the lower shrouds. From its neck hung a blue silk leash, like some kind of perverse neckerchief. Like the neckerchief on that American captain. Fluttering in the breeze, laughing at him.

From now on, he would be the butt of a thousand jokes, jolly farces and banter in smarmy Cockney pubs and gambling parlors, where would spread the tale of James Gordon's burlesque command aboard the HMS *Absurd*. His name would float forever in tobacco smoke and weedy rums, and in time, his mother and grandmother would hear the story and the laughter.

He touched the white linen of his shirt. He had run out of his cabin in only his shirt and breeches. No jacket, no hat, no sign of his rightful rank.

On the dock, someone was laughing. Then someone else joined in, then some women. So it began.

The monkey showed its teeth and spat at him.

The Great Heart

The mountain top, the meadow plain,
The winding creek, the shady lane ...
Those sunny paths were all our own,
And you and I were there alone.

Francis Scott Key to his sister Anne about their childhood.

"WHAT DO YOU SEE over the wall, Frankie?"

"Madam, I am not a giraffe."

"Do you think you'll be taller next year? Enough to see far away?"

"I will see as far as I need to see in this earthy life. Please be patient."

Tucked in the cuff of the Blue Ridge Mountains, the boy Frankie and his sister huddled behind a tall curved brick wall, spying. At the age of twelve, this was Frankie's first year to see over the wall and still he could only get his nose to the wall's stone-blocked top and only by tilting his head back. As yet, Anne had no hope of looking over it and relied upon her brother to be the master spy. That was well, because Anne preferred to have tales told to her, while Frankie yearned to be in them.

And this would be a tale like those. Frankie anticipated making grand orations about the day the whole world visited his parents' plantation. With his chin up on the top brick of the divider between the grounds and the courtyard where his father addressed the slaves every morning, he closed his wide blue eyes and inhaled deeply. The aroma of venison, turkey, ham and pheasant dizzied him as he imagined the bustle going on in the cookhouses. Already he was mad with hunger at the scent of baking—bread, sweet pastries, muffins in the hundreds tumbling forth from a four-day frenzy of cooking. This was the great day, an appointment with destiny. A bead of perspiration broke between the boy's drawn brows.

He and his sister were accustomed to their home's being the meeting house of Frederick County. Their parents' hospitality drew every gadfly in Maryland to the ever-open gates. Every traveler from old soldier to vaporous lady knew the benevolent hospitality of the family that was the crucible for these two children, and all were welcomed in the white-plastered manor with the four stately two-story columns in the front and the gracious gardens here in back. Anne enjoyed the cooing of fine ladies and tagged behind them, imitating their postures, and Frankie gloried in the tales of the soldiers who once fought on the Potomac with his father and Lafayette against Arnold and Cornwallis. They, in fact, had given him the nickname "Frankie."

But this particular day saw guests arriving by the hundreds, leathery farmers and tattered Fighting Cocks still carrying their long rifles, neighbors of every stratum flooding down the red soil of Frederick Road, seeping from the tree line, clattering in carts, treading on foot, prancing on pedigreed steeds. The guests of honor had arrived an hour ago, before a long parade of dignitaries and escorts, coaches and grooms and footmen. Impending rain had held off all morning and there was a sparkle in the air.

"I see a horse!" Frankie rasped finally, stretching his neck.

"Is that all?" Anne asked. "A horse."

"A wonderful horse!"

Cued by his enthusiasm, Anne ventured, "Does it have wings?"

"It's gray as a cloud and bears the scars of battle!" Frankie hooked his fingers onto the top bricks and dug his toes into the lips of mortar on the bottom. He forced himself up another inch. "Anne, do you know what that is?"

"A gray battle horse with scars on his wings," she attempted, trying to remember all the adjectives. "I think I'll walk around and have a look."

She stood up from where she had carefully arranged her satin skirts into a tuffet.

"No!" Frankie pushed her back. "Everyone will see you. Do you know what that horse is? Quick—follow me!"

He curled his body and crept along the wall.

Anne followed him, not bothering to curl up. After all, she lived here.

Frankie kept his head low, lest hidden enemies spy his golden hair.

At this historic moment the children were interrupted in their reconnaissance by three of Terra Rubra's slaves hurrying down the walk with baskets of aromatic bread. It was the rolling butterball Maybel and her two skinny adopted daughters, Corabel and the other one.

"What is the game today?" Maybel called out in that crackly voice. She cocked her round body, fixed her glower on the boy, and spoke with deep-throated elegance as Frankie's grandmother had taught her as a child. "Mr. Frank, are you storming the Bastille again?"

Frankie did not straighten up. "I'm doing reconnaissance."

"Don't you go interrupting your elders at their business, mind. This is a so-important day, a so-important day."

Frankie nodded and crept past her and her skinny daughters. "Pardon, ma'ams."

"You are pardoned," Corabel or the other one said.

Frankie came to the end of the wall with Anne behind him, and peeked around into the courtyard, seventy-five-feet deep to the structure of the house and beautifully gardened terrace.

And there, tied to the hitching post, was the horse.

The horse. The horse of glory and victory.

"Do you know what that is?" Frankie whispered. "Long neck, short back, high withers ... look at the legs. Long legs. Lean, muscled body ... good hindquarters ... and the small head with a dished face, large wise eyes ... Oh, my dear sister, that is an *Arabian*!"

"Why do you start sentences with 'oh'?"

The boy studied the body and form of the chalk-gray horse as it drew a breath and sighed it out, showing a sculpted rib cage which carried the heart of a champion.

"All thoroughbreds can trace their bloodline back to three Arabians, founding sires from the Orient. They were mated with the best of English mares. Their offspring are marvelous racers, riders, hunters, and battle steeds. They exert themselves to the point of death if asked of them. That horse is the father of all the best horses. I *must* ride that horse."

"You're going to steal it?"

"I'll return in it good condition and groom it myself every hour it resides here."

His sister's mouth made an "O" of her own, but no sound.

"Here I go," Frank announced. "To the last man!"

—⁂—

The great heart thundered beneath him. The engine of a racing horse, the natural pump of an athlete, flooded the body with oxygen from the giant lungs, increasing blood through its chambers with every beat—the boy felt it between his knees. Wind tore at the horse's charcoal mane; the mane beat the boy's face, the boy's heels beat the stallion's flanks, and the stallion beat the earth.

The boy's booted feet moved heel to toe with a pause between, over and over. His imagination soared. In the measured seconds, he circled the courtyard, raced out into the terraced gardens and down them as if they were the Vallum at Hadrian's Wall. He reconnoitered behind the jardinières, took down two enemy sentries in the marigold beds, destroyed a guardhouse, and slew an Indian at the edge of the tobacco field. Worthy nemeses for him and his powerful steed-of-war! In seconds the boy and horse were in the woods, surrounded by a thousand redcoats disguised as trees. He bent forward over the stallion's withers. The black mane whipped his cheeks.

Heel, toe, heel, toe, heel, toe. He thundered at breakneck speed around the mansion, past the four white pillars, along the picket fence on the front grounds, trampling the five-foot-tall hollyhocks, then up, up, and over the gate like a big gull.

The shaded lanes raced past him, the brooks flowed beneath, the flax fields laughed as he conquered them. The power of the Arabian's thick neck and gathered thighs and shoulders chewing up the land surged their energy through the saddle leather into the boy's body and he was suddenly a god. In the kennels the foxhounds began to bay wildly, sensing they were being left out of something important.

A sudden shadow passed over his face. Things began to go suddenly wrong. A massive brown form crashed across his line of sight, blocking almost everything. Under him the gray horse twisted, balked, and flung its head back, then changed course against the will of the boy at the reins, a change so sharp that the boy went dizzy for a moment. Everything was wild—turning—

Had he fallen? Unthinkable! He hadn't fallen off a horse since—

Beneath him the light-gray Arabian gathered its experience, shook away uncertainly and the weight of its rider and plunged in a new direction, now with a companion—but the boy knew that brown hide, that deep bay color, and the scent of the hay from his own stables and the aroma of saddle leather burnished with the oils from his own tack room. This newcomer was one of his own, one of his father's favorite hunters.

A complete stranger rode the hunter, a man in a draping layered cloak, now charging alongside the boy and steering him and the stolen destrier back toward the mansion. The man rode tall in his saddle, but not up on his stirrups despite the jolting. His shoulders were back and curved downward in a frictionless posture, his deeply carved eyes were bright blue in the streams of breaking sunlight as he glanced again and again at Frank. A fan of silvering hair that had once been auburn framed the big man's rosy face and broad cheekbones.

The boy added up the facts of the case against him and realized with a shock to his chest just whose horse he had taken. Joy rushed up against panic and was consumed by the fragrance of adventure. The boy, the man, and the two horses hammered through the trees, over rocks and through thickets, hooves clattering and underbrush cracking beneath them. They bobbled in their saddles as they splashed through a stream, broke out onto the terrace, and then they were a cyclone again. The boy clung to his mount, stupefied, for he was no longer controlling the stallion. The gray would no longer answer the boy's hand on the reins nor his shifting weight in the saddle. Somehow the other rider was steering both horses with superb technique and grace. The man's hands came down with every stride to perfectly match the dip of his horses' heads.

Frankie's riding skills drained away and there was nothing he could do but totter in the saddle and cling on.

For a hair-raising moment he thought about falling off on purpose, rolling away, stumbling on his bloodless legs to the slave dormitories and hiding for a few days or months. Wouldn't work. Anne would find him, or Corabel, and then everybody. Maybe he should join the Army for a few years. In Egypt.

Beneath him the dappled stallion abruptly broke stride and gamboled sideways. Someone had a grip on its bridle now—a strong angry Negro man, who had come along in the big coach parked under the trees.

"Get the lad, Billy," another man's voice instructed.

Frank's legs flew into the air, his hands fell from the reins; he was dragged by the body from his mount and spun miraculously onto his feet. His palms felt suddenly cool and wet from the sweat that had formed as he gripped the reins. He stumbled backward just in time to miss being throttled by the furious stallion's head, the frantic reeling protests of a horse that wanted to run onward, harder, longer. Frank just wanted to run away.

"Francis! What is this?"

John Ross Key. Here already.

All at once there were more people around him, many more curious people with appalled expressions and two old mountaineers who were laughing. The faces around him made a sea of salt and pepper, all the white people who could get here today mixed with all the slaves who served them and those who lived here, invited by his father to see the eminence who had given them their nation. Scowling down at Frank, with both big hands on the boy's shoulders, was a thickly built mulatto man who looked very angry.

Even more appalling for him were the eyes of the women now appearing behind his father. His mother, whom Anne was named after, stood just over there, where in the mornings when the weather was good she taught the slaves to read, write, and sing hymns. She was arm-in-arm with his pious and poised Grandmother Key, brought from Belvoir to attend this day. Long ago blinded while rescuing a slave from a house fire, his grandmother could not see him, but he knew she would listen for his voice, judge his resonance, his breathing, his posture, his enunciation, text, and subtext with her Puritan code of manners.

More for her than anyone else, Frank squared his shoulders and summoned up a voice he hoped would be as elegant as hers. "I've ridden an Arabian, Father."

"The question was rhetorical. I've barely tamed your Uncle Phillip and here you are, complicating my life with indecorous pranks. Defend this barbarism."

"Ah ... I ... I ..." Frankie heard his voice, but didn't recognize it. If his actions were indefensible, why did his father bother asking? Aware of the many eyes on him, he squeezed out a noise. "I *saw.*"

"You saw? The horse?"

"The ... opportunity."

"What does *that* mean?"

"Americans should ... seize opportunity."

"Nobly said." But these words were not his father's. Somehow Frankie knew that voice, despite never having heard it before in his twelve years of life.

His father's voice was very different. "Turn around, Frank."

"Must I?"

"Mm."

The boy's stomach dropped. He turned and looked up, up, and more up. Towering over him, the grand gentleman smiled with lips pressed flat. His fog-silver hair and dark blue jacket had become legendary over the course of Frank's young life, and everyone knew him. For Frank, though, General Washington had been an unexpected riding companion, which complicated the moment.

"Good morning, Master Frank."

As the bravado of youth withered, Frank's voice was pitiful. He did try, however, as Grandmother Key had taught him, to make a single dramatic gesture with one hand. "I do beg your pardon most sincerely, Your Excellency."

Finished, he drew his hand back to his chest and waited.

"Pardoned," the whip-hand of history said. "But not *Your Excellency*. We dismiss royal titles. He who is Mr. President must know that he is no king."

Drawn down, the boy felt coldly absurd at his own arrogance. From now on everyone would recall the legacy of the silly stripling who had exhausted George Washington's warhorse on the John Ross Key plantation. Terra Rubra would become a subject of mockery throughout history.

"My son has a nature for the theatrical," his father said to the general. "Our grooms will rub down your stallion and cool him."

"Kind of you," the general responded. "He is none the worse for a gallop. Nor am I."

Two more women appeared at the front of the gathering crowd—it was Mrs. Washington and her servant girl, whom Frank recalled being introduced to his mother as Oney Judge. The mulatto girl had a very fair freckle-peppered face and looked almost white.

The general turned a spiritless eye on Frank and spoke slowly and with difficulty. He had a contraption in his mouth that Frank did not understand. "Would you like to meet my charger formally?"

"Please, your ... president."

The general waved at his footman, who brought the snorting gray around to face Frank. The horse's flaring nostrils put droplets of foam on the boy's face. The horse looked right at him. *Right* at him.

"His name is Blueskin," the general said. "He's very old."

"He's an Arabian, isn't he?" Frank gasped.

"Half Arabian. He's big for his breed. I ride him only for show, now and then," the general told John Key.

Frank's father looked at the boy again. "Tell Mr. Washington you're sorry."

Again, the boy was brutally aware of his grandmother just over there, listening.

"I can beg his pardon," he told them, "but I'm not sorry."

John Key turned a color or two.

Everyone looked at Frank. Everyone—the sun, the moon, the gods, the winds—

"Is that so?" the general asked.

"I will cherish the experience, sir. I cannot regret it!"

"Frank," his father droned in warning.

"Integrity," the tall man said. He didn't smile, but seemed satisfied as he looked at Frank. "You're a capable horseman, young man. And you have a sense of honor."

Frank simply stood there, shaking and sweating. Was the general making a joke?

"Blueskin is one of my favorites," the general said with difficulty, and patted the horse's sweaty neck, a gesture of deep familiarity. "I lost Nelson, my excellent sorrel battle horse, just last Christmas. He was twenty-seven." But now the general was no longer speaking just to the boy, but to all the people gathered around. Everyone wanted to hear everything, anything, he had to say.

What must that be like? For everyone to know your name?

Speaking was a struggle for the tall man, Frank noticed again, as the general hesitated over the letters *f* and *s*, and kept his mouth almost closed even when speaking. The *s*-sounds came out like *sh*.

Battle horse. Frankie heard the words over and over. Suddenly he had a thousand questions. Had it been grand? Was it song and story, glory and pride? What was battle *like*? Was it like anything?

But humbled as he was, he had no courage to ask.

The general gazed around the grounds, so calm that at any given pause he might have been posing for a portrait. "What is Terra Rubra's acreage?"

"It began as one-thousand-six-hundred in 1750," John Key told him. "A thousand acres of forest, almost a thousand, were cleared by slaves and hired whites. They built the stables and slave quarters, dug the wells and surveyed the land. Later the property was enlarged to two-thousand-eight-hundred acres and a road was cut from Philadelphia to Williamsburg."

"What do you produce here? I smell tobacco."

"Tobacco, wheat, buckwheat, corn, and flax."

"How many bondsmen have you?"

"This month I believe it is one hundred seven, a little fewer than usual. I freed a man and his family in the early spring. My

wife had taught him to read and do arithmetic and he had become a good ironsmith, thus we let him go so he could work in
Philadelphia and support his brood. There's a teacher there who
accepts Negro children. He planned to travel back and forth to
see his wife and children, but I saw no advantage in breaking up
his family."

The general nodded with what seemed to be appreciation.
"Marriage between the bonded must be respected. I never dis-
perse families nor separate a man and wife. Billy," he called
then, and turned to the mulatto man who had seized Frank from
the saddle.

"Right here, sir," the man responded.

Washington went on without a pause. "Mr. Billy Lee has
been with me since he was fifteen. He is my constant companion through many expeditions and through the war as my *val
de chambre*. I appealed to my purchasing agent to have Billy's
wife brought to us in Virginia. It rubs against my nap to hurt
anyone's feelings."

"And Neptune's wife also, sir," Billy added.

"Yes, our bricklayer's wife. The laborers in my family are
never made to pine or hunger, though were I to give them too
much they would simply sell it. They tend gardens to add to their
allotments. I often purchase sweet potatoes from them. I have
two baskets in the wagon. I would like to give you one basket."

"Thank you," John Key said. "Do your servants fish? We
have a bounty in Big Pipe Creek. Our Maybel makes a mouth-
watering chopped trout."

Billy, sensing an interruptible moment, raised a shiny brass
dial as some sort of illustration. "Sir, the audience is waiting."

"What's that?" Frankie blurted. He was unable to control the
child in himself at the sight of the gleaming contraption.

The slave looked at the general. Mr. Washington nodded.

Billy turned to Frankie and held the dial in both hands so
the boy could see.

"This is Mr. Washington's ring dial. The Marquis de Lafayette made it a gift to him."

"Is it a sundial?" Frankie nosed his way closer to the dial,
which was about the diameter of a grapefruit and possessed
two engraved brass rings, one inside the other, the outer en-

graved with scrolled decorations and a ruled scale of numbers by the tens. The inner circle was engraved with Roman numerals. There was also some kind of brass fitting on the axis that was engraved with letters and lines. The whole thing looked like some kind of circular slide-rule.

"These leaves are acanthus," Billy explained, pointing to the scrolled decorations. "This ring is the meridian ring, this the equatorial ring, and this is the central bar. One tells the time by turning the dial until sunlight falls on the hour ring and one peers through this small hole. This is a precisely calibrated timepiece, accurate at any latitude except—"

"Would you like to try it?" the general offered to the boy.

"Oh! May I?" Frankie gasped.

While Billy showed the boy how to work this elegant contraption, all manner of persons crept onto the lawn beneath the portico from where they had camped under the trees over there or waited in their carriages by the meadow. The crowd represented every stripe of American, from the grizzled veterans of the War for Independence to proud ladies from plantations around, to the stately attorneys, thin or round, old and young, of the Key family's connections in the field of law, since John Key was a judge and his brother an attorney. Some other judges had also come, hoping to be able to say they knew the great general.

There were no grand reminiscences, no gloried battle tales, no victory whoops, no raucous jokes at the expense of the English, nor even any mention that the Revolution had happened at all. Instead, the men were discussing fertilizer, slaves and sweet potatoes. What was inspiring about that?

One of the house servants appeared with a tray of crystal glasses properly filled with Old Madeira wine and offered a glass to the general first, then John Key, as the gathering of special guests turned toward the manor doors. Other servants floated about with trays of strawberries, crab and oysters. The host led the way, with General Washington by his side, still talking again about agriculture. John made a friendly gesture, as he was inclined, by taking the general by one arm, only to have the famous man step sideways and skillfully pull out of the grip. Frank squinted, wondering whether he interpreted the action correctly. The movement communicated that Mr. Washington did not tolerate being touched.

After them came the governor; the administrators of Frederick County; Mrs. Washington with Frank's mother and his elegant blind grandmother; the aides and Billy Lee; more guests of importance who had come along with the general in his entourage; and everyone who would have the honor of standing on the portico with the general, Mrs. Washington, and their hosts.

Frank watched them go with a quaver in his chest. The general was a *very* big man ... every president from now on would have to be big.

He almost tagged after them as if drawn by some cosmic magnetism, but was drawn backward by a small set of hands biting into his arm.

"Frankie!" It was Anne. She was dragging him back, out onto the crowded lawn.

"Th—thank you," he gasped and sank to his backside on the cool grass next to a pink-bearded old man in buckskins.

"You did it!" his sister gasped. "Was it wonderful?"

Frank had no answer. With Anne sitting beside him in her satin frock, he sat there too and shook.

The children turned quiet. Their plantation garden between the two bracketing brick walls was now crowded with strangers. Hardly anyone spoke.

Though the sun shined, there were clouds moving in. Out over the terraced gardens, beyond the paths and shaded lanes, on the tops of the Blue Ridge an electrical storm was growing.

Above them on the beautiful plastered portico where Frank and Anne had watched so many sunsets and played guessing games, John Key and General Washington appeared first, then their wives and a few of the more highly titled guests. In spite of the dithers caused by his visit, General Washington was steady as Gibraltar, the man who had spent tortured years bending posterity to his will, dominating the scene with the power of his mind and the resonance of his place as consultant to history. Standing with practiced poise, he was nearly a statue of himself.

How many times had this happened in the past few days, and how many more would it happen before the general and his wife arrived at their destination in New York for his inauguration as president? In how many villages, ports and farmhouses had he looked out over the people of America, who knew him by his reputation better than they knew each other in person? He could be a king if he wanted to, but he didn't want to.

"My countrymen," he began, "I am about to leave your good land, your beautiful valleys, your refreshing streams, and the blue hills of Maryland, which stretch before me. I cannot leave you, fellow citizens, without thanking you again and again for the true and devoted friendship you have shown me. When in the darkest hours of the Revolution, of doubt and gloom, the succor and support I received from the people of Frederick County always cheered me. It always woke a responsive echo in my heart. I feel the emotion of gratitude beating in my heart. My heart is too full to say more ... God bless you all."

The words did not echo, but they seemed to do so.

Polite applause began among the ladies and quickly swelled into cheers and whoops. A couple of old soldiers shot their turkey guns into the air. On the portico, General Washington waved and made a flat-lipped smile.

Frankie Key stared up at the master-hand of history and wondered where the rest of the speech had gone. Where were the retellings of glorious battles and danger? Why wasn't he recalling his coolheadedness at facing the most skilled fighting force in the world, or his long-sightedness when most men couldn't see past breakfast? Hadn't everyone come to hear from his own mouth the resonance of his trials? Where was the jubilation? George Washington was a man to whom the future was a craft to be chiseled and formed by the hand of justice. They would have stood here and listened for hours, yet he spoke only a few seconds. During his progress through town after town, manor after manor, had he used up all his good speeches?

The cheering was still going on. More than just a response to a speech, this was something else. Frankie looked out among the visitors. They had come, many of them, from far away, or had given up this day at their ploughshares or offices just to be here, he thought, to hear heart-swelling descriptions of eight years of war and final victory. Instead, they were smiling, cheering and clapping tirelessly. Their smiles were poignant, their applause without eddy. General Washington bowed his head and waved solemnly to them again. The audience's effervescence didn't diminish. The other people on the portico actually stepped back, sensing something, and gave the general his moment in the sun. He had come, it seemed, not to impress these common people, but to thank them. They had come, it seemed, to thank *him*. The boy with the wide poetic eyes and the caramel curls sat humbled in the puddle of his own assumptions, and in this void something else rushed in—an adult thought, perhaps, an idea completely new to him after his twelve years of experience.

He would think about this. He would walk the paths and ride the red lands of Frederick County and whenever he was alone, he vowed to himself, he would think about this moment and try to understand it. He sensed there was more than he was able to digest, something these men and women around him already knew, but if he asked them they would scowl at him and shake their heads. He felt his natural shyness creep up. Instinctively, he stayed quiet.

The cheering continued. The general—*President* Washington—oversaw the crowd's felicity, somehow completely at ease in the eye of the world. There might have been a hundred people here or a hundred thousand, and he would command them. All day he would shake their hands and talk to them about farming, rifles, yams, timber, and mundane things that mattered. This evening he would leave, once again on the progress to New York, with his battle steed beneath him and Mrs. Washington in her coach, their servants and footmen and grooms and escorts, and Terra Rubra would return to its eternal springtime where never a harsh word would be spoken nor a heart hurt. There would be only the lingering echo, like something out of a myth, of the general, two children, and this idyllic place.

1812

Tug of War

*"America certainly cannot pretend to wage war with us;
she simply has no navy to do it with."*

THE LONDON STATESMAN

NEW YORK HARBOR
MAY 1812

"SOMEONE'S BUBBLING A CAULDRON of pig fat."

"It's Congress, back in session. Throw yourself in, John."

On this sparkling day, New York Harbor was spindled with topmasts. The usual bustle of seagoing ships laden with goods and passengers was overcrowded today by hundreds more vessels and thousands more people flanking the channels. From barges to pilot boats to Indian birchbark canoes, every possible floating platform was crammed with spectators, every deck and patch of wharf a rental space. Today was the first Parade of the Fleet of the United States' Navy.

A Marine of nineteen years heard the voices of men conversing as he climbed a questionable ladder to the top of a chandlery, clumsily balancing his musket on his two arms as he made his way up. *Wouldn't be seemly to drop the thing, would it?* He had been ordered to the roof as a guard. *To guard what? Seagulls?*

Orders were that he climb, and repel anyone else from climbing. *By gosh a'mighty, I'll blow the hair off anybody coming to my roof.* Orders were orders. He liked orders. Made life clear.

As he nosed his way to the top, he saw three men, elders, standing at the roof's north edge, looking out at the harborscape, while behind them three empty rocking chairs nodded in the sea breeze. *Odd ... only three men?* Many dozens of citizens coveted this high vantage, to view the Parade of the Fleet. Were these men aristocrats who had paid dearly for this privacy?

The Marine surveyed the rest of the wide roof, where a long table with a bright white draping displayed plates of biscuits and cheese, strawberries, apple wedges, fried chicken legs, finger-cakes, and a pitcher of lemonade surrounded by crystal cups. Three men and a maid tended the food tables while a servant boy with wide shoulders, Negro or possibly mixed, with pleasant features and strong black brows. He wore a red brocade jacket, and batted an ostrich feather at springtime's opportunistic flies. Behind the three aristocrats were three sturdy-looking rocking chairs, wagging a bit in the breeze.

The servant boy waved to the Marine to come forward. Moving quietly, the Marine shifted this way and that to gain footing on the roof without fumbling his musket again. If these were newspaper owners, perhaps they would have a good word for a young soldier.

His name in a newspaper? *Famous!*

At this moment of heady self-delusion, the Marine tripped. The musket went clattering onto the roof before him. He landed on his chest, with his legs splayed out behind him, legs wagging in mid-air.

The servant boy winced in empathy, but didn't move away from his post.

The tallest of the aristocrats turned to look. In a moment the other two also looked.

"Oh," expressed the shortest of the three men. "A visitor."

"No need to genuflect, soldier," said the rosy-cheeked man of middle height, who appeared younger than the other two, though all were clearly senior. This man was dressed entirely in black, except for a white collar. Probably a minister.

"This Marine must be a fan of yours, Jemmy," the tallest man remarked in a quiet voice, speaking to the man in black clothes.

The middle one was fairer of face than the others, with a complexion that still clung to youth despite his platinum hair, and he was slight of body. But there was something in his eyes that caught the Marine by surprise ... amusement, intelligence. Something.

The three men were rather an unlikely trio, seeming to have nothing in common. "Jemmy" was frail-looking, with nothing adventurous about him as he stood there in a long black velvet jacket offset by a white shirt. The next man was the shortest, but also portly and solid, leaning on a cane to relieve what appeared a sore left leg. His jacket was dark blue. They looked like ... barristers. Or professors.

Jemmy ... Jimmy? James? The Marine squinted at the short man who was younger than the other two and suddenly added up his situation. He knew who that man was! His head swam at the realization. He felt both inadequate to his assigned task and thrilled at the privilege. He would be able to tell his older brothers, *"I was there that day for the Parade of Sail and I guarded the president of the United States!"*

And two of his friends.

For the first time in his life, he would have a tale to tell! A reason to speak ... *a reason for folk to listen to me!*

He shouldered his musket and scanned the scene on the roof, and well beyond to the harbor. He would have to plumb every detail, remember everything, and tell it right. Today's was a gathering of modern Americans, and from the roof of this three-story chandlery the privileged trio before him seemed to be the winged side of a coin struck a generation ago. In those days, there would've been thousands of powdered heads bobbing about, but white wigs had fallen out of fashion. His uncle had been a wigmaker, but now told him that wigs were "too derivative of Europe" and had changed to making wool-felt hats for frontiersmen. Not fashion but finance had caused that change. American craftsmen like his uncle were busy making field weapons and deerskin coats for adventure in the untamed-wilderness territories of Michigan, Indiana, and the Niagara frontier, not threading and powdering faux coifs for parlor intrigue.

The stout and solidly built man named John leaned on his cane and wrinkled his nose at the odor of potato skins, meal

leavings, cabbage hearts, and turnip flakes burping in a pot
somewhere on the street below. "Seems the Irish can't leave the
Ould Sod behind even in the city," he said.

The Marine tucked his chin, aware of himself. He had taken
a dipper of that soup from the vendor on his way to the ladder.
He'd thought it earthy and good.

The pleasant scent—pleasant to him—mingled with that of
molten bee's wax from the shop below, where a display of candle-dipping stood in the front window. The display had begun
a few days ago, he recalled, with strips of dried rushes tied to
a pole on a rack, hanging above a long trough of melted tallow
kept hot by a bed of coals. Each morning and each afternoon the
rushes were dipped, showing a method of candle-dipping used
since feudal times.

"Witness this metropolis of New York," the president said.
"Nearly doubled in population since the Revolution. We were
four millions of Americans then. Now we are nearly eight millions. I'm heartened to see what the spirit of free enterprise has
done in thirty-five years."

"It's thirty-four years," the man named John said. "Can you
count ships any better?"

The president—James Madison —smiled. "Well enough to
see six strong frigates and a corvette, and a worthy-looking fleet
of sloops, brigs, and gunboats. What do you see?"

"American ships built with American timber," John said.
"Three-thousand trees for each frigate."

They paused from their conversation and looked out on the
harbor as the Frigates USS *Chesapeake* and *President* passed
under lower sails in the favorable breezes.

The tallest of the dignitaries tamed a flip of pale hair that
still held its tint of red. "There's the *Constitution*," he said in
his delicate voice. "I've toured her. The architecture is inspiring.
And it was brilliant to build each of the frigates in a different
port."

"Yes, it was," President Madison agreed. "Six ports full of
American wrights and smiths making the Navy. Was that your
idea, John?"

"Partly," the stout man said.

The tallest man pulled out a small telescopic spyglass from

where it had been apparently stuck in his waistcoat. He focused upon the *Constitution*.

"Hercules with a raised club. Her figurehead. Very elegant."

They paused and watched as three more frigates, the *United States*, the *Constellation* and the *Congress* floated slowly after the first three. The black-hulled ships were heavy and noble, dressed with signal flags flicking like a hundred snakes' tongues, and the flag of the United States lopping grandly off each stern. Each ship moved under reduced sail, and there was a bit of interest to see that different sail plans moved them, showing that each ship was individual in handling, despite that they looked very alike. To have all six frigates in one harbor—would this ever happen again?

"I like the figurehead on the *United States*," the shorter, rounder John said.

"I can't see it from this angle."

"A sculpture of a lady who is supposed to be the Genius of America. She holds a portrait of George Washington on a chain, a belt of wampum in one hand, and the U.S. Constitution in the other hand. I saw it while they were carving it. Excellent artwork, really. Ships' figureheads, I mean."

"What is that sloop-of-war across the harbor?" the tall man asked.

"That's the *Enterprise*."

"Wasn't she at the Battle of Valcour Island?"

"I think so," the president said, "or a sloop of the same name. Twelve guns. I wish she had more."

The man called Thomas, with hardly any volume behind his voice, said, "The government must never have more guns than the people, else you have guns pointing in the wrong direction."

His face was like his voice, with soft wide-set brown eyes, and straight pinkish brows like watercolor strokes the Marine's mother made on her little canvasses on Sunday afternoons. She painted clouds. Clouds, all the time.

The young Marine thought of his defenseless mother and opened his mouth to add to the conversation, but thankfully was saved from childishness by the crew of the *Constitution* as they cheered at the three men on this rooftop.

The president laughed and waved back.

Stout John waved his cane. "Thank you," he said. "Thank you, good men all."

"Look at their faces," Thomas said. "They're proud."

"It's not their faces that worry me." John squinted into the bright reflection of sunlight on the water. "A fleet of seventeen ships that doesn't stretch across this harbor, and we're about to go up against a fleet of nine hundred veteran warships that stretches from horizon to horizon. This predicament is your doing, Thomas, cutting the military budget."

"I remember. I was there." Thomas waved again at the cheering sailors. "I endeavored to reduce the influence of the government."

The president waved also, changing to the other hand when his arm grew fatigued. "America may not be able to contend with Britain on the seas, but we also can't be defeated on land. Our militia will rise to win again."

"Oh, be warned!" John snapped rudely. "General Washington is not here to build you an army this time."

At this venerated name, a sacred moment dropped upon the trio like goose-down. The great icon rose before each of their minds, so clearly that the Marine could almost see him floating above them.

The president asked, "Do you think we'll need a large regular army?"

"Yes, I do."

"Even with England drained of resources? After using all their arms and men fighting Napoleon, this might be the perfect time—"

"Reckless! We're far more depleted than they are."

"Most communities have militia companies. We won the Revolution with armed citizens, not a regular army."

"We won by the trick of audacity and the bulwark of George Washington. Never has such a man existed at the right time, and since then we have hunted among ourselves for anyone who could rise to his example. We all fell wanting. He was the man of his century."

"Of the millennium," the elegant Thomas agreed.

Spontaneously each man raised a glass of lemonade.

"To the general," John said, and they all drank, repeating,

"The general."

When that moment had passed, with all its gravity, Thomas went on, saying, "We had a chance to avoid unnecessary military investments, so I took it. We were no longer at war. I endeavored to cut the national debt."

"You did," Mr. Madison agreed.

"I question the expenditure for a military academy at West Point. Do we really need trained officers and gentlemen to fight the red Indians?"

"*Not* to fight red Indians," John argued. "To fight the drilled regulars of England and France. Is no one listening to me? Again?"

Thomas waved again to the passing sailors on the frigates. "France has no interest in this continent. That's why Napoleon sold us his possessions here. Oh, look—a spicebush swallowtail."

He stepped quickly to a corner of the roof where a colorful butterfly had lited. He stooped and carefully enticed the little creature onto his finger, then pulled a small magnifying glass from his waistcoat pocket and began examining the creature, whose black-velvet wings were dotted with white marks and a crescent of blue dots on the back part, inside the white dotted border. He held the bug so professionally that it began moving its wings placidly open and closed, open and closed, as if inviting his gaze.

"I had some of these on my sassafras last spring," he murmured, barely audible.

President Madison watched him thoughtfully. "I don't blame the English for being afraid. The French betrayed their own revolution with ten years of weak government and radical leaders, only to let a tyrant seize power. General Washington refused a crown. Napoleon crowned himself."

Turning the butterfly this way and that to have a good look, Thomas responded, "While we sold exports to both sides."

"We should've taken Canada years ago," John mused, almost to himself. "Benedict Arnold was right."

President Madison waved a dismissive hand. "Let's not raise his spirit here."

"We could have used a thousand Benedict Arnolds," John said, "before he met that Loyalist girl."

"Congress dealt him a cold hand," Thomas mentioned. With that, he gave his hand a shake. The butterfly flipped away, and he watched it fly. "He was wounded in more than just the leg."

"Many are wounded," the president said. "Few change their coats. If we go to war with Britain, will we not then be Napoleon's allies?"

John clacked the end of his cane on the hard roof. "We are *not* Napoleon's allies!"

"We are if we make Britain weaker," Thomas cautioned. "Forcing them to fight on two fronts helps us, but it also helps Napoleon."

"And it would force us to increase our government's control over trade on the seas."

"Do we have the revenue for that?"

"Not for a bigger navy," the president answered.

"You see?" John seemed to be rather enjoying himself. "We need a *strong* federal presence with *money* to support a standing military."

The president frowned and looked down at the roof beneath their feet, as if thinking about the foundation they all stood upon. "Strong federal government means more government employees and more money funneling to them, which means more chicanery. I fear you and I and all of us failed to protect liberty well enough in the founding documents."

"Or to protect the documents themselves enough," Thomas added.

"A lovely speech," John spouted. "Too bad only we pigeons are hearing it."

The Marine had almost forgotten that he himself was here, listening. He glanced at the servant, who only nodded back at him as if he'd heard these talks a dozen times. Probably he had.

John huffed a rebuke, looked out over the sailing fleet and controlled his tone. "Too many people think war talk is a bluff." He turned directly to the president. "Is it?"

"If you mean we will posture toward war, then back away if the bait is taken, then, no, it is not," the president said. "We will not back away. If you're asking whether Britain will cease its offenses once it realizes we're serious, then I sincerely believe there is a chance. Napoleon has them engaged and spread very thinly."

"Our borders are very long," John said, "and will spread us thinly too. *And* many men will not cross state borders to defend other states. Several governors have sworn not to commit their troops over state lines. If we go to war, there had better be a firm national motivation. Firm enough to move all their souls and impress England and France that we are serious."

President Madison abandoned them to get a little plate of food from the beautiful table, attended by the Negro boy in red velvet. "I ask you both here for suggestions and what I get is deeper quandary."

The Marine took the pause as a chance to move to the edge of the roof and look around. Below were hundreds of people crowding the waterfront, watching as the Parade of Sail began to come back along the opposite bank, giving everyone a second look at each ship.

The president accepted a small dipping bowl of honey for his biscuits from the servant. "Thank you, Paul. Do help yourself."

"Thank you, sir, I will," the teenaged boy responded pleasantly. "First let me refresh your lemonade."

The Marine found himself looking at the boy, who was not dark-skinned, and had real nice features, strong eyes, and a satisfaction of self beyond his years. He couldn't have been more than fifteen, and here he was tending these elegant and important men. *I wonder if I could do that.*

"Thank you." Mr. Madison turned again to his guests. "I had hoped the United States could remain neutral in European conflicts."

"Ironic," Thomas said, "that we may have to go to war to secure our right to be neutral."

"There seems no such thing as 'neutral' when one trades, does there? England is in financial disaster after years of battling that maniac. If we posture toward war, perhaps they'll negotiate and we'll win free trade on the Atlantic without firing a shot."

"Oh, fantasy!" John roared, so loudly that people on the street below looked up.

The Marine flinched at the great insult. Training begged him to be quiet, but his youth and Irish blood erupted all at once.

"Sir! I beg your pardon!"

All three elders turned to him as if just noticing him all over again.

"Something?" John asked.

"Sir, your tone!"

John's brows went up. "My tone?"

Committed to his interruption now that he'd made it, the Marine shrank inside his jacket. "It's ... you are ..."

"'Abrasive' is usually the word," John offered.

"Fire-eating," the president said with his mouth full.

"Cranky, bombastic, intemperate," Thomas added.

The Marine stammered, "But a ... a ... after all, Mr. Mad— Mr. Mad—"

"Mr. Mad," John chuckled.

"He ... *is* the president ..."

John turned to Madison. "Are you?"

Madison tipped his face downward. "Witness the configuration of my many chins."

The three elders laughed and so did the boy servant.

Confused, the Marine shrank further. They were laughing at him.

Thomas smiled at the president. "I would congratulate you, but no man who has held that office would wish it on a friend."

Again, they laughed, but this laugh was different, more private.

"Young man," the president then said, directly to the Marine, "before we discompose you further, may I introduce to you the Honorable John Adams, he who began the Navy passing here today."

"And a mighty mallet it took, too," John added.

The Marine swallowed his musket. Right down to the bayonet.

"He's turning blue," Thomas warned.

"And this," Madison went on, "is the Honorable Thomas Jefferson."

The last thing the Marine heard was Thomas Jefferson's soft voice saying, "There he goes—"

There was a twirl, a buzz, then nothing.

—⟋⟍—

When his mind began to reawaken, the Marine sensed his body rocking backward and forward. Something touched his lips. Sweet and tart ... moist ...

"Drink. It's lemonade. With sugar." This must be the servant boy, because it was none of the three other men's voices.

The warm liquid ran down his throat and choked him awake. He jolted and struggled, saw his legs kicked out in front of him.

"Remain seated, young man," Mr. Madison instructed, his face just coming into focus.

An order from the president. What should he do now?

"But who will guard you?" the Marine stammered, spitting lemonade.

With a funny lilt, Mr. Jefferson offered, "Oh, I will. After all, I have your firearm."

"You?" Mr. Adams commented. "Thus is conquered the last thing Thomas has not yet done in this earthly life."

Mr. Jefferson aimed the musket at a passing gull. "Just a hobby to keep me busy when we're not pinching the presidency from each other. This is a solid fowling gun. Did it belong to your father?"

The Marine couldn't speak yet. He was young, but not so young that he didn't know the story of his own nation and the eminence of the men whom fate had sent him to guard. Not only were they all presidents, but Adams had been vice president to George Washington, Jefferson had been Adams' vice president, and Madison had been Jefferson's secretary of state. These men had risked their lives and done treason to make the United States out of a bunch of owned colonies, then had stepped up to be its first administrators, to shove it off down history's trail in the right direction.

The president extended his own plate to the Marine. "Have a chicken leg."

"Sir, I must guard you!"

"Against what?"

Mr. Adams made a derisive snort. "Jemmy, don't bait him!"

Madison looked up. "Am I being naive? There's no danger here, is there?"

"Only from the hooded highwaymen we call *government*." Mr. Jefferson proclaimed, still toying with the musket.

"Tom," Madison scoffed.

"It's John's fault," Mr. Jefferson added softly. "He got me into this."

Mr. Adams shook his head. "Now, don't blame me!"

The three dignitaries laughed, the depth of their amusement completely lost on the Marine.

A companionable silence fell again as they watched the beautiful Parade of Sail. The American Navy's eighteen-gun brig *Hornet* and ten-gun *Viper* were just sliding by, barely able to contain their speed in a breeze stiff enough to move the bigger and heavier frigates.

"How capricious the winds of international troubles, John," James Madison mused, "to have seen the French seizing American ships in your presidency and England seizing American sailors in mine. Paul, may we look at the cartograph, please?"

Out there on the water, the six frigates were returning along the other shore, fluttering with flags and pennants, sailors standing on their yards, high up there, as straight as rows of pins. Somehow they no longer made the Marine feel better. The ships had been brought here to showcase the American Navy, but instead had proven its inadequacy.

The three elders gathered around a small wooden folding table, put up quickly by the servant boy called Paul and another of the servants, then Paul unrolled a good-sized map and put little sandbags on the corners so the map would not roll up again.

The president put his hand on the map. "The War Hawks justify annexing Canada and Florida on the basis that the Crown's allies have shelter there."

"A war to justify having a war," Thomas said sadly.

"They insist that Britain is drained of resources after the long struggle with France and that Canada has few soldiers, arms, or supplies along this area of the border, which is probably true." He ran his fingers along the cartograph. "General Hull can move from Detroit into Ontario and toward Quebec. Quebec is still the most populated area. Most people there are French. Would they be loyal to Britain? Do you think they will flock to us in a war?"

"Impossible to know," Mr. Jefferson told him honestly. "We

do have good military presence on Lake Erie, of course."

"We have ships and coastal gunboats," the president said. "The Brig *Niagara* is there. We could attack Fort Detroit, and the British are probably unable to defend York. Lake Ontario would be ours."

Thomas added, "Including Sackett's Harbor. Good defensive position."

Mr. Adams looked down from the roof at a common sight on the water below them—a thirty-foot-long birchbark canoe sliding by the shore, loaded with what appeared to be two or three families of Indians, all wearing calico and hats with feathers and strips of fabric decorating them, and an American flag hanging from a stick at the back of the canoe.

"What about the Indians?" he asked.

The president peered over the roof's edge at the full canoe. "What about them?"

"The tribes in the Western Territories, I mean. Michigan. Ohio. They'll defend their fur trade with English. And the English have always supplied them in their attacks of white settlers. They may be a factor against us."

"Or for us," Thomas said. "If war weakens Britain's Indian alliances, expansion will be easier for settlers. More Americans might support a breakdown of those relationships."

"Such support would be fresh air to me. I asked for revenue for increased military to defend the sovereignty we have won, yet I've received obstructionism, as if Americans don't understand. Anti-war sentiment in Massachusetts and Connecticut has clogged the wheels so much that I'm afraid a war will not accomplish its objectives. Great differences of opinion exist as to the time and form of entering into hostilities. Negotiation has failed—"

Mr. Adams snapped, "It always does when from the weaker side."

"We could suspend commerce or engage embargos with foreign nations, but—"

"But we know *that* doesn't work." Mr. Adams flicked a ferocious glare at Mr. Jefferson, who simply made a nodding shrug with one hand. There was some kind of past in that gesture that the three seniors recognized.

"I'm vacillating, aren't I?" the president said unhappily. "Not the truest mark of a statesman."

"Your hesitation shows your strength of conscience," Mr. Jefferson told him. "If nations go to war for every degree of injury, there will never be peace on earth."

Mr. Madison turned and suggested with sincere passion, "Thomas, why don't you come to Washington and address Congress? Surely you could influence a more rational state of mind—"

The pleasant man shook his head. "You know I am no public speaker."

"Do you still believe," John charged, "that war is better for business than unresisted depravation?"

"Things do change, John."

"But do you *believe* it?"

"Yes."

"*Et tu, Brute*?" the president said with a little smile.

"Yes, *et moi*."

Again, they laughed, but not with much mirth.

"So some kind of action is supported by two men I admire, and one of them isn't me," the president contemplated. "We haven't been able to protect our merchant shipping. The French raid our trade even more than the British. At this pace, we'll have no trade at all. Should we now have a U.S.-Franco-Anglo war?"

Mr. Adams snickered. "Yankee Frankie Limey. That won't give us Canada."

The president accepted another cupful of lemonade from his servant. "Thank you, Paul. I need suggestions, gentlemen, if you have any."

"Grant letters of marque and reprisal to American merchant ship owners," Mr. Jefferson suggested. "Let them go on the offensive. Turn dolphins into sharks."

"Turn honest businessmen into pirates, you mean," the president said. He then quickly held up a hand when Mr. Jefferson inhaled to make some point. "No, no, I'll do it, of course. All vats must be tapped."

The Marine quietly asked, "Your honors ... may I speak?"

He flinched, shocked to hear his own voice, right out like

that.

The eminent Mr. Adams clapped him on the back. "We had a revolution so that you might speak. Have at us."

The boy stammered at first, but then found himself. "Are we going to make a war? Right on our own soil?"

Mr. Adams flicked the president and Mr. Jefferson a glance meant more for Madison, then looked out over the quietly moving ships and boats and canoes. "What do you say, Jemmy?" he asked. "Shall I give this fellow an honest answer?"

"A United States Marine deserves nothing less."

Mr. Adams nodded. "Well, young man, we're skating rapidly toward war, yes, on our own land, that we are not ready to wage. There are simply not enough of *you*."

The Marine found his legs and stood up. He found the steel inside himself to face the three presidents.

Three presidents! Would anyone ever believe him?

He licked his lips, but it didn't help. "Should we swaller the Britishes pulling men off our ships and pressin'em into the Royal Navy?"

"Or that we cease to defend immigrants as rightful citizens of the United States?" Mr. Madison added.

Adams shook his head. "I don't suggest those at all."

He looked out over the harbor at the small red-white-and-blue banner of the United States flicking over the stern of the Indians' birchbark canoe. The flag rippled in the harbor breeze, its little white stars glittering in the eyes of this roof's company.

Former President Adams turned to current President Madison and spoke in a very balanced tone.

"I suggest we put bees in our bloomers and *get* ready"

Upper Marlboro

"IT'S ELEVEN O'CLOCK."

"It is not eleven o'clock yet. If it were eleven o'clock, he would be here. Not one minute after, nor one before."

Dr. William Beanes closed one eye, pulled his spectacles down on his nose so he could see over them, and sighted a picketed fence line leading from his heavily gardened estate down Academy Hill toward the center of town. "Six of these properties have misaligned fences along the fronts. Make a note to instruct the mayor to have them straightened before there's anymore talk of laying a boardwalk."

"Noted," his wife responded, shielding her eyes to look down the street, but she was not looking at the fences.

The street was luxuriously wide here, with enviable estates and elegant homes on both sides, an arrangement interrupted several houses down the long street by the saddlery and farrier, a boarding house, the lumber yard, a cobblery, a fabric mill, tea and cake shop, the courthouse, more shops, and lanes leading to the small port landing at the western branch of the Patuxent River, established long ago for tobacco boats, the grist mill owned by the Beanes family, and to the horse racing track south of the town. It was a pleasant and exclusive place to live, and the doctor prided himself on keeping the finest house, the finest garden, the finest wines, and the finest wife.

He looked at her. She was ready with a wink and a grin, as if she knew what he was thinking, and, of course, she did. A little taller than he and just enough younger, with hair still mostly brown and hardly a wrinkle around her eyes, Sarah Beanes pushed back the lace of her cap and gave him a kiss on the cheek. Theirs was the unspoken affection of a long and quiet marriage.

"Oh, I see him," she said quickly and pointed down the fence line.

There, Frank Key came toward them on a big bay mare at a polite canter, so as not to disrupt the pedestrians or carriages poking about. On his saddle were mounted huge bags, which usually carried books about the law, ethics, or theology, and probably some poetry by Keats, Burns, Donne, Shelley, Khayyam, or a slave named Jupiter Hammon. Frank Key always had a book of someone's poetry tucked away for moments when he had to wait. No one ever had to wait for him. He had a clock in his head and was impeccably punctual. A scholar of no poet in particular, Key touched like a butterfly upon each, drank of the nectar, altered his own writing for a bit to test a new pattern of speech, but though he loved to read poetry and was prone to write it, he would never make much of a poet. Better to say he read poetry, but wrote rhymes. Very different.

It was a quirk of nature that he was inclined to write at all, because he was a far better spontaneous orator than ever he could commit to paper. He could spin a sermon, a prayer, or a patriotic speech to swell the heart of any, and do it without preparation. He had it all in his soul, armed and ready. Erect of posture and introspective of mood, Key had a voice as sonorous as cello music, with the most precise of elocution, as if he were singing his thoughts, though he couldn't sing a lick.

The thought occurred to Beanes once again, as every time, of what a truepenny Frank Key really was, and the doctor could recall no one who disliked him. What an accomplishment was that in this earthly life? His face was often as expressionless as a painting, but the eyes set within it were warm and complex and bore the turbulence of the world. He did not like even hearing about controversy, yet he was always in a swarm of it because of his booming law practice and his family's proximity to politics and all its concubines. His father a judge, his brother-in-law a prominent banker and litigator, his best friend a maverick congressman, his uncle and law-partner a circuit court justice and also a congressman; the list was heavy to bear for an upright fusspot who should have been a minister.

Beanes watched as, down the street at the saddlery's corral gate, Frank Key swirled out of the saddle like a dancer, gracefully considering his lanky frame, turned his frothing mare over to the stable hand with a brief discussion involving how long he would need his horse minded, gathered a parcel from a saddle bag, then came striding toward the doctor's house. The younger man had a bouncing gait when he walked, a springy affair that seemed to use too much energy. While he rode a horse like a bird on a branch, his style of walking was curious and looked uncomfortable, as if he were taking steps just a little too long even for his twenty-foot legs. They waved at him and watched as he strode toward the mansion. Just before their guest arrived, the doctor turned to his wife and pushed his spectacles back up. "It is now eleven o'clock. Just as his letter said."

Sarah Beanes nodded as the younger man approached. "And how is Maryland's leading barrister this morning?"

Frank Key smiled and paused at the gate to make a small polite bow, then responded to her familial hug in kind. His sky-blue eyes were bright, but not piercing as some could be. "I'm well, cousin, though I'm sure Uncle Philip still holds that title. I've brought each of you a gift. Moccasins made by Indians."

He handed her the parcel wrapped in paper, which fell open at her touch. "How thoughtful, Frank," she said. The two of them had always liked each other despite the age difference, for they were second cousins and had always had some idea of what the other was doing in life.

"I know how William's feet are," Key added. "I hope these are helpful."

William Beanes took the larger pair of dark brown footwear and rubbed the thick dimpled leather. "Is this deerskin?"

"Buffalo."

"Where did you get these?"

"I accepted five pair as payment for defending a mulatto who made them."

"Can I walk in the garden with them?"

"I should think you can walk anywhere with them. The Indians do. I hope they fit. You see, there is a drawstring for adjustment."

"We shall wear them with joy and leave them to you in my will."

"Hardly necessary ..."

"I know how sentimental you are."

Mrs. Beanes sat on a carved marble garden bench to try on her slippers. "How is your school project in Georgetown?"

"Thank you for asking," Key said with another little bow. "And thanks again to both of you for your most generous donation."

"A school for the poor is a noble cause. We thank you for the opportunity."

"There are two hundred students now, in only one year. No white child is refused. They pay for nothing but notebooks. Those who are able pay only ten dollars a year."

"A wonder of benevolence," Mrs. Beanes lauded as she tested her new slippers along the stone walk. "Some day you'll be even more famous than you are now, and I'll be waving a little flag and shouting, 'I'm his second cousin!'"

"I would never pretend to fame, but my soul is glad. As I secure financial support, I hope more schools like the Lancaster can be opened in other locations as acts of Christian charity."

"Are you the headmaster of the Georgetown school?"

"No, no, the president of trustees. My time is dominated by our law practice."

"I could see you as a professor," she added with a smile. "Perhaps you'll retire from the law someday and have a whole second career. Have you visited the Wests yet?"

"No, but I'll stop by before I leave town. If only my life were consumed with nothing but visiting my relatives, I should be a contented man."

"You're related to everybody," Dr. Beanes commented while tugging one of the moccasins over his toes. "Richard was just here this morning. He and your sister-in-law are anticipating a visit to Terra Rubra in a week," he mentioned. The doctor stood up and padded about in the buffalo moccasins. "I like these. They're hardy. And there's room for my little toes. Come in out of the sun and take a quench."

"May I wash my hands first?" Key asked with his usual perfect manners as they entered the impressive three-story mansion.

"Sarah, will you have Pearl get a basin of fresh water and bring it to the smoking room, please?"

"Please, be at home, Frank," Sarah offered, and disappeared into the house to fetch the cook.

Together the two men stepped in the front door, across the richly flagstoned foyer, and onto the only carpet in town. In a matter of minutes they were together in the smoking room, a masculine room lit charmingly by several well-placed whale-oil lamps, even in the daytime. Key dried his hands with one of Sarah's embroidered French hand-towels.

"You've wallpapered this room!" the lawyer exclaimed, making sure to sound happy about the new and shiny green-and-gold leaf-patterned walls.

"It's machine-printed," Beanes said as he fetched a crystal carafe of red wine. "Ordered it from New York. Sarah liked the color on the sample. I'd have preferred something in the plum spectrum. Now, I have a sparky new Sangiovese here. Quite different from your father's oily Madeira. If you like it, please sing its praises. If not, down it anyway, for your good health."

"The blood of Jupiter," Key said, and smiled sheepishly, giving Beanes the impression that he knew he was showing off and that it embarrassed him. "It's barely the end of morning."

"Wine isn't drinking. I wouldn't ply you with whiskey. I know you disapprove." The doctor made a serious expression, knowing that even the prim Mr. Key would not turn down a nip from the world-famous Beanes wine cellar. Or was the world not quite wide enough to describe its glories?

Beanes glanced through the doorways toward the kitchen to see whether his wife and the cook were within earshot, and confirming that they weren't he turned quickly to Frank Key.

"Well? Did he do it?" he asked. "Is it done? Has the president signed it?"

"Yes," the lawyer said. "He signed it. The House voted earlier, then the Senate on the seventeenth, and he signed it on the eighteenth."

"So, a declaration of war."

"Yes, war with Britain."

As the doctor filled two goblets halfway up, Frank Key paced to the front window, stood beside the pianoforte, and gazed out, plainly looking at nothing in particular. The afternoon sun lay upon his burgundy coat in such a way as to caress his spine and lay like honey on the curls of his hair around the collar.

"For a third of my life, this has been portended. I can scarcely believe it's finally here. God will chastise America for this wicked misstep. For all the multiple arguments for war, I've yet to hear a truly honorable one. Or to have my heart moved."

"What about *an eye for an eye?*"

Key turned and looked at the elder man with a disapproving expression. "But that phrase does not mean revenge."

"What else?"

"Justice, not vengeance. The punishment must not *exceed* the crime. Never take *more* than an eye for the loss of an eye."

The doctor raised his cottony brows, took a sip, and pondered his loss of a convenient excuse. "Hm. What a pity."

"Some say it's for national honor that we do this." The lawyer again turned to the outside, seeming to be relieved to have a pane of glass between himself and the world. "I don't know what a war means for us. For me."

"You're against it," Beanes supplied. "So what? Half the nation is."

"How will our lives change, I wonder? I've never been through a war."

"You grew up during the Revolution."

"I was born when it started and was a boy when it ended. I have the privilege of living and practicing in Georgetown," Key went on, "in the eye of events in the chambers of Washington, but I feel somehow as disengaged as I was as a child. Terra Rubra was like a garden oasis then, for Anne and me, almost a dream world. If our parents had not entertained so much, I think we might never have known the Revolution was happening at all."

"Yet General Washington bivouacked in the hills around you the whole time. Your father was an officer. Maryland Rifles, wasn't it?"

"And a cavalry captain later, but the war never came to our door. Even when Father came home and we listened to his tales,

I felt as if I were a student hearing the day's history lesson. I feel that way again. Will I be always on the outskirts of events? But I don't know what I can do."

"Join the military," Beanes suggested.

"Without conviction, what kind of soldier could I be?" The younger man asked this in such as way as to suggest that he didn't want an answer, or at least not yet.

Beanes watched him. "There's more than soldiering. You could be a clerk, an adjutant, a quartermaster, a currier, a cook—"

"A cook?" The lawyer smiled. "Pity the men! I suppose there might be some capacity in which I might serve. What do you think will happen now?"

The doctor cocked his head casually. "Somebody will attack somebody."

"But where?"

"I'm a doctor, not a dragoon," he said.

"While I was visiting President Madison," Key told him, "Colonel Monroe came in with a plan to defend the Chesapeake. He said there were also plans to strike into the Great Lakes and Spanish Florida too."

"I suppose the war will be mostly on the sea," Beanes said by way of agreeing with what he had just heard. "That's where we're the weak and they're stronger. But strategy will be left to generals and lords. The rest of us will sweep up."

"Did you know there are almost seven-and-a-half millions of American citizens now, despite families getting smaller?" Frank Key asked, more of offering conversation than asking a question. "When President Washington fought the British before, there were only four million. We will soon be doubled in numbers."

"I have a feeling Mr. Washington would not be surprised," Beanes responded. "He saw the future like a gypsy, they say."

"Despite doubling in population, we have only a tenth of the standing Army that was expected by this time."

"How many is that?"

"Mr. Madison says about three thousands." The younger man seemed briefly to go off into other thoughts, which now and then he did without announcement. Then he said, "I met him in person once. President Washington."

"Did you? During the war?"

"After. He came through Frederick."

"Was he as magnetic as they say?"

"He was a force of gravity."

"Was he tall?"

"He seemed very tall to me."

"And here you are, yourself a willow."

"Unless I'm still growing, God forbid, he was a good two or three inches taller than I am now."

The doctor brushed a dead fly from one of the imported teakwood tables beside his wife's favorite wing chair. "And did he say anything memorable?"

His demeanor as usual very gathered, Key answered, "My father and he spoke of myriad topics ... crops, fishing, tariffs, slaves ..."

"Slavery?"

"Slaves. Negro lifestyles at Terra Rubra and Mount Vernon. Management, obligations, that sort of thing."

"I don't deal with it," Beanes said. "I only have the two in the house. I think there are a few at the farms, but we pay them, so I suppose they're not strictly slaves in the old sense. Then again ... eh." He shrugged and took a sip.

Key parted his lips to speak, then did not speak. Fluidly he came back to the center of the room and he and the doctor took seats opposite each other across a foreign rug so expensive that only certain guests were even allowed to step upon it.

Though seated, Key's posture remained upright and proper. His tender eyes scanned the room's flocked wallpaper. Seconds passed. His glass of wine remained untouched where the doctor had put it on the side table. "I hoped he might offer some insight ... I was just beginning to think about slavery, as an issue, at that age. I thought he might explain why they didn't end it when they had the chance."

"They had their arms full just bucking that king off our backs."

"Every new venture has embedded flaws, of course," Key went on, contemplating as he spoke. "As long as slavery is tied to commerce, we shall have to deal with it."

"What's to be dealt with?"

"As long as slave-holding is the law of the land, I must defend it."

"But you defend Negroes before the bench."

"They have rights too," Key said firmly.

"Slavery is part of human life, Francis. Always has been, since Noah and the Egyptians."

"Moses, of course."

"Moses, Noah, Jonah ..." Beanes paused to burp. "Some say that slavery is the hidden reason for this war."

Key looked at him. "How could it be?"

"By giving us a reason to conquer Canada. That's where escapees run. If we seize Canada, we can take back our Negroes harboring there."

The lawyer frowned. "That's stretching the hat out of shape, isn't it? I will not fight the unoffending Canadians. A true patriot should never invoke his country to imperialism. We should find another place for freed Negroes."

"Where else would they go but Ontario?"

Key shrugged, for him almost a cannon shot of expression. "I suppose ... Africa."

"They're not Africans," the doctor pointed out. "Haven't been for generations. Send them to Ireland! At least they'll speak the language." He took another sip, noticing that Key had not participated in the joke. "Mayhap someday we'll let go some of them, then later some more, and like that."

"Freeing some without freeing all only contributes to the advantage of owning them. Those who own them will profit while those without them will go out of business, leaving slaveholders to dominate their industry. The only mechanism to end slavery is to free them all at once, by Constitutional law."

"A high-minded stump speech for a Supreme Court justice! I shall whip every vote in the county your way."

"Justices are appointed." The lawyer tucked his chin rather like a shy girl might do. "And I'm not that sure of myself," he demurred. "Where's the humanity in freeing them without helping them establish themselves? They're incapable of taking care of themselves. It would be like sending children into wilderness."

"Helping them? Crippling them! I know no slave who wants to trade one set of chains for another."

"The Bible gives us no divine instruction, neither permitting nor prohibiting slavery. For thousands of years servitude has been the natural order. It will end on its own, I suppose, collapse of its own weight. Slavery is contrary to America as a theme."

Beanes grunted a wordless response.

"I have emancipated some of my slaves," the lawyer went on, almost speaking to himself. "I find myself haunted while lying in comfort in my own bed. How will they fare on their own? Once again enslaved in some Northern factory? In time they will be infirm, cast away to starve in a slum without advocacy. What does an old Negro do without a master to care for him? What good is freedom if it defines itself in squalor?"

"You're indulgent, my boy."

Key looked up. "Do you think so?"

"I do."

"My mother has always read to them, taught them hymns, letters, numbers. I teach my slaves to read, right beside my children. Is that indulgence? Why would we be teaching them to read and calculate if not to one day direct their own destinies?" He paused to ruminate again, since he never spoke before thinking, and his gaze fixed on some knot in the floorboards. "Perhaps we could make a country for them. Somewhere they can go ... a nation populated by—"

"Heaven behold us, stop it! If you want to direct the nation, cease chattering in the parlors of stuffy physicians and get thee to Congress. You could be there in a matter of months!"

Crystal goblets in the French corner cabinet vibrated and jingled, a small but piercing sound, like the laughter of children in the distance. Off in the kitchen, somebody dropped a pan that rang briefly on the tiled floor.

Frank Key sat utterly still, his hands folded upon one knee. "I haven't the mettle."

The aromas of johnnycake and roasted chicken from the Beanes farms drifted in from the kitchen, where lunch was warming on the German cast-iron stove, new just last month. The doctor's practiced ears, though his eyes were weakening, still heard every footfall in every part of the house, and he knew the cook and the maid were setting the dining table and laying out lunch.

"Does it have a name yet?' he asked, almost surprising himself with the sudden change of subject.

Key blinked. "Pardon?"

"Wars have names. The Hundred Years' War, the War of the Roses ... You're a poet. Come up with something."

"In Washington some are calling it the Second War of Independence. Or the Second *Half* of the War of Independence. Rather lumpish."

The two men fell quiet again for a few moments, each trying to see in his own mind what would come, but neither was good at predicting—nor could either imagine—what might be going on in the minds of military strategists who saw coastlines and rivers much differently than a gentleman lawyer and a crusty doctor might.

Beanes didn't have to think about his role. He was a physician and in his sixties. No one would expect him to be anything else. He would do what he could as humanitarian ethics and his bones allowed. He would treat the wounds that came before him and let the politicians and generals deal with the dirty complexities beyond blood and bone.

For the lawyer, though, as Beanes gazed at the younger man, there were the troubles of a pacifist in a time of war, of a loyal patriot when his country went against his morals, a man of extraordinary Christian devotion, with five children and a wife for whom he was responsible, an adored son and husband—such a man could not simply think of himself. Here he was, considering how freed slaves would live out their destinies, yet he hardly knew how he would live out his own.

Just as Beanes heard his wife and their cook clacking about with the lunch dishes, heading from the kitchen to the dining table, their immaculate guest sighed heavily and asked the kind of question that doesn't want an answer too soon.

"I wonder how I will fit into this war."

The Royal Navy Blockade

"SO THE UNITED STATES has declared war on Britain. Amusing. And insulting at the same."

Lieutenant Gordon paced the command deck of the *Helen*, which moved along at only two knots in a slacked breeze, probably moving only with the current. Very hot, sticky, but clouded over, so there was no scorching sun as was common here.

The ship was quiet. Two watches were asleep below decks; those on watch were involved in all the little tasks that could be done when there was no appreciable wind. Mending sails, making mats, splicing, carpentry. The rectangular sails hung nearly limp, only now and then stirring in a weak puff.

As usual he was alone except for Victor Tarkio, who sat on the deck, polishing Gordon's shoes. Gordon padded the afterdeck in his stockings, reading a newspaper he had just acquired from a passing Royal Navy cartel full of piratical American prisoners.

"The war is barely begun and already Fort Mitchee-lee-mackinack has fallen ..."

"Mackinaw," Tarkio corrected. "Fort Michilimackin*aw*."

Gordon pointed at the article. "But it ends in a *c* ... like Cadillac."

"Still."

"Is that French or Indian, or what?"

"French."

"Well, it's British now, isn't it? Without a drop of bloodshed in defense of it! We captured several American ships on that island—two schooners, two cartels. The governor of Mitchigan heard about it and abandoned his invasion of Canada and retreated back to Detroit. The coward! He had superior supplies and more troops, but he blew like paper before a flame. So, your Great Lakes and Canada are proving better at defending themselves than you Americans predicted. Oh! Listen to this—the governor then surrendered Fort Detroit too! You're having a grim summer, Tarkio, grim, grim, grim. It seems America is being chastised back to her rightful station."

Tarkio looked up at him and shrugged, as if trying to remain unmoved. After all, what could he say? The war was out of his hands.

"A terrible massacre at Fort Dearborn," Gordon read on. "The fort has fallen to the Pot—poe-ta-wa—"

"Potawatomi."

"How do you know all these names?"

"I read newspapers to my uncle when I'm in port. He was blinded in the Revolution."

"Their chief cut out the heart of an Indian agent and ate it raw." Gordon continued reading, but then glanced at Tarkio and held back the description of the massacre. Torment was not his purpose here. These details were nothing short of cruel. "Savages ..."

"They're your allies," Tarkio commented.

"Seems you're losing this ill-conceived war even as it has barely begun."

This time Tarkio smiled and shook his head.

Gordon glared. "Is something funny to you?"

The other man nodded, bemused. "You gloat like a school boy."

Humiliated, Gordon's air of confidence shattered. "And you carry the smell of insubordination."

"You're not concerned with me."

"Really!" Gordon put the newspaper down on the chart table and tried to figure a way to annoy the unflappable American. "You keep thinking about your future, even though you know you don't have one. I can see you doing it. Thinking like that. If you survive our encounters with enemies, you'll spend years un-counted right where you are. But you still think of other things, don't you?"

"Think like a free man? Yes."

"Why?"

"Because I am one." Tarkio put one buffed shoe down and picked up its mate. "I know my future. I mean to have a dozen children at least. I might found an entire town. A city, maybe."

"Hah! Tarkio Town? Victorville? Sounds like a lot of muck-ing about for no reason. Why would you do all that?"

"Same reason any Englishman wants to be a master of land and treasure. To surround myself with stability."

"A dozen children doesn't sound stable to me. Why would a man want so many needy dependents clinging upon him?"

"To have a family. Never had much. Just my uncle left now."

"So you will build an edifice of Tarkio." Gordon paced to the taffrail and gazed out at the quietly rolling ocean. "Do all of you think this way? You Americans?"

"Oh, I'd say most."

"Where would a humble-born wretch get such elevated ideas?"

"We get that from being American. We're born with it. Grow up with it. Freedom means something, y'know, it's not just a word. Means being free from the power of others. Mr. Madison says freedom means being free from government. The whole idea is new to the world. Had fate dropped me anywhere else on the face of the earth, my fate wouldn't be mine, but a king's or a master's or a lord's."

"Or an earl's?"

Tarkio smiled at him and chuckled amiably. "Or an earl's."

Self-conscious, Gordon let a brief silence fall between them. A weak breeze stirred over the taffrail, pulling the sweat from his face.

For weeks now, many weeks, only Tarkio had been allowed in the captain's cabin, to tend his clothing or bring his food. The rest of the crew noticed, but they didn't seem to care. Gordon thought at first there would be jealousy, but when it hadn't ma-terialized he assumed it was because they disliked him as much as he disliked them, and they thought Tarkio's position was some kind of punishment. Still, he couldn't read them.

The only person he talked to, other than to give orders, was Tarkio. Gordon was curious about the American character, why they would wish to live as they did, with no single purpose, no guidance or rules. How could they trust each other when no one knew his place?

"Why would someone want to go live in a wilderness like Fort Dearborn?" he asked. "Some mad field with ravenous Indians and people clomping around in animal hides? What's the attraction of uncivilized places?"

"Men like me can build their own places," Tarkio explained. "So we go out to the wilds and stake a claim. Born with nothing, you build something."

"Seems that poor men would not be so attracted to places where they have even less."

Tarkio stood up to stretch his legs, and looked out over the empty expanse of ocean. "Look where you are."

"What? Where am I?"

"Is there any place more desolate?"

The two stood together, looking at the steel-gray ocean, rolling before them in every direction, as if they and the crew of this frigate were the only human beings on the planet.

"Yet," Tarkio added, "here you are."

Gordon fought the desire to agree. Here he was, locked on a relatively small ship, with relatively little reputation, eating dried elephant meat, drinking water growing daily more fetid, in the company of men he didn't trust.

"I have a duty to perform," he attempted. "Service in the Royal Navy is a time-tried honor for the greatest men of England throughout our history. There is nothing desolate about it."

"Except your daily life."

"Are you trying to tempt me to defect? Sir, that is an insult."

"Did you choose to be in the Royal Navy?" Tarkio asked. "Or was it a family tradition?"

The young lieutenant shifted his feet and felt a sudden desire to be candid. "My mother decided. I am privileged." He looked at Tarkio, suddenly with more confidence. "But don't take that as if I've been forced. I am here willingly. I'm as much a patriot as you. I am devoted to my country and I have a duty. I am compelled."

"What you really are is desperate," Tarkio told him bluntly. "Britain is so short on sailors that you have to steal them."

Not waiting for an answer, he sat again on the deck and continued his work on Gordon's shoe, which had thrown its heel. Tarkio fitted the shoe awkwardly over a belaying pin and began tacking the heel back on.

Gordon watched him. The other man seemed to be content in his menial labor, a contentment that was entirely mysterious and somehow attractive.

"You Americans are ingrates," he complained. "The only reason you won independence is that we were not willing to be brutal and burn you out during your revolution, which we could easily have done. You didn't *win* independence. We let you go. America has never appreciated that, ungrateful children of the Crown as you are. This time we should burn you out."

He watched Tarkio for a reaction. He got one—absolutely nothing. No smile, no shrug, none of the American's typical versions of a silent response. This time there was only the silence.

Uneasy, Gordon paced along the taffrail and felt the warm wood beneath his hand. "We English must remain stalwart against Bonaparte. No other motivations matter. Who we are, what we want ... the nobility, the gentry ... it's nothing now. He has conquered every power in Europe from the Balkans to the Arctic to the Atlantic. Once Valencia fell, Bonaparte became superior in Europe—"

"Except for England."

"Except for England. Europe under a single power and now America has turned hostile again. Once again, Britain stands alone. All British citizens must rally against this Corsican menace."

"He's busy in Russia."

"He won't stay there," Gordon said bluntly. "Russia's too big. No one lives there. All the people are west of the Urals. You will have the same troubles in your country. America is too big, too. It's doomed to become another Europe, fractured into regions that barely speak each other's language. You'll collapse of your own weight. Pioneers rush west, never to return. Eventually they'll become so different that neither will recognize the other.

You'll be at each other's necks. If you know what's good for you, for your America, you will help us defeat Bonaparte."

"I do help you," Tarkio said. "I take your orders and work your ship."

"No, *really* help me." Gordon squatted to get eye to eye with the other man and grasped Tarkio's wrist to keep him from starting work again.

Tarkio stopped working, surprised.

"Tell me how the American privateer ships out-sail everything else on the seas," Gordon asked. "What gives them their superior quality? How do they carry so many men in proportion to their sizes? They can't be comfortable and they're certainly not safe. What makes them so fast? Is it the angle of the rake? The wood they're made of? What sorts of bulkheads separate the lower decks? The Royal Navy has captured a dozen of your privateers, then we can't make them sail right. Tell me what it is!"

Tarkio paused. "It's the skill of the captains and crews. Things you can't copy."

"You know what I mean! Is it the style of rigging? The gaff spars? Why are the masts so tall? Aren't you afraid you'll turn over?"

"Sometimes."

"So it's true that these ships are dangerous?"

"You bet."

"And you sail them madly in spite of that? How do they point so tightly into the wind? How can they be so lightly built and so heavily sparred without tipping over? Is it the shape of the keel?"

Tarkio leaned back against the aft dockline, coiled and hanging behind him. He let his arms slump and simply looked into Gordon's intense eyes. "What would you think of me if I told you? If you're trying to get secrets out of me, I don't know half of them and I'll never tell those I do. There's no time for you to learn the skills of a lifetime. Some things are just done by instinct. Sons learn from their fathers, grandfathers. There's no book about it and no model carved that shows it. None of you—not the best English sailor or the best admiral—has time to learn how to sail our ships. Unless this war lasts a hundred years, you'll never prevail against captains like Tom Boyle."

Gordon surged to his feet again and glared down. "Tom Boyle ... Tom Boyle!" He snatched the newspaper off the chart table and shook it at the other man. "The hunter has become the hunted. There's a price on his head now!"

He opened the paper to the article he had been reading and dashed it to the deck. The crisp paper, damaged by rain and the fingers of those who read it before him, flew apart and danced over the deck to land in a flurry around Victor Tarkio.

James Gordon glared at the paper, his eyes unfocused, his mind fixing on a target.

"I mean to collect it."

Trim to Fighting Sail

THE SARGASSO SEA
FORTY MILES WEST OF BERMUDA
SEPTEMBER

"SAIL SIGHTED, TOM. SQUARE tops'ls on two masts. Still hull down."

"Trim to pursue. Get a lookout up."

"Trim to pursue, aye. Trim for broad on the larboard reach! Pursell, put some eyes on the maintop. Ready about!"

"Ready about!" "Ready about!" "*Ready about*," the crew chanted back unevenly, with great cheer.

Subtle, but a curious point about ships with plenty of experienced hands—the chief mate could've called out for hands to the braces and sheets, helm this, helm that, but with so many seasoned schooner men aboard, such calls would've been almost insulting. He only shouted so everybody could hear him, and it was pretty much the kind of experienced shout that traveled only along the deck, and not out along the water.

Tom Boyle left the starboard rail and crossed the crowded deck to the other side, midships, to look for the new sighting. There he found grizzly prize-master John Hooper scouting the horizon as well, where they could just see two masts with main and fore course sails puffed out and two tops'ls each as well. Hooper was a competent captain in his own right, as were a dozen others here, and equal that many qualified mates who could be captains in a pinch, and some of those were still boys.

Hooper had his own two sons aboard, aged eight and ten years, and made a good practice of ignoring them, leaving it to officers on the other watches to deal with them. It was well for a father to be aboard, but not a daddy.

Every few waves under the schooner, they caught sight of a hull painted brick-red just coming up over the horizon.

"She's big," the heavily bewhiskered Hooper said in his high voice, sensing Boyle's presence without looking. "Cargo ship."

"Brig-rigged and big, I'll be jigged. Must be headed for London," Boyle responded, since no other destination except maybe Bermuda made sense here in the constantly clockwise North Atlantic Current. "Do you see any banner?"

"No colors yet. I'll bet she's double our burden, though. Three hundred tons, anyway."

"Let's assume we like her." He cast a shout over his shoulder without taking his eyes off the prey. "Clear for action, boys."

"Light breeze," Hooper commented, looking up at the state of Maryland flag flying off the topmast as a weather gauge. "Little better than the day you picked me up."

"You mean when we cracked out at a whopping two knots?"

"When Yorktown tried to overtake us."

Boyle smiled, remembering that attempt to sail off the dock of the historic site of Washington's victory over Cornwallis. "Well, anyone can sail in heavy wind. Where's Ring? Tommy!"

"Here," Ring called from the other side of the main deckhouse.

"Cram on all canvas."

"Cramming."

Still over there on the starboard quarter, Tommy Ring yipped a few hoisting orders and men moved as swiftly as conditions allowed without literally stepping on each other. With a crew of ninety-nine and fifteen prisoners stuffed into the ninety feet between *Comet*'s stem and stern and her twenty-three-foot beams, there was no room for *pardon me* where most of the men slept literally sitting up. The next half hour was a clatter of activity. The Marines hurriedly dived below to make room for sail handling until their muskets were needed. Seamen who weren't manning halyards and stuns'ls and tops'ls began the process of passing up boarding pikes, swords, cutlasses, then loading pistols and muskets one by one, all of which were laid side-by-side on the decktops upon flaked ropes that would keep them from sliding off as the schooner dipped and tipped. Gun crews prepared the powder and shot for the ship's twelve-pounder carronades and the two nine-pounder long guns stationed at the beams. With a calculating eye Boyle watched all this going on around him and was glad he had spent the last three weeks drilling every last man till his fingers bled. Sometimes he wasn't popular for that. He hoped they had some pride in what they'd learned.

The mid-Atlantic airs were breathy and fresh, which favored the *Comet*, with her much lighter body than the other ship, in fact lighter than most of their prey. In minutes the schooner was a giant puff of ivory canvas with a little yellow blade underneath. She was a pretty bird under her lower sails, but with the topsails and studdingsails set she was something out of heroic myth. Away she sliced, heeling over with her starboard shoulder down, sending her crew scrambling for the high side so they wouldn't be bounced overboard as she buried her rail.

This quarry, if they caught her, would be their second prize-ship. The first had been the month before, in mid-July, a good prize loaded with sugar, wine, and fustic for yellow dyes, and she'd be worth a hundred thousand dollars to the owners and crew, and another fifty thousand in duties and charges to the United States government. That had been a good day.

Boyle thought back to their first capture and his chest swelled with anticipation for the next one. Sailing a ship for profit was a joyous thing, but add to that the blood-rush of the privateering hunt—there was nothing like this. They were raiders now, representatives of the United States, carrying a license to raid. He had an entrepreneur's taste for risk, and the war now allowed him to bring out that extra measure of dodgery that went unpracticed before. What good is a predator, after all, if he doesn't love a chase and a good fang-and-claw?

These who had been merchant seamen only a few weeks ago were something else now, something on the edge of maritime law and the rules of commerce. Rather than passing other vessels with friendly salutes, a wave of a hand and an exchange of news, they were hunters and other vessels their prey. They could attack, shoot, kill, steal, seize, or destroy, and claim authority on the high seas to do so. They were armed soldiers how. Only one thin document kept Boyle and his raiders from being ordinary murderers and thieves. That one document was a letter, stowed away lovingly in the captain's cabin in a leather envelope, in his desk next to the box of new signal flags Mary Pickersgill had delivered to him, to protect it and the important signatures upon it from moisture or hot shot. That little piece of paper turned Captain Tom Boyle from a merchant sailor and land speculator into a privateer—a captain with permission to run down enemy shipping and legally steal both cargo and vessel, to take and hold prisoners and sometimes to decide their fates, and to cash in on the value of both ship and load. They were armed for more than protection or salutes. Aboard were government-sanctioned heavy guns and a phalanx of United States Marines. So was he a soldier or a mercenary? Pirate or patriot or opportunist? With that piece of paper, Boyle could call himself any of those. And others would call him other things, but he didn't care.

Pretty sure he'd been a panther in a previous life, Boyle looked up at the patches on the fores'l where repairs had been made from grapeshot during their wrestle with their first victim. That battle had lasted twelve minutes.

Everything depended upon factors he could not divine. What was in the minds of the other ship's owners? Were they loading their ship so full of cargo that she was manned only by seamen, or were they betting that half a cargo was better than none and loaded the other half of her burden with heavy guns and armed mercenaries? And of what kind of spirit was her captain? Was he a hired merchant who would heave to at a warning shot across the bow? Or perhaps he was a former Royal Navy man, with twenty years' experience and the stones for a fight? Or a combination of both—a merchant captain with part ownership of his vessel and a huge personal stake in evading the privateers or battling them down to the last man? Was he a fair-weather sailor who had enjoyed good luck and favorable passages, or was he a grizzled bare-knuckled tar who had been around the Horn and seen the notorious house-high seas?

Quickly, but not too quickly, the schooner bobbed, leaned her shoulder into a swell, and climbed. If the tiller were swung too aggressively the schooner would go too far over, then the helmsman would have a nasty time steadying her up as she wagged back and forth in a mess, and she would lose way as the seas passed inefficiently by her rudder. A good helmsman's touch was a light, slow, firm, anticipating touch, and Webb was a good helmsman. Handled right in the right seas, the schooner would climb a swell, lean into it, crest the top, then skate down the other side and even gain speed. She began to do this dolphin-like movement, slicing forward and a bit to the starboard with every swell and skate. At the helm Isaac felt his way along, reading the sensation of changing water pressure against the hull. The breeze against the sails and the feeling of the current on the rudder would communicate through the tiller to his hand, as if he were taking a pulse.

A dozen possible patterns of behavior chewed at Tom Boyle as the *Comet* closed on her larger prey and he tried to guess the unguessable. The other ship turned northeast to bring the wind to her stern. In these light airs that square-rigged brig had also rolled out every bit of canvas.

Boyle got a little shiver up his neck. While very few British seamen had experience aboard American fore-and-aft-riggers, he had to assume that captain knew some key facts about schooner handling.

The schooner's saw-up and skate-down motion began to lose its ballet and the yellow hull bobbled inefficiently as the course changed and the wind moved from a halfway decent starboard tack to a clunky gust from over the stern.

"He knows," Boyle mumbled. Over his shoulder he called, "Wing and wing, Tommy. Let's run before it. Catch him."

"Wing and wing," the second mate responded. "Hands to put the main over!"

"And soak the sails."

Ring relayed that order and men scrambled for buckets, filled them, arranged themselves into bucket brigades on both sides of the ship, then climbed the ratlines until they were over the sails. They dumped bucket after bucket of water over the eggshell-white canvas. Swollen with water, the cloth was less porous, and the sails puffed out a bit more than before, catching a little more wind, and the ship moved that bit faster. Anything was an advantage.

Over the Sargasso Sea's sapphire waters, notorious for color and depth of clarity, the distance began to close between the two vessels with each commander trying to use the endless current in his favor.

When his instincts started to buzz, Boyle interrupted the curious silence that had fallen as those men on deck settled to watch the chase and spoke less and less with every half mile crossed. When he was ready, Boyle spoke to Tommy Ring again.

"Call all hands."

"All hands on deck, all hands—somebody go tell 'em." Ring had the sense to somehow yell without yelling, and the men were trained well enough to keep their responses low. Sounds traveled over water like a skimming pelican and no one wanted to announce each movement to the other ship.

No more than seven minutes passed, long minutes, before a crowd of drowsy crewmen erupted one by one from the crowded hammocks below, shaking away their sleep, then chief mate John Dieter appeared at Boyle's side, carrying the box of signal flags. He blinked through the bright sunlight to the square-rigger. By now they could see its dark-red hull when the swells were right.

Dieter was the kind of mate considered by the crew to be the de-facto captain of the ship while Boyle was just making the decisions. No one really could explain that, except that like any truly effective chief mate, Dieter was somehow everywhere at all times, aloft and below, forward and aft, wordlessly knowing what the captain was thinking, divining every change, and breathing down the neck of every jack who might be too clumsy or too groggy to do his job ten seconds before it was expected to be done. A wiry young man with stovepipe legs, a narrow but strong upper body, and arms completely covered in tattoos, Dieter went about with his long sun-brassed hair twisted up into a kind of Oriental bun from which the blanched ends fanned out above his face like a twiggy halo.

"Standing by your favorite gun again?" he asked as he approached Boyle.

Boyle glanced down at one of his newly acquired carronades. "Well, she is a virgin, after all." And he patted the fat, stumpy, sun-warmed iron body under his resting foot. There were nine more like her aboard, all fresh from the foundry. "The finest of Scottish gunnery, all dressed up and never a bit of red on her lips ... but she's quaking for it, John. Can't you feel her? She wants to do more than drill."

"Clement wants to do that too. He's getting the powder boys to cheer and gambol around below."

"Told you he'd make a good gun sergeant. His uncle runs a powder mill." He smiled and tried to imagine his third mate frolicking with the youngest boys below, making up gun rhymes and arming chanteys. Even at the age of thirty, Clement Cathell was a boy at heart himself, eternally in a good cheer, and could find a twig of hope in any grimness.

"I like this business," Dieter said, peering out at the ship they were chasing. "Any clues about how they're armed?"

"No ports, so guns'll be on the weather deck. If they know war's been declared, they'll have some firepower aboard. I would."

"I know you like your twelves, but what if she's got twenty-fours?"

"We have speed and maneuverability."

"Tom, do you know what a twenty-four-pounder can do to us with one shot?"

"Not yet."

"Pretty soon we'll be near enough to find out."

"The schooner, the better." Boyle felt the wind turn cool on his face, as if it were trying to tell him something. He sat down, straddling the carronade's fat body. "She's a pleasant companion. Just this morning, I was talking to my gun about life—"

Dieter smiled. "Did the gun answer?"

"You discuss your problems, then you shoot them."

"If we keep shooting our problems as we did last month, we'll be famous."

"I'd rather be anonymous," Boyle said. "Leaves me free to be shrewd. And we have to do better than one capture a month."

One of the crewmen, a boy of fourteen, son of a watchmaker and in need of income for his crippled sister, appeared and didn't quite approach. He had a limp when he was nervous and hair the color of fire, which made him easy to spot on deck, even in the rain.

"Should I load, Tom?" the teenager asked. He had loaded the carronade three times for drills, and now finally would load her for a possible real engagement. He would fire her too, if needed, and learn to do the hardest thing about being a privateer. He would learn to kill.

"Oh! Certainly. Load all of them." Boyle cleared out and moved midships so the boy could make ready the carronade in case the other ship put up a fight.

Dieter followed. "What's that buck's name again?"

"Sigsby. Steven Sigsby. Reminds me of somebody. Makes me think."

"'Bout what?"

"Lieutenant Gordon and the sea."

"Ah ... who?"

"That squirrel who seized our flags and pennants last year."

"The one who took Tarkio and Bristow? That boy?"

"A smart boy. He was talking about Napoleon. The French have an interest in anything that draws the British off them. That's us now."

"Does it give you concern?"

"Every day," Boyle answered. "I sent Victor Tarkio because he was the most likely to survive life in the Royal Navy. He could be anywhere by now, on any ship. Bristow too. We could fight a Royal Navy ship and discover we've killed or maimed our own shipmate. That's what bothers me, and that's all. I don't want to help Napoleon rule the world, but I've no sympathy for emperors or kings. They deserve what they get."

"Aren't the British right to fight Napoleon? Y'know, right, wrong, up, down ..."

"I'm no priest. But the only dictator I want to work for is myself."

"And a sweet tyranny it is."

They laughed, and together climbed the lower shrouds a few ratlines up and hung there, to get a better view of their prey. On the deck, Steven Sigsby wrapped his hand in a gun truck line and tried to pull it.

"Steven, don't wrap your hand," Boyle instructed.

"Oh?"

"Never wrap your hand in a line."

"Oh." The boy uncoiled the line from his wrist and hand.

"Sorry," Dieter muttered. "He should know that by now."

Under his breath Boyle said, "All I could see were his broken fingers dangling before my eyes. You know, Gordon was right about the sea."

"I don't remember what he said."

"It's the bottleneck for controlling the land. Who controls the seas, the land must do his bidding. Britain knows that."

"He said that?"

"That's why Napoleon will eventually collapse."

"Why do you think that? He's making his way to London, via Moscow."

"That's what I mean. This invasion of Russia. He's bitten off a huge land mass. Unless he can move supplies from port to port at sea, he can't keep a grip on all that land. It makes me think."

"About ... attacking Napoleon?"

"Why not?"

"By yourself?" Dieter made a mirthless chuckle of both alarm and concern. "Thomas, control your ambition, eh? Just for the next two hours."

"How's the crew bearing up?"

"Excited. Maybe some shivers."

"Fear?"

"I don't think so ..."

"What, then?"

"Well, they've never fired a gun at another human being before last month. Some liked it, some not."

"Nobody had to sign on," Boyle told him. "They're seasoned now. They've shot and been shot at in a rousing battle."

"A twelve-minute battle," Dieter reminded. "Two shots, both out of range."

Boyle strained upward a bit. "Look—she's hull-up. We're gaining. Thank God for light airs. She must be fully loaded. I can see her stern ... no name board. He's trying to stay anonymous."

"That means they know there's been a declaration of war."

Boyle turned and called, "Marines, on deck!"

Below the weather deck, a muffled shout answered and there was a sudden clamor of boots on the companionway steps.

Armed Marines in red jackets came piling back up onto the weather deck, led by their captain, a meaty disagreeable Irishman named Robert Cascadden. No sooner was Cascadden himself on the deck than he crossed paths in a narrow place with Tommy Ring, who clearly tried to give him berth, and the two men shared a long and bitter glare as the Marines formed up along the rail.

Boyle leaned toward Dieter and asked, "What's that about?"

"I think Tommy called Cascadden a cornshucker."

"What's that mean?"

"No idea."

"Well, he's Irish. You could call him 'sweetie' and he'd hear 'fire-crotch lepercoon.'"

"Want me to have a word with'm?"

"They have to work it out themselves or it's not worked out."

Boyle jumped down to the deck and put his attention where it wanted to be.

"Bear on her stern. Raise 'heave to and wait for my orders."

As Dieter opened the flag box and sifted for the right signals, Boyle addressed the crew.

"All right, boys, listen! Stand by your lines and guns. For the second time we will engage in the business of privateering for ourselves and our nation. By these acts we weaken the resolve of those who would dictate their oppression upon our free trade. Know that they are no longer our rivals in trade, but our nation's enemies. Be steady, follow orders, and remember ... every ship wants to be a privateer!"

—◊◊◊—

The schooner boiled with anticipation. From the ensign halyard flew the signal flag ordering the prey ship to cease his forward progress and wait for Boyle's orders, but the other ship responded only by turning more sharply away.

Clement Cathell, armed with his explosion of sun-bleached hair, clean-shaven face, and eternal smile, and his powder boys popped out of the hatches and scrambled up and down the deck with pretty good efficiency, carrying buckets of gunpowder and toting round shot, systematically supplying the carronades, but placing the buckets amidships where they wouldn't catch a spark when the guns were fired. Or so everyone hoped. The guns were already loaded, needing only supplies on deck to load them again, a portent of trouble literally on the horizon. More buckets were dipped into the sea for sponging the barrels. Thus began the gut-twisting struggle of waiting.

In a half hour the ships were within two thousand feet of each other and the captains were able to look into each other's eyes while their crewmen hopped about them like ants with each of a series of small and devious course corrections. Boyle tried to be a gentleman about it, tried to approach the merchant ship without firing a shot, posturing clearly to board her, coming in from upwind of her and parallel to the hull in an attempt to steal her wind, only to have the other captain swing the square sails around just enough to twist away at an angle Boyle wouldn't have expected the heavier vessel could even manage while fully loaded. The distance between the two began to widen.

"Knows his ship," Boyle muttered. "Then we'll take him to leeward."

The other captain was maneuvering so that the wind stayed behind them and *Comet* was forced to maneuver in following wind. It was risky, considering that the schooner could jibe and correct and come about quicker and was just plain faster, but so far the other had kept himself out of gun range.

"Lee helm," he finally said. "Tops'ls only. Scandalize."

"Lee helm, Isaac," Ring called aft.

"Lee helm, aye," the helmsman repeated.

"Scandalize the main!" Ring could call out louder now, because the changes in the sail handling would be obvious anyway.

"Trim to fighting sail," Boyle ordered. "Shout it right out."

"Trim to fighting sail!" Ring called.

This time there was no shuffle to grab the sheets and braces and main peak halyard. This time only the men assigned to each line handled each line. This was part of the drilling—not just guns and shooting, but sail handling. The studdingsails, topgallant, and jibs dissolved into laundry and, empty of the wind, fluttered in frustration. At the top of the mailsail, the long gaff spar drooped, spilling wind out of the main. Now *Comet* was free of the force of that mainsail, so her stern could turn, and free of the jibs, so her bow could turn. Propelled only by the foresail and the square topsail in the middle of her body, the schooner could wheel on a dot. She wheeled like an attacking eagle and bore down.

Eighteen hundred feet ... fifteen hundred ... men huddled by their guns, holding glowing linstocks and blowing gently on them to keep them burning, each man itching to fire first yet also afraid he might be called to do that. They weren't killers. Not yet.

The square-rigger in front of them suddenly raised two flags—English banners. So she was declaring herself finally. No sooner than the flags shimmied up on their ensign halyards did the starboard guns erupt in a skull-pounding race of explosions.

A black monster of smoke enshrouded the other ship.

"Down!" Boyle shouted.

—⁓—

Boyle crashed to the deck, dragging Steven Sigsby with him, and prayed everyone else had time. His innards quaked. Absurdly he realized this was the first time he had ever been shot at, within range anyway. The same for everyone else. What a feeling—a kind of orgasmic shock.

The sea on the *Comet*'s larboard side blew upward in a silver fan, splashed over the rail and soaked him, then immediately scrambled down the deck and out the scuppers like a terrified animal. The gunners in the other ship had aimed too directly, no arch, hitting a swell instead of the *Comet*.

"All right, then," Boyle muttered and jumped to his feet. "Larboard nine, fire!"

"Fire in the hole!" Clement Cathell shouted as he touched the linstock to the fuse.

The nine-pounder long gun on the larboard beam fizzed, then roared. Boyle clutched the shrouds and waited to see what happened. There were only seconds to check the distance, seconds before the other ship reloaded. They'd been foolish enough to fire all their guns at once, a critical mistake. Boyle knew those were seconds for him to use. Nine-pounder gun, eighteen hundred feet or less—

The *Comet*'s round shot landed in the water also, but was just a foot short of the other ship's hull, actually striking almost under the angled stern. She might have taken some damage below the waterline, but Boyle had a splinter of instinct that said no.

"Clement, adjust the angle."

Cashell and two crewmen quickly adjusted the quoin on the gun truck while the boy Sigsby reloaded. They knew how to do this just from the drilling, but firing at an actual target—well, anybody could hit water.

"Larboard carronades, fire!"

The response took too long. The men were somehow surprised by the order to actually fire all at once. Cathell himself grabbed a linstock from the stunned man holding it and lowered it to a gun's touchhole and the other men were shaken out of their stupor and touched their linstocks to the fuses.

Poom poom poompa poom—five fat carronades blew their tops off at once and the whole body of *Comet* rocked sideways away from the blasts, then staggered to regain her footing in the swells. The helmsman had to fight his way back

Two of the five shots slammed into the brig's side, disintegrating the planks amidships. With so little support on the main mast now, the other captain was forced to trice up his fores'ls and try to stop using them. Suddenly there was a squid-like creature of smoke obscuring the view of the other vessel, enough to disguise the report of three guns firing back at the *Comet*. Another splash, and this time a thunderous strike on the gunwale below the rail, which broke and took a kevel cleat with it as if some big shark had taken a bite.

"Damage to the gun'l," Dieter called.

Several men were moving. No screaming, no pain, yet. They gathered themselves and began, more nervously this time, to reload.

Shot, and shot at. Ice broken.

"Captain?" It was Cascadden, his face red with anticipation.

"Not yet," Boyle answered.

Frustrated, Cascadden and his Marines crouched on the deck and waited with their muskets loaded and their stomachs knotted. How many of them, too, had never fired a shot at a living person? Untested, how would they perform?

"On the fores'l brails and sheets, stand by," Boyle called. He calculated the shifting of the ship under his feet, the slight heel of the deck, and ordered the fore brailed up for a few seconds, then almost immediately sheeted out again. The men worked together, slacking the brails as the sheets were hauled. The big sail, with its free-foot and no boom, was able to open and close like a curtain and almost as fast.

The schooner paused at the top of a swell, then jumped and skated downward as the sail filled again. Boyle waited, watched, felt, then ordered, "Starboard brails, peel off."

The starboard men's arms spun as they brailed up, pulling the sails away from the wind and spilling air. The schooner fell into a trough, turned slightly, and with one hand Boyle quickly signaled Isaac Webb at the helm, who adjusted the tiller as the signal instructed. Immediately he ordered the fore sheeted out again to catch the wind and sheeted over just a foot or two.

"Brace over," he ordered, and the square tops'l swung around. The ship heeled sharply, climbed a swell, and he ordered the fore filled again.

With each of Boyle's finely tuned orders, the wind either caught or released the sails, the ship's position in the water pivoted a little this way or that, not just closing the distance to the other ship, but making use of the attitude of those swells to change the angle of approach. Boyle kept the bow from smacking into a swell head-on, which would've taken way off the ship, instead causing the vessel to flow nearly parallel to the swells and use the swells as slides. *Comet* magically gained speed every time the fore was set, then slipped down each chute when the sail was brailed up. In, out, in, out, this way, that ... with the stays'l pulling the ship along up front, until Boyle was where he wanted to be.

"Fire the nine!"

To his left, Cathell was ready at the only remaining loaded gun on this side. The nine-pounder long gun blew a funnel of black smoke and made a hell-shocking boom. The solid shot slammed into the side of the brig, blew straight through the planks, out the other side, and took out the corner of the main deckhouse. Someone on the other ship wailed pitifully—a man in blistering pain.

Cathell and the powder boys jumped up and down at their good aim.

Through burning eyes Boyle saw the brig turn sharper and begin moving away at a new angle. The *Comet* was lighter, sweeter in the water, the brig more loaded down, but the brig also had two masts of square sails and could catch more wind. Boyle ordered the *Comet* on her best running course for these airs, yet still could only parallel the brig's skillful movements and tight, subtle course corrections. Again he fired his carronades and the long gun, and again was answered by another broadside. Again the shots scratched temptingly at each hull, but this time the carronades ripped several lines of the brig's rigging, and that was almost as good as a punch in the side. The shredded lines danced as the brig tried to swing away, to put its stern to the schooner and make a smaller target. As she turned, she fired off another two shots before losing the ability to aim at the schooner. She had no stern gun, so relied on her broadside guns.

One of the two shots flew wild over the schooner's bowsprit, but the second tore high, right at the square tops'l, and severed both braces to shreds.

"Whore that!" Dieter snarled, glaring upward.

Now or never.

"Captain Cascadden," Boyle called, "rake that deck, if you don't mind."

Cascadden tried to jump to his feet quickly, but stumbled on stiff legs, shouting, "Marines! Ready! Aim!"

An awful pause—most, now all of the Marine detachment arranged themselves side by side, and brought up their muskets, which caused each man to turn to the oblique, like an archer drawing a bow. The formation seemed to shore them up mentally. Resolve showed in their faces now, thinly masking their inner quandaries.

"Fire!"

A breathy, shaggy blast rumbled down the rail. The balls seemed to travel together, side by side, like the Marines, through their own smoke on a mission of their destiny. Each ball had only one life, this moment, forged for its own fate and the fate of one man somewhere at the end of its flight.

A singular long moan rose from the deck of the other ship, shrouded now in smoke, human voices in pain and shock. The airs were light and the smoke cleared slowly. Boyle watched impatiently the most important single thing in his life right now— the English royal standard hanging from its staff on the brig's stern. The flag waggled as if it were sick, and fainted downward.

On the schooner's deck, a short blast rang. Another musket. It was Cascadden himself, discharging his own gun.

Boyle swung around. "You cock, they've struck!"

Cascadden seemed shocked, then called, "Cease fire!"

But everyone already had ceased.

Boyle craned to see what was happening on the brig. Was it over? Or would someone on the other ship take offense and answer the wild shot?

Silence. Shorn lines hung useless on both ships. The brig's rigging was in tatters.

"Dieter," Boyle croaked, needing to hear a voice if it were only his own.

"Yeah?"

"Check damage."

"Sure."

But a second or two went by before he roused himself.

"Deploy the boat," Boyle added. "Tommy, get on the tackle fall yourself."

Somebody responded, and the crew began to rouse themselves and to realize they had won. No one cheered or dishonored himself in any way. Several men stiffly moved to the dory boat stowed on the amidships deck and made the gantline to it. The work cleared their heads, gave them focus, and in short order the dory boat was floating and Boyle climbed in, along with Hooper, two Marines, and a man to row.

—⁓—

After the Marine guard secured the brig's deck, he boarded the smoldering deck and immediately stepped in a smear of blood. Boyle looked down at his foot and paused indelicately at the sight, but managed to rouse himself and hoped no one noticed.

He forced himself to walk across the bloodied deck, through the shredded lines and splinters of destroyed planks, to where the captain of the brig sat amidships on a deckhouse top, unable to stand because of a devilish leg wound.

"You are the captain," Boyle said, just to be clear, since the two of them had been watching each other for over an hour and knew who was in charge. But there was always the chance of a mistake.

"I am," the Briton responded. He was a man of middle age, perhaps forty-five, with a short silver beard sparkling with sweat, no moustache, and a head completely hairless. Upon his head was a white dome of skin where he normally wore a hat. He pressed a hand to his leg wound, but allowed no pain in his face.

Boyle stood back a pace to allow the man some room to move his legs. "You should've heeded my signal to heave to."

"It was my duty to resist."

"This vessel is English in origin?"

"Yes."

"Very well. I am an American cruiser in a time of war with England. I will capture English vessels, if I can, that are on the high seas, the common highway of all nations. The high seas, rightly, belong to America as much as any other power in the world and I am determined to exercise the authority I have been given by the president and Congress of the United States of America."

"You're a pirate, Captain," the Englishman said, unimpressed. "A dishonorable pirate. You fired on us after our standard was struck. It's reprehensible."

"That was a mistake," Boyle said quickly. "The man couldn't see through the smoke."

"He's a liar."

"That's for me to judge."

"You? You are hiding behind that fraudulent letter of marque in your pocket."

"It's not in my pocket. It's in my cabin and it's signed by President James Madison and Secretary of War James Monroe. Your identity, please?"

"William Anderson, shipmaster." He nodded toward a man with a severely bleeding ear wound who was sitting beside him. "Our bosun, Mr. Pomroy."

"Where are your first and second lieutenants?"

"Both are wounded by your musket volley. Being tended by our surgeon."

"Name of this ship?"

"This is the *Hopewell*."

"Out of ..."

"Surinam."

"Bound for?"

"London."

"Burden?"

"Three hundred forty-six tons."

"Cargo?"

"Cotton, sugar, coffee, molasses ..."

"Cocoa," Pomroy supplied, almost whispering.

"Cocoa."

Boyle pulled a kerchief from his back pocket, folded it, and pressed it to Pomroy's bleeding ear. The man took it and nodded silent thanks.

"How many aboard?" Boyle asked.

"Twenty-five, including officers," Anderson responded. At this, a British seaman who had been standing by leaned to his captain and murmured privately. Anderson nodded. "Twenty-four. Our carpenter has just died."

Boyle paused. He thought about offering condolences and requesting that the sentiments be conveyed to the man's family and friends, but he held back rather than imply that he or his crew might be guilty of anything. The fight had been fair. The *Hopewell*'s choice to resist might serve all sides better as a warning to surrender sooner.

He motioned to Hooper, who came up behind him.

"This is John Hooper, prize master," he said to Anderson. "He and a prize crew will board your vessel, which will be taken to Baltimore, where condemnation proceedings will be instituted for the value of the ship and cargo. Your crew will be imprisoned aboard my schooner, with the prisoners from our previous exchanges. They will be treated decently and their wounds attended. However, I shall allow you and the worst-wounded of your men to remain aboard the *Hopewell*, thereby to be returned to land sooner and be treated of your injuries."

"Most considerate," Anderson responded without emotion. "In return, I shall give you the latest news of your nation." He then ordered one of his men to go to his cabin and retrieve a newspaper. "When did you set sail, captain?"

"July 12."

"From Baltimore?"

"That's right."

"Then you might know that your General Hull invaded Canada at Sandwich on that day."

Unsure about how much to divulge, Boyle simply nodded.

"This newspaper is recent, as of only a week." Anderson received the paper from his crewman, then handed it to Boyle. "The *Niles Register*. Baltimore."

Boyle looked at the paper with surprise that he couldn't hide. "How did you acquire a Baltimore newspaper?"

"Exchanged from another vessel just yesterday. There is much interest in Baltimore these days, what with the Federalist riots and all."

Inwardly raging to read the paper, Boyle instead folded it and handed it to one of his Marines, who thankfully had the sense to tuck it in his coat rather than look at it.

"Your wounded who remain here will be considered prisoners, but will be allowed common comforts to mitigate their suffering. I expect to have their words of honor that they will not rise against my prize crew, who are honest men engaging in legal control of this vessel. I will therefore refrain from imprisoning you and them below, and, if they're able, allow them to assist in splicing and re-reaving adequate to sail the ship. Is there anything else I can do for you, Captain?"

"What could I want from you?" Anderson asked bluntly.

"Medical supplies?"

"Thank you. No."

The other captain's cold resentment toward Boyle and disappointment in himself moved Boyle's humanity an inch. Unnecessarily, he explained, "We are no longer enemies, Captain. That part is over. This is the time for civility. You sailed skillfully and defended your ship with vigor. I shall note so in my log and report it to the *Hopewell's* owners. Thank you for the newspaper."

Boyle returned to his dory boat, leaving Hooper and the Marines aboard to hold the *Hopewell* secure until the prize crew could join them, but he was sure to get the newspaper from the marine before leaving. He quaked to read it, managing instead to hold it calmly in his hands as he was rowed back to the *Comet*. News ... news of Hull's victories in Canada, news of marvelous successes in the western territories of Michigan, Lake Erie ...

As the dory drew up to the *Comet's* side and Boyle climbed

back aboard as easily as if the ship were simply sucking him in, a disturbing volley of angry words and the sounds of a scuffle caused him unhappy distraction. On the foredeck, Cascadden was at Ring's throat with both hands, his teeth gritted and lips peeled back like a badger. Ring was spitting obscenities and laughing as he endured being strangled, and he responded by twisting the Marine captain's ears.

"Not this again!" Boyle headed for the quarrel, boiling that this unshipmatelike behavior was being seen and clearly heard by the crew of the *Hopewell*, as the sound skated over the water. Without a pause he barreled into Cascadden's bulk and drove an elbow into the man's ribs and a fist into his head and slammed him to the deck. Cascadden skidded on his rump and glared up at Boyle.

"What happened?" Boyle demanded.

"Ring called him a pudnigger," Dieter said.

"Spudfucker!" Ring snarled. "I'll say it again!"

Boyle spun on him and roared, "Do and I'll knock your head off!"

So rare was this vicious side of his temper, so seldom seen and yet constantly perceived, that the whole company fell to cryptic silence and feared to catch his attention. His voice carried from bow to stern and below, carrying the authority and the anger of a prudent captain pushed too far.

He turned again on Cascadden, who was just getting to his feet. "You fired on the prize after their colors were struck!"

"I ... I ... thought the flag had been shot away!" the Irishman sputtered. "I didn't think they'd struck!"

"You're a captain! You're supposed to know!" He tipped forward and sniffed at a distinct odor on Cascadden's breath— something not even allowed on board. "Whiskey? Are you drunk?"

The Marine officer sputtered, but made no sense.

Boyle snapped, "Dieter, put him in irons."

Cascadden gasped, "What?"

But they dragged him away before more could go wrong.

Eminence Grise

"CAPTAIN! CAPTAIN BOYLE!"

The friendly call took a bit of effort to elevate over the noises of one of Fell's Point's famous shipyards. Sounds of industry were everywhere, wall to wall, earth to sky. Carpenters' mallets clacked, backbeat by their own echoes, discordant with the clangs of ironwork, the rasps of saws, the barks of foremen overseeing large crews of workmen among dozens of rope-workers and chandlers rushing about with armloads of ordnance. Horses and mules clumped by, drawing freight wagons large and small, the largest carrying four-ton loads of lumber, wreckage, iron parts, bolts of rope in varied diameters, folded sails ready-made for each order, and looming above them at every turn was a dry-docked ship's hull, some without masts, others already rigged but landed for repairs. Among them were cranes for setting the masts into the hulls, and dozens of beasts of burden, mostly mules, but here and there a draft horse or an ox with its horns sawn off.

The draft horses were the most fun to watch, he had learned. They loved to work and often stamped the ground or shook their livery impatiently while their wagons were loaded, and some of them had to be tied to docking bitts or they would strike off on their own. He recalled the same teams of giants hauling loaded sleds last winter and mused briefly on the industrious all-year-around partnership between men and beasts, keeping each other alive and constantly moving forward, and how the ships of the sea wouldn't be possible without the beasts of the land.

Along the dock floated a small fleet of ships—some new and being rigged for the first time, others damaged and awaiting attention. One of these latter vessels was an unpretentious schooner with a yellow hull, shaggy and beaten up, still in the water at the dockside, without any advertisement of her heralded adventures over the past many weeks. She was the stuff of newspaper stories and midnight dreams for those on land who awaited any dribble of information about the war at sea, and indeed there were some people hovering about the dock who were clearly not shipwrights, but who had come to see the famous little ship. The schooner's deck was a mess of loose blocks and gasket-coiled lines, metal parts and tools, rags, scraps of discarded rope, and smelly buckets of pitch. Her sails were unfurled and draped about the deck like laundry, seeming much bigger than when they were set into the sky. Her crew, crowded around the deck or on floating rafts around the hull, were painting, splicing, stitching, sanding, reaming, hammering, packing deck plank seams with oil-soaked raw cotton or unraveled rope fibers—the French Jew was exhausted just watching them. He had an idea of what they were doing, but not the skilled part of *how* they were doing it. He had been here every day for two weeks, waiting, watching, and learning. They toiled with a deliberate urgency, for much of this work would have to tolerate the coming winter months at sea. The whole operation had a distinct industrial smell that he would forever associate with ships.

On the deck of the schooner, Tom Boyle heard his name finally and looked over toward the source, then recognized the not-quite-familiar round face, dusky complexion, the bowler hat, and the beard.

"Oh—hello, Mr. Yemmick, is it? Yelbrick?"

"Yambrick. How joyous to see you again! I'm so pleased you're safe and hale after your long adventure. You recall Sophie, my niece ..."

"Miss," Boyle said, nodding to the funny-faced woman beside the Frenchman.

She made a clunky curtsy but, as previously instructed, said nothing. The Frenchman thought for a moment that others would find it too odd, too quirkish, that she never spoke, and toyed with the idea of giving her some cursory lines to say, but had no confidence that she would say them correctly and not get carried away. Silence was better.

Thomas Boyle made a polite bow in return and thankfully didn't try to engage her in conversation. He wiped his hands with a rag and climbed up onto the dock, then stepped through a gauntlet of barrels, wooden hoops, and fenders, and excused himself passing through the folded legs of a team of three boys who were passing oiled fibers of old unraveled rope through used sailcloth as if hooking a rug.

The captain reached out to shake the Frenchman's hand, then quickly withdrew, for his hands were nearly black with the filth of shipboard work. He wiped them on his trousers. "Sorry. Got oakum and pitch all over my fingers."

The Frenchman seized the captain's hand anyway. "Now I can say I helped you on a ship and I'll smell just right."

The two men laughed, and mousy Pdut chimed in with her ridiculous chortle. She thought it was safe to laugh, but botched it.

Minutes later, the three were stationed around a small round table at one of the port's popular cafés, on the cobblestoned Thames Street, not far from where the Frenchman and Pdut rented a suite. Flanking the street were bright orange-gold trees waving their autumn jewelry in the pleasant sunshine. Warm mugs of Irish coffee steamed from the table, mingling with the eternal aromas of commerce—sweat, horses, grease ...

"Do you have business here at the shipyard?" Captain Boyle asked.

The French Jew drew in a long poetic breath. "If it were true! Growing up in the countryside, locked between hedgerows and gardens, I imagined the grandeur of seafaring, of travel and adventure. Sadly I missed that opportunity and went into business with my father as a real property agent. All I know is land. But for one expedition over the Atlantic to bring me to this nation, I have never realized that wish. Of course, no one would look at me and see a prince of adventure such as yourself anyway. I'm clearly not constructed for it."

"And yet," Boyle said, "this is not a chance reunion."

"You're quick," the other man said, smiling. "I was told you might be in Fell's Point today."

"By whom?"

"By the owners of the *Comet*."

"I'm one of the owners now," Boyle declared. "But you already know that, don't you, Mr. Yambrick?"

"Samuel, please." The Frenchman blushed a bit and chuckled. "I would say all this is your own fault, Captain. Your expert advice on my nephew's model ship inspired me. I have hardly been able to think of anything else! I read about you in the newspapers. You're famous now! An intrepid privateer, the cunning intriguer cruising the open ocean, sultan of the seas prowling for enemy victims to vanquish, riches to seize—"

"Sounds piratical, sir. We're not pirates."

"No, no! Patriots, to be sure. You would never take a ship in time of peace—I know that. Everyone knows. You're soldiers. You're a navy."

"With different tactics. We don't confront enemy cruisers. There's no point to it. We aim for the merchant fleet. For privateers, there's no dishonor in running."

"Please accept my apology."

"Not necessary, but accepted." Boyle paused and savored a sip of the Irish coffee, then gave his shoulders a stretch.

"Do you live near here?" the French Jew asked.

"Albemarle Street."

"Oh? Pdut ... Sophie had some alterations done by a lady who lives on that street. Dress alterations. Ladies' things. Petticoats, I believe they're called."

"Mrs. Pickersgill?"

"Why, yes! So you know her."

"She lives across the street. Everyone knows her. Certainly every captain. She makes ensigns and signal flags. We would be crippled without flags. Mute. Where would we be without people who know how to sew?"

"A most pleasant woman. She seemed like the sort who will always make her own happiness."

"And the happiness of any man who might have the sense to court her."

"How true. Not me, of course—I'm too old."

"Don't misunderstand," the captain repealed, as if he thought he had said too much. "I've never seen her flirt, though she's certainly young enough to make a fine wife and new mother. I don't think she's interested, but I wouldn't speak out of turn."

"Has she always made flags?"

"She comes from a flag-making family, back at least a couple of generations."

"She showed me some pennants and household ensigns. Dazzling, some of them. The embroidery, I mean. I believe the dress tailoring was done by one of the darkie girls in her house."

"Mary's skills are far above ordinary tailoring," Boyle said, "but she trains girls to sew. She's interested in making women self-sufficient. Those two Negro girls live there. One's an apprentice and one is a bonded servant. A cook, I think. I've always respected Mary's treating them just as she treats her own daughter."

"Quite a household."

"She hosts many parties and brunches. Without her, I think Fell's Point would be nothing but a den of pubs and brothels. Pardon me ... miss." The captain blushed and shifted, looking at the silent woman at his side. "Too much time among sailors."

"Not at all," the Frenchman said with a smile. "For what you are doing for this nation, you deserve to speak your mind in any fashion that inspires you. Oh, look ... cows."

They paused to watch a herd of cattle tread by on their way to the butcher, kept moving by three boys and a girl with shepherd's crooks.

"Steers, probably," Boyle mentioned.

"When will you be, shall we say, striking out to the briny main again?"

"No specific date. Repairs, provisions, new crewmen ... weather ..."

"Oh, of course you'll want to keep that information undisclosed. I retract my ill-considered question." The Frenchman fell silent for a few calculated seconds, then spoke again, infusing great sympathy into his voice. "But you have an uphill battle. There have been many wins for you privateers, yes, and the Frigate *Constitution* made a legendary victory against that ship with the French name—"

"*Guerriere.*"

"Yes, that story will become naval lore for the future. But I've heard the British Navy is still supreme on the seas. And we've lost many land engagements, sad to say. We simply have had no effect on Great Britain. But you know that."

Boyle shifted his feet, as if a secret had been revealed.

The Frenchman let the moment move his way. "I've also heard the enemy is having notable success in recapturing your prizes even after you take them. Not just yours, I mean all the privateers' prizes. Then they make prisoners of our best sailors. You must feel sometimes that you're wasting your time and effort—"

"We're not doing this for profits alone," Boyle declared.

"We have a war to win. This is a war at sea. And a war *for* the sea."

"Certainly, yes."

With practiced self-control, the captain retracted his temper. "It's discouraging when prizes are recaptured," he admitted. "If for nothing else than the British get to use that ship against us again. Part of our mission is to deprive them of useful vessels."

The Frenchman lowered his voice. "Have you ever thought of ways to do more damage to the enemy?"

"Why? Do you have a suggestion?"

"I?" The Frenchman tried to appear shocked. "Oh, I could never be so clever. I'm asking ... curious ... if you were the president or an admiral what would you do to have more effect? Or even better, have you ever thought about what you yourself, with your ship, could do to cause Britain deeper pain?"

Boyle rubbed a muscle in his neck, gazed into his Irish coffee, then looked out the window at the passing pedestrians and the endless parade of wagons lumbering over the cobblestones.

"I have thought," he said. "I'm thinking still."

—⁂—

In the aromatic Thames Street café, strangers from two continents sat across a tiny walnut table from each other, silently contemplating the problem that had crawled its way into the moment. Like the Irish coffee, there was just enough spirit in it.

Timing was critical with a man like the captain.

As was not pushing.

"Well," the French Jew slowly said, "I've asked too much of you. Please forget about it."

The captain took his time drawing in the scent of the Irish coffee he had finished drinking. "Not likely."

"I'm so very sorry."

The captain waved a dismissive hand. "Nothing."

"Allow me to make up for my indiscretion."

"Sorry?"

"I would like to invest in your ship."

Boyle looked a little surprised, or at least momentarily confused by the change of subject. "You didn't discuss that with the *Comet*'s senior owners?"

"Cash only. No records. Dealing with you alone."

"That's not an investment. That's a donation. *Comet* is not a charity."

"Oh, no! Oh, certainly not. But I am a patriot too. Now, look at me. I am no soldier or any kind of a sailor, but in my own way I too wish to fight for the flag. I want to support the war effort, and I don't expect a profit."

Boyle wiped his hands on the linen napkin, which already was smudged from his morning's work. "You are neither an unintelligent man nor an unthoughtful one. You know that anyone who fights for a flag is a mindless fool. We fight for what the flag represents. And we must mind what it represents, that it is worth fighting for."

The Frenchman smiled with genuine delight. "Well said. Captain, I know you have endured some unsavory publicity about your using portions of prize cargoes for your own crew, consuming the foodstuffs, confiscating weapons—there has been some legal wrangling as to the ethics of that. But what else should you do? I find the questioning to be petty. I would like to help. Perhaps my *silent donation* could go to provisions for your vessel so that you have no need of such confiscations. My means are considerable. Bottomless, as they say."

"The source, may I ask?"

"Toothbrushes."

"Pardon?"

"I founded a new line of bone toothbrushes with horsehair, and tortoiseshell hair brushes with boars' hair. But the toothbrushes are the anchor, as you sailors might say. Allow me to supply your entire crew."

"An entrepreneur."

"Much like yourself."

"Such generosity might be construed as a bribe."

"But I'm not asking for anything in return."

"The future remains undefined."

"True, but to protect you we shall have no written contract and I shall have no hold over you. A silent, and mute, partner."

"Still, it has an odor. No records, no paper trail—Why would you do this?"

"I trust you, Captain."

"Why would you trust me?"

"I'm an excellent judge of character."

From the look in his cool blue eyes, Boyle disclosed himself as also an excellent judge of others. There was curiosity in those eyes, maybe a touch of opportunity, but caution too.

"You're a gambler, Captain," the Frenchman goaded, with a slight change of tone. "You wouldn't deprive me of the same pleasure, would you?"

The funny eyebrows went up, then down again.

Caution finally closed the door.

"I must get back to the schooner," Boyle said as he stood. "Mr. Yambrick. Miss ..."

"A captain's work is never done." The Frenchman stood also, but did not move to put his coat on, indicating passively that he would not impose further on the captain's company even to walk out to the street.

"Let me know if you think of any way to enhance your effectiveness against Great Britain. I will help in any way, spiritual or corporeal, that I can. If I were a younger man, I should be glad of a chance to serve under your command. I am proud to say I know you, Captain Boyle. I hope you will not be discomposed if I tell people that we are friends."

"At your own risk," Boyle said with an uncharacteristically humble smile. "And I will consider your offer, sir."

"Samuel."

—ₘ—

Leaves blew down the street on the harbor wind, carrying the captain away as the Frenchman and Pdut watched through the slight coating of grime on the café window. Pdut was less interested in the complicated man who had just left them. She finished her Irish coffee, pushed it aside, then took what was left of the captain's and finished that too.

The French Jew kept watching the corner where the captain had left his sight. "He certainly is hard-boiled."

"What you talk him for?" Pdut asked.

"About. What did I talk to him *about*."

"About talk?"

"You're hopeless," he muttered. "You heard us, didn't you?"

"Heerd, yis."

"But as ever you do not understand. You can't put one and one together at all, can you? You lump around with that numb brain."

He glanced around at the self-concerned patrons of the café. Too many ears. He switched to French for the lecture, yet still kept his voice down.

"The best way to help Napoleon is to stir up these colonies. These *states*. At this very moment the Grand Armée of France is moving into Russia. Britain must be kept busy while the Russian conquest is completed. When the emperor returns, he will have wealth, weapons, power, territory. Britain will be weak and we will cross the Channel. Then America is nothing. Napoleon will control the world. The Rothschilds banking empire will control Napoleon. And I will have been here first."

Realizing her attention was drifting, he snatched the second cup of Irish coffee from her hand and slapped her away from it.

"Napoleon has broken the old monarchs and established a world bank, while in America they cannot even decide upon a leader. Thus they will have no consistent goals. We have Napoleon now and forever. We are secure. I mean to engage Captain Boyle's help in our cause, though he will never know it. At least, not until it's too late."

1813

THE MAN CALLING HIMSELF, for now, Samuel Yambrick sat on the outside steps of the house he had rented, basking in the rare winter sunlight that mitigated the bite of cold. He sat in his wool knee-length overcoat and hat as if waiting for a coach, but he wasn't going anywhere. Between the coat, hat, his whiskers, and the sun, he was comfortable enough to remain out here. He wanted to be cold. His own comfort was a shame to him.

As he sat he thumbed the edge of a used newspaper, as he had thumbed the same paper every day since December when it first arrived, smuggling in from his contacts in London. Thus it was in English, a somewhat irritating language for him to read. He wished newspapers could be in Latin. Much more precise.

He was about to read the article yet again, when a ceramic chamber pot shot past him three feet in the air and shattered on the cobbled street. It blasted into shards, leaving no hint of its original form, immediately to be further crushed under the hooves of a pair of draft horses drawing a beer wagon. The horses either didn't notice or didn't care. Their feet, the sizes of dinner plates, made a pleasant sound on the stones and broken bits.

Behind the flying pottery came a freakish scream, which then twisted itself into a howl, then fizzled out and was followed by more smashing inside the open door. Then a teacup, still with its saucer, flew madly over his head and went into the street, there to commit complete suicide. Later he would come out with a whisk broom and collect the destruction.

He heard angry footsteps inside, if footsteps could be angry, and he believed they could. Knew it, in fact. Had it well memorized. Inside, Pdut was involved in one of her fits of fury or frustration. He knew not which, for she was a blunderer when it came to explaining herself, or anything.

The howling and wrecking went on without pause. Mirrors, dishes, windows, the entire set of salt-glazed dishware, the porcelain dog he bought her last week. He had of course kept the breakables in the house at a minimum, or at least breakables of any worth. After all, she had to have something to break or the episode would migrate outside to the windows of others.

People passed, peering curiously at him as they heard the frantic noises of rage and destruction inside, offered help or worry with their expressions, but he merely shrugged, waved, and assured then with his own expression that he was monitoring the war inside the door and waiting it out. So they walked on, with something to gossip about tonight.

He was satisfied to be alone here on the open street, thumbing his newspaper and digesting yet again the crushing headline. Disappointment chewed at him. Rarely surprised by events, he had been attempting for weeks to suffer the dire news as the rest of the world moved forward. Were things changing, or were they merely different for now? How should he revise his plans? Would his sponsors still move on his advice? Would those who moved above the thunder and rush of ordinary life yet have confidence in him or in the world as he described it to them? He was a spinner of possibilities, a measurer of investments, a diviner of futures. His success depended upon the faith of others and that faith upon his record of wins.

This was not a win.

Half of a shattered saucer skidded beside him and landed on the step, accompanied by a mad shriek and quite a lot of foul language in French. He was glad it was in French, for the sakes of the passing shoppers and merchants. Their glances told them nothing and his rolled eyes and little waves permitted them to be on their ways, for the havoc, while out of hand, was in hand.

Firewood. After she was finished razing the rooms, he would have to get more firewood to warm the place again after having the doors open all morning. If the doors weren't open, she would come barging out. He had no idea why.

So the doors were open, the windows were shattered, the heat flowing out. Appropriate, somehow.

He gazed again at the newspaper in his winter-reddened hands.

BONAPARTE RETREATS FROM RUSSIA
GRAND ARMÉE FROZEN TO DEATH

The International Highway

THE COAST OF BRAZIL
JANUARY 14

THE *COMET* STOOD TEN miles off Pernambuco on the east coast of South America, as foreign a land as the world could offer, a sea of a different kind—a green sea of jungles and insects, predators and victims. The poetry was not lost on Tom Boyle as he hailed the very large brig that had hove to at his approach. Obviously it was not an English ship, so he had not fired a warning shot. The high-bulwarked brig had backed its two course sails and slowed to be hailed. Now the two ships, big and small, rode a current within half a cable's length.

In the rigging, Mary Pickersgill's signal flags flew, asking the question of identity. *Who are you? What is your home port?*

Too much to spell out, the questions were represented by only two flags whose symbolic meaning was known internationally.

On the stern of the other ship, an officer in an unrecognized military uniform had ordered his own signals raised. *WASA, Lisbon.* Then the signal for *cargo* and the individual letters "C-O-O-K W-A-R-E-S C-O-F-F-E-E" were spelled out in English. Boyle knew that Dieter spoke Spanish, but fortune favored him today and he could deal with this brig on his own. If they had to speak directly, translation was always awkward and reading the other man's inflections and tones would have been difficult. He reminded himself to learn Spanish one of these days.

"Raise 'pass on,'" he said to Tommy Ring, who was manning the ensign halyard with Steven Sigsby's help.

He waved at the Portuguese officer as the lone flag went up into the schooner's rigging.

The officer gave him a salute, and the brig again hoisted her courses and moved onward toward the port of Pernambuco.

Boyle sat back on the schooner's rail and watched the other ship move away toward the mountainous land mass to his west.

John Dieter appeared at his side, and leaned with those tattooed arms on the deckhouse. "Well, you were right. How did you know there would be activity here, of all places?"

"Seasonal alterations in commerce. It's winter up north now. More trade in the tropics."

"And this is a trade route?"

"Everything from flannel shirts to johnnycake."

Dieter shook his head and twisted up half a grin. "Wish I were you."

Boyle smiled at the compliment. "Just one problem."

"Yeah?"

"That's not a trading ship."

Dieter watched the foreign brig braced around to sail away. "Huh ... what's his game, then?"

"Don't know. Could be what he says. Maybe they're short of ships."

Above them the mainsail was scandalized to keep it from filling, and forward the brailed foresail waited to be hauled out again. The *Comet* floated easily with just a jib puffed out before her.

The early day was dark, with glowering clouds from horizon to horizon, but no storm. The ocean was rolling quietly, enough to carry them slowly along, as if it were rocking a baby.

"Make sail?" Dieter asked.

"Not yet," Boyle said. "Let's lie off here a while. Do some repairs."

Dieter simply nodded, too exhausted to engage in chatter, and went off to arrange repair parties and oversee the work.

Boyle watched in silence as the man-of-war moved away, and every man left aboard the *Comet* also watched until he was ordered away into a work group, those who were awake anyway.

He had fewer than one hundred aboard now, after leaving prize crews on several captured vessels. Capture after capture, he had taken a bite out of British commerce, he and the other privateers who had set out of the United States' ports up and down the coast. The Royal Navy still tried to blockade the US coastline, but there was simply too much coast and too much ocean for them to sentry. Privateers, in small brig-rigs and schooners such as the *Comet,* slipped out like little birds, their captures slipping back in, past the palace guards, along a thousand miles of land-falls, bays, and inlets leading to America's bustling port cities, where auctions transferred the prizes to dollars. Still, too many of the privateers' prizes had been recaptured by the British before reaching an American port and thus offered no profit or win, but only a cost. The blockade had greatly reduced trade and crippled the American economy. The Royal Navy was dominant in the world for good reason. They were competent.

As the day wore on, he watched the coast of South America. He felt the pulse of the ship and the men around him, those who were left. The prisoners also had been put off *Comet* and transferred to a prize ship, thereafter to be landed in the United States to become someone else's problem to house and feed. Or perhaps, of course, they might be captured by the Royal Navy and put right back into service against the United States. Skill and cleverness were part of the equation, and luck everything else.

Comet was chopped up with battle fatigue, her lines spliced and spliced again, filthy and blackened from gunpowder blasts, the deck scored by the iron wheels of the gun trucks, rails chipped and blown out, fitted with new wood, then blown out again, sails tattered, repaired, tattered again, and the port watch was busy making a new main stuns'l boom after the last one had been shattered almost in the middle. The crew's grimy clothing told of days at sea broken only by the tempers of weather and strife, of bad water and dwindling food supplies, of exhaustion of the body and weariness of the mind, a state in which all adversaries melted one into the other, kept in order only in the captain's log book. Many wounds but so far no deaths aboard, by the luck of the stars. Boyle counted his blessings and drew in a deep breath of the breeze off the aromatic jungle just barely in sight.

The deep breath made his ribs hurt on the left side. Until now he hadn't realized. Had he fallen? Been struck by a flying fragment of wood? Been elbowed by someone?

He rubbed the sore spot absently and continued to watch the place near land where the brig had left his sight, disappearing into the distant coastline and ultimately the harbor at Suape.

"Tom?"

John Dieter again. How much time had passed? Hours. Boyle noticed he was hungry now. His thoughts had consumed him. When the ship wasn't moving, he sometimes forgot to be alive.

"Tom."

Boyle buried a flinch and came out of his concentration. "John—sorry."

"We're squared away, if you want to get under sail at change of watch."

"Mm."

"You don't want to get going?"

"Not just yet."

"Should we put in to the port for supplies and water?"

"No, we'll just lie off here for a while."

"Drills?"

"No ..."

Dieter lingered at his side, waiting to see whether there would be an explanation forthcoming, then went ahead and made a guess. "That Portuguese man-of-war?"

Inwardly impressed at how well Dieter knew him, Boyle wondered, "Why is he here? What's his true business?"

Dieter folded his arms and sighed, staring out at the horizon. "Gambling?"

"Only if I were her captain," Boyle commented. "Could be a sign."

"Of ..."

"Of something."

Morning chipped away into afternoon accompanied by the constant percussion of chisels and mallets, the smells of oakum and hot tar, sweat of the men and stew to feed them. Stew, again. There were no maneuvers except to hold the ship more or less in place, which took its own kind of skill at the tiller tackles and at sail handling. A very dreary and monotonous kind.

Boyle knew the men, at least his officers, were watching him, noticing his obsession with the coastline. His senses were piqued, his mind racing. So much had changed in just these few months of predation, political changes, the fortunes of war—not just the war of the United States and England, but other wars in the world. There was no such thing as isolation anymore, not for any nation, ever again.

Some time after noon, Dieter approached him again, somewhat tentatively. Boyle saw him out of the corner of his eye.

Dieter didn't speak.

Against the stern, water lapped like a big dog drinking out of its bowl.

The first mate waited.

"There," Boyle spoke after a time. "Look there."

Dieter squinted out over the water, saw movement against the still land, climbed up into the shrouds for a better look, and hung there like a candle sconce on a wall. "I'll be damned…"

Boyle handed him the spyglass and asked, "How many?"

The other man steadied his feet on the ratlines and peered into the brass tube. "Four sets of sails … a brig … a full-rigger … another brig … and in the rearguard that Portuguese ship. Sails are set for a southeastward course, I think. East-southeast."

"That's what I see too."

"Seems he wasn't quite forthcoming with us. How did you know?"

"What time is it?"

"Almost three."

"Note the sighting in the log. Let's let them get another league or two out from land. Then make all sail and sheer up close. Call hands and get the guns loaded. Both round shot and grape. Quick march."

"Quick march, aye!" Dieter shot away to follow that command with specific orders to the gun crews, and to get the deck cleared for action. "All hands!"

"Hoist 'stop your intentions,'" Boyle said. "Let's see what he does."

—⟨⟩—

Not more than one hour later, the Portuguese man-of-war floated between the *Comet* and the three other vessels, which were obliged to trice up and wait to see what would happen. The three-masted cargo vessel and both two-masted brigs made a pretty picture floating so near each other against beautiful sky and the streak of jungle in the distance. Boyle took a moment from his calculations to enjoy that picture and wish he were a painter.

The foreign ships had done as the *stop intentions* signal ordered, and Boyle wasn't quite sure why. That man-of-war was big and could be intimidating if its captain wished, but the *affirmative* flag had been raised and they seemed to be complying with his order.

The Portuguese man-of-war dispatched a boat to approach *Comet*, and in it was the officer whom Boyle had just this morning signaled, being rowed over by only one uniformed man. The Jacob's ladder went over the side and the officer nimbly climbed aboard, where Boyle and Dieter stood waiting with the phalanx of Marines standing ready behind them, just for show.

"*Boa tarde, senhor,*" the man said immediately, facing Boyle. "May I call you by name?"

"I'm Captain Thomas Boyle. *Boa tarde.*"

"I am Vascouselos de Millo, *capitão* of the Man-of-War *Libra.*"

"The Privateer *Comet* welcomes you aboard, *capitão,*" Boyle offered. "What is your ship's purpose in these waters, sir?"

"We are a Portuguese national vessel, sir."

"Yes. What is your armament?"

"Twenty thirty-two-pound heavy guns. One hundred sixty-five men-at-arms."

"You're bristling indeed. What is your mission? Why are you sailing with these three cargo ships? What is their nation of origin? They are flying no banners."

"They are under our protection. Our government's protection, I should rather say."

"Their nation of origin, please?"

"They are ... the ships themselves are of English origin."

Now it came out.

"They are bound for Europe, not England," the Portuguese

captain quickly added.

"Are the crews English?"

"Oh ... yes, most of them."

"Names of these vessels?" Boyle's tone communicated to the other captain very clearly that he thought it inappropriate and sneaky that the English vessels quite purposefully bore no name boards or identification pennants.

De Millo paused, deciding, then pointed at the nearest brig and evenly said, "That is the *Bowes*. The other brig is the *Gambier*, and the three-masted ship is the *George*. Why do you wish to know this information? You say you are a privateer?"

Boyle nodded once, firmly, and went into his favorite speech. "I am an American cruiser in a time of war, sanctioned to subdue English merchant vessels on the high seas. The seas are the international highway of all nations and the United States claims as much right to use the open waters as any other nation. In time of war, we will capture English vessels if we can, and confiscate them, their cargo, and their crewmen."

"Disturbing," the other captain said. "Show me your authority to engage in such molestation."

"John, if you will," Boyle called.

Dieter instantly produced the letter of marque, which he had kept tucked inside his trouser belt at moments like this. He whipped it into Boyle's waiting hand without taking his eyes off those of the Portuguese captain.

Several quiet moments went by as Captain de Millo studiously read the letter of marque with the patience and interest of a historian. His eyebrows went up and down each time something fascinated him in the wording of the document, until finally he scanned the signatures of the president and the secretary of war.

"You see now," Boyle began, "that I am authorized to restrain shipping involved with English trade. As a Portuguese-flagged vessel, you have no right to protect English merchant ships."

"In fact I do, sir. Those ships carry Portuguese-owned cargo. They are not carrying goods bound for England. You will not be seizing the stuffs of English commerce—"

"Then Portugal should not be engaging in deals with the English while England is at war. It is interference."

"Portugal has no strife with England. You are one ship, sir.

We are four, armed, ready. Like you, I have no desire to engage
in unpleasantness. Portugal wishes to be friendly with America,
of course. As such, I am an ambassador of my country, charged
to make only the most benevolent of gestures."

"Nor is it our plan to harass Portugal," Boyle said. "Your ship
will be allowed to pass freely through these waters. However, the
English ships must heave to and surrender to us."

"Does America have this allowance? To molest the trade of
anyone it targets?"

"As much right as any nation at war. We have the right to
harm our enemy. Captain de Millo, you look confused."

"You say you are a privateer."

"Yes."

"But you talk of nations and enemies. If there is firing of
guns, there will be damages done to all our vessels—"

"Certainly."

"—and thus damaged the ships will not likely make port so
far away as the United States. You will have no profit from them.
Why would you risk so much for a low return?"

"We are privateers, but we're also patriots. Americans defending America. Tactically, we seek to deprive England of those
three ships."

"So you are soldiers."

"At home, I was company commander of Baltimore's 51st
Regiment," Boyle said lightly. "I liked the uniform."

The other captain smiled, and even laughed. "A man of all
seasons!"

Boyle smiled too. "A few seasons, anyway. I didn't care for
the hat, though."

They chatted briefly about anything other than business—
the weather, fine for sailing, the passage from Lisbon, uncom-
fortably warm, the harvest season of plump fruits enjoyed by
the *Libra*'s crew and replenished in Pernambuco. There was a
brief—very brief—tour below decks to look at the configuration
of the cabins and the hold, deliberately a distraction from touring the deck and counting ammunition and marines. Both captains knew what was going on, and both played the game. Boyle
showed off his new collection of signal flags, without a single
frayed stitch, de Millo marveled over the manly woodwork of

Boyle's cabin, done by the expert hand of the ship's carpenter, who in private life was a decorative woodcarver for Baltimore's wealthy. And finally, unavoidably, back to the subject of the day—that their missions were mutually exclusive.

"Then we are at an impasse," de Millo said as he was escorted back to the Jacob's ladder. "I regret any unfriendliness that should pass between us, Mr. Boyle."

"If it does, you will be the aggressor," Boyle promised. "I will not fire first. As you can see, my ship is well appointed for such events and we will not shrink. Better that your charges should surrender themselves and their cargo rather than engage in a costly battle."

"My vessel is a man-of-war, built to engage in battles," de Millo responded reasonably. "The English vessels are armed also and prepared to defend themselves. They carry fourteen, ten, and ten guns, a formidable force when combined with my twenty. I shall go aboard my ship and convey this communication to my officers and to the English ships. Will you do the same? Confer with your officers?"

"Of course."

"Be honest with them about their chances of catastrophe. Then also convey to them that they will be attacking ships carrying wheat to the nation of Portugal and would be harming Portuguese investors and the people of Portugal, not the English."

"You have my word." He held a hand out again to John Dieter, who produced a long-necked bottle with a ribbon tied around the neck. "Please accept this wine as a gift. It's from the cellar of a prominent Maryland doctor who is an oenophile and a valued friend. Good body, round, toasty, with a lingering finish. It's my favorite."

"Elegant," de Millo said as he held the bottle up to the sun. "A rich color. After all is over, perhaps you will swim over and join me in a glass."

"If your raft is big enough, I'll be there."

De Millo smiled again. The two men shook hands as if they had known each other for years.

—ᴍ—

"Ready about!"

The fifth tack. Turn, turn, turn, the *Comet* tacked and jibed again and again. She was simply much faster than the *Libra* and the English ships, and not loaded down with cargo. That and one aspect usually regarded as a good thing, today rather a hindrance, and that was Boyle's own brilliant sailing ability. He knew he had it, everyone said he did—and he didn't mind saying it himself, for it was his greatest accomplishment and he was proud—still he couldn't eliminate the quickness and teamsmanship of his officers and the crew they had unremittingly trained. When *Comet* approached the convoy and made a formal demand that they back their topsails and heave to, the schooner then shot past them like a raging rocket and was forced to twist around and come back. The only hole in his system was that Boyle hadn't figured out how to dial down their efficiency at the right moments. The maneuvers were purposefully threatening, designed to show the English ships and their Portuguese guard that they couldn't hope to outrun the privateers.

The three English ships bunched together on the rolling ocean water in some kind of effort to pool their firepower or protect each other, but that only helped Boyle. They weren't trying to run, but huddled together as the shark of Baltimore circled them, assuming the *Libra* would take on the *Comet* and do their defensive work.

By now it was eight o'clock and soon the sun would dip and darken. The sky was clear and he hoped there would be a bright moon.

De Millo was true to his word—he did not fire his guns yet, but held his temper and tried to maneuver the much-larger battleship between the schooner and the English vessels. This proved impossible, because like a fly the *Comet* could spin around and be everywhere at once, while the man-of-war could not shift position that quickly, but opportunity was a living thing and had its own idea. Finally, inevitably, when *Comet* came abeam de Millo shouted a muffled order and the *Libra* opened up her starboard guns on *Comet*.

Solid iron balls and hot grape shot blasted into the *Comet*'s yellow sides. The tremendous blow shook the whole ship and made her stumble. Half the men were knocked to their knees, but the aim was low so the deck wasn't raked nor was the rigging damaged. Cries of pain and surprise erupted, but almost instantly faded as the men controlled themselves, even the injured. Part of the training, yes, but also pure bravery. They gritted their teeth and held their voices even as they watched their own blood flow, for they were experienced fighting men now and knew orders had to be heard. The wounded were dragged below very quickly and even the Marines took their places if necessary, so no position went unmanned as the schooner blew forward.

De Millo had made a tactical error—he had fired while *Comet* sped between *Libra* and one of the brigs. Some of the man-of-war's fire blew past *Comet*'s stern and smashed away two of the brig's gun ports.

Finally free of his promise not to fire first, Boyle called, "John, right now!"

"Both sides, fire!" Dieter shouted.

Comet shuddered to her bones as both batteries opened up. But this was a different kind of shudder, a controlled and useful kind. Because both sides fired at the same time, the schooner's way was not disrupted and she shot forward out from the gauntlet of the two vessels, leaving behind a dirty mess of wreckage. Through the smoke Boyle could see that the *Bowes'* fore and main channels were both shattered and several shrouds had come undone, leaving both masts unevenly supported and waving as if they were sick. Nothing was so disarming to any sailor than to see masts wobble that way.

And on the *Libra*, her high sides were in splinters. Boyle's stumpy, powerful carronades had pounded her bulwarks as if she were a punching bag, cracking planks and smashing deadeyes. The choice in armaments was making a big difference at close range.

"They're trying to move apart," he said as the English vessels bobbled around, disorganized, probably hoping to give *Libra* more room to move. He glanced at Wade. "Circle him when I say."

"Standing by," William Wade assured from where he and two other men worked the tackles that moved the heavy tiller this way or that.

Even though Dieter was forward at the jibs, flashing about like an animated figurehead, he saw immediately what Boyle was up to and ordered the heads'ls dumped again, but faster this time since the schooner wasn't going to make a complete tacking maneuver, and also brailed up the fore long enough for the ship to twist to a new course.

The men's arms spun like wheels, the foresail shot out again and caught the wind, the headsails were sheeted home and filled so smartly that each actually made a loud *snap*. The *Comet* jumped forward, slicing through the water with her nose down and a purpose in her heart. She shot past the other ships before another shot could be armed and fired.

"Ready about!" With one hand Boyle gave Dieter the signal they'd agreed upon to dump the headsails during the maneuver. "Helm's alee!"

While Wade and a deckhand worked together on the tackles to haul the big tiller to leeward, the men at the headsail sheets cast off, dumping the air out of the staysail and jibs. Those huge headsails whipped violently, but the men at the lazy sheets on the other side did not haul in yet. Instead, they held on to those mad sheets and waited for Dieter's signal.

The *Comet* spun around on her keel in the manner of a weathervane, seeming almost to lift itself from the water, turn, then drop in again. Once she was around and pointing back between the *Libra* and the *Bowes*, the sail handlers hauled in the sheets. The jibs and stays'l cracked full of air again and drove the ship nose-down like a hunting dog charging into a quail's nest. Given those seconds, the gunners had reloaded.

The *Comet* came around so fast that the English ships almost bumped each other in trying to stay away, obviously shaken by Boyle's fearlessly tight approaches at such speeds. The schooner skated past them like nearby lightning, causing the men to duck and cower in case the guns went off or the marines opened fire.

Gratified to see the English crews cowering, Boyle bit back a smile.

The *Bowes* and the full-rigger *George* tried to separate, probably to give the man-of-war room to fight, but it didn't work. *Bowes* turned without allowing enough room for the other brig, the *Gambier,* to also get out of the way, and those two nearly bumped. Boyle took the moment of wild confusion when the Bowes' crew was distracted, to fire a broadside into the full-rigger, almost beam-on.

The *George*'s starboard mizzen shrouds dissolved, making the mizzen sails useless and forcing the crew to quickly trice up and hope the mast held long enough without snapping. They succeeded, but maneuvering by the stern was almost impossible now.

Boyle's crew gave a little cheer, then immediately got back to work.

The breeze grew suddenly stiffer as night approached and the sun's warmth dropped away. He watched the *Libra*, which was being blown downwind. Square-rigged, she simply couldn't come back against the wind and would be forced to go around in a big circle. In desperation the man-of-war fired its stern chaser guns at *Comet,* which did some damage, but only to the name board.

"God love a schooner," he said, and patted the *Comet*'s rail. "De Millo has never fought one of us."

"And his first one had to be you," Dieter said from over his shoulder.

Boyle looked back and up, to see John Dieter standing on the main boom, hanging on to the mast hoops even while the sail was right out behind him. He wore a gray striped shirt with the arms cut off, giving his long tattooed arms a good audience and allowing him to move freely in all his thousand mate's duties.

When had he come aft? The man was a phantasm.

From here Dieter was surveying the damage on the other ships.

"What do you think?" Boyle asked.

"Keep shooting. Don't let 'em breathe."

"Reload all."

"Already done."

"Let's hammer the full-rigger," Dieter suggested. "They're already crippled, with the mizzen shrouds blown. Let's go for the main."

"The main on the other side," Boyle refined.

"Mighty!" Dieter plunged through the crowd of deckhands and Marines.

Only then did Boyle recognize that the Marines were all armed and ready, and clearly annoyed that they hadn't been able to shoot yet.

"Bear on the full-rigger's larboard side," Boyle said loudly, communicating to Wade at the helm as well as Clement Cathell and his gunners and powder boys. "Fire as your guns bear, Clement!"

"Aye!" Cathell shouted back. "Fire as your guns bear!"

The ungodly loud carronades filled the darkening night and blew fire at the *George*. The ship's starboard main deadeyes were blasted to pieces and the shrouds sprang free. What a hit! Several men behind the shrouds crumpled.

"Reload!" Cathell shouted without even waiting to see the full effect.

"Ready about! Helm's alee!" Boyle called again, and again the schooner cranked around, almost under the *George*'s spanker boom, and came back along the other side, but this time opened the other side's guns on the struggling *Bowes*.

Night folded around them, and the moon rose, almost full and very bright. Still, Boyle had a funny sense about the weather. He felt the barometer dropping and knew his luck would not hold.

"Pound the full-rigger!" he shouted. "Marines, fire at will!"

The Marines brightened and began shooting madly, doing as they had been trained to do—firing at other human beings. All over the *George* and the *Bowes*, men fell or ducked. The English ships had no Marines to fire back and had not anticipated having to fight, relying upon the *Libra* to defend them, which was now far out to the east and trying to crawl back into range.

"Clement!"

Cathell looked aft at Boyle.

"Ready the long guns!"

There were only two of them, one amidships on each side, but the long nine-pounders had good long reach.

"We're ready!" Cathell called. So those were loaded and primed.

"Fire on the *Libra* as you bear!"

"Fire as we bear, aye," Cathell repeated, delighted, then told his men to hold back until *Libra* approached close enough to make the shot a good one.

"Aim for the sprit," Boyle suggested. "Snap her whisker stays."

Cathell nodded, but was concentrating too hard to speak. He

and two other men put their backs into aiming the long gun with the quoin and shifting the heavy gun truck.

"Help them," Boyle said to Wade.

The *Comet* turned just enough to put a narrower target before the *Libra*, but still give the gunners what they needed.

While all that was happening, Boyle used the eye in the back of his head to calculate the positions of the *Bowes* and *Gambier*, both trying to hide behind him. He pointed back at the two ships. "Cut them up, Marines! Shake 'em to their royals!"

All bets were off. Clement Cathell's gunners opened fire on the *Libra* while the Marines skittered aft along both the schooner's rails and opened fire on the two brigs. The roar of the gun and muskets was maddening.

Boyle knew he was making de Millo's prediction come true—that he was cutting up his four prizes to the point that they would be impossible to sail back to America. He mourned that loss on behalf of his men, but nobody seemed to mind. They were still eager at their work. Somehow they understood without his having to explain.

In the tropical moonlight the four ships engaged in maneuver after maneuver, firing broadsides at each other, the three English ships often making the mistake of shooting at *Comet* while the schooner was between one and another, causing damage to their own partner ships. Perhaps it was the murkiness of night or the inexperience of the commanders, but this mistake took at least an hour for them to correct. The English were completely befuddled by the way an American-built privateering ship could race in almost any direction, turn almost in place like weathervanes, and come back up in defiance of the wind itself. In that hour, Boyle's gunners and musketeers chopped them up.

The *Bowes* wallowed in the water, listing badly to starboard, down a noticeable several inches by the stern, advertising that her hull was damaged below the water line. The *George* was even more smashed, unable to use two of her three masts, with those shrouds cut to pieces and waving around drunkenly from the mast tops. At eleven o'clock, the *George* surrendered.

"Order her to stay in place and wait," Boyle told Dieter, who immediately went to the beam rail and yelled the order across. The ships were so close together that neither signal flags nor lamps were needed to communicate.

The *George* dropped her heads'ls and hove to, bobbing in an increasingly jumpy sea, subject to the whims of the waves, and waited as ordered. She could do little better than move her rudder this way or that in the current in the attempt to hold position.

Bowes hadn't surrendered yet, but she was clearly out of the action. Seeing the *George* reasonably give up, the *Bowes* almost immediately did the same. Dieter ran up the signal flag to hold place.

"Let's get a crew over there," Boyle said when Dieter asked what was next. "Take possession for sure."

"They gave their words of honor," Dieter reminded.

"Just to be sure."

Dieter quickly assembled a prize crew, taking away a few of the gunners from active duty, and a quartet of Marines. A boat was put in the water for them; the *Libra* came barreling back on a good wave just on the other side of the *Bowes*.

"What's he doing?" Dieter growled, but he could sense something.

On his last word the *Libra* opened up her forward guns and piled a horrible explosion into the *Bowes*.

"Damn! Denying us the prize!" With a gazelle's leap, Dieter raced for *Comet*'s forward shroud and climbed it to see what the damage was on the other side of the *Bowes*.

Boyle watched while keeping one hand extended to Wade for subtle helm changes. De Millo was trying to protect the *Bowes* by denying it to the privateers, probably hoping to save at least the cargo of wheat aboard.

"Meet him on the other side," Boyle told Wade. "Position to rake her." He raced forward to meet Cathell and get the starboard guns ready. There were only seconds, no time for relaying orders.

Comet sped past the stumbling *Bowes* more quickly than *Libra* came past on the other side, and the soft-handed Wade and the two men helping him with the tiller tackles turned the ship in front of the *Bowes* so close to the sprit that Boyle could've spat on it. In moments the *Comet* was abeam of *Libra*'s bow.

Boyle waited until the *Libra* went down into a trough and shouted, "Forward guns, fire!"

The starboard carronades barked. The man-of-war lurched as the iron balls slammed into her forward deckhouse, crashed through it, came out the side and mowed down the gunners and sail-handlers on the length of the larboard side. Then one ball got stuck somewhere and two others continued crashing through the bulwarks and into the ocean. The *Libra*'s deck was in splinters.

But as the *Comet* blew out of her way, *Libra* came up close and a keen-eyed Portuguese gunner opened fire.

The single blast so close by was as accurate as a bullet. It glanced off the foremast just above the pin rail and smashed a gun on the larboard side.

Comet wobbled sickeningly.

Dieter called, "The mast!"

"Oh, vetch!" Tom Boyle snarled.

He didn't have to give an order. In seconds Dieter had the fores'l brailed in to take pressure off that mast.

Libra passed behind the schooner and distance opened very fast between them. Boyle signaled to Wade, and the *Comet* bore away on a course impossible for the square-rigger to follow. When the distance was good and wide, Boyle called, "Fall off!"

The schooner immediately turned and went off the wind. Her sails luffed and fell into confusion. The ship dropped into a trough and rested there just as the moon went away. Clouds were moving in.

"Is anyone killed?" Boyle called. "Anybody dead? Find them!"

Everyone looked about, oddly silent as his words bounced around the ship, until finally Clement Cathell shrugged and said, "I'm dead."

A roll of appreciative laughter rippled through the filthy, bleeding, and exhausted men. No one called his attention to a corpse. Grateful for that, he began thinking about the condition of the ship.

"Damage reports, anybody," he called, but he was mostly interested in what was going on forward, where Dieter already had a lantern shined on the base of the foremast. In an instant, Boyle was there himself.

"It's sprung good," Dieter said.

In the stark lamplight, Boyle ran his hand up and down the

front part of the mast, and there found a crack wide enough for a finger to fit in.

"Get the tops'ls down and house the topmast," Dieter said. "Put some gammoning around this until we can tend it better."

"Either we put to shore and hunt for a new mast—"

"We need a fir tree. This is the tropical jungle. We'll hunt all year in that leachy rot before we find one. We'll fish it and gammon it tight with the winch. Do we have a spar the right diameter?"

"I doubt it. We'll have to go ashore like it or not."

"That's easier to find than a whole mast. Find one a good two fathoms long at least. Longer, if you can. On second thought, get two or cut a good one in half. We should reinforce with a fathom below the deck also."

"Right." He went off to get a repair crew together.

"Tom," William Wade called from the tiller. "The other brig is signaling."

Boyle squinted over the water through the dimming moonlight. *Gambier* had struck her sails and was hoisting a flag of surrender. He looked now in the direction of the *Libra* and saw that the Portuguese man-of-war was presenting only her stern—the only part of the ship left that hadn't been turned to pudding—and was making all possible sail to get away.

"I see why. De Millo's given up on them."

"Don't blame him," Cathell said.

"There goes my goblet of the doctor's wine."

"We'll drink their health with rum."

"I'll write to the Portuguese government and tell them of Captain de Millo's courageous defense of his charges. He deserves that, I think. Well done, everyone. Clement, well done, very well, on the gunnery." Boyle went aft, giving the hearty well-dones to every man if possible and noting in his mind the visible damage on deck and the condition of the wounded who hadn't yet been taken below.

On the command deck, well astern of everyone and everything, he patted Wade on the shoulder and said, "Superior work, Will. I'll take it for a while."

Alone, he touched the long wooden tiller. He felt the current below the surface push and pry at the rudder as the ship bobbed on choppy waves. They would still need a tree with a good girth and a strong grain to hollow out and lash to the cracked part of the foremast. Within easy sight even in the dark, the three English ships bobbed also, sails mostly furled, waiting for Boyle to give them their orders.

He watched them hypnotically. His only comfort came from the machinelike work going on around him as the crew cleared their heads and set about repairing the hammered rails and hull. The rigging was in fair shape, maybe a splice needed here or there. They were taking care of it. They knew their jobs. Working would be good for them after so many hours of tensions and guessing and battle.

Boyle stalked the afterdeck, smoldering. Minutes stretched out into more time, but he did not keep track.

"All right, Tom?"

Dieter again, checking on him the way he checked on everything, every stitch, every nail. Having asked, he waited instinctively until the captain arranged his own thoughts.

Finally, Boyle drew a sigh of frustration. "It's not enough."

—⁂—

"Not enough of what?"

Being a man of practicality and a first mate, someone who's entire world consisted of details, Dieter wanted specifics.

"We're not doing enough damage," Boyle told him. He had at last narrowed in on what had been bothering him since ... well, since Baltimore.

"Oh, lovely," Dieter rasped, his throat burned by gun smoke. "My captain's turned daffy. You don't recall cutting up all four of those—"

"We can only sting the Crown, John," Boyle told him. "Deprive them of a dozen ships and cargoes here and there, but they have ships all over the world in their empire and all you or I can do is prick them. I want to slice them open. I want to strangle them. Make them choke. I want to hear them *gasp*."

Dieter thought about that, but could make no sense out of it. "How?"

The Home of Francis and Mary Key

THE HOME OF FRANCIS AND MARY KEY
GEORGETOWN, WASHINGTON, DC
MAY 3

THE KEYS WERE EXPECTING guests, but not the one who appeared at the Bridge Street entrance in the early evening, just as the sun sank behind the neighborhood of Georgetown, nestled on the Potomac in the cradle of Washington, DC.

Frank Key answered the door in the tidy entrance of the brown-brick house that also held his law office in its wing, with a greeting on his lips intended for a joyous friend, and instead found himself facing a short red-haired woman in her fifties with a shabby cotton cap and a lace shawl that needed cleaning. She carried with her a bitter odor, perhaps of a stable or butchery. Her face was almost as red as her hair, she had one eyebrow going over both eyes, and there was something familiar about her the longer he looked. He never got a chance to invite her in. She simply spun inside as if she had lived there for years.

He almost had the door closed when it was shoved open again, and in came two burly men with chests like barrels and very unhappy faces.

"Oh—" Key backed away as the two men came all the way in.

The door hung open.

"You're Mr. Key," the woman declared as she swung to face him. Her skirts were saturated with filth and urine from the street, indicating that she had not had her hands free to hold them up. In fact, her hands were hidden under the shawl.

"Yes ... I know you, do I not?" He kept an eye on the two; all he could think to call them was ruffians. They hadn't done anything. They just looked as if they wanted to.

"I'm Mrs. Verity Flett. I clean the floors at your church and look after the char and the candles. St. John's Parish Church."

"Of course, yes. How may I—"

She leveled her small marbly eyes on him and peered fiercely from under that eyebrow. "You are a pious man of charity and good works. You visit the sick. You minister to criminals in the jail. You do errands of Christian mercy. You deliver sermons. You write hymns."

She suddenly stopped.

He waited, glanced at the two bulls standing silent at his doorway, but finally sputtered, "Um ... I do ..."

"You're humble in the service of the Savior Jesus, you're in his glory. And all that."

"Is there some way I may help you, Mrs. Flett?"

She looked at the two men, steeled herself, and drew her shawl away from her bosom. There she cradled a tiny bundle the size of a kitten. With one hand she drew back the bread cloth in which the bundle was wrapped, there to reveal a tiny head no bigger than a peach. At first it seemed to be a doll, a child's toy, but in a single moment of crushing truth Key realized it was not a doll at all.

"God save us!" he gasped as his chest constricted.

"This is my grandson," Mrs. Flett said. "He's dying. Save his soul. Baptize him, Mr. Key. I beg it."

The level of determination in her unbalanced little face left no room for alternatives.

She saw in Key's face that he was trying to invent other ways to solve this dilemma, other places for her to go, better people for the task, and she instantly added, "There's no time. Do it now. We beseech it."

"But I'm—I'm not ordained!"

"Any breath might be his last."

"But where's the mother? The father?"

"The mother's down in the bed and he's right at your door."

In his spinning mind, Key couldn't figure which of those men fit that role. In a mad instant he decided they must be brothers. The father and the uncle.

He looked at them. "Get water!"

Never before had he seen a man of that bulk move so fast. The other one stood in the doorway and dragged off his hat.

"Give him to me." Key reached for the infant, clumsily. There was hardly any substance to the tiny package. Though he had experienced five precious infants of his own, he had never seen any this small, this impossibly frail. Tiny blue hands no bigger than grapes flared out at his touch.

As he and the woman crudely arranged the bundle in his arms and exposed the cherubic face, another man came down the steps between the doorway and Bridge Street.

Key had forgotten anyone else was expected.

"Good evening. What's—" Captain Tom Boyle, otherwise a most welcome presence, added a sudden gravity to the moment. He looked around, then paused over the countenance of the buffalo at the doorway and the other one who just now returned with a china tea cup of water. He pulled his own hat off and stepped in, and deliberately stepped to Key's side.

"Frank, you all right?"

"Tom, please come in."

The captain moved closer, until their arms touched. "Do we need to repel boarders?"

"No ... one moment."

Mrs. Flett reached up—way up—and seized the hat of the other man who had come with her. "Cap off, brat."

"Yes, mum," the man squeaked.

Key drew a shuddering breath and sighed it out, trying to clear his mind and collect his thoughts at the same time. Even so, he stumbled for the rights words. He closed his eyes and steadied himself. He could not address God in a rattling voice.

"Heavenly Father, we thank thee that by the Holy Spirit you bestow upon this innocent child your forgiveness and raise him to new life in grace ... Enfold him in your arms and keep him safe in your mercy. Sanctify this water, we pray ... that he is cleansed from sin and born again to rise at the right hand of Jesus Christ, our savior."

Key dipped his hand into the water and let the cool liquid

drizzle over the infant's little face and hairless head, and he spoke to the baby. He thought for a moment that he was the only help for this helpless one, yet around him stood the infant's family, desperate to save him, but helpless themselves. Born too early, though he looked like nothing more than an idea unfulfilled, he was a full human being, exactly right for his age. He was surrounded by all these, who wanted him to live.

"Child of God, whose son was thus anointed, know that you too are purified and absolved of all sins of this world, for the soul but waits in earthly form ..."

A hopeless calm came over him then. Key was rambling, stringing together senseless platitudes. With great inner will, he focused his thoughts and got on with business.

"I, Francis Scott Key, in the name of the Father, the Son, and the Holy Spirit, baptize you—"

He paused, then one of the men quickly said, "Joshua John Butterford."

"Joshua John Butterford, and commit your immortal soul into the hands of God, our Heavenly Father, if He should deem it so. Dear child, in innocence you were born and in innocence remain. May you dwell with angels in eternal paradise ... Amen."

"Amen," the others chanted.

Key lowered his head and kissed the tiny boy's forehead.

Silence folded in. To speak now seemed crude, to interrupt the moment at which God would dip down from Heaven and take this little life, if that were His divine will. Key hoped it had sounded all right, and that they wouldn't notice he had literally run out of words.

Only the rock-hard common sense of Mrs. Flett finally put an end to it. She reached up, wrapped the small body again in the bread cloth, and took him back under her shawl.

"Done," she said, with a heave of relief.

Visibly shaking, Key stepped back and let her go past him. He felt Captain Boyle's hand around his arm as if to steady him or keep him from doing anything else, and remembered that Boyle had lost a son in infancy himself, while Key had been graced with healthy children. So far.

"Bless you, sir," Mrs. Flett said. Whether the baby was alive or dead as she stepped out the door was known only to her and

God. "Bless you, bless you, bless you."

Her voice faded as she went up to the street. One of the two men nodded a silent thanks at Key and the captain, then followed her.

The other man shook Key's whitened hand. "Bless you, Mr. Key." He started digging in a pocket. "I have—"

"No." Key stopped him sharply. "Not a thought of it. Go into the kitchen and tell Mrs. Key that I request a basket for you with two roast ducks, fresh fruit, and bread. And honey. Go, please. Go."

The big man sheepishly pulled his hand from his pocket, held his hat as if it were a life line, and nodded before moving past them in the direction Key had pointed through the house.

When he and the captain were alone, the shaken lawyer pressed his hands over his hot face. "Did I do that?"

Boyle pulled him aside, away from the door. "Have you slipped your wig? You're a layman!"

"I told them. God help me, Tom, I made it up as I went."

"The bishop is going to baptize you in a whole new way, I think."

"Did I sin? What've I done? My pride is my undoing—"

"Shh," Boyle cautioned. "It'll be all right. Have a sip."

He picked up the teacup of consecrated water from the corner table where one of those men had left it and handed it to Key, who almost made the colossal roaring scandalization of actually drinking from it.

"Not that!" he choked.

"Right—" Boyle pulled it away. "Something stronger. Let's go downstairs."

In a dither, he tried to find a place to put the teacup, but had no idea what to do with a handful of holy water.

Key stammered, "Give ... it to me ... I'll..."

He took the cup, but likewise had no brilliant solution and only clutched it to his chest.

"Below." Tom Boyle seized him and together they disappeared into a hole in the earth where Frank Key could only hope to keep going onward to hell.

—◊◊◊—

"His wound was a horror. Most of his thigh was torn away. I was sad to hear that he later died of it. We could've been friends, I think, in another life. When they told me he had died, they also said he was noble enough to send a letter to Lisbon, regaling what he called my 'superior sailing abilities.' He must've been in unspeakable agony, but he did me a kindness even so."

Tom Boyle stood at the dining room's window on the lower level of the Keys' home, holding a glass of wine and measuring in his mind the distance between the moonlit swells of current on the Potomac River outside. The dining room provided a view of both the Potomac on the riverside, with the lovely terraced gardens sloping from here down to the water, and the street on the front side. The room was graciously decorated, a sanctuary in the basement of the home, warm in winter and cool in summer. Moonlight came through the window, softly moving as it shined through the huge walnut and poplar trees and the orchard, and turned the yellow cotton of Boyle's shirt to a buttery cream.

Beside the captain, the staid presence of Frank Key provided a kind of philosophical gravity. Key raised his own goblet. "To Captain de Millo."

"Captain de Millo." Boyle raised his goblet and together they drank the tribute. "Thank you, Frank."

"Truly the least I can do. Too often we forget that there are decent souls among our enemies."

"We must forget it in times of conflict. Or we couldn't find it in ourselves to kill them. War makes murderers out of angels. There's no other way."

"Uncivilized."

"To you, the manor-born poet."

Key smiled, rather sadly. "I wasn't born on the manor. I was born outside, on the road to Frederick."

"Born outside? Like a little colt?"

"I wonder to what that entitles me," the lawyer mused.

"You'll probably turn feral. A little honey badger with curly hair."

They managed to laugh, in spite of the clumsy beginning to the evening. They hadn't forgotten the immortal soul of little Joshua Butterberry—Butter something—but as adults were forced too commonly to do, they had learned to move past the death of a sick infant. Only if a child lived past the age of five was he considered safe from the deadly state of infancy.

For the sake of his guest, Frank Key forced himself to accept the unchangeable and leave the details to God.

He filled the captain's goblet. "I'll be a gentrified badger. Are you getting too hungry to wait? It's not like the doctor to be so late."

"Oh, I'm not wasting away."

"I can offer you some biscuits."

The captain smiled. "You're the only man I know who can be high-strung and composed at the same time. Well, other than Dieter, I guess. Do you have tattoos all the way up your arms?"

"Sorry?"

Boyle chuckled. "Nothing. By the way, I may have need of your legal services, if you're free to take on another client. There are some challenges about the distribution of prize cargos. If my agent calls for your fees, don't be surprised."

"I never charge veterans."

"Veterans?"

"No one is more a veteran of this war than you, Tom."

"But I can afford to pay. Save your pro bono services for the wounded soldiers and the Negroes." He hung a comforting hand on Key's shoulder. "And desperate grandmothers."

The lawyer shrugged with just his eyebrows and thanked his friend with a sniff and a nod.

"Are you available?" Boyle asked.

"For you, always. But the war has depleted my practice anyway, the same as so many businesses. No one needs explain the hardships of the blocked to you, certainly."

"Still disapproving of the war?"

"You know what I think. We claimed to strike in defense of free trade, then moved to seize Canada. Better the flag be lowered in disgrace for such un-Christian acts."

"Have you given further thought to running for an office?"

"I suppose, yes."

"Well?"

"Makes me go dead inside. Political parties have ruined politics. I find that the worst men in a party will be uppermost in it. So there is no great gain from change of personalities."

"Does seem to attract more bugs than honey. But you are an emollient, my friend. If anyone could unkink the ropes, it's you. Even President Madison enjoys to see your face at his office door, the poor man."

The bell at the front entrance rang.

"There he is." Key raised his gaze to an imaginary hole in the ceiling through which he could see as well as hear the presence at the front door.

"Good," Boyle said. "I'm starving!"

Key smiled. "I may have to cross-examine you."

They turned to the stairway as Dr. William Beanes' walking stick made its first clap on the top step, but as they met the older man at the bottom of the stairs they could see from his expression that their evening of conviviality was at an end even before beginning.

Beanes came down the stairs so fast that they thought he had taken a tumble.

He looked at each of his friends, one then the other, as if a strict glare could set them up for what he had to tell them.

"It has finally happened," he said. "They've come."

—⁂—

"They're in our bays and inlets, right in the top of the Chesapeake, sculling barges up our rivers, blocking our ports. This morning before dawn, they went in on barges to get past the shoal. When they rounded Concord Point in Havre de Grace, a man at the battery fired on them and tried to hold them off. They landed, captured him, turned the guns on the town, and started shooting."

Beanes' words were cannon shots across the expansive dining table. Light from the chandelier reflected in the rosewood as if to display the enemy firestorm delivered to a small town in the north of Chesapeake Bay. The British were starting at the top.

The dining room was warm, windows open to capture any moment of breeze off the Potomac, but Washington had been built on a swamp and the pestilence of heat and humidity were already weighing down the spring air. Beanes and his host across the table were sitting, but everyone else in the room was either pacing or trying to find a place to hide his or her expression.

At the other end of the impeccably set table, Francis Key sat with his eyes fixed on that reflection from the chandelier. His curls framed his solemn expression. It was as if he and his wife, who stood a few paces behind him, were from a painting come to life.

Mary Tayloe Lloyd Key, whom for some reason everyone called Polly, was a myth-made match for Frank, a charmer with long arms, a swanlike neck and pretty hands, who had a queenliness about her, but was also approachable and open-hearted, and whose youthfulness had not been worn away by having had five children and carrying their sixth, expected in the autumn. She was almost tall enough to look her husband straight in the eyes, but not so tall as to be awkward or unwomanly, which was probably why she wore her expectancies with such grace. Her high-set eyes and cameo complexion were lovely in a frame of lemon-zest curls caught up in ribbons, showing her throat and shoulders just open like that. She enjoyed entertaining and was supportive of Frank's very common dinner parties with his myriad friends, clients, associates, Congressmen, the clergy, and all manner of luminaries. She was the *arbiter elegantiarum* of Francis Scott Key's social position as a prominent barrister in the Washington/Baltimore tableau. This dinner had been arranged in good cheer, but Beanes was now forced to ruin it with grim news upon his arrival only minutes ago.

He knew he had been late for dinner and that they had held it as long as possible for him, but the news from Havre de Grace had delayed him, and now they all knew why he had been so rude as to let the roasted ducks go dry on the warming plates.

Polly Key stood near the fireplace with her daughters Elizabeth and Marie and son Francis Scott Jr., who were crowded around her for the kind of security children seek from their mothers' arms when dire tidings are delivered. The children, at ten, eight, and seven years, were old enough to hear, and if the British brought their brutalities to Georgetown, these children would be expected to help with their two—and this autumn, three—younger siblings.

But the fear in their faces as they read their elders' expressions—Beanes found their countenances troubling as he described the terrors of Havre de Grace. Until now the war had seemed a thing to talk about, but beyond the horizon.

This evening they were no longer chatting about the theo-
retical pros and cons or strategies in the Western Territories,
but heard the crushing details of real attacks, brutalities leveled
upon their Maryland neighbors—not soldiers or sailors, but ordinary folk. Like those in this room.

At the window, gazing out, probably to hide his expression
as he might have done on the stern of his ship, Captain Tom
Boyle was uncharacteristically quiet as he now heard the dreadful announcement of the attack on the small Susquehanna River
village. He looked like something out of a Barbary Coast story,
with his yellow shirt, black waistcoat, and blue neckerchief. His
day coat was over there on a hook, because of the heat.

The doctor continued speaking, as he knew he must, and
knew that Captain Boyle wished he could drive his schooner up
to the top of the bay and take revenge.

"While the women and children ran into the woods, the seamen came with hatchets and torches. Rear-Admiral Cockburn's
orders. They ransacked every building, then set it afire. They
took what they wanted, like common pillagers, delivering revenge. People's private possessions— clothing, bedsteads, sofas,
shoes, heirlooms—your grandfather's chessboard, your mother's rocking chair, whatever they saw fit to steal. They took an
antique globe and used it for target practice in front of the terrorized family. Go on and guess which part of the globe they shot
at. They did the same with milk crocks, wig boxes, anything to
scare the families. They smashed furniture they could not carry
off. They set alight each house and moved to the next. They set
fire to the herring boats and nets. For four hours they plundered
and molested. Featherbeds cut open, shaken into the wind. Mirrors shattered for the shameless delight of it. They rolled rain
barrels and butter churns down a hill, aiming for the people in
the trees, then cheered when they knocked some poor sot over.
The pitiful citizens were driven out, to look back and see their
houses fall into red ash. This the British did till the whole town
blazed. When nothing was left but burned-out hulks, the ras-
cals climbed onto their barges, cheered Admiral Cockburn, and
moved on to plunder other towns."

Frank Key suddenly interrupted, "What other towns?"

"I don't know. I only know they've moved on through the upper bay for more marauding and conflagration."

"Cockburn," Boyle snarled. "That son of a freshwater gondolier."

"You know him?" Key asked.

"I know about him. He's a vain sadist. He's also brilliant and notoriously thorough. That's why he's an admiral at only forty. His methods are right out of the most vulgar backstreet barrack and quarter no discretion for the harmless civilians in his wake. His own sailors deplore serving under him. His ships are like prisons. He creates a lot of deserters."

The captain paused, took a swig of wine, then turned to those at the table. He put his wine glass down.

"Well, Frank," he said bitterly, "there's your next rhyme. 'The day they laid waste to Havre de Grace.'"

Beanes looked up at Tom Boyle, but found neither mirth nor satire in the captain's eyes. Boyle simply glared at their mutual friend, communicating some silent punishment only those two understood.

But then, as he thought about it, the doctor understood. When the British finally came to Georgetown and the Capitol, would this famous young lawyer, this pacifist, stand down or stand up to defend his own home?

The brick house, with its many keystone-linteled windows and two dormers with their own arched window, provided three and a half stories and two framed porches to the Potomac in back and two and a half stories in front to the street. Both the river and the street were avenues the British would certainly employ in their invasion. The house would be an obvious target for English gunners coming up that river. It was not the most aristocratic home in Georgetown, but it was settled and appealing, flanked by two chimneys on the sides that always reminded Beanes of raised ears on a cat's head. He always enjoyed coming here, or most of the time, to attend Frank's dinner parties and hear the latest bubblings from the political pot.

"Even when upheaval is so long portended," Beanes went on, "its arrival is still a shock. Since Napoleon retreated from Russia in that mess last December, the British have been plotting how to turn their concentration on us. And now they have finally done it."

"Napoleon isn't defeated yet," Polly Key reminded them.

"No, but he is substantially weakened," her husband said, "for now. We pray for the poor souls who—"

"Five hundred thousand men," Boyle interrupted sharply. "Reprehensible behavior for a commanding officer. Half a million men, starved and frozen in that Cossack wilderness. The time to pray for them has passed. They were eating their horses even before the horses died. Some were even eating—"

"Captain," Polly warned, "another time."

He glanced at her, at all the little Key faces. "Sorry."

"Children, you've heard enough for tonight. Upstairs for your reading hour."

Disappointed, the three children slogged toward the stairs. Nothing they could read would be as salacious as listening to the adults tonight. At least the elder two perceived what the captain had been saying—children always knew more than their parents realized. And these were particularly quick-minded and observant children with minds like wicks. Beanes knew their education was their father's pride, for he devised their lessons and taught them himself, as he was taught at home by his own parents. He could easily have foisted them off on some elite school, but instead he took this task upon himself.

Polly herded her daughters and son upstairs and went with them, courteously giving the men a chance to descend into men's kind of talk if they wanted to.

"Napoleon will not suffer long for the loss of his army," Boyle went on. "He hasn't given up the crown. But he'll need time to gather more men. Until then, Britain's anger will land hard on us. This is a world war, my friends. We're in grave danger."

"We are," the doctor agreed. "The word is that the British were infuriated by the burning of York, the capitol of Ontario, last week. We can look forward to more attacks and more anger. If Havre de Grace is any template, they will not target uniformed militia alone. They will target our homes and families. Since the militia is all of us, I don't suppose we've given them a reason to spare anyone." Beanes pushed to his feet and took his walking stick in hand. "I must take my leave."

Key stood up and protested, "But you've barely arrived. We

made a duck for you."

"Thankee, but I shall have to take my grim tidings and return to Marlborough. I've left Sarah alone to ponder this news
without comfort. And of course I must prepare my clinic for the
wounded who will come my way. I had thought to retire to a
passive life of gardening or winery, and here I've been handed
another war in the sunset of my service. It changes everything.
Francis ... Captain."

"Doctor." Boyle extended his hand.

Beanes took it. "I'm glad to see you in good health after
your latest cruise, Thomas. We all worried about you when they
clapped a bounty on your head."

The captain seized his day coat and dragged it on. "I must
see to my wife and children's protection. *Comet*'s still docked
in Fell's Point. I'll have to get her and myself to another port
before the redcoats turn on Baltimore or they'll target my family." At the foot of the stairs, he turned to his disappointed host.
"Brace yourself, Frank. Washington will be a tasty target and
that means Georgetown and this house, smack on the Potomac
in the line of fire. You'd better do more than pray. You'd better
find a warrior in yourself."

Wool

CAPTAIN BOYLE OPENED THE door of his home himself, handsomely, for he was carrying a two-year-old asleep on his shoulder.

From under her white bonnet and dark ringlets, small-statured Mary Pickersgill smiled at the sight of them.

"Mary," the captain said, "good day. How nice."

"Look at your littlest sweetie," Mary cooed. "God loves a happy child."

"Especially when she's sleeping."

Mary whispered, "Oh, Tom, look how hale she is. I'm glad for you."

He stepped outside and carefully closed the door behind him. "Let's talk in the garden. I've succeeded in getting the whole houseful to take a nap at the same time. I am lord and master of all I survey. That is, until this one wakes and the world begins revolving again."

With his daughter molded to his body, he managed to sit on a stone bench and lean back against the house, then beckoned Mary to the bench across the tiny pebbled path.

"Is everyone well inside?" she asked.

"All's well," he said, rubbing his child's back distractedly. "It's good to set sail and good to come home. Though coming home these days is a bit trickier. Well, so's getting out, but you know."

"What is the blockade like now?"

"Dense," he told her honestly. "More Royal Navy ships and patrols, angrier captains ... we follow the darkness and fog and hope not to hit the shoals. We can outrun them, but it's safer to see them without their seeing us. It's a gamble every time."

"But you love a good gamble."

He grinned in that rascally manner that showed what he was thinking. "I do, don't I?"

His manner was born of his courage, she knew, as was his desire to shield her and the women in his life from the grim truths of privateering.

Mary was not one to need coddling, or to be fooled. "It's not a game, dear. If they capture Captain Tom Boyle, they'll hang you just to say they did."

"After they parade me though the streets of London and nail my hand to Lloyd's front door."

"Tom ..."

He gave her a one-shouldered shrug, since the other was occupied under a baby head. He could have stated outright that he and his crew were soldiers in a war, but she knew already and they sat in companionable quiet, listening to the birds sing.

"How is the packing going?" she asked then.

"We've moved two wagonloads a day for two days. I've had some shipmates come to help."

"I'll be sorry to see you move away, Tom. I'll miss you and your family so."

"We're only moving one block down and three blocks over," he told her reasonably. "Hardly 'away.'"

"For which I'm very glad. I'll be strict about visiting and looking in on them while you're gone, and I hope you'll do the same. The only thing Caroline seems to truly enjoy is taking care of your children now and then."

"You know, Mary, I've found that we see our dearest friends even more often when we're not right next door. I suppose it's because there's some effort involved in keeping them in our lives and we all like to have results from our efforts."

She laughed. "Or we take each other for granted when we're

close by."

Across the street, Mary's daughter Caroline came out the front door of the Pickersgill house with two buckets, accompanied by her cousins Eliza and Margaret, who had arrived to live here for a while. They also carried buckets, so Caroline was probably showing them the way to City Springs, six blocks away, to collect the day's water. Grace was not with them, so she was probably stoking fires and ironing flags, the almost-constant sub-stratum of their business. Hard worker, that girl. If only she would sneeze on Caroline and pass on the habits.

"All right," she finally said. "I need some advice or help, if I can get it."

The captain shifted his daughter a bit as she slept. "Anything I can do, of course."

"There's a new commandant at Fort McHenry, a straight-up young man with unalloyed patriotism that I deeply appreciate. He has made a request for an ensign of rather alarming proportion. Says he wants the British to be able to see it from quite a way down the Patapsco. He also wants a smaller storm flag, but even that one will be massive."

"What can I do?" Boyle asked.

"These two flags require a great reserve of English wool bunting. There's not enough immediately available and I need it all at once so the dyeing can be done correctly. There's no time to place an order through the usual channels. I've inquired as far as New York. Stocks are so low."

"Have you tried Jesse's connections?" he asked, about her brother-in-law, another sea captain and owner of a Fell's Point shop which usually would be perfect as a source, were times different.

"I have," she said. "He's in the South Atlantic, out of contact."

"Oh—that's right. How much do you need?"

"Almost two-thousand square feet."

"Feet? He must mean inches."

"We were very clear about it. The big ensign alone will be twelve-hundred-sixty square feet. Thirty feet on the hoist, by forty-two."

The captain let out a low whistle, and almost wakened his

child. He rocked her and she settled down again. "That's the size of a gaff main. Where will you lay this creature out? In the street?"

"I'm pondering that."

"Explain to me what you need."

"It must be Worstead wool, combed, not carded, loosely woven, high quality and light of weight, and all the same size of yarn and weave. The standard size is fine. Length doesn't matter, since the stripes will have to be pieced anyway."

A twinge of doubt jumped in. So much to think about, to figure out.

"This will be a very important flag, Tom," she told him, suddenly earnest. "It will be a proclamation to the enemy that we mean to fight. We will defend our port and our homes. We want to show them that we won't be bullied."

The captain simply fixed his pleasant blue eyes on her. His black hair reflected the morning light and made an appealing portrait of a daring adventurer holding a sleeping child.

"Yes," he quietly agreed. "This McHenry man ... I like him."

"Do you know him?"

"What's his name?"

"Armistead."

"The same Armistead who was second-in-command?

"Yes. He went away, but now he's been assigned back here."

"Never knew him personally. But he thinks as I do. As you do." Boyle smiled again, this time seeming to admire Mary herself for being the kind of person he and his crew were fighting to protect, and in some kind of gratitude for her demonstrating that she would do her part. Somehow he got his message across so effectively that Mary felt herself blush a little. They were partners of the best kind.

"I'll get the word out to the privateer fleet," he promised. "I'll keep it private, captain to captain. We could rely on luck, of course, but if you want a better product, and sooner—"

"Then pay for it," Mary anticipated. "I shall advance five hundred dollars, which I have calculated as the cost of the bunting."

"That will guarantee our success. Somebody'll simply make a landing and purchase the yard goods, if that can be done.

There's always the problem of finding it, then having a landing party of Americans flocking into some textile factory in England. But as you say, we love a challenge."

"Dare I ask how soon?"

"I can't take the message myself. Not yet. *Comet's* in the south of the Chesapeake, patrolling—well, hiding, mostly. I sent her there because I thought the British were coming here, but they haven't yet. There are two schooners shoving off tonight after midnight. I can get this order to them this evening. Can't tell how long it'll take for them to run the blockade, but after that, serendipity's in command. Messages going ship to ship as fate has them passing, then the goods coming back the same way. This product may travel the length and width of the Atlantic before it finally makes landfall, God knows where, and finds its way here. Bunting might be available in the Indies, some English colony maybe. One of us will find it."

Mary felt the nervousness about the project suddenly become a bit easier to suppress. Her level of hope cranked up a notch. "You're wonderful."

"*We're* wonderful. Let's show the world how to be wonderful."

With a little laugh of relief and enthusiasm, she wordlessly agreed.

Boyle stretched his back carefully and patted his little daughter's round rump. The child opened her bright eyes, blinked in rediscovery of the world, and sat up on her father's lap. Abruptly the singing birds caught her attention and she craned toward the trees.

"What lives we have," the captain mused. "Smuggling English wool to make two majestic American flags for the English to see as the lay siege to Fort McHenry. What a privilege, to be alive and enraged in Baltimore today!"

National Ensign

"MAMA. ARE YOU AWAKE?"

"What, what? Come in, cupcake."

Mary stepped into her mother's room, glad the old woman was still awake and alert. Rebecca Flower Young—Mary had always liked her mother's full name—sat in bed under a cloud of white linen, but she was sitting up and knitting, listening to the birds from outside her open window and to the buzzing of a dozen flies that had come to circle the soup bowl on the tray at the end of the bed. They were an unavoidable consequence of open windows in the summer.

Mrs. Young was industriously knitting, working on the second of a pair of tan stockings. She had reached a level of manual infirmity and trouble seeing that prevented her from doing much sewing other than perhaps basting, so she had taken up knitting stockings and shorter socks, which were sold at Frearer's dry-goods in town. On the dresser top was a pile of stockings of various sizes and colors, waiting to be delivered. Her physical force may have flagged, but her sense of purpose was still youthful.

"I need advice," Mary said as she sat on the edge of her mother's bed.

"Find a man to marry."

"That's not the advice I'm seeking."

"A grown-up one with his own store."

"I've accepted a new client. Fort Jefferson's commander."

"That Armistead fellow?"

"How did you know?"

"Gossip, of course."

"Oh. Good. He wants a very large national ensign for the fort. Dauntingly large. Thirty feet by forty-two."

"You misheard, cupcake. He meant inches."

"I heard perfectly. The flag will be as big as this whole house. I must admit that I'm intimidated."

"You should be. Oh—I missed a purl."

"Stop knitting for a moment and help me think."

"I can knit and think."

"Well, then, what do you think about this?"

"Let's see," Mrs. Young said, and stopped knitting. "You'll have to piece the stripes. How wide will the stars be?"

"Almost two feet, point to point."

"They'll have to be pieced too."

"They'll be three layers of fabric through. I'm concerned they'll be difficult to see with that much fabric blocking light."

"Reverse appliqué."

Mary sat straight up. "Oh!"

"I did it on the Valley Forge union jack, the white stripes and St. Andrew's cross. To make the white shine."

"Mama, that's it. That's it! Will you remind me how to oversew the reverse side?"

"This flag is wool? Bunting?"

"Yes, of course."

"If you make the fifteen stars out of cotton, they'll be more luminous."

Mary laughed. "Mistress Young, you've done it!"

Her mother began knitting again. "Still a twig or two to offer."

"If I put the girls on basting, will you supervise?"

"When will you start?"

"Right away, with a pattern in muslin. Now we can start cutting and piecing the stars. We have plenty of white cotton."

"Have the girls come to me in the morning and I will show them a manner of basting that will keep their hands from getting tired quickly on large projects."

Springing to her feet, Mary said, "All these years and you're still teaching us."

The elderly woman made a crooked grin. "It's why we women live so long, isn't it? To teach the grandchildren. After all, their parents can't be counted upon, can they?"

"Thank goodness you are. This is encouraging, most encouraging. I'm beginning to think this mad jim-jam can actually be done! Pardon me—I have walk around the block. I must speak to the proprietor of Brown's Brewery."

"Oh?" her mother responded, with narrowing eyes. "Are you planning to become an imbiber of malt spirits?"

Red-Blooded Legend

"GOOD AFTERNOON, CAPTAIN! OVER here, Captain."

Samuel Yambrick's round elfish face, made only a little more masculine by the whiskers, grinned at Tom Boyle from the doorway of the ship's chandlery.

"Mr. Yambrick," Boyle began as he paused there in the street. "Another chance meeting? I'm sensing a pattern."

He peered past the man, to see whether the shadow's shadow lurked there also, but there was no sign of the niece or daughter or whomever she really was. Boyle approached the habitually cheerful gentleman.

"Sir, am I your new hobby?" Boyle stepped to the chandlery door while John Dieter, Tommy Ring and two of their ship's boys waited in the street with armloads of parceling strips, boxes of surgical supplies, and two new checkerboards.

"Provisioning the *Comet*?" Yambrick asked.

Boyle shrugged. "Eternally."

Vague answers were always best, especially with this wily fellow who always seemed interested in the whens and wheres of Boyle's business, and always seemed to know the answers before he even asked the questions.

Boyle turned to his mates and boys. "I'll be along shortly. Carry on."

"Aye, Captain," Tommy Ring said jovially, making a good

show for passing pedestrians and the two boys.

As his crew headed back to the dock, lanyards wagging from their belts to the knives sailors always carried, Boyle leaned on the doorframe and pocketed what was left of his provisioning money. Then he looked at Yambrick. "And your story is …"

"Perhaps you'd like to join me for—"

"Not today."

Yambrick smiled in that accommodating way that revealed nothing, and said, "Perhaps again some time."

"If fortune favors," Boyle said, equally elusive. "I don't mean to be sharp, but I have iron-casters to meet."

Yet he did not step away.

Finally Yambrick broke the uneasy pause. "Your instincts are correct, of course. I am the bearer of some news."

"Please don't make me ask."

"I've had a meeting this morning with the owners of the *Comet.*"

Boyle stepped forward to let a woman and three children pass behind him. "That's artful of you, considering I'm one of them and I was not summoned. Courting subterfuge?"

"Oh, it wasn't that kind of a meeting, that you should have been bothered from your more important concerns. I'm doing some menial legal paperwork on behalf of Mr. Carerre, and I happened to meet over breakfast with—"

"I'm sure you did. And they sent you with a message?"

"Nothing so graceless," Yambrick said. "But something was discussed that concerns you, and I suggested that it should be brought to your attention before you set sail without knowing about it. Since no one knows when you'll set sail—"

"You thought to bring me this information yourself, since you were coming here on your way to having your whiskers curled or the city hall moved underground."

Yambrick laughed, which seemed genuine enough. He might have been easier to read were he a smuggler. "Well, I did offer. They seemed to have no reticence about it, but if you are uneasy, I shall—"

"Fire away."

"Here? You wouldn't like to get a cup of—"

"No time."

"Ah … well, then … I hope this is not jarring."

"Mr. Yambrick, I'll knock you silly and turn you over to the nearest barge master."

"Sorry, sorry." Yambrick leaned on his walking stick and drew a stabilizing breath. "I'm just not good at difficult news."

"I am. Let's have it."

"You see, it's possible to do a job too well. You've gained considerable fame, and the *Comet* herself great notoriety. For those who expected the war to be over by now, your red-blooded legend is more than fulfilled."

"But the war isn't over."

"Nor does it seem to have a resolution coming any time soon. At this juncture in events, it's worth discussion that your company and the nation might both profit from a few key changes."

Unshrinking, Boyle gazed at him, but refused to ask the obvious question. He didn't like being led blindfolded through a maze.

The mysterious man nodded. "The time has come for bigger privateer ships, able to carry more men and more guns."

Boyle's legs went cold and his ears started ringing. Like a shot out of hell, he suddenly understood. Unable to hide his frown, he turned partly away and tried to control his reaction. The best he could do was not pull the propped-open door off its hinges.

The other man gave him a few moments then cautiously continued. "*Comet* is famous, fast, and has taken many blows. And I suppose this is why the conversation came up when you were not present. No one wanted to ambush you."

"What you mean is that no one had the plums to face me."

The other man nodded and shrugged, heeding his responsibility to agree with no one or everyone.

"The *Comet* is tired, captain," he said. "She's earned her legend and her rest. Suggestions have arisen that she might be retired. Or sold."

As his mind raged with a thousand details, twisting with the conflict between a devoted captain with a ship that had saved his life over and over, and a businessman with other responsibilities to other people, Boyle muttered, "She's not a horse."

"But like a horse, she has run her maximum. Perhaps she

could see new service as a pleasure craft ... a yacht."

Boyle scowled. "Yacht!"

"But even more, your partners would like to make optimal use of their best captain. They want to find a newer, larger ship for the dauntless, impetuous Thomas Boyle to command. It's good advertising, good use of ... em ..."

"Resources?"

"It's meant as a reward, Captain, please take it so."

"They want me to be their big flag."

"Sorry? I don't understand that."

Boyle shook his head and made a dismissing gesture. His mind was somewhere else. This was not a conversation he wanted to have.

"As an owner, you have options," Yambrick said. "You could appeal to them to keep both ships in operation for you."

"A captain must be monogamous. One wife, one ship—"

Boyle cut himself off. His mind, unbidden, flashed to the many ships he had commanded since his sixteenth birthday. Ships come and ships go.

But now and then, not often, there's a ship with a sense of herself. A ship that saves her crew's lives again and again, that hits the shoal, gives herself a shake, gets up on the next swell and carries on as if nothing happened. A ship that takes on water up to the weather deck and still doesn't roll over, that gives the crew time to scramble, a fighting chance to save their own lives and hers. Some ships came off the ramps with a certain undefined quality of being that proved itself out over years of stubborn service. With right combination of lumber, iron, and workmanship, somehow the right captain and the right procedures, a perfect balance was discovered, an amalgam of all the unknowable thousand things that fuse and end up on the ocean together in the same place, at that one moment of danger where it all demonstrates itself at once. And out the other end of the tube comes a human devotion to this object underfoot, this battered gathering of wood and rope that has taken on a personality.

But not every ship. Just now and then.

"When do they want to do this?" he asked, hoping to drown out his thoughts.

"When you're ready."

"We've just done repairs and re-rigging. New foremast."

"Certainly, Captain. When you're ready."

Boyle knew what that meant—when he was ready, but as soon as he could manage to become ready. They were planting this in his head, but allowing him time to get used to it. They knew he was provisioning and mending the *Comet* and would not yank her away quite yet, but would give him one more voyage with her, a chance to let the idea sink in that the marriage was ending. He could almost hear them say it. They didn't want to make him angry enough to change companies and leave them behind while he was so valuable an asset. A big flag.

"I'm not ready yet," he said. "Excuse me. I really must be on my way. Thank you for ... that."

He tried to step back toward the street.

The other man's voice called him back. "But, Captain—there is more."

Boyle hung his head and groaned. "Mr. Yambrick, please release me."

"Please ... in here, sir."

Yambrick moved into the chandlery's wood-floored shop, waddled a few steps, then turned. When Boyle followed him in, with his cane he poked at two large burlap-wrapped parcels the size of couch cushions lying next to each other in front of a display of ship's cabin lanterns and binnacles.

Tired of riddles, Boyle asked, "What's this?"

"Suffice to say your message was received. It sounded urgent, so action was taken to satisfy the request. I humbly say that I had a small part in finding these goods. They arrived through the blockade at three o'clock this morning."

"But what is it?"

"Bunting, Captain. Four hundred sixty-nine yards of first-quality English bunting."

Amazed, Boyle reached down and lifted one of the packages partly off the floor. "Is that right?"

Yambrick gazed down at him, pink-cheeked and almost bashful. Mischievously, he asked,

"To whom would you like it delivered?"

Fortifications

STICKY HEAT BLANKETED THE city of forty-six thousand, seeping into every clapboard seam, plaguing every beast of burden, cooking manure in the streets until it steamed, seeking entrance through every crack like an infestation. Thick air clogged every lung and turned hair to wire as Major George Armistead climbed out of the rowboat that had brought him from Fort McHenry across the inner harbor to the City Dock. He ordered his rower to wait, then began to walk up Great York Street.

Sweat dribbled down his back under the blue wool uniform jacket. He felt it on his neck, his scalp under the hat, and was almost tempted to stride right into the blacksmith's furnace, where at least the heat would be dry. He paused for a moment at the smith's open yard to inhale the hot dry air and look at the chimney backs, anvils, stovepipes, and bathing basins arranged for sale between him and the furnace itself, where three men without shirts worked as if hell were their natural home. He started to move on, but paused again at a temporary wall of pegs hung with fishhooks, loops of wire, metal buttons, and sewing needles. On the ground was a large box full of cart springs. Wise sidelines, he thought, marveling in the ingenuity of business people. Where there was a demand, some industrious citizen would conjure up a solution.

His chest felt heavy, constricted. Every breath was tight. He felt people's eyes upon him, noticing him, thinking about him. The city was watching him, wondering which day might be the last day of their lives or the last day of being Americans. They were going on with their daily lives, but there was more happening in every unspoken word, every silent glance. They read every day about the battles in the north and the west, the dangerous hunts at sea, and almost every one of them knew someone who had fought, or someone who had been lost to a British warship out there on the ever-present sea. What did he mean to them, a man in an Army officer's uniform? Could he come through on the promise his uniform made?

He walked on, wishing he had arranged for a horse. The faint breeze from the harbor dissolved as the neighborhoods folded around him in a brutal blanket. The less pleasant smells of city life began to assault him, an oily scent of industry overlaid with the aromas of fresh cabbage, onion, turnips, and all manner of ripe vegetables being transported by wagonloads from farms to the markets. There was also, unfortunately, a whaling ship currently docked at the inner harbor and even from this far away he could still catch a whiff of the ghastly soup saturating that ship. It would never go away and that old brig would never be anything but a whaler. He hoped it would sail away soon and take its boiled-down cargo on to the Nantucket lamp makers or wherever it was going.

Feeling nauseated, he increased his pace through the neighborhood, looking forward to going back to the fort, where the smells were familiar ones and the at least the chance existed for a breeze off the Patapsco.

At 60 Albemarle, he approached the Queen Street door, as he had been told was the door for business clients, and knocked.

When no one came, he knocked again, louder. Then again.

"Hello!" a voice called from behind him. "Ahoy!"

He turned to see a milkman holding up his wagon only paces away.

"Yes?"

"You'll get no answer there today, Sergeant," a grizzled and very short gentleman croaked.

"Oh?"

"No, sir, not today, or tomorrow, I don't think, General. The ladies are all off at the brewery."

"I beg your pardon? That is slander, sir. Do you claim that this fine family is—"

"No claims, just truth, y'know. They're off at Brown's, stitchin'. Been there every day for days and weeks now. Working."

Armistead stood down his defensiveness. "Oh, I see. And where is this *Brown's*?"

"Jump up on the wagon, Admiral. I'll take'ee there."

The next block. That was the entire ride. A few houses.

Still, the little man had taken great self-satisfaction from ferrying Armistead these few steps.

There, occupying almost the entire block, was Brown's malt house. This was a brewery, a business, so the major didn't bother to knock, but just stepped in. He spoke to a boy of no more than ten, who gestured through two more doors and up a short stairway to a non-descript storage room. He knocked, then opened the door.

There, Mary Pickersgill was just pulling a roll of thread from a wooden box. She looked flushed with the heat, and was wearing a simple blue cotton dress, a white apron. and an ordinary cotton cap. Her hair was tied up under the cap.

"Major," she greeted. "What a joy. Come in, please. How are you?"

"I feel like an egg being poached," he admitted.

She laughed. "But this is what we dreamed of during last winter's raw frosts!"

"True enough. I'm about ready to swim back to the star fort just to get some relief. A milkman told me that you were here. I'm sorry to come without announcement."

"Perfectly fine. How are the fortifications coming?"

"Satisfactorily, I would say. The men are drilled every day in operations for repelling a landing party from several directions. We've covered our powder supplies with sandbags and built battery platforms. I'm also provisioning in anticipation of extended siege."

"Oh, Major, such frightening portents."

"We must curb our fears and be ready. We have no idea when these things will happen in Baltimore, but we are certain that indeed they *will* happen. The inevitable is not such a burden when one is prepared."

She nodded. The dread lingered in her eyes. "Our city ..."

Armistead was lost for words. He could explain the fortifications, the drilling, the preparations and provisioning, but at the end of the lecture there would be only that void of the unknowable. There was no promise he could make that her home and her family were safe from invasion. If Fort McHenry were to fall, then Baltimore would fall. The British would be victorious and encouraged, power mad. The Chesapeake would collapse, commerce would vanish, and martial law at the whim of the Crown would be here with no resources to push it off again as once the United States had done in its slim and reckless beginnings.

The lady's voice shook him out of his inadequacies. "You've come to see your flags in progress."

"If it can be allowed?"

"Certainly. This way. We found enough bunting, thank goodness. We were able to get to serious work by the second week. Well, of course, we did other things to start, like cutting patterns and laying them out."

"Patterns? Of what?"

"To get the proportions of the stripes right, for instance. And the size and placement of the stars. I wanted to see the cantons before actually cutting the bunting or the cotton. I had to decide how to place the stars."

"Really," he uttered, displaying his complete ignorance of women's commercial operations. His wife was fond of tending honeybees and growing flowers, but she did little in the form of domestic making. She was one of the nation's very important people called customers. Without customers, who could have a business? She bought the family's clothing rather than making it, bought curtains and pillows, bought churned butter and baking supplies—well, she did bake quite a lot. She supplied the cakes and cookies and pies for the fort, and for three churches when they had their little ice-cream socials.

And she cooked masterfully. She oversaw all the victuals and cooking for the entire complement from their little officer's quarters there.

But sewing—a complete mystery. Being situated at the

mouth of the harbor next to a city, Fort McHenry's men had the luxury of sending clothing and boots, livery, and belts to the city's professional shopkeepers for repairs or replacements. Unlike a frontier fort in Michigan or Indiana, they needed not repair things themselves. It was a comfortable place to be stationed and at times he wondered if he and the men weren't spoiled.

"I hope the heat in the loft won't make you dizzy," Mary said as she led him up two sets of stairs.

He smiled at her, enjoying her unshrinking personality.

In this building, the smells were completely different from outside. The cloying and somehow exotic aroma of fermentation, smelling like sweet oatmeal and potatoes, was in the air and the very walls. Not a bad smell, actually. Manly.

As Mary led him into the loft, Armistead muffled an emotional gasp. In the room about twenty feet square, was a large and somewhat rumpled American flag, stretched almost wall-to-wall, with two young women on their knees at work with needles and spools of colored thread.

Both young women had their hair tied back in kerchiefs, as Mary did, and one girl's hair was also braided tightly, probably to avoid its falling forward while they worked in this awkward face-down position.

"These are my nieces, Margaret and Eliza Young," Mary said. "Girls, this is Major Armistead, who commissioned these banners. No, no, stay where you are and continue work. So, Major, it seems your authority extends beyond the fort, for my girls almost came to attention." Armistead started to speak, but was overtaken by a sudden cough. The loft was dusty.

"This is your storm flag, Major," Mary went on. "Twenty-five feet by seventeen, as you requested. As you can see, the stars are five-pointed, just the same as Fort McHenry. I rather like that." She knelt beside the field of blue and picked up the edge of the fabric. "You can see here that the bunting is a very open weave."

"I can almost see through it," he agreed.

"In order for the flag to hold together and not beat itself to shreds, the stitches must be angled slightly up and down every stripe and every place the flag is pieced."

"May I touch it?"

"Yes, of course."

He knelt and rubbed the fabric between his thumb and fingers. "Very light-weighted, isn't it? You said it would be."

"But durable. Notice that we have double-stitched around the outside edges and the sleeve on the hoist."

"Will the big flag have a sleeve also?"

"Oh, yes. The strain will be distributed evenly up and down the hoist."

"Ingenious."

"Skills passed down for thousands of years, then from my grandmother to my mother, to me, to my daughters, nieces, servants, and any other woman who wants to learn to support herself."

Mary was proud of the work, but also she was proud to be working. Armistead, a soldier all his life, often took for granted the position he held, assuming the Army of the United States would be a permanent fixture. But Mary Pickersgill—civilian, craftswoman, widow, mother—was appreciative of the chance to work and, through work, rise.

"Seems downright magical to me, ma'am." He tilted his head, scrutinizing the field of stars. "The stars don't look ... straight. Is it the way I'm standing? They don't look lined up."

"They're not soldiers," she told him with another knowing smile. "The points of the stars are canted slightly to the left or the right. This provides an illusion similar to sparkling when the flag waves. A kind of flashing effect."

"I must say, ma'am, this is admirable skilled work. I had no idea there were so many elements involved. I can say with confidence that I certainly came to the right person. Have you begun work on the big flag yet?"

She appeared a bit surprised. "You did say you wanted it as soon as possible."

"I did, but now that I see the level of expertise required for such a process, I know I shall have to wait for all the elements to be correctly done, and gladly I will. I had no idea. No idea! Please accept my compliments and take it positively when I say you and your troops are as martial as the best brigade of Army Engineers."

"I wonder what you'll call us when you see the next loft. Come with me, Major."

Armistead came to his feet. He knew an order when he heard one. He stepped after her, following as closely in her footsteps so as not to accidentally step on the storm flag's edges.

At the other end of the room, she led him to an unmarked door, very old and made of the same wood as the wall. She went in first, and stepped aside for him to enter the main loft.

For all his chatty ways among civilians, George Armistead fell as dumb as if he had been physically stricken. In his periphery he saw Mrs. Pickersgill smile like a fox beside him, but he could not make his neck move to look at her. Only then did he realize he had stopped breathing.

For there it was.

—⚒—

The main loft was endless as a magic mirror. It stretched into the distance before George Armistead and seemed almost to fade into the haze of floating dust shrouding the farthest wall. Not one bit of the floor escaped being carpeted by red, white, or blue. Simple, bright, new primary-colors.

The scale shocked him. Until now, there had been only numbers. The vast loft could barely accommodate the masterpiece stretched out before him. Now he felt the first sensation that he had done something historic. Here before him was the picnic blanket of titans.

Armistead looked down at his feet, where the blue field began, a solid blue field except for a single star that had been sewn in. To his left, a Negro girl was down on her knees and elbows, placing a second star—canted the other way from the one near him. The flashing effect. But this star was two feet across. Two *feet*. Next to the star, his boots looked like little doll boots. He felt like a speck.

"Grace is placing the second star," Mary explained. "We use a method called 'reverse appliqué,' which means that we sew the star onto the flag, then fold it over to the opposite side, then cut the blue field away from the star and sew down the edges. That way, the stars are only one layer thick and light can shine through them. It also reduces weight, of course."

"Do you have an invoice for me yet?"

"When we're finished," she said. "I will be charging about

four hundred dollars for the big flag and another hundred fifty for the smaller one."

"What? You can't be serious! That can't cover the cost of the fabric alone!"

"Oh, it pretty much covers the cost of the fabric," she assured.

"What about the thread? The time and labor? Your assistants?"

"We don't mind."

Bewildered, Armistead said, "I don't understand."

"Yes, you do." She looked at him. "It's our country too."

The flag lay peacefully as a cat being combed. Not as elaborate as most national flags, this flag proclaimed a hope for the pieces, the industrial pieces of it, to come together in something new, like the states themselves. It was, after all, just a symbol. A gathering of yarns, of thread and dye, patched together the same as any quilt. Pull it apart, rearrange the patches, and any symbolic gravity would disintegrate. It did not proclaim perfection, since perfection was an elusive puzzle of a million pieces, nor did it pretend to grandeur, but made its statements simply, grasping no regality or representation of any family or name, holding no subordinations, no heraldic devices. No royalty could claim it or tame it. The world had nothing else like the flag of the United States.

"So this is it," Armistead finally uttered, scarcely above a whisper.

At his side, the proud mother of the miracle asked, "Pardon me?"

"This is the reason I was born." He laughed, overcome. "I've always wondered."

She was smiling. Her round face made a joyful glow when she smiled.

Together they gazed at the spectacle before them. In a riot of impropriety, the major took the lady's hand and held it in both of his own.

"And you, Mary Pickersgill, my superb artisan. All generations of Americans will know your name."

Into the Fray

"WHY DO I DO this?"

"Stand still. You'll fall off the stool."

"Farm boys, country gentlemen, church elders, cattle ranchers—this one's a street cleaner!"

"Then put him in charge of sanitation."

"Oh, I can assign them. How am I going to arm them?"

"Let them bring their own rifles."

"Shall I also have them bring their own heavy guns and caissons? Perhaps one can bring a cart of apple pies for dessert. At least most of them are well-off sufficient to afford their own uniforms."

"Yes," she said. "And they dream that they can dazzle the English with the sparkle of their epaulets—stand still!"

"And who's going to train them with every new term of enlistment?"

"I'll train them."

"I'd let you. You can teach them to swab out the guns and load them and fire them. Of course, that would require that we could actually *find* a gun."

Major George Peter had been a soldier all his life, a veteran of the Ninth US Infantry, the Army Corps of Artillerists and Engineers, the Regiment of Light Artillery, commander of the field artillery company that had made the march from Baltimore to

Washington at an astounding six miles an hour just to prove that it could be done, and then had marched to New Orleans to test the stamina of the artillery they were moving. Still, he didn't know what to do with the patchwork of recruits that came and went from his sphere of influence running a militia company here in his own neighborhood. He tried to remain stationary as his sister-in-law pinned the hem of his new uniform trousers while he stood balanced upon a kitchen stool.

"If only the damned British would make an attack, we could just bring everybody forward and have it out."

"Your language, please."

"I do apologize—no, I don't."

"And don't be inviting evil. Sure it will answer."

"Let it come." He balanced as he scanned the list of new recruits. "If I could just have these men for longer enlistments ... then I could train them effectively, instill solid discipline and make—"

"Then they would be regulars instead of militia and none of their jobs would get done on the home fronts," she said. "You would've had them drilling and marching about for the past two years, all for nothing."

"Not nothing," Major Peter insisted.

He started to say more, to go into the timeless arguments between army regulars and home-front defenders, for he knew them all, but he was interrupted by a knock on the front door.

"There's another one."

"Stay on that stool while I answer the door," his sister-in-law said, and climbed to her feet.

As she went into the hallway, he warned, "I will not receive a guest from atop a perch like some drunken sparrow, madam."

But he was still up there when she came back.

"It's Mr. Key," she announced.

"Thank goodness. See him in."

Finally he did get down, dismaying of his appearance, for his uniform jacket was in some other room, having a seam repaired, and his suspenders were showing.

He turned just as one of his more pleasant neighbors appeared in the archway.

"Frank! Do come in. I was afraid you were another starry-eyed fool with the Union Jack in his sights."

Francis Key held his hat at his side and seemed to be working on his posture. "Thank you for seeing me."

"Some legal matter?" Major Peter asked. "Or is this a social call?"

Self-conscious, Key smiled. "I would never make a social call in the middle of the day without announcement."

"So a legal issue?"

"No ... no, not a legal one."

"Well, very well, then, what can I do for you? Do you want a cool drink, or—?"

The skinny lawyer took a long glance at Peter's sister-in-law, who was simply standing by, not even pretending that she wasn't busy and that he wasn't interrupting. She didn't care whether he was comfortable or not. This was a woman who had seen and judged soldiers and citizens all her life. As the granddaughter of General Washington's wife, she had lived in the midst of a mosaic of every kind of American. She folded her arms and watched him, waiting to see whether the hemming of the trousers was going to continue or there was some other business worth doing which she could horn in upon.

George Peter knew she had that effect on people. He counted on it.

Uneasy, Frank Key went from one foot to the other, quite uncharacteristic of him, for usually his physical demeanor was subdued and drew little attention.

"Yes, I did come for a specific reason," he said. He looked at the major. "I would like to offer my services as a recruit in the Georgetown Field Artillery. I want to be a militiaman."

1814

"WHAT IS HAPPENING TO this world?"

The French Jew sat in his rocking chair in the parlor of his rented area, a place he had taken as a temporary affair but had come to regard as his home. He had been thinking of purchasing the building, since Fell's Point too had become so comfortable for him. His neighbors had become accustomed to Pdut's occasional explosions of temper, so that barrier had been eliminated. She had become less eruptive over the past several months, another incentive to remain as long as possible. She did not take to new places. That small mind of hers.

She sat on top of the sideboard, certainly looking absurd to anyone who passed by the window and happened to glance in. At least she was doing something not so absurd while she perched up there—she was sewing. She never made anything useful, but only made stitches up and down rags. Sometimes she hemmed the rags. When she ran out of rags, she began tearing apart their clothing in order to stitch random hems in them. He had hired a darkie girl to teach her how to make rosettes in order to keep her from dismantling their entire wardrobe, which resulted in every bed sheet's now having a thousand rosettes. Quite uncomfortable. He was about to hire the girl again to teach the idiot how to make nose snoods or sleeping caps. Napkins, anything. At least there would be some use to the useless.

He was sitting in his rocking chair, but he was not rocking. Instead, despair and defeat darkened his whiskered face to a point that Pdut had stopped talking hours ago.

"It is a disaster," he moaned. Again he held a newspaper in his hands, as he did every day, but this was a Dutch newspaper. Each week several foreign newspapers were delivered to his house. The news was not always accurate nor always the same, but he could at least piece together a reliable picture.

At the foot of his chair lay four other newspapers from four other sources: Spain. Belgium. England. Paris. They all delivered the same suffocating news.

Napoleon defeated at Leipzig. His army shattered, retreated, a bloody litter of corpses left behind by the tens of thousands. Paris captured. The Emperor finally forced to abdicate. Banished to an island in utter humiliation. That ugly word. *Exile.*

"We will save him," he spoke aloud to no one.

Pdut sewed and nodded. *Stitch ... stitch ... stitch ... stitch ...*

"It's only an island," he thought on. "Men like the Emperor are not so easy to crush."

He stood up and began pacing the room slowly, thinking.

"We are a banking empire. We span Europe. We are bigger than France, bigger than England. And I ... I have influence here. If England is no longer distracted with Napoleon, they will come here to beat down the Americans. While they are distracted with the Americans, we can rebuild Napoleon. He will build a little army and we will add to it. We will crown him again. Yes!"

He clapped his hands then paced with more vigor.

"Yes ... yes ... this is challenging."

Pdut's beady black eyes turned up from her sewing to look at him with an uncomprehending expression, as usual.

He waved a dismissing hand at her and went back to pacing. "I wanted to own a privateer, to keep the English spread thin on two fronts. If the English make a full-scale war here now, they will be distracted while we build our plans to crown the Emperor again. By drawing the full fury of the English here, the Americans will crumble under the assault of the Crown and be destroyed. If this is destined to happen anyway, we have the power to make it much worse. The English will have to defend this continent, and their own land in their own waters—weakened. It's at least a chance, is it not? A strategy? We must antagonize the English, fire the furnace. How ... how?"

He paused to think further, letting his mind grow quiet as it combed possible outcomes.

"If men like Tom Boyle are supplied with sufficient artillery— bigger ships, more guns—they will be more likely to challenge armed ships. That sounds like him, doesn't it? His partners want to give him a new ship anyway. What if we find not just a new ship but a *great* ship? A ship that will give him ideas? Exploit their intrepid nature. If those men like him, if they have enough power to challenge the blockade itself ..."

Stitch ... stitch ... she was watching and listening. Sewing without even looking at her work.

"I shall write to my contacts immediately, tonight," he said. "This minute. We shall use our resources to stir up trouble and see what bubbles out of the pot."

Stitch ... stitch ... stitch ... stitch ...

A New Ship

A YEAR ON GUARD. From summer through winter and into summer again had been a shuddering time. Skirmishes, battles, attacks, raids, feints, a stumbling calendar of activity that left no one feeling victorious.

Tom Boyle stood under the porch of a cobbler's ship and watched the rain drill into the street as if it had an attitude. Despite all the tricky travel between Chesapeake Bay and New York, he had managed somehow to arrive early. His thoughts were spinning. He had spent much of the winter on the hunt in the West Indies aboard the *Comet*, but with diminishing success. Though he captured other vessels, the Royal Navy blockade had become thick and efficient enough to recapture many of them. Flying around the Indies with a heavy price on her head, *Comet* was a tempting target had taken heavy damage. Many merchant ships carried guns now, and were ready to fight back if they weren't protected by Royal Navy brigs or frigates. Though a swarm of American privateers now prowled the Atlantic, their effect had been blunted.

Five months at sea, dipping into ports now and then for provisions and repairs, then out again, *Comet*'s legend grew and so did the price on her and on her captain. When he finally made port in Beaufort, North Carolina in March, he carried in his chest an unshakable foreboding that he wasn't doing enough even as he grew more notorious. All this time, news of the war on land dribbled aboard maddeningly. Sieges on forts and towns, Indians slaughtering settlers in Alabama, the inspiring victory of Commodore Perry in Lake Erie, followed by a half-dozen disheartening defeats, invasions, sieges, captures and burnings. To be at sea was a cocktail of torments—he knew what he had to do and what he was capable of doing, and that the United States needed him and every privateer to harass the enemy in place of a true armed navy, and he could do all that well enough, but where were the British today? Where would they be tomorrow? Where would Boyle himself be when an attack came on Baltimore, on his own neighborhood, his house and family? Would his wife and children be forced out and be running in the streets with British regulars shooting at them, tossing torches into the residences? Would the family of Captain Tom Boyle, the famous privateer, exemplar of all American privateers, be the focus of some English officer's revenge? How would other privateers hold their mettle if the spiteful British could capture Boyle's family?

When he was home, all he could think of was his purpose at sea. While at sea, he thought all night long, every night, of home.

Now he was a captain without a ship. On the orders of the owners, he had delivered *Comet* to Wilmington, North Carolina. Clement Cathell had taken over and sailed her here to New York, where she had been sold to a syndicate. Boyle hadn't been able to bring himself to follow her fate, but like the sad owner of a loyal dog he could no longer keep, he hoped she would get a good enough home, have her bruises and cuts mended and live the softer life of a coastal schooner. Then, there might be only the fate of being broken up for salvage.

Now he too was in New York, but not for *Comet*. He felt her presence here, somewhere, in some little dock in some cove, wondering where he was.

Not very rational. Boyle could calculate and strategize as coldly as a shark, usually. He tried to keep his heart out of his adventures. But there would always be a cloying hurt about losing a ship like *Comet,* which had saved his life and his crews' a dozen times and more. She'd been quick and answerable—not all ships were—and he knew every moan of every plank and creak of the leather on the gaff jaws. He and the spunky schoo-

ner had been together for a long while, longer than usual even
for just the merchant trade. From his cabin in the dark he could
tell whether she was on course or not. Even if he were asleep,
Comet would waken him if something came amiss.

Could he expect that from his new ship? A *new* ship, only
a year and a few months old, built in Fell's Point, at least, in
Thomas Kemp's shipyard. He and Kemp were partners in ownership, along with a roster of Baltimore merchants. He had an
idea that since the keel was laid on this new vessel, his fate had
somehow been linked to hers.

"Going to stand on the porch all day?"

Boyle flinched at the familiar call, he hoped not too visibly,
and shook out of his thoughts to look at the street, where John
Dieter, Paul Mooran and Thomas Coward had just pulled up
in a loaded open wagon drawn by one horse. He trotted out to
meet them.

"How are you, Tom?" Mooran asked.

"All balls." Boyle put his hat on. "When did you arrive?"

"This morning," Dieter said. "Picked up your parcels at the
shipping yard and here we are. You're early."

"Are you hungry?" Paul Mooran asked. "I'm hungry."

"You're always hungry," Boyle said. "Good to see you, Paul.
Thomas—you've gotten skinny!"

"Maybe I'm hungry too," Coward said as he took Boyle's
handshake.

"What's in these boxes?" Dieter asked.

"Mementoes," Boyle told him. "I took *Comet*'s halyards and
docking lines."

"Won't she miss them?"

"They're selling her, so they'll be refitting anyway. The halyards
are spliced and sprung anyway, but we'll weave mats or baggywrinkle out of them. Actually, they offered to give to me, but I bought
them honestly." He smiled. "I want no hints of collusion."

"Surprised you didn't win 'em in a bet."

"Also pins, small ropes, some brass fittings, lamps, gantline
hooks, hemp, four deadeyes, ten blocks, robands, the main gaff
tops'l—"

"What are we going to do with her tops'l? Won't fit the new
ship."

"I'll cover my bunk mattress with it if I have to. Or make a new pair of breeches. But some of *Comet* is coming with me."

"Sailcloth hats," Coward suggested. "Ditty bags."

"Sounds like work," Mooran complained.

Dieter got a thoughtful expression. "Wouldn't you rather honor *Comet* in some way? Have a little ceremony and drop this stuff somewhere out at sea?"

Boyle shrugged at the sentimental idea and pretended to give it some thought, but he knew what he was going to say.

"The sea honors nothing, John."

The others remained quiet, recognizing that Boyle was engaged in a moment of reverie with his lost schooner. *Lost . . .*a word that means something to sailors and captains. When a ship was lost at sea, sunk in battle, taken by storm, there was a story to tell in one's old age and a memory to hold as if the ship were still there, just a few thousand feet of water away. But when a ship outlives her working life and is broken up for parts or sold, the ignoble end warrants no story of heroism and sacrifice. It is just lost.

Breaking his own moment, Boyle hopped into the wagon and took an uncomfortable seat on the edge. "Drive on. Let's have a gander at this new barge."

—⟩⟩⟩—

By the time Dieter pulled the wagon into the shipyard marina, the rain had stopped. The dock was busy, but still less than if the rain had not drenched the morning's activities and driven as many people indoors as could do their work under a roof. They would come out now in droves, but for a few minutes Boyle and his officers would have some quiet.

They pulled up directly abeam of her. They paused without speaking or even getting off the wagon.

She was a black-hulled banshee, strong and young, furious and waiting to be run out. Like a raven-haired woman she hovered at her dock, looking dangerous. Her profile was sharp, her bow deeply angled, not like the round bow of *Comet,* an arcane and new design. Her masts were wildly raked, high into the sky with their topmasts still raised, her sprit, jib-boom, and flying jib-boom spearing far out from her bow with a bright new net spread on her whisker stays. Her main boom hovered well over her stern, boasting of an enormous sail plan. All her sails were bent on, every line belayed, coiled, and hung. The pin rails and belayed lines were well appointed, mystically looking the way he himself would have arranged them. How could that be?

And she was big—seemed very big—compared to *Comet*. Would she be fast? Would she be able to spin on a pin and come back almost into her own wake as *Comet* had?

Boyle scanned the schooner forward, then aft, then forward again. Somebody had done a great deal of what he would have done himself. She was more than ready to sail. She was ready for *him*.

Dieter stood up. "Looks like she's going ten knots standing still."

No one else spoke.

The ship was clean, but even more she was new. Her fir deck wasn't soaked with filth and saturated with ocean salt as was *Comet*'s. The black paint on her hull had no chips, her channels no splintered edges from cannon shot. Her shrouds gleamed with coats of fresh tar and the ratlines were so new that they were still white, and all the same shade of white, probably recently replaced. She wasn't a patchwork of repaired parts. Boyle was suspicious of the sparkle. What were her weaknesses? What were her quirks? What would crack under strain and what would hold up beyond expectation?

"They said there'd be an agent here to meet us," Mooran commented when the silence became too uneasy to bear.

Boyle hopped off the wagon and stepped to the edge of the dock. The schooner was now only inches away—a silly concept, but somehow significant.

His officers came up behind him and together they studied the schooner with experienced eyes. Dieter immediately went forward, leaned over, and looked at the shape of the bow.

"Sharp-built," he said, "like a hatchet blade. Keel's probably deeper farther aft. If there's no half-model aboard, I'll take a swim later and have a peek."

"I'll go with you." Somehow Boyle restrained himself from diving in and having a peek right now.

It was the hull form upon which speed and balance depended, and of course maneuverability, packaged with the rig—the masts and their placement, the engineering of the shrouds and deadeyes, blocks and lines. The myth of the Baltimore privateers and their unnatural speed was tied to all these elements, although by far the most striking characteristic to the untrained eye was the rake of those masts.

No one knew for certain the history of the deep tilt of those masts, for it had been an organic development rather than one sudden invention, but Boyle had his own ideas after years of merchant trade and now privateering in the Indies and South America, where there were ample trees but scarce land for farming rope materials. Masts with larger diameters had come from those virgin forests on the islands and if they were set with a pronounced rake, they could hold themselves up and resist wind, while Europeans, after a thousand years of culling out their own native forests, used narrower masts set vertically with lots of rigging to hold them up. Dramatically raked masts still required shrouds, but those supports could be dropped vertically from the mast top to greet the hull farther aft of where the mast was stepped into the deck. The resulting triangular formation made for extra strength and prevented the masts from tipping forward, giving them support while needing less tension on the stays. A larger fore-and-aft-rigged ship like this one, with stout masts, that triangulation of light rigging, a V-shaped hull with lots of drag to the keel, and a big sail area, could be easily driven forward and turn quickly indeed.

Well, that was one theory, anyway. The one he liked, in the elements he saw before him. Size changed everything about the way a ship moved. How would she really handle in open water? In light winds and heavy? In big seas? With an enemy biting at her heels? When he asked her to twist herself around like a dancer on a toe shoe? Was she *too* big?

"Ahoy!" he called, and stomped twice on the dock.

Almost instantly the fore hatch slid open and an unexpected face popped up, a bearded face with rosy cheeks and clever eyes, peeking out of the forward hatch like a cuckoo out of a German clock.

"Ah," Boyle uttered. "Mr. Yambrick, the agent of everyone and no one."

"Who's he?" Coward asked.

Boyle sighed. "I can honestly say I have no idea."

"Captain! You're early!" The unlikely presence climbed the rest of the way up the companionway ladder and extricated himself from the hatch, managing to carry a leather satchel under one arm.

"Permission to come aboard?" Boyle requested properly.

"Oh, my! Yes, yes, please do! It's my honor!"

Putting one hand on the larboard shroud, Boyle stepped over the gap of slimy water between the dock and the ship, onto the ship's rail, and dropped to the deck.

The portly Frenchman met the newcomers at the fore shrouds.

"Welcome to the *Chasseur,* Captain Boyle."

"Many thanks. Allow me to present my chief mate, John Dieter, and lieutenants Paul Mooran and Thomas Coward."

"Gentlemen, as Captain Boyle's associates, you have my deepest respect. Your chambers are ready for you. There are fresh blankets aboard the boat, and provisions for—"

"It's a ship," Boyle said, "not a boat."

Yambrick stammered a bit, then nodded. "Forgive me."

"Let's get to business, Mr. Yambrick."

"Certainly." He pulled a paper from his vest pocket and unfolded it for reference. "You probably already know that *Chasseur* is the largest privateer ever built in Fell's Point. Her hull is one hundred fifteen feet, she's eighty-five feet at the keel, twenty-seven at the beam and she draws sixteen feet into the water."

"So much for the shallows," Dieter commented.

"Something called 'sparred length' is one hundred sixty-four feet and six inches. What does that mean?"

"Means she's big," Coward commented.

Paul Mooran pointed forward, then aft. "It means measuring from the point of the jib-boom to the end of the mainsail's boom."

Yambrick nodded mechanically. "Oh ... charming."

"It means how much space she takes up of the dock," Dieter explained. "The length overall."

"Oh! Of course! Thank you." Just as he started stammering, Yambrick actually blushed. "I'm sorry. I am infatuated with these vessels, but I know shameful little about them, speaking technically. I cannot seem to retain the details."

"You would if you worked 'em."

"Oh, no doubt, no doubt."

"Want to join the crew, Mr. Yambrick?" Boyle asked.

"In my younger days and my older dreams!" the round man accepted. "I shall boast always that Captain Tom Boyle himself attempted to recruit me!"

He was rewarded with laughs from the four sailors. They seemed to be more at ease with the big schooner by the minute. Dieter and Coward were now on the fore shrouds and halfway up the ratlines on each side.

Aware of himself, Yambrick turned back to business. "Extra spars and canvas are coming which will allow you to rig her as a ..." At this he had to consult the paper again. "Pardon me. As a foretopsail schooner, a double-topsail schooner, brigantine, or a brig should you desire to do so. A brigantine, is that the one with the two—"

Boyle sharply said, "Two masts, squares on the fore, gaff on the main."

"Oh, later perhaps you can draw me a picture?"

Dieter laughed. "Coward likes to draw, don't you?"

"An artist, I am," Coward responded, distracted. "Flowers and kittens."

Yambrick nodded merrily and went on. "Last year she carried fifty-two men on her first voyage, eight carronades, and two long twelve-pounder guns—well, here is her log from that spring and summer, for you to examine."

Boyle and Yambrick paused to watch Dieter and Coward climbing down again. The two men jumped down from the shrouds almost simultaneously. In a matter of days, they would be rushing up and down and all over like squirrels in a new tree.

Coward recovered from a clumsy landing. "What's the name mean?"

Yambrick seemed happy to answer that question. "It's French. It means 'raptor.' Like an eagle or an owl."

"Like *chaser*. Like chasing something."

"Yes, like that."

"Good name for us," Boyle approved. "We're in the chasing

business."

"We didn't paint it on the hull yet. Best that decision should be yours."

"Paint it on. I'm not hiding."

"Where's she been?" Dieter asked.

"At first, she attempted to go to France," Yambrick said, "but the voyage was cancelled—some conflict between the captain and crew. She spent most of last year docked because of that, I'm afraid, but in December she was re-commissioned as a privateer. Her new captain was a man you know. William Wade."

"Wade!" Boyle exclaimed. "That explains it."

"Explains?"

"Why so much of the rigging looks familiar."

"Does it?"

"Is Wade here?"

"No. He went home. He had quite an active winter in the Caribbean and took five prizes."

"Has she been out in the Atlantic yet?"

"Yes. Wade took her to the coast of Portugal and took six more prizes. When he returned, he couldn't push through the blockade to reach Baltimore, so he came here to New York instead. When your syndicate purchased her, he prepared the boat for you. The ship. She is beautiful, isn't she? It's not just my wistful imaginings?"

Boyle nodded, still studying the manner with which the blocks and halyards had been run. "If she performs stretched out, she'll be a good scamp."

Yambrick didn't seem to know whether that really complimented the ship or not, but he said, "Captain, I think if we had a fleet of her, we could take the war to England as they have brought it to us."

He paused over his own sentence and stood silent while Boyle breathed in the new ship. Then Yambrick put the paper he was holding into the satchel and handed it to the captain.

"Here are your Articles of Agreement, *Chasseur*'s letter of marque, and her log book. Oh—and a copy of the Instructions for Private Armed Vessels of the United States, which I'm sure you know by heart. As of now, you are her captain and can set sail at your discretion."

"Just the four of us?" Dieter mentioned, now examining the gathering of hoops at the foot of the main mast.

Yambrick was proud to be ready with an answer. "Downstairs I have a list of potential crewmen who want work, including carpenters, sailmakers, a surgeon, surgeon's mates, an armorer, stewards, experienced gunners, master's mates, several qualified prize captains, two cooks, and a long list of seamen. And several boys."

"Below, not downstairs," Coward corrected, taking the precedent from Boyle's correction.

Yambrick smiled. "Yes, below. Sorry. Oh, I should mention several of them are freed or escaped Negroes, and there are a couple of Spaniards, if that matters to you."

"Can they work a ship? It's all that matters to me." Boyle then gave his first order aboard the stately vessel. "Have them line up over the next week and report to Mr. Coward for consideration."

"I shall send the requisite notifications."

"I have my own list of sailors whom I would like you to contact also. John, if you'll board those boxes, you'll find several pins from *Comet*, her compass, several of her sail ties, ratlines, and small ropes and ends. Go ahead and see if you can blend them into this big girl."

"Good luck charms," Dieter said with a grin.

"And I want more long guns."

"Oh?" Yambrick looked surprised. "We thought you would want your usual carronades."

"No, I want more twelve-pounders. At least eight more."

At this, his three lieutenants turned to look at him but said nothing, only questioning him with their expressions.

Thus he answered.

"I may need to fight at long range. This cruise is going to be different."

A Year on Guard

THE MORNING WAS PERFECT poetry. It would have to
be, or Mary would not have been paddling her canoe across the
outer harbor on the Patapsco River.

She enjoyed this kind of morning, a sapphire-skied morning,
warm but not too hot, with just enough breeze to flip the lace on
her bonnet and flutter the old groves of trees along the shores,
but not enough to push her canoe in some maddening direction.
She was able to breathe deeply and paddle occasionally, letting
the birchbark craft skim along the river's glassy surface.

The canoe was new just last autumn, to replace the old one
that had seen its fill of service getting her around, and this was
a good one. Vessels of this type were common conveyances for
the citizens of Baltimore, made by a local Indian family of birch
transported from their connections in the West. There was nothing as pleasant to the soul as canoeing. Mary paddled, then rested, and lifted her face to the breeze, then paddled softly again.

There were things about the old canoe that she missed—its
tendency to wander to the left, as if it secretly wanted to keep
going out to Chesapeake Bay and the distant ocean far south
at Hampton Roads. She had enjoyed fantasizing about letting
it go, leaving her responsibilities behind, but everyone felt like
that sometimes and the old canoe always let her turn it around

without much struggle. This new one would have to develop its own quirks and she would get used to them, as if she had a quiet dog that always wanted to go for a stroll.

As she drew closer to the Whetstone Point peninsula, on the opposite side of the Patapsco from Fell's Point, she began to hear voices. Men's voices, of course. Snapping orders, crisp responses, bustling and muttering, the clop of horses' hooves, the crackle of wagon wheels. McHenry was a small fort, tidy and well-placed, and from here on Whetstone Point it stood guard over the waterways into the Basin, Baltimore's inner harbor. Along one of the outer paths and inside the walls along the barrack buildings, upright spires of Lombardy poplar trees created a soldierly attitude. Though she was down at the water's level, Mary could see the tops of the trees over the fort's straight brick curtain walls, and she could see the huge flagstaff that had been installed just inside the parade grounds area, more toward this side of the fort. The tall pine staff had been made like a ship's mast, in three segments of gradually smaller diameter, to be strong and flexible as it carried the huge new flag. Today there was a standard-sized garrison flag flying up there, as it did every day, hoisted at reveille, struck at sunset.

She glanced like a mother duck at the two burlap-wrapped bundles at her feet. There was a lot of fabric wrapped and lying on the bottom of the canoe, quite a lot.

And every man in the fort knew the big flag was coming. They started to line up on the wall and were looking at her, while a quartet of them came running from the fort down the long stomped-down path to the shoreline. From here the fort looked like a blocky structure of angled brick walls, but Mary knew those walls formed star-point bastions much like the spikes of a snowflake, except with five points rather than six. Angled walls had been around since the first medieval wooden forts, so armed men along one wall could protect those along another wall, and no enemy could sneak around a corner without being seen.

Pretty, she thought. The fort must be lovely from the air, if she could be a bird and cavort above. Architecture attracted her. Structure and form. Artifice and effort. To make a plan, then take a brick—or a thread—and turn out a vision ... only mankind could build like that.

All at once, as if she had been slapped, the loveliness of the day drained away. The curtain walls of the fort exploded into pebbles. Men were blown into the sky, limbs severed from their bodies, their freedoms in tatters. She was surrounded by British warships all headed toward the inner harbor, each firing broadsides into the fort on one rail and toward Fell's Point on the other. Homes and businesses were demolished in a gasp, years and generations of effort, struggle, and hope, flattened. Screams of horrified people and confused animals crawled over the trees to her ears. The sun crept behind ugly clouds from horizon to horizon.

And the soft gray water lapped upon the birchbark hull of her twenty-foot canoe. With its little gulping sound, it called her back.

Again the sun shined, but with less meaning. The trees were calm and the fort walls had reconstructed themselves. But the false peace of the morning had been thoroughly ruined.

She would know no peace, she realized. At the age of thirty-eight, Mary had never known herself to be anything but an American. She knew many people who had been British once, and had married one of them and born his children, lost him and rebuilt her life here in this nation where prosperity had a chance and ingenuity was rewarded, in the only system in history that had ever actually raised the poor out of poverty.

Not now, she understood. Now there was a dangerous chance of being forced to once again become British, subject to the whims of a king and an unknowable authority far away. This moment of floating gently upon the water outside of Baltimore, city of great promise, hinge-point for exploration and commerce, had already been wrecked. The British blockade choked the American coast, driving down trade, driving up insurance rates and costs of doing business, causing shipbuilding to suffer and agriculture to stumble, and cutting America off from Europe and all roads to the world. Her friends, the many sea captains of the merchant fleet, were either land-locked or out risking their lives as privateers, like Victor Tarkio running the very real risk of being captured and fated to a life of squalid naval service or in some British prison. She still had her little soirees for neighbors and friends, clients and city officials, but there was always a pall over the party these days. The happy chatter had given way to a dimmer muttering of tactics, skirmishes, rumors, and anger, always anger.

This peace, this moment, was a lie, a woman's fantasy. Up there at the fort, those men weren't engaged in the secure lifestyle of peacetime soldiers, but were touchy and preparatory and knew their moment would come to face fire. Baltimore had so far gone unadulterated, though there was always talk of threats and strategies of attacks from land or sea. The constant tension was worse than a real battle.

And the British knew that, clearly. For them, this was an effective tactic of war. They had cannily made feints toward this attack or that attack, then made no attack, or had twisted at the last minute and gone somewhere else. They were magicians, causing panic and preparation, teasing militiamen into sleepless nights and drawn-out days, only to have nothing happen and the preparers slump into their beds, clutching rifles and worn-down faith in their chains of information. Or the attack would happen somewhere else, which in many ways was even more frightening, because it was really happening somewhere. America was a sleepless nation, exhausted and afraid.

There were enough battles that the air was full of their bloody details, of ransacked settlements in the west, of conflict on the Great Lakes, and in dozens of places she had hardly heard of and others that she knew. Just enough to keep her and everyone worried, anticipating. The war was no rumor, but it was moving on rumors like a snake.

"Mrs. Pickersgill!"

Mary flinched out of her ruminations. She pushed the fear down deep inside, as she had learned to do, and dealt with the matters at hand. The delivery of this bundle to Major Armistead marked a moment both dark and thrilling, the beginning and end of something important—her part in the war. Had she been a man, she would have enlisted already.

"Come this way, please," one of the men requested, and motioned her to a grassy bump on the shore.

With two good strokes, she was there. One of the men caught the point of her canoe and two others drew her alongside the land. The fourth man reached for her hands and pulled her up and out of the canoe, always a bit of a clumsy affair given the obstacle of her petticoat and skirt. But she was used to it and easily popped onto the land.

"Welcome, Mrs. Pickersgill," the officer began. He was an attractive man with brown-sugar curls and an infectious smile. "I'm Captain Joseph Nicholson, second in command."

"Yes, I've heard of you, Judge Nicholson. I'm pleased finally to meet."

"Actually, I've been to one of your parties."

"You have? Oh, yes, you have! I remember now." She flushed. "I'm embarrassed!"

"Not at all. It was a crowded party, spilled all the way out into the street. You were flitting around like a happy butterfly. I'm not surprised you didn't commit every face to memory."

"Yes, but a sitting judge ... I should have paid better attention. I read about you now and then in the newspapers. I've seen your advertisement for volunteers. You're still on the bench, aren't you?"

"Oh, yes. I split my devotions between the courtroom and this garrison. We're determined that Baltimore will be defended when the British come, and they will."

"I wonder when," she mused.

A moment later she was treading eagerly up the path toward the entrance to the fort, flanked by soldiers on either side, with Nicholson carrying the smaller of her two bundles, two others carrying the eighty-pound burlap bundle.

She was glad the day was sunny. She needed sun.

Major Armistead and more officers were waiting inside the fort's parade grounds, the bright center of the circular formation of barracks and fortifications. They were uniformed and proper, yet had the expressions of little boys at a picnic, waiting for the watermelon.

"I was surprised to receive your note yesterday, ma'am," he said immediately. "Six weeks and you're delivering the flags! Allow me to voice my amazement that you've finished all that work with such dispatch!"

"The project was inspiring," she said simply. "This is my fort too, Major."

"Of course." He seemed to truly value her sentiment. "Let's

have a look. Nicholson, your knife."

Armistead stood over the eighty-pound parcel as the judge sliced the strings and laid open the burlap. Then Nicholson stepped back and Armistead stepped forward.

There on the grass of the fort's center grounds lay the thousand and more yards of English bunting, folded into a square, with the blue field and two of the stars showing on top, two feet across each.

"My, my, my goodness ..." Armistead took a step, then another, and actually circled the folded flag. Next to those stars, his boots looked like little doll boots. "It is big, isn't it?"

Mary smiled.

"You see just there," he said, pointing off to one side of the parade grounds, "there is the flagstaff for it."

The ninety-foot pole, painted white, stood ready, with a small United States flag flipping at its top. Well, the flag probably wasn't all that little, but just seemed that way, flying so far up.

"That pole is stabilized with two seven-foot cross-braces sunken into the earth," Joseph Nicholson explained. "I supervised the hewing of the timbers myself. Very strong. Oak."

"Most gratifying, Judge," Mary said. "Wouldn't be sporting if it fell down, would it?"

"No, no. Ma'am, it is my determination that this war has changed complexion. We no longer fight for free trade or to absorb Canada, but for the very existence of the United States. We'll show the enemy that we embrace that change."

His commandant nodded in complete agreement.

"Let's get some men out here, captain." Armistead nodded to Nicholson, who turned and made a motion to someone else, and in moments a phalanx of United States Army soldiers trotted into the center of the grounds, out of formation.

"Let's unfold it," the major ordered.

Mary stepped back and let the soldiers do their work. The first motion was to gather around the parcel and lift it off the ground, freeing it from the burlap wrapping.

"Be careful now, men," Armistead told them. "Don't let it touch the ground. More hands, please, Captain."

Again the judge motioned and this time shouted for more

help. Another squad of soldiers came boiling out of one of the barrack buildings, then still more as word spread that the new garrison flag had arrived, to be their signature before the forces of the enemy.

Fold by fold, man by man, the flag was opened. Yard by yard it expanded across the parade ground, the blue field coming first. Until now, Mary had seen it only in the dim expanse of the malt house loft. In the sun, today, the flag seemed almost alive.

Now the stripes. She remembered every stitch. Her intimacy with the construction of the flag filled her mind now and made her fingers hurt as they had night after night, stitching in a pattern that seemed never to end. Six weeks? Was that all that had passed, truly?

She felt as if her body had been beaten with a cane. Weeks, hunched over in that loft, doing a significant portion of the work herself, much by lamplight, to be sure it was done exactly right. She trusted the girls, but she trusted herself more, and there hadn't been time to make a classroom of the important project. They had done what they could do well, and she had done the rest. Then she had, every night, checked their work, every stitch, every meeting of each strip of fabric through the process of piecing them into these long stripes, until she could see no colors but red and white anymore.

Longer and longer the fifteen stripes were unfolded. More soldiers came to support the edges of the flag, until it covered almost half of the entire parade grounds. Like an ocean it sprawled out before her, waving in the middle as if it knew what it wanted to do up there in the sky. Several times Major Armistead warned the men not to let the flag touch the ground. Finally he ordered four men to climb under it and support the middle of the huge field of colors.

Mary almost spoke up, to warn them to be careful with the edges, for if the flag were to unravel itself, that would happen where it was handled the most, and that would be the edges, but she didn't speak. They would have to learn, for theirs would be the hands that would open it and raise it from now on. But it was like a child, wasn't it? Her child, and she couldn't help but want to bat away unkind hands and protect it around the edges.

At Mary's side, in a rare expression of pure delight, George

Armistead clapped his hands and laughed. "Magnificent!"

He surveyed the superb expression before him, surrounded, as it always would be—if he had anything to say about things—with the soldiers of the United States of America.

The men were not at attention, and let their expressions say what they were thinking. No one but Armistead spoke, but some moments didn't require words. The enormous flag waved and pulled at the men's grips so that they were obliged to constantly adjust their hands to keep hold of it.

Had the sentiment of the United States ever been demonstrated in any banner so large before? If it had, she would have known.

"What a miracle," Armistead gasped. "A few hundred dollars, a hocus-pocus of colors, and here it is! So much more than the sum of its parts."

Judge Nicholson leaned over the flag and examined the hem closely. "How many stitches did it take, I wonder?"

"Over three-hundred-fifty thousand."

The judge stood straight and gaped at her. "I didn't expect you to actually know!"

Mary stretched her shoulders as if every stitch still rested upon them. "We didn't count them, but we did the mathematics."

Armistead laughed and shook his head in appreciation. "Do you have an invoice for me?"

"I'll have one sent over."

"Very well. Of course, it will have to make its way through the bureaucracy, but I'll do my best to hurry it along."

"Fine," Mary said. "I've never encountered a problem with the Deputy Commissary."

"I'll give you a note confirming that you made the delivery of both flags today."

"Thank you."

"Shall we hoist it, sir?" Nicholson asked.

Armistead blinked. "No! No, not yet. This is not its moment. This banner is for the British to see. It has a mission. We'll wait."

Mary sensed disappointment from the men, and felt some herself. Yet, the major was wise and knew his mission too. He had a picture of it in his mind, of that moment yet to come, when the statement of this giant would be made to the enemy and to the world.

The major took a steadying breath and made his decision.

"All right, men," he spoke out. "Now for the tricky part ... let's see if we can fold it up again."

—ᴡ—

Word had leaked out across the New York docks that the big privateer schooner with her famous captain was warping out today. Boyle had kept the date of his leaving the harbor as quiet as possible, but when recruiting a hundred fifty sailing men and boys, Marines and prize captains, the news took on a life of excitement. A crowd had gathered at the shoreline, families of the men aboard, dockworkers and every stripe of attendant to the needs of ships and commerce. Here in New England the sentiments in favor of the war were sparse, but Tom Boyle saw nothing but encouragement along the shore today. Even those Americans who remained against the war were today proud of the record of their privateers.

All the spectators regarded the spirit-stirring beauty of *Chasseur* as she was moved out of her dock space by heavy cables drawn by a four-mule team on the shore. The sail ties were off, sails ready to be hoisted, depending upon which Boyle decided would best get the ship out of the harbor. The mules would take her to the first bend, where another team waited to take over if necessary, unless the winds were favorable. Boyle had held up three extra days, waiting for the wind to change direction in his favor. It was nearly six o'clock.

The crowd cheered and waved American flags as the schooner was drawn slowly forward. Boyle stood on the aft deck next to Paul Moran and two of the new boys, who worked the tackle system on the enormous tiller and kept the ship from pointed inward at the land where the mules worked.

Inwardly, Boyle's stomach was quaking. Never before had his confidence in himself as a sailor been so challenged, his concerns wrapped up in doubts and uncertainties. Doubts in this ship—was she too big to be handy? Sluggish? How did the shape of her hull work with the sail plan? How would she handle with so many men aboard, and how as they were gradually put off in prizes, lightening the vessel's burden by the weight of several men? He wished he had had the chance to speak to Wade.

Now the ship would have to teach him. He was setting sail with a giant mystery beneath him. The sensation was unnerving.

He glanced around at the two dozen or so other vessels escorting them. Canoes, sloops, rowboats, all manner of small craft had surrounded the schooner whose legend hadn't even begun. There was only the sense of it so far, what they thought of as the legend of Boyle himself, a legend that had not yet completely fulfilled itself. What did they really expect of him?

Being legendary carried a burden, a weight upon his chest every moment, the unresting concern that he might never be able to satisfy them completely, that the war would overtake him and shrink the effect of the privateers to insignificance. His fame was an anchor he might never be able to raise.

He looked up at the weather gauges and noted the wind— almost following, but coming more over the port quarter. The wind over the trees, no longer blocked so much by the buildings, was aligned to the axis of the harbor's shape. If he wanted the bow to go downwind, then the stays'l and jibs would be the working sails.

"Haul away on the stay and lower jib. Signal the second warping station that we will bypass their assistance."

Thomas Coward went amidships and called out those orders. The signal flags were run up to communicate with the mule drivers as the stays'l and inner jib crawled up the stays on their iron rings, evolving from taffy-folds of furled canvas into flapping triangles, finally to be hauled up snug to where their pointed tops met the foremast. The sails fluttered along their inboard edges, signaling to Boyle what they needed.

"Give me five points to larboard, Paul," Boyle requested. "Let's see if there's enough wind to take her."

"Five points to larboard, aye."

The men on the tackles hauled the tiller over, then had to correct for going too far. On the decktops and lining the rails, keeping out of the way of the assigned sail handlers, the entire ship's company of one hundred fifty men watched.

Boyle held his breath. This would be the ship's first movement for him under her own power.

The bright canvas heads'ls shivered like the triangular wings of a gull sitting on the water, then made great flaps as if trying to break the sheets that held them to the pins.

"Release the warping team."

The warping cables were unmade and tossed into the water, from which the mule driver would reel them in.

"Paul, let's have another two points."

The tiller tackle blocks creaked. Far forward as Boyle and everyone watched, the bow turned with surprising agility. The huge triangular heads'ls made an abrupt *crack* in unison and snapped full with air, harnessing the wind as it increased over more open water.

Chasseur shot forward suddenly, her black shoulder dipping into the water as her keel took a good bite sixteen feet below. A half dozen men were pitched sideways right off the decktops. Others laughed as they grabbed for handholds to keep from stumbling. Boyle had to replant his feet as the speed abruptly increased. The ship charged forward, leaving her escort fleet behind to cheer their goodbyes in her wake, for she was clearly and very decidedly leaving them.

As they cleared the point, the water opened up before them and there was instantly more room for maneuvering.

Boyle clapped his hands once. "All right, let's set that fore."

At the fore sheets, John Dieter barked the order, "On your sheets and braces, let go and haul!"

The brails were released, the sheets hauled. The graceful foresail draped out like a theatre curtain and snapped firm. *Chasseur* took another sudden leap forward and heeled over on her starboard shoulder.

Boyle listened the *shussh-shussh-shussh* of the water's ageless voice against the hull. The hull sliced through the waves like a sword blade. There was nothing sluggish about her.

He cast a glance at the ungasketed main sail, taffy-folded on its boom, ready to be hoisted, and saw that the men were ready. "Set the main."

The helm team eased off a little, letting some wind out of the sails so the main could be raised. Dieter sharply shouted. "On your peak and throat halyards, haul away together!"

The colossal mainsail crawled upward, tugging on the hoops,

rising as if commanded by the titans until it dominated the dimming sun.

"Put us on the wind again, Paul," Boyle ordered, and the ship screamed forward so smoothly that there was no rocking motion at all, but only a sensation of speed. Boyle began to calculate how much time at this racing speed would bring them out into the open ocean and then in danger of being spotted by the blockaders. He had originally estimated a slower pace, which would let night close around them as a shield, the clouds in the sky assisting by covering the moonlight. His mind spun with calculations and an adequate memory of the chart for these shores.

A singular cheer reached Boyle's ears. He turned to see the people in the flotilla of escort boats and the people on the shore reveling and waving their good wishes as they were swiftly left behind. The wind pulled at his dark hair and made him blink. He waved at them and hoped he would not let them down, for his plan was a mad one this time.

Flag receipt.
Courtesy of the Star-Spangled Banner Flag House, Li1938.12.1

A Coastal War

"SAIL TO L'WARD!"

The lookout's call brought Tom Boyle out of his cot. He'd slept all night, for a change.

Dieter was handing him the spyglass even before the captain was all the way out of the hatch. "Just hull-up."

"How cooperative of them to appear at change of watch."

"I arranged it that way," Dieter crowed.

"Call all hands. All lowers and the square tops'l."

"All hands on deck! Hands to hoist the foretop!"

"Oh, more than one," Boyle observed through the spyglass as the *Chasseur* turned—and turned with a little jump, as if she knew.

Comet had been handy and quick, making course changes fast as a bird flying. *Chasseur* was something else—bigger, heavier, longer, deeper, yet so well-balanced, so ingeniously crafted that she responded to her helm's smallest adjustment smoothly even on choppy seas. Each ship had her own good qualities, rather like the difference between a feisty pony and a long-legged racehorse. *Comet* had been quick and sly, hiding in the smallest, shallowest inlet, disappearing in a light fog, slipping away as if she were a specter. Then, *Chasseur*'s ability to accelerate was shocking and the power of her sails to drive the bigger, deeper hull carrying more men and bigger guns was a tribute to the minds of her makers. The slightest adjustment in trim could send her shooting forward and she did not like to stop. He had discovered that even completely dropping the main might not be enough to slow her down. Her design was something new in the world, a fresh idea for seafaring—this sharp hull and wave-cutting prow, and a hundred details in the minds of her designers and shipwrights, sailmakers and then those who sailed her. While *Comet* had been built like a typical American schooner, created to make the best of the winds, currents, bays, and rivers of North America and the Indies, *Chasseur* had been built as a privateer—a fighting rig balanced to carry heavy guns, designed to twist and rush and crank around, offering the widest possible changes of rigging style while underway that anyone could imagine. She was a ship of war, built to fight.

Of course, the deal was not done on the best ship in the world until her crewmen also were trained and attuned to her finest of adjustments. Then, there was the sea.

Boyle shook out of his ruminations as men piled up from below, having already eaten and dressed to take over the watch.

"Captain!"

He turned as two of the ship's boys, chubby Yankee Sheppard and wild-haired Adam something, came bare-footing to the after deck.

"Yankee," Boyle greeted. "Adam. Good morning."

"An abundance of storm petrels today, Captain," Sheppard boy said, pointing into the sky.

"Good. Thank you for being observant."

Adam, who could never quite control all his arms and legs at one, bounced as he asked, "Why's it good?"

"Remember that I asked you to keep watch for cape pigeons and storm petrels?"

"Yes ..."

"Those are Wilson's petrels. That puts us at the converging point of the Labrador Current and the Gulf Stream. It's right where we want to be."

"Just from the birds?"

"Animals can help us navigate very well. How do you think the ancients traveled the seas without charts?"

"How did they?"

Yankee asked, "From the birds?"

"Birds, fish, whales, even more. At night, the color guides in the sky are unreliable, but luminous marine organisms occur where there are reefs."

"Water temperatures," Dieter told them.

"Go on, John."

"Knowledge of charting warm and cold currents, like here where the two big currents meet, one warm, one cold. We take the temperature of the sea at certain intervals."

"Can I take it?" Yankee bubbled.

"Me too!" his scrawny shipmate demanded.

"Of course, you both can."

"I knew a man in the Indies," Boyle added. "He would paddle south in a canoe, absolutely nothing in sight, no land, and all at once he would finally just turn right to get to his island. I asked him how he knew when to turn. He said, 'When the water turns warmer.' And I think he tasted it, too, whatever that did for him."

"Tasted it?" Dieter repeated. "Salt content?"

"Honestly, I've no hint. I tried it, but it didn't work for me."

"Can I taste the water?" Adam asked, still bouncing.

Boyle smiled and cupped his hand over the boy's knobby shoulder. "That's not a call I would standardize. Are you coming on watch?"

"Yes!" Yankee gulped, still excited about the birds.

"Go talk to Mr. Thompson. Have him pay out about a hundred fathoms of line for you. Braid and whip some new sail ties and another length or two of baggywrinkle. Off you go."

The two boys rushed forward, madly spotting birds and telling the other boys what they'd discovered, but not before skinny Adam whirled around and shot Boyle a spanking good salute.

"Keep them busy below in case there's action," he said to Dieter. "Send your watch to breakfast, John, but bid them eat quickly and come back up."

"Will do," Dieter answered, and made the order for which the men on his watch were grateful after the chilly night.

They soon drew close enough to see that their prey were three ships, at least three, visible in the morning haze.

"Two brigs and a three-master," Isaac Webb noted from his place at the helm tackles, when he could count the sails with his naked eye. "Either they're bound for Canada or they thought they could avoid privateers by taking the northern route."

Boyle nodded. "That's what I think. Let's run up on them. Close haul."

"Close haul, aye."

The helm was put tight toward the wind. The fore-and-aft sails were drawn inward as far as they could be without coming completely amidships, and the wind pressed into towers of canvas almost straight flat as dinner dishes. The schooner heeled over, then over more, until her crew clung like monkeys and her rail went down into the pale pink waves of dawn.

"You know, I'm thinking about changing our watch routine," he mentioned casually to Dieter as his mate reappeared, precariously carrying a plate of biscuits and a pot of coffee.

"Oh?"

"We have plenty of men aboard and officers to relieve you and me of watch leading. Divide the crew into thirds instead of halves. Let the lieutenants lead the watches. Instead of two sixes, we could run eight-on, eight-off, with two dog watches at four and six. The men will be rotated in such a way that duty during the night watch is shared. They get more rest."

"I've dreamed of that for years. Why the sudden change?"

"This ship's big enough for more people to be asleep at the same time."

"I like that," Dieter agreed while gnawing on a biscuit. "I revile the midnight-to-six watch."

"Do you? You never told me."

"You couldn't divine it from my bearlike snarling at change of watch?"

"I figured you were just nasty. After dinner, let's rewrite the duty roster. Give it a try."

"That's well." Dieter pointed at the ships they were pursuing. "They've seen us. Turning away. You intend to take all three?"

"Always bite the big bites, John."

"I'll ready the gun batteries."

"Finish your coffee first."

With the ship heeled so steeply, they could only load the guns on the high side. By running those guns out, and with a little help from the helm, the balance of weight brought the lee-

ward rail out of the water and they could at least load the forward and aft guns on that side.

"Oh—look at this!" Boyle squinted, then used the spyglass.
"That brig's a man-of-war. Royal Navy guarding the two merchant ships. That puts a different color on the cake. Isaac, bring
us up close, but stay out of long-gun range."

"Understood."

After telling Dieter his plans, Boyle moved to just forward of
the main, where he could bark orders to anybody on the deck if
things had to happen suddenly.

The schooner skimmed through the morning swells, which
were shallow enough that the hull could cut through them rather
than riding high over crests and down into troughs. *Chasseur*
was able to close on the three-ship convoy in less than an hour.

"Fire a gun, John," Boyle ordered.

"Larboard bow gun, fire!"

The crew covered their ears. The long gun's heavy bark made
the water quiver under it. The gun's range was long, much longer than the carronades of *Comet*. If their quarries had any
doubt that the schooner was a privateer seeking to raid them,
they would no longer.

They waited, drawing closer with every swell—dangerously
close. Isaac was estimating the range of the Royal Navy ship's
guns, with Boyle keeping a vigilant watch over movements on
the warship's deck, measuring what they might be doing by their
positions on the deck. A gun answered—probably an eighteen-
pounder, from the sound.

The ball soared toward them. The crew scrambled, but there
was nowhere to hide. Only by the thinnest of margins did the
ball miss the stern and splash into the water, shooting up a huge
asymmetrical funnel of spray.

Dieter shouted, "Look out, Nanny, we're in range!"

"Bear off downwind," Boyle called to the helm. "Let's run
away."

"Bearing off."

"Ease the main out. Back the tops'l, John, brail up the fore.
Take some speed off her. Let them think they can catch us."

The schooner bore away from the convoy, running beautifully with her main sail all the way out over the water. She balked

a little in the breeze from behind and tried to turn against her helm, like an anxious dog pulling at a leash. But he must rein her back, Boyle knew, as he watched the British man-of-war easily fall into the chase. The square-rigged warship was very fast in a following wind, so he moved *Chasseur* to a position that did not favor her—with the wind almost straight behind.

"Unback the tops'l and back the stays'l," he ordered. "Luff the main."

Sailors came aft to handle the main sheet and bring the big main boom, which of course was a de-branched fir tree trunk, back to the middle of the ship, where the sail did almost no good. Its leech began to flip and starve for air. The schooner stalled under them, barely moving forward. For *Chasseur*, that was still a good six knots, even with only her square tops'l and heads'l working. Fast banshee.

Boyle looked behind. The man-of-war was closing on them. Almost back in gun range. Farther behind them, the two merchant ships tried to escape on their western course.

For a good two miles they drew the English ship downwind. A couple of times Boyle made sure the schooner appeared to be struggling in the following wind. They had to work hard to make it look like a struggle. *Chasseur* just wanted to race.

Calculating maneuvers, wave strength, wind, and time, Boyle ticked off the minutes until he estimated the moment had come.

"Wear ship," he commanded.

"Wear ship!"

"Clew up the square and set the fores'l."

Isaac Webb brought the helm across the wind and the schooner wheeled smoothly around, turning so sharply that the square-rigged English ship could not match her movement. By the time the English ship even began to turn, *Chasseur* was going almost into the wind like some kind of sorcery of physics.

Boyle rubbed his hands together and put the English warship out of his brain. He looked now forward at the two fat merchant ships, probably loaded with wonderful aromatic cargoes like coffee and cotton and rum.

Dieter appeared at his side, but he was looking back at the English warship as it batted around and struggled to come back into the wind. They would find it impossible to come back at any useful angle, giving *Chasseur*'s crew time to capture both merchant ships. "I wonder how many times we can get away with that before they figure it out. Someday they'll stop chasing us."

"Someday," Boyle agreed wistfully. "But not yet. Take care, because those merchantmen could still be armed. When we get to there, let's take one and put a prize crew aboard, then have them get cracking to New York while we take the other one. We'll get an accounting of the cargo when they reach a port. By the time the man-of-war gets back in range, I want both those ships under my prize captains and escaping."

Dieter motioned for two of the prize captains to meet him amidships, told them what was expected, then let them go quickly to gather boarding implements—pikes, pistols, cutlasses—and organize their prize crews. That done, Dieter came back to the command deck.

"So what did you mean?" he asked, keeping an eye on the man-of-war, just in case.

"Mm—pardon?" Boyle turned. "'Bout what?"

"What did you mean, 'this is it'?" the chief mate asked.

"Oh ..." Holding on to the shroud as *Chasseur* bit down and heeled insanely over, Boyle glanced up at the taut sails, then forward at the excited collection of sailors and Marines whose lives were in his hands.

"You're going to have to tell me," Dieter said. "I'm your chief mate and I need to know. If anybody kills you before I do, I'll need to complete the mission. So what is 'it'?"

"This schooner, John." He clapped a hand on Dieter's shoulder. "She's the devil I need. And by the souls of the damned, I think she knows it."

"Right," Dieter answered in true facts-only first-mate style. He shook his head, making the fan of hair from the knot on his head wave like a child's toy. "No ... no, I don't have a clue what you're talking about."

"England, my man. They're blockading our trade, so we will plunder theirs in their own waters."

"England? *The* England? You mean ... we're going to England? Itself?"

"England itself. We'll strike where they're vulnerable."

"Where in hell are they vulnerable?"

"Their pocketbooks."

Dieter's face screwed in incomprehension. "What can sixteen guns do against the English in their home waters?"

Boyle sucked in a big, long, clear breath and turned his face into the wind.

"Attack the pound sterling."

Respect

"There it is!"

History's doorway. Portsmouth, England. Lieutenant Gordon almost jumped out of the boat right over the oars when he first saw the American ship moored out, minding its own business and awaiting its fate.

This ancient and venerated place had seen more monumental seaborne happenings than any hundred lifetimes could carry. Here King John had formed a naval base. From here Henry III and Edward I had struck out against France. Here the French had raided in the 1330's and the first dry dock in the world had turned out the first English warship. Here Henry VIII witnessed the disastrous turnover of his top-heavy warship *Mary Rose*, saw her sink with more than five hundred lives, including irreplaceable archers whose skills had taken their entire lives to develop. One couldn't just go and hire another skilled longbowman. Here the founder of the Royal Navy had planned his assaults during the Dutch War and the war with the Spanish, and the first colonists had embarked. Back into the echoes of time, Portsmouth was there, with the Normans, with the Saxons, with the Romans, and all those who had walked the twisted, time-carved roads, rusty outskirts, and fog-shrouded farms.

Of all that had happened here in the past thousand and more years, James Gordon was sure another such moment was dawning as he looked with tight scrutiny at the captured American privateer ship. The rake of these two masts was almost as deep as Thomas Boyle's *Comet*, against which he measured all privateer ships—the rake, the speed, the hull, the arcane maneuverability, and that American dash of recklessness that could never be predicted. There was something, though, that this ship possessed that the *Comet* had not. Gunports. This was no converted merchant ship tempted into service by James Madison and his desperation to have a shadow navy. This captured American ship had been specifically built for armed privateering.

"Destiny," he spoke out.

"*Atlas*," Victor Tarkio corrected vaguely as he rowed his captor toward the vessel, which was rigged with schooner sails and two square tops'ls on her foremast.

"What?" Gordon asked.

"*Atlas*, not *Destiny*. It's written right there on her bow."

"Oh ... no, I didn't mean the name. I meant destiny. Delphi. Fate."

"Whose?"

"Mine. And yours. And hers." Gordon knew he was taking a risk letting Tarkio row him out from the *Helen*'s mooring, with land just over there, not only in sight but close enough for a brisk swim. Once free in England, how then would an American escapee conceal himself? How would he find refuge and perhaps transport back to the rogue nation?

Tarkio was better off here, in this boat, rowing around. He had nowhere to go if he jumped ship. Gordon knew, and so did Tarkio, that out on the open ocean Tarkio could at least entertain the idea of being recaptured by Americans and finding his way back home, though that hope was blunted by the simple fact that the American privateers, their only real navy, did not challenge English ships of war. That wasn't their mission. Facing an armed vessel, they ran. They always ran away.

As the boat drew closer, he heard the sound of hammers inside the gray hull, audible from the line of gunports, just above a thin line of white paint that ran the length of her hull.

"This will do," he uttered to himself as the rowboat came up close to the dove-colored hull. "Your best guess, Tarkio. How long is this ship?"

Tarkio stopped rowing and took a good look. "'Round seventy at the hull, I suppose. Hundred fifty, maybe, with her jib-boom out. Pretty big."

"Pull up to her side."

In moments they were tied up and climbing aboard, dropping onto the battered deck, which had many broken seams and must certainly leak like cheesecloth.

"Oy!" a shout greeted them—or perhaps it was not a greeting. A strong-looking man in filthy clothes, not a uniform, came trotting at them from the afterdeck. "You aboard for some reason?"

Gordon had assumed his uniform would say something, but this creature was clearly not impressed. "I am James Gordon, in command of His Majesty's Ship-of-War *Helen*, anchored around that spit head. You will address me properly hereon."

"Yeah."

"Who are you?"

"Farquarson. Shipwright." This beefy laborer was rough in all ways with the exception of a pair of striking emerald eyes ringed with thick black lashes much darker than his stubbly hair. He would probably tidy up well and be completely unrecognizable.

"How did this schooner come to be here?"

"Captured by the squadron under Admiral Cockburn, s'all I know."

"I know. Your assignment?"

"Same as ever. Refit. She's going into dry dock tomorrow, like do all the Yanks."

"Specifically for ... ?"

Farquarson shifted unhappily, debating whether to explain his purposes to Gordon, but then deciding not to care one way or the other. "Add bulkheads, straighten up these masts, add to the keel, shorten those tops, shift the ballast, ehm ... cover the gunports so they don't take water when they go under, reinforce the weather deck so the guns can go up there instead of the—"

"But these will change her center of balance, her ability to move as she was built to, the steepness of her heeling?"

"That's the thing, isn't it? Make her less dangerous. Don't want to turn arse-up in a puff of breeze, do you, dump a dozen men overboard?"

"Please stop!" Gordon snapped, holding up both hands as if he could push the big man over the low-slung rail. "Please do nothing more to alter this vessel. Nothing!"

"What?" Farquarson actually laughed. "You taking charge, then? How're you doing that? Don't you have some papers at all?"

"Patience, man. I mean to take command of this ship. The only thing I want changed is her name, do you understand? I personally guarantee that you and your carpenters will be paid for this assignment, but only if you cease work today until I can secure the proper orders. Is that clear? Or shall I post a guard?"

The bulky man shrugged. "It's your neck, admiral."

"You will address me properly."

"Why?"

After so many months among Royal Navy seamen whom he could punish or even hang at his will, having failed utterly to get Tarkio to do him that simple respect of class distinction, Gordon began to finally digest how poorly that tactic worked for him in the general populace.

"When do we get paid?" Farquarson asked.

"You don't trust me?"

"Should I?"

"I'll arrange that you'll be paid in full for any work you have done or were told to do on this vessel, and that will be done within one week. I'll give you something today as a security. But there will be some alterations I may want, so I will keep you on retainer."

Farquarson bobbed his straight eyebrows and frivolously waved a hand. "Take her."

He started back the way he had come, to stop the work going on below, which indeed did stop as soon as the big man disappeared down the main hatch.

Gordon's legs felt like solid iron. He had never seen himself as a man with an imagination, one who would take wild risks, yet here he was, devising a mad plan because some higher power in heaven or hell had put this American prize in his path. Here he stood upon her deck, having just given his first order aboard. And she wasn't even his yet.

Victor Tarkio folded his arms and coughed, or was it a sigh of some kind?

"Yes," Gordon muttered. "Yes, this will do what I need. The world is entirely new now. Napoleon has abdicated and sits rotting on his island, the last bit of land he can call his own. May he rot there. They still call him 'emperor.' Absurd … an 'emperor' with an empire of one island off the Tuscan coast."

"They say there are twelve thousand people on that island," Tarkio recalled. "He's even created a navy and an army."

"Probably to parade himself about. He makes decrees about farming. How pathetic." Gordon glanced at him. "How do you know these things?"

"The crew got mail from their families yesterday."

Swinging all the way around while testing the stiffness of a shroud cable, Gordon merrily said, "Britain has regrouped and we can now turn our attention, and our hardened military forces, on our little American problem. The Americans, with your little militia civilians stumbling from their beds to march around like dolls and pretend they know how to defend their—"

"I know," Tarkio interrupted. "That's why we're here instead of in the blockade squadron. Your own navy doesn't need the *Helen* anymore. They don't really need you anymore either."

"Leaves me free to pursue my own devil." Gordon deliberately didn't look at him. "That swaggerer has changed ships. Your man. Boyle. He has abandoned the *Comet* that made him famous. He left the ship behind and much of the crew."

"Maybe they just went home. Americans can do that, being free and all."

"Still, he's left them behind."

"How do you know this?"

"Spies. Are you angry that I didn't tell you when I found out?"

Somewhat stiffly, Tarkio said, "No point to that."

"He's sailing a large privateer now. A ship with black sides. A ship built only to be a privateer, like this one, to carry heavy guns and disguise herself by changing her rig like a woman changes her dress. So my sources say."

"Not so rare," the American commented, holding back his true thoughts.

"You're wrong, Tarkio. His new ship, it *is* rare. And it's new. He's only had it a matter of weeks. He and the ship are strangers. It's big and black, a symbol of its kind, with that American stripey flag dancing off her—we can see a ship like that. It will stand out. We can follow the viper. Hunt him down. I want to see how your Captain Boyle fares when facing a Royal Navy ship instead of unarmed merchant ships with inadequate crews."

He rubbed the base of the foremast on this captured American ship, vengeance proudly brewing within him.

"I won't help you," Tarkio anticipated.

Gordon looked at him. "What?"

"I know what you're planning. I knew as soon as we came around the Spithead and saw this schooner. I won't help you destroy Tom Boyle. Put me back in chains down in the bilge. Make me a prisoner again."

"You won't even work this ship? You won't help us learn to sail ... this?"

"Did you really think I would?"

Shaking his head a little, Gordon knew his disappointment did show. "You've been poisoned by that nation of turncoats. I've given you my trust, against my own better judgment, but I have no more expectation of devotion from you than from any other of the maggots in my crew, do I?"

"Take them with you."

"What does that mean?"

"Take them, your crew, the men you have now, when you go out on this ship. Don't get new men. Take the ones you know. They'll go with you."

"What's this? Are you giving me advice?"

"It's your advantage." Tarkio turned and leaned back with his legs against the deckhouse as if he had been there all his life. For this moment, he was back on home soil. "You think you can't trust your own crew, so you put your life in the hands of a captured foreigner. These hands. I could've strangled you a hundred times. Easier, I could've let the elephant crush you."

"Are you sorry you didn't?"

"Not yet."

"*Why* not?" The question erupted without the reins Gordon had used inside himself to hold it back before this. "It makes no sense! You had the perfect opportunity. Why would you kill the animal instead of me?"

Tarkio stood there for a moment and seemed to be waiting for Gordon to figure it out for himself, as if it were written somewhere and all the young commander had to do was find it.

When nothing happened, Tarkio spoke more quietly. "Because you fight for a purpose that's clear to you. Not because you think Americans are vulgar dogs or a nation of mutineers, or you'd never have taken me as your steward. Even if you don't like us, that's not enough to make you into a killer. You're not fighting because some admiral ordered you or because you want to climb the ranks and impress the fancies at a dinner party. You're not a fop and you don't care if you look absurd as long as things get done. The crew respects that about you."

Taken by surprise, Gordon discovered that he could neither move forward nor away.

"Even Moycroft," the American continued. "But you've never stepped forward of the mizzen to discover that most of them are just as loyal to England as you are."

"They're drunkards and pressed men," Gordon said. "Why should they be loyal?"

"Because you are. You don't want to spend your life in a Royal Navy sweatbox any more than they do. But here you are anyway."

Squinting, Gordon felt his throat grow tight like an embarrassed little boy's, so tight that he couldn't respond.

"Never thought of that?" the enigmatic Tarkio went on. "That the attitude of the captain could sink into the crew, even drunkards and pressed men? Don't you know they've been watching you? Deciding whether or not to die for you? You don't give them the respect of holding the same cause in their hearts as you hold in yours."

"Stop," Gordon managed.

But Tarkio did not. "And me. Why do I protect you? Why didn't I poison your food or strangle you in your bunk?"

"I would've done it to you."

"You wouldn't," Tarkio said with a revealing smile. "We're not so different, all of us, you and me, American and English. There will always be some bit of England about America. After this is all over, England will discover we're pretty much related for all time. I hope we never fight again after that. Not against each other, anyway. It shouldn't be like this between children of the same womb."

Gordon noticed his hands were shaking. He clutched them into fists and pressed them against his thighs. "Why are you speaking of these things? After all the months, why now?"

"If you put me in chains and I'm not there to protect you, remember this," Tarkio told him firmly. "Your crew saw you run out in front of a monster to defend your ship. Just like England, running out in front of Bonaparte and standing alone."

The American walked to the rail of this captured princess and gripped a shroud, seeming the perfect idealization of a sailor, as if he had been painted there in watercolors.

"We do understand," Tarkio said. "So when you face your foe, stop looking over your shoulder like a man with no friends. That's my advice."

Attack!

WILLIAM BEANES HAD SEEN war before and had not en-joyed it. His role as a surgeon in the Revolutionary War involved frantic attempts to save lives of men whose gore was flowing out from their bodies, and if he could save them, to patch those bod-ies together from the tattered pieces and hope against the odds that they did not die later after months of indelible pain.

As the enemy marched into Upper Marlboro from the North Road, he was there holding a flag of truce. A few other citizens stood with him, hoping to ameliorate the destructive bent taken by the British Army bullies in so many communities. As Upper Marlboro's leading citizen, he carried the white flag himself and led the little group of Americans to the front line of the impres-sive enemy force and stopped before the officers in the front line.

He gazed up at the highest-ranked officer, a tall and hand-some aristocrat, who was right out in front, glorious in his red uniform, white breeches and Ostrich-plumed hat, riding an ab-solutely stunning pure-white Arabian horse that clearly was a personal steed, not an Army mount. It might've been a comman-deered animal, but to Beanes' experienced eyes the officer could control the creature with barely a touch of the reins, indicating that he was used to the horse and the horse was used to him.

Behind him a few paces was another officer on a red horse, a wiry man with a severe face and intelligent eyes, clearly keeping back from his superior, but also clearly a close aide. And after them, dozens upon dozens of British marching men, not boys, but men of obvious experience, comfortable in their roles, at ease with their weapons, and looking at the Americans with a sense that they were completely entitled to invade here.

There were only a few dozen houses in Upper Marlboro's rolling hills, aromatic with fields of hay and tobacco, meadows with grazing sheep and its ancient woodlands. Beanes himself owned considerable land and of course the gristmill. In a considered effort to keep it all from being set afire, Beanes waved his white flag and adjusted to the inevitable. He straightened to attention and gave the officer a snappy salute, or his best version of one.

He rolled out his favorite Scottish accent. "Welcome aboard, sir. Doctor William Beanes at your service. You are welcome in our humble village."

"I see nothing humble here," the high-ranking gentleman commented. "You're a physician?"

Northern Irish aristocracy, that accent.

"A surgeon," Beanes answered, wondering now whether the Scots accent was helpful.

The officer steadied his horse with one hand upon its withers. "I am Major General Robert Ross, commanding Wellington's Invincibles and Royal Marines."

"Welcome to you, Major General Ross. I would like to offer my house at Academy Hill as your headquarters. I have a reputable wine cellar, a farm, milk, bread, and victuals. Your brigade can be comfortable camping in this field. You may take leisure."

"Why should you do this so lightly, sir?"

"I am not in favor of this war and disapprove of the president's decision to wage it. I am British by blood and believe our nations should be amicable. I begin my philosophy in my own home and live what I preach. Thus I welcome you and offer you the comforts of Upper Marlboro. We are not all war hawks and savages."

"Very well, I suppose." Ross nodded toward the officer behind him on the other horse. "This is Lieutenant George De Lacy Evans. He will be your liaison. I will convene a council of war here and plan my next movement."

Comfortable enough with Beanes and the countenance of the other townsmen standing with the doctor that he had revealed his lack of a decisive plan, Ross flexed his shoulders.

"If I may, sir," Lieutenant Evans spoke up—also Irish— "this would be an opportunity to collect Admiral Co'burn and bring him here for your counsel."

"Let me have a day to ponder."

Evans seemed irritated, but said, appropriately, only, "Yes, sir."

Co'burn, the lieutenant had said. The English pronunciation for *Cockburn*. Cockburn, the devil of Chesapeake Bay, the plunderer himself, the devastator. Coming here.

"Doctor ... 'Banes,' did you say?" Ross asked, pronouncing it in the old way as Beanes did.

"Yes, General, sir."

"You and your party will be considered spies if we are betrayed while we camp here. You will also be under guard at all times. That said, we accept your gracious hospitality and will spare your private properties of retaliation for the reprehensible behavior of Americans in Canada and the west, that your countrymen learn cooperation reaps rewards. Lead on."

Surrounded

POLLY KEY PACED THE terrace of steps in front of her house, her heart thudding so hard that her chest hurt. Her body trembled with a hundred unfading fears, for she was watching her neighbors on the street, militia, soldiers, cavalry, running for their lives. Horrifying to see these people fleeing, compelled by the dread that had been gathering for so long. Her hands trembled, her stomach churned, and her mind would not quiet from imaginings of what was happening now and what would come tomorrow.

The afternoon was brutally hot and clouded over, depriving these sorry people even of a comfort of sunshine. As early as July her husband had begged her to stay at Terra Rubra, but she would have none of it if he were not there. Why?—she knew not even herself. Perhaps it had been the magnetism of her presence that she hoped would hold him at home. They had been here only a day, and thank God the children and most of the servants were still at Terra Rubra, looked after by Frank's parents.

Frank was a man of his word. He had enlisted in George Peter's militia for reason of his own conscience, thought he had no experience with artillery or strategy, and now that the British were taking focus on this area he had insisted upon being here, moving with Peter's artillery. He had paid for his own uniform and weapons and supplied his own horse, and despite being a superb horseman he had succeeded in being pitched over his horse's head into a river. Thus were his accomplishments during the one month of militia activity last summer. The Field Artillery had remained on alert, constantly teased and exhausted by the redcoats' half-hearted taunting with hardly any real attacks to purge the tension, so the tension kept building. The militia, citizens with families and work that needed to be tended, made no real progress toward training or experience, but simply wore themselves down with the burdens of expectation.

Today, though, the British had finally revealed themselves, gathered thousands of warriors, and begun to move through this countryside.

Frank had gone off with Brigadier General Walter Smith from the Keys' church, to act as a civilian aide, whatever that meant. While riding away he had turned and looked back at her with those misty eyes, as did the knights in the olden times stories he read to the children. He tried to be gallant, to be the man of the family and of the nation, not a peacock like so many other militia men pretended to be, but she knew he was ill-fitted to his task. Since that moment, Polly had trembled.

"Polly!"

She jumped at the sharp call. Ellen Martin, the choir leader from church, ran toward her, flushed and mussed, her cap entirely missing and her greasy black hair pressed down to the sides, undone. She grasped Polly by both hands and shook her unkindly.

"Why are you still here? You must go!"

"Not without Frank. Have you seen him? He was with Walter Smith. Do you know what happened?"

"There was a battle at Bladensburg," her friend gasped.

"Is it over? What happened?"

"We lost!"

"Oh, Lord!"

"There's nothing to stop them now! For Jesus' sake, run for your life!"

And the other woman was gone, racing so passionately that she held her skirts all the way up and showed her knees. Polly let her go and scanned the flowing crowd for more familiar faces.

"Leonard! Leonard Bates!" Polly called, and rushed out to meet the area's most successful barrel maker.

The thickly built Bates' militia uniform was intact, but dirty from the knees down, and he didn't seem to be wounded, but he pulled behind him a lame mare that didn't want to walk anymore. Confused at the sound of his name, he wiped his sweat-caked face with his sleeve and blinked at her.

"Leonard, have you seen Frank?" Polly rasped. "You were with Peter's artillery, weren't you?"

"Frank? No—"

"What happened?"

"I can't pause, Polly! My shop will be burned! I must empty it!"

"Please!" Polly shrieked, clawing her hands into the cooper's clothing. "Tell me!"

"Somebody named Ross," he stammered, "Major general commanding Wellington's Invincibles, battalions of them, hundreds of men, thousands, God save, God save—" As he talked, speaking very quickly, he bent over and tried to do something to his horse's lame hoof with a small knife. "Stones, damned stones."

A loud report of cannon fire in the distance jolted them both. Polly pressed her whitened knuckles together. "Leonard, I beg you!"

"Winder, you know, General Winder from Baltimore—"

"Yes, we know him!"

Bates gasped out the words. "Tried to block the enemy from the way to Washington, so we went to make a battery in Bladensburg. We had six thousand militia and volunteers, cavalry, riflemen, I don't know what. I saw Frank at the earthworks, only once. Stand still, Aphrodite!" He put his shoulder to the horse and pushed her over a step, fighting to keep a grip on her up-turned hoof. "No one thought they would bother with Washington!"

"Please!"

"The president was there and the secretary of state. Joshua Barney came with guns from the Navy yard and some men from the flotilla. George Peter's gunners, we were to the right of Barney, but we didn't have enough rounds or charges—the civilians driving the ammunition carts were running off God knows where."

"But what *happened*?"

"It was chaos! Skirmishes broke everywhere, rockets firing, the Royals surrounding us, men running away. We shot at them and Barney's boys did, but everybody else was running. We didn't know which orders were real, what Winder was thinking or anything, whose orders to obey, whether to retreat, take a stand, retreat again—and we didn't know *how* to retreat, you know, there was no plan! Were we supposed to meet somewhere and form up again or make a stand at Washington at the federal buildings? Nobody knew what to do, so we just ran, we broke and ran. Heatstroke killed more redcoats than we did!"

"But where are the artillery men?" Polly demanded. "Where is Frank?"

"Don't wait for him. Sorry, Mrs. Key, very sorry. Come on, Aphrodite!" Bates tried to haul the horse into movement, but she only walked a few steps on the cobbled street, clearly in pain. "Damn you beast of hell!"

"I'll take her," Polly offered. "I'll put her in our stable."

The man simply dropped the reins, put the horse in his past, and sprinted away into the rushing throngs more nimbly than she imagined he could. He was in a complete blight of fear, and he left his fear with her.

She had hoped for some comfort. Instead there was only more dread. She clamped her teeth tightly to hold back her own panic and drew the mare off the cobbled street to the path that led down behind the house to the stable. Able to walk on softer ground, the relieved horse followed her. She made it to the corner of the house, and there saw the Potomac River flowing as it always had past the terraced gardens and old trees.

There, ominous in its silence, traveled a single two-masted ship with square sails and tall sides, like a ghost under the cloudy sky. It was loaded with British Navy men in their blue and white uniforms, officers wearing those awkward clamshell-shaped hats.

How had they gotten past the shoals and oyster banks at Kettle Bottoms? Were they miracle workers? Were more warships coming? She had been told they couldn't possibly attack

Washington from the Potomac, yet there they were!

There was no sound, no talking, not an order, traveling over the water. The men on those vessels were not talking to each other. They were listening to the panic on the Georgetown road. They were all looking at the shoreline, scanning, peering at the houses, the federal buildings, looking at *her,* stunned as they looked at her, her home, her gardens. Polly gasped out a senseless sound. The mare shook her head, not understanding why they had stopped.

"Mildred!" she called, her voice a throaty squeal.

The cook, a slave girl just transferred here from Terra Rubra, appeared magically beside her, and probably had been watching her all this time. She was a good girl with fair skin and a red birthmark across her left eye that made her seem always half in shadow.

"What's happening, ma'am?"

"Take this horse to the stable. Give her water and grain. Then go inside and shut the doors!"

Mildred, taught to ride by Frank himself, whom she worshipped almost as her own father, was able to swing up into the saddle as fluidly as a nymph and urge the mare along the house to the gardens and down toward the stable. Thankfully she asked no questions about the strange-looking ship moving past their home and spared her mistress from having to explain what a Royal Navy warship could wreak upon them.

Frantic, Polly rushed back up to the street. She tripped on the steps, jamming her hand hard into a concrete slab and hardly felt it. There was no solace for her from frenzied families and defeated militiamen trying to get away from Washington by retreated past her house. The volcano of war was finally erupting after spitting smoke for so long. The Second War of Independence had come to her doorstep.

She gave up counting how many of the fleeing citizens she knew personally and stopped trying to run out to meet them, to get answers, but where was he? People rushed by on foot, driving wagons, dragging cattle or goats or children, pushing garden carts or wheelbarrows, and militiamen stumbled past, many without their weapons. Clamping her lips tight, Polly Key summoned all her will to resist calling out to them, *"Where are your weapons?"*

The bleak swelter of afternoon blended into sunset. Watching the street became more and more difficult, the people harder to identify.

She never recognized her husband even as he rode toward her. He was almost to her when she recognized the horse. Her husband was a changed man from the tidy patriot who had left this morning. This flying waif was plastered with dirt and streaked with sweat, his hair the same color as his dirty face and clothing. The black horse, painted with foam and filth, was almost as disguised, but Polly knew that gait and the arch of those withers.

"Oh! Frank! Frank!" She waved as if he wouldn't know to stop at his own door.

Frank Key galloped to her and swung off the horse without even bothering to stop the animal, which immediately trotted on down the path to the back of the house and the stable where he would find his own stall.

"Go in!" Her husband seized her arm and together they rushed into the house, their refuge, which today might mean nothing at all.

Frank slammed the door and rushed into the kitchen, where he terrorized the slaves who were cooking bread and cakes. He found a dishcloth and soaked it, then peeled off his jacket and began to rub the dust from his face and hair.

"Are you hurt?" Polly begged. "Are you wounded?"

"I'm not."

"We've heard the cannons firing all day." She tried to control her tone. "Bladensburg ... tell me."

"The town was almost abandoned," he said through the muffling washcloth. "Smith and I scouted for places to station the artillery. We chose a high place and I stayed to direct the militia. I tried to help, Polly, I made suggestions. I know the land at Bladensburg—I thought I could help. The excitement caught me up in its spell. I tried to decide the position of the artillery, but Smith and George Peter argued about the position I chose. General Winder came and chastised me for trying to arrange his men. I must've been wasting his time, but the commanders couldn't decide on positions. They disapproved of each other's deployments. They were moving each other's men around as if there were time to play. Laval's cavalry ended up in a ravine where they couldn't see anything!"

"Were you the only one—doing that?"

"I wasn't. Others tried to find good positions, other gentlemen of the militia, Madison, Monroe, some of the cabinet. Suggestions everywhere, confusion—communications broke down completely—lock that window."

Though it was a distraction, Polly rushed to the kitchen window, pulled it shut and turned the latch.

"They were shooting," Frank went on, words pouring out like grain, "so we opened a six-pounder barrage. Our aim was off half the time. Joshua Barney's sixes were firing away too. He was the only one whose men seemed to know what they were doing. When British soldiers fell, the others kept marching forward, right over the bodies of their own, wheeling—" He threw his hands in the air, a gesture of tragic appreciation. "—wheeling with glorious perfection and forming new lines without even having to look at each other. We tried to keep shooting, but shot right over their heads. Our shots and rockets fired on them, and sometimes whole platoons were cut down, but the holes fill up with men from the rear like water draining into empty spaces. They were impervious to fear! They couldn't be confused! Wellington's Invincibles—hardened soldiers. The discipline—it was ... it was ..." He paused, fell back against the sideboard and grasped the edge. His eyes glazed. "It was beautiful. Terrifying."

Polly saw it in her mind as if she had been there. "Frank—"

But he was in his own world. "Rockets screamed every which-way. Congreve rockets. They aimed right at *us*, at the militia instead of the regular army. They knew we were untried. They were right; we cracked. Whole regiments dropped their weapons and ran. Poor Winder tried to hail them to take a stand, but the British had everyone consumed with blind terror. Our front lines disintegrated. The carnage was sinful ... more and more of them came. Battalions of them! They marched after us in columns so steady that the very sight of them was a weapon. They seemed to be growing out of the grass like poppies. With bayonets!"

"Bayonets!" she echoed.

"One English officer's horse was cut down under him. The man got up, drew his saber and charged us, just like that, as if he never gave it a thought. Nothing stopped them, Pol. They just kept re-forming their lines until we were overwhelmed. We broke, abandoned our guns. Our regiments cracked. It was a rout."

Lacking even a groan of empathy, Polly lowered herself to sit on one of the three-legged stools near the oven.

"They're already calling it 'the Bladensbug Races,'" he went on. "Disgraceful. The day the Americans ran like rats. Even the president ran."

She looked up. "Did you run?"

"What? Barney's men and Peter's? ... We held out, or at least tried. But at a certain point, we were forced to break. I heard that Barney fell."

She couldn't help a gasp at the thought of having lost their greatest and steadiest commander. "Killed?"

"I don't know. Our defeat left the Bladensburg road completely open. The road to Washington open. They're on their way here."

She rose and fetched him a cup of water, then dried his face with a fresh cloth.

Staring at a crack in the stone floor, Frank made a forlorn sound. "I made egregious mistakes. I was unqualified, untrained. I'm no tactician. What business did I have directing the placement of troops? Acting the part of an officer? I let my ego carry me away."

"Oh, Frank!"

"It's true, Pol. A good horse and a uniform are not the ingredients of a good soldier. It's all façade—without substance. Useless."

This was too much for her. She pressed her hand to his cheek. "But remember, and promise me that you will *never* forget for the rest of our lives—"

She stopped. Frank was forced to look up, seek out the end of that sentence, that vow. "What?"

"Never forget," she said solidly, "that you stood your ground with your comrades. You did *not* run in the Bladensburg races."

Those gentle eyes, so angelic in church, so striking in the

courtroom, stinging from the dust and disarray of humiliation, squeezed shut briefly, then fluttered open. He wiped his hand across them as if to clear away the fog of so much unfamiliar action.

"Oh, well, thank you for that," he murmured. But he could not be comforted. He had seen something this day that no one trying to be a patriot should ever have to see. His inconsolable eyes moistened. Tears broke on his cheeks. "I know one thing for certain now. Tom Boyle was right about me. The battlefield is no place for me. I am no warrior."

She was about to argue with him, to say he was the best kind of warrior in God's kingdom, a warrior of the heart, of morals and right, of the law, but the opportunity was crushed by a shriek from outside—a woman screaming in the street.

Frank bolted for the front door. Polly followed.

Darkness had fallen completely now. The dreadful day had turned to night, pretending everything was normal. There were no stars, no moon, nothing but clouds horizon to horizon. Reflected upon the low-lying clouds were colors of a false sunset—orange colors, yellow, white—moving constantly as if to display their primitive power.

Other people in the street had stopped running, some of them. Droplets of rain had begun to fall upon their faces. They stared back the way they had come, to the place only a mile from here that held such important symbolic meaning for them, the swamp of only nine hundred houses and a cluster of buildings, a place so strategically unimportant that no one thought it held any attraction for the enemy.

"It's Washington." Frank's voice was scratchy, raw, as he spoke to his wife, to God or anyone. "They're burning Washington."

—⁂—

"Don't stop me."

"No! Please, Frank!"

Even the beseeching of his beloved wife could not dislodge Frank Key from the sudden and irrepressible urge that rose in him.

"Stay here!" Polly locked her hands around his arm. "Don't

leave again!"

Drawing his arm back, he clasped her by both shoulders in the fiercest message he had ever given her.

"I have to see!" he blurted.

Without jacket or horse, he sprinted through the gathered people, his long legs stretching with every stride, toward the glow of flames beyond the shadowed tree-line. Just as she lost sight of him and the anguish of separation crushed her again, she heard his voice like an echo in a cave.

"I have to see!"

Red Heaven

WASHINGTON, DC
EVENING, AUGUST 24

FIRE AT NIGHT. FRANK Key entertained no satisfaction of having been right as he stood a mile away from his Georgetown home and, like the last lingering Americans standing around him, here to witness the face of hell. He had been against the war and still was, but when the invaders came he had taken arms in defense of his country, however clumsily, and the taste of utter defeat was bitter even for a staunch pacifist. He had predicted disaster and divine punishment, and there it was.

The night was ebony, glossed by rain. Heavy clouds, invisible under normal conditions, tonight glowed an angry vivid red, the same red as the coats of the enemy who held the torches. Before him the president's mansion was no longer a silent symbol. Tonight, it roared.

Flames licked from every window. The ceilings had collapsed and enormous hellfire snarled where there had once been a roof. The building looked like a giant toy set afire by a mischievous giant child.

As the heat from the flames cooked sweat and rain off his face, Key wondered dizzily about the federal governments papers. Had they been saved? Had the president and his wife escaped? The nightmare of not knowing roiled in his empty stomach.

To one side burned the Capitol building, a monument designed by Key's friend and frequent guest, William Thornton. Watching the elegant building roiling with orange flame—a pain rose in his chest for the loss of something personal.

Over there the Treasury, the Senate Chambers, the House of Representatives, and a further roster of national insults around the curves and behind trees, all burned. In some places he saw the buildings themselves, in others he could see only surreal columns of flame. Against the black horizon over there, the Navy yard glowed. Were they burning private homes, or keeping the destruction to government buildings? Was his home a target? Washington was not a good military target and no one had expected it to become one, but this was not a military attack. It was an attack of punishment and revenge, pure resentment for American audacity, which the British were doing just because they could. War had been declared by the unready, a gesture of defiance and a tactic of conquest, and this was the pathetic, humiliating result—the landmarks of the United States drenched in oil and set alight, to be baptized in ash. This was the supper of the unprepared.

A voice caused him a painful flinch.

"There they are."

It was a boy, a teenaged boy, standing close by, whom he thought he recognized as the son of someone he knew. That was a good bet, since he knew almost everybody.

Key looked in the direction the boy was pointing.

Officers. British officers. Some in Army uniforms, some Royal Navy. They stood well away from the Americans, flanked by a laughing, mocking phalanx of regulars and flotilla men drinking from crystal glasses and merrily refilling them from bottles of Jemmy Madison's wine and throwing papers from the humiliated administration into the smolder.

"Who are they?" he asked.

"Ross and Cockburn, with their marauders," the boy said, pushing the impolite part of the admiral's name. "Ross had his horse shot dead right from under him. Just made him mad. Cockburn's going around saying we can blame Jemmy for this. Madison. The president."

"I know," Key uttered miserably.

There they were, just over there—the architects of the British assault campaign, one by land, one by water, personally super-vising the spectacle of England's grudge. These were the men who had only this morning charged a larger force of Americans and scattered them like insects, including Key himself.

What a moment this must be for the two of them, he thought. Revenge for Americans' burning of Canadian towns and instal-lations on the Erie frontier.

His body, exhausted, felt as if it were made of strings, still as death, as he witnessed the insult of the British conflagration here in the capitol named for that greatest of men, a man he would never and could never forget. The reserved gentleman of Virginia, that exemplar of noble behavior to a misty-eyed boy who believed in heroes, tonight stood just behind Francis Key's right shoulder, watching the American catastrophe from the veils of eternity.

Aroma of Destruction

THOUSANDS OF CITIZENS CLIMBED onto their rooftops or opened their third-story windows, or ran to Federal Hill, there to be joined by neighbors who did not have such vantages. Mary Pickersgill herself had a prime vantage, knowing as well as she did the structure of Brown's Malt House. She stood on the roof of the now-familiar building, in a pall of helplessness with Caroline, her nieces, and Grace Wisher. Other neighbors stood here too, as well as the owners of the brewery. No one spoke.

Usually the forty miles between Baltimore and the Capitol was the same forty as any other. It took a certain amount of time by land and another amount of time by water to get there.

Forty miles—a distance shrunken tonight by a fire so historic that the two cities were joined by it. Showing in all directions, the display of enemy rage illuminated the black horizon in a manner so arcane and otherworldly that mere human hands could not have created it, but they had.

Mary thought of Major Armistead. At Fort McHenry, from the tops of the walls, he could surely see the burning of Washington far to the southwest. That glow was a message to him, to her, to everyone here. Baltimore would be next. The major would think of the burlap bag with eighty pounds of English bunting folded inside, tied closed with string and tucked in a corner of his office for more than a year. Warned by the orange paint on the southwest night sky, he would go to his office and cut that string. She could almost see him doing it.

She drew a breath and was startled by the scent on the air that had just arrived. It was the aroma of destruction. The smell of smoke on the wind.

More effective at communication over a distance than any flag, pennant or banner, the firebox of Washington carried a message from the Crown to the Americans, drawing their eyes in the same hypnotism with which fire had mesmerized humans since the first cook fires glowed in the first caves. The wordless message read that this rebellious fledgling nation was finished, the experiment turning to cinders, finished before it had really even begun to find its place on the stage of the world.

Rivers of Soap and Whiskers

THE ENGLISH CHANNEL

"SQUALL! SQUALL, BOYS! SOUND the bell! Get your gear!"

Chasseur was as wild as her name. She was insane. She was a menace. She was possessed. And Tom Boyle was in love with the black witch.

Now wearing two stripes of bright yellow along the length of her hull, to commemorate the *Comet*, the muscular schooner crashed along under all lowers and the foretop at a dizzying fourteen knots with her starboard rail buried as if she liked it, doing that dolphin movement schooner-men both loved and feared. There was no comparison, no other ride on earth that could replicate that stomach-pulling sensation of going up twenty-five feet, hovering for the briefest of moments, then dropping suddenly into a bowl of white foam, only to be propelled up again, always hanging on for dear life to the half-tipped-over devil beast as she laughed her demented way along.

The wall of rain approached as straight and sharp as a razor scraping the ocean's surface.

"Hurry or you'll miss it! Get your gear quickly! Tommy, blow the tops'l sheets!"

With one hundred men left aboard and a hold choked with prisoners after—what was it now?—thirty-three days into the cruise, Boyle held on to the larboard shrouds and smiled, watching the crew boil from the hatches with their gear as the sudden squall dropped upon them out of the gray sky. This one had come fast, before they could see or even smell it, closing rapidly from the port bow.

"Turn into it," he cast over his shoulder to the four men manning the huge tiller. Only in the slimmest of definitions were they able to control the schooner. She had her own mind and was doing what she was built to do. No sailing ship was moving with true efficiency until she was heeled over.

The squall combed the water's jumping surface in a boiling line, while before it the water danced in as clear a demarcation as he had ever seen.

"God's combing the water, boys! Hit the deck!" he called. Then leaned over the main hatch and requested, "John, pass me my kit, will you?"

Dieter was already up before Boyle's voice was completely snatched away by the wind, carrying two canvas ditty bags.

The squall rattled over the port side as if someone were shattering dishes. In less than fifteen seconds, it hit them. The temperature suddenly dropped by ten degrees. Above, the foretops'l flopped like laundry, its sheets cast off and belayed in lazy fashion, just enough to keep the ends of the lines from going wild and fouling in the other rigging. *Chasseur* made a groan of strain and went violently over on her starboard side, as steep a heel as she could take without rolling over and dumping them all off. Every man aboard hung on desperately, some to the rigging, some to each other. There was not a man aboard whose mind could banish thoughts of sudden turnover in just this manner, a violent arm of wind pushing her over and farther over till she failed to recover. She would right herself, of course, but she'd be under water.

Boyle glanced at the open main hatch, then shook off the dismal pondering and, knowing the men would take their cue from him, casually opened his ditty bag.

He spoke to the helm team. "Francisco, break this heel, would you?"

Lead helmsman Francisco Pedre and three helpers eased the tackles and gradually relieved the tiller until the ship righted herself at least enough to let them actually walk on the deck, although it was that crab-like side-to-side amble on a slanted deck. Boyle moved over the tiller tackles and out of their way, to the larboard rail and to the main shrouds where he could get a better grip.

Like romping children, soaked by sheets of rain, the crew stripped off their clothing down to the waist, pulled out cubes of soap and shaving tools and went about joyously dancing and soaping up in the torrent of fresh water from the sky. They hadn't had a good squall in four weeks. Shaving by salt water was a sticky, skin-drying business, and there was no way to wash their bodies at all, unless they took a swim. Boyle pulled out his shaving gear, hooked his little mirror from its frame on a ratline, still holding on with one hand so he didn't go tumbling onto the deckhouse and probably right off the ship, and soaped up his hair and face. Beside him, Dieter untied his long hair and worked up a healthy sudsing from the molded bar of soap, and they both laughed at their clumsy attempts to get a stable-enough foothold that they dared take straight razors to their faces.

Five of the ship's boys bubbled out of the hatches with empty buckets and put them on the high side of the tilted deck next to the deckhouses, to collect as much fresh water as nature would provide. All around the weather deck the men held mirrors for each other and some dared let shipmates shave them, then pulled out the toothbrushes provided by that oily-tongued rascal known only as Yambrick, and went about scrubbing their teeth as if they'd just rediscovered that they had any. Then the boys joined the men and things became a circus.

"This is good," Boyle commented. He had one arm looped tightly into the shrouds and a leg up against a deadeye. The ship rolled severely under him. If he's had the desire, he was sure he could wait until the right moment and dive from here on the larboard side straight into the water over the starboard rail and touch absolutely nothing. "We'll be sparkly and sweet-smelling for our audience with the king."

He pulled off his soaked shirt and scrubbed his upper body with his own somewhat shrunken bar of soap.

"You were right, so far anyway," Dieter chatted.

"'Bout what?"

"The Royals have put so many ships to the blockade and the Indies that they haven't guarded their merchants this far over the Atlantic. We've had easier pickin's with the ships that think they're safe going from Canada to Spain or the Canaries to Scotland, while the king's favorites are back on our coast, looking for us."

"Cargos have been meager, though."

"You didn't paint any pretty pictures about that. We didn't come for prizes. We all knew that."

"No grumblings below?"

"None I've heard," Dieter said, "but then, they're all terrified of me."

"Yes, you're very scary."

The ship's company reveled in their toilette, lathering their bodies and fingering their heads into crowns of suds, going after their armpits and even dropping their trousers and continuing the process. They laughed and assaulted each other with handfuls of lather like snowballs, and scrubbing each other's backs in that shipmate way that always works. The squall's great freshwater faucet was a sailor's joy for sure.

Merry as a Christmas mouse, Boyle shaved his muttonchops down to nothing, glad to be free of the insulation that had felt so good in the winter. As quickly as that, he caught a glimpse of the horizon line as the sky lightened and the rain thinned.

"Hurry, boys! She's waning!"

The crew threw up their arms to rinse themselves while they had the chance. Rivers of soap and whiskers and hair ran to the starboard scuppers and wept into the ocean. The hard rain decreased to a drizzle. Refreshed, the crew inhaled the crisp air and let out great sighs of happiness, except Dieter, who now ran about the ship sticking his head into the last drips from the booms.

"I'm not rinsed!" he cried.

The crew was, of course, sympathetic. Boyle laughed with them and said, "At least we'll have a good deck brush! Up-end him and we'll clean the scuppers!"

"I don't want to be a deck brush!" Dieter wailed and ran to catch drips from the stays'l leech.

"Sad, soapy John. Have a good thought that we'll get another weather cell this week! I'm taking wagers on the quarterdeck! Date and time!"

He caught Steven Sigsby by an arm as they boy tried to step

past.

"Take some of those buckets below and let the prisoners wash and shave."

"Aye, Tom," the skinny black-haired boy responded.

Boyle watched him collect other boys with a commanding manner but not being a tyrant, and start a bucket brigade. There wasn't much fresh water, but enough. Steven was a good young man, and had matured into a very good topman. A couple of years and he'd be a captain. The most telling characteristic was that the boy was happy with his position, whatever that may be at any given time, as the crew complement shifted and men came and went with prize ships. Steven had both gained and lost authority as things changed, and always accepted each new position amicably. If he was a topman, he did that without complaint. If he was in charge of the younger boys, he did that with a stern but not unkind hand, and did not look back at whomever might have taken the job he just had. Once he was an emergency cook. The food was questionable, but Steven kept a good spirit, so everyone pretended to like the fare, and of course like any ship's meal they ate it anyway. For Tom Boyle, tall and lanky Steven was in the "solves problems" list. The other list was "causes problems," something with which every captain dealt on any ship. Often many of the "causes problems" people were involved with dock work and provisioning, and he always enjoyed that moment of leaving them behind, but there was always the odd personality who had to be handled by Dieter or one of watch officers, who were the layer of protection between Boyle and the common daily troubles.

They had been prowling the mouth of the English Channel, getting familiar with the winds and currents. Two days ago they had run down a convoy of ten merchant vessels, then discovered a brig and a frigate guarding them. Knowing when the bite was too big to chew, *Chasseur* had turned close to the wind and handily escaped, leaving the square-riggers floundering while trying to chase the chaser upwind.

He had also primed his reputation by putting English prisoners off on a small sloop of little prize value and sending them back to England, relieving the *Chasseur* of added men to guard and feed, a logistical problem of privateering. Yesterday Boyle had seized a topsail schooner and a brig, just a few miles apart, but they too were too small to be prized. They got a shipment of wine for their trouble, then put a torch to the schooner, and later the brig experienced the same fate. Privateering off the enemy coast required a rethinking of tactics, now to include leaving burning hulks sending smoke signals high into English skies.

"Sail ho!" called Henry Bettys, now on lookout.

At Bettys's alert, Boyle and Dieter—well, pretty much every-body—scanned the slowly lightening horizon until they spotted sails in the lingering mist, moving on an easterly course.

"Glass," Boyle requested. One of the helmsmen reached into the main hatch to the protected little shelf where navigation equipment was kept out of the weather, and provided the of-ficers' spyglass.

Training the scope on the new sighting, Boyle said, "Brig ... another small one. Riding high. Let's run'r down, John."

"If she's riding high, somebody else probably already stopped her."

"Let's irritate them anyway. Give them a story to tell."

"Clear the decks!" Dieter called. "Sheet home the foretop! Hoist the main tops'l! Ready about!"

For a ship of her size, *Chasseur* was swift to answer, then stabilized without much bobbling back and forth at the bow. The intelligent fit of her rigging to her hull design was paying off, and the good helmsmanship, anticipating the swing of the bow and correcting early. The combination made movement efficient as water flowed smoothly under the hull.

The square foretops'l turned stiff in the wind again, while the crew hoisted the triangular gaff-topsail over the main. *Chasseur* rolled firmly on her side and gained speed. At this inopportune moment, four crewmen crawled carefully along the high side to the aft deck. It was Elijah Badger and his helm team.

"Change of watch," Badger reported.

Boyle did not even glance at them. "No change right now."

"No change, aye." And they about-faced.

Boyle leaned his legs on the decktop to keep balanced and watched Pedre and his helm assistants for a moment. He wished sometimes to take the helm, to let his mind go numb to anything but the compass points, and orders given by somebody else. To feel the ship rise and fall beneath, sense the coming of a new swell--helm was the most satisfying duty in the world.

"Here you go, Tom," fire-haired Steven Sigsby showed up from the main cabin with a fresh white shirt for the captain.

"Good man! Bring up the signal flags and run up 'heave to.'"

The wind was still stiff and the flags boiled madly on their halyard. High up at the main peak, the United States flag batted madly at the remaining droplets of rainwater shedding off the gaff. The flag was sassy, or was it just his own defiance? He liked the sass.

The prey ship turned away, bracing its square sails over as tightly as they would go, clearly recognizing the nature of an American ship in these waters, with this design. Reputation had preceded the *Chasseur*, though Boyle knew the credit was not all his. He was part of an active fleet of raiding American privateers out of several ports, though Fell's Point held the most infamous reputation for spitting out the dangerous and effective design with risk-loving captains and white-knuckled sailors for crews.

No reason not to be proud of himself, though, was it? Of his ship and crew.

And he was the first to hunt these waters. He knew, though, or hoped, others would follow him here, scatter predictability to the north wind and knock the Brits' personally in the teeth.

"Put the brig to l'ward," he said. "We'll steal her wind."

"L'ward, aye," Pedre responded with a reckless gleam in his eye.

Chasseur bore down in a lovely arch on the sixty-foot brig. The faces of the crew over there were clear to see now. They were ignoring the signal order to clew up and wait.

"Put one across her bow. Clew up the square. Ready on the fore brails."

The forward gunners were ready and adjusted the aim of one of the twelves. An enormous report pounded the atmosphere, blown forward of the brig in a column of rushing smoke. The ball streaked visibly forward of the brig and struck the water with a satisfying splash. At almost the same moment, *Chasseur* straightened up and came abeam of the other ship, like a big bird, and the brig's sails went limp and flapped pathetically. With *Chasseur* between her and the wind, the brig went gasping.

Boyle instinctively knew the momentary indecision had ended. The brig's sails fluttered up at the corners and the ship surrendered. Her little stern Union Jack was struck. Never a good moment for a ship.

"Brail the fore!" Dieter ordered from where he stood amidships at the fore sheets. "Back the stays'l."Wind spilled out of the sails, and the schooner's speed magically dropped away.

"Prepare to raft," Boyle commanded.

"Fenders, starboard!" Dieter called.

The ship's boys dropped woven rope fenders over the rail, measuring in their minds where the two ships would bump.As the conqueror, Boyle had the privilege of boarding the other ship rather than be boarded, unless he requested that, which he rarely did. Climbing onto another vessel when he had seized it was an ego-feeding moment and he might as well enjoy it. He dropped to the deck of the tidy cargo vessel, where the crew of five along with two passengers waited for him to decide their fates.

He introduced himself and made his usual boarding speech to the disheartened captain of the *Marquis of Cornwallis,* who irritably said, "You are too late, Mr. Boyle. Your comrades have stopped us no less than four times already, stripped us of our cargo and told me that my ship is not worth a prize crew."

"Not something a captain wants to hear, certainly," Boyle replied. "You have passengers?"

"Two. Their valuables have been spared by your cohorts."

"Understandably," Boyle said. "Most privateer captains choose not to rifle the possessions of private citizens."

"How noble."

Boyle smiled, not without sympathy. "Don't worry, Captain. You'll sail on. But this time you will have a reputation."

"What's that?"

"John!"

"Right here," Dieter called from *Chasseur*'s amidships deck.

"Bring our guests and transfer them."

The other captain watched, curious, as *Chasseur*'s prisoners from other ships paraded out of the hatch, blinked in the brightness even of this overcast day, and climbed over the two rails to the deck of the *Marquis of Cornwallis*. They were the captains and crews of the *Reindeer*, the *Favorite*, the *Prudence*—Boyle's captures of the past couple of days. Dieter followed them, carrying a rolled parcel wrapped in brown butcher paper and tied with sail twine.

Boyle accepted the rolled parcel from Dieter and addressed his prisoners as well as the other captain. "This brig is now officially a cartel vessel. You are all hereby paroled, free to return to your home country, on one condition. I required your words of honor that you, singularly or collectively, will travel immediately to London and that this document shall be affixed to the front door of the insurance underwriters' office Lloyd's Coffee House, in a pronounced manner for all to see."

"What is it?" the *Marquis*' captain demanded. "Does it involve becoming a traitor, because I won't do it."

"I know what it is," said the Scottish captain of the *Reindeer*. "I'll do it." An older man with arthritic hands and a full beard that did not hide his emotions, he all but snatched the parcel from Boyle's grip. "You're a brassy man, Captain Tom, and your schooner's a muckle minx. That said, you've been humane tae us and left us wi' our dignity. Your crew has been respectful. You therefore have m'word of honor as a fellow shipmaster and an Aberdeen gentleman that your message will be delivered swiftly and posted as 'e direct. This," the old man added, wagging the roll, "is the most vexatious dispatch in the history of seafaring. You may not enjoy the results. However, I must say, sir, you're a cheeky Caesar among us."

"Thank you."

"It's no' a compliment."

Boyle smiled and shrugged. "Fair weather to you."

"And to you."

"Captain," he added, nodding to the current master.

The *Marquis*' commander nodded in return. "Captain Boyle."

"Hands to rafting lines and fenders!" Dieter howled and followed Boyle back to *Chasseur*.

As Dieter orchestrated the crew, Boyle retired aft to let it all happen. He felt the surge as the sails filled and the ship heeled elegantly to larboard, and instinctively adjusted his balance, taking that athwartships stance that kept sailors on their feet.

He hardly thought about it, but today for some reason, he noticed the motion under him. Feeling the eyes, and the multiplex emotions of the people on the other ship watching *Chasseur* as she bore away from them, he looked down at his feet, braced apart there beneath him, and felt completely alone.

By tomorrow it would be done. For good or ill. But done.

On a starboard tack *Chasseur* slipped away from the other vessel, in no particular direction except to put distance between them, going where the wind went. The clouds thinned, allowing a haze of sunlight to penetrate as if shining through gauze. The gray water slowly hinted at turning blue, but even gray water had a metallic manliness about it that drew the eye as he stood gazing off the stern at the eternal scene.

Only as the *Marquis of Cornwallis* became nothing more than a handkerchief on the horizon did Boyle notice the unusual silence aboard his own ship.

He turned and looked forward. There were the silent faces of his hundred men, looking back at him.

Standing with the stiff white fores'l as his backdrop, John Dieter sharply raised both his tattooed arms and shouted. "Hail, Caesar!"

And the cheer rose from every throat.

"Hail, Caesar!" the crew answered.

As they laughed and cheered for him, Boyle hung his head and smiled. It wasn't easy to surprise him, but they had. He had no doubt, too, that the riotous cheering traveled across the open distance of water to the ears of the ship that carried his bizarre declaration.

He waved at them in gratitude, somewhat shyly, quite against his nature but genuine anyway, and hoped they wouldn't feel otherwise any time soon.

The Royal Exchange

LONDON, ENGLAND

"DO YOU THINK IT'S too late to take it down?"

"We gave our words of honor."

"You gave yours. God knows what demons have driven *me* here."

"You know what demon."

The two captains, of the *Reindeer* and the *Marquis of Cornwallis*, stood together across the excessively wide street from the Lloyd's of London insurance market in the massive Royal Exchange complex at Cornhill, the world-renowned center of British commerce chartered by Queen Elizabeth I. These, of course, were not the original premises of Lloyd's Coffee House, which had been an actual coffee house, though mostly a place where insurance brokers could do business regarding the maritime trade.

London was very different from the sea. The sea was quiet and lonely, changeable and dangerous. London was a vast, overbuilt, overcrowded, unsleeping city both ancient and modern, founded by the Romans who were still here in spirit and in form, their echo very much present in the vaulting arches and columns all around. Never mind that people called it "London town," this was the eternal definition of a metropolis, with breathtaking stone edifices like St. Paul's Cathedral just over there, and monuments like the Royal Exchange to ground all passersby in both past and future.

The captain of the *Reindeer* was enjoying himself. Being a Scot, he couldn't help but find enjoyment in their handiwork, the placement of Captain Boyle's cheeky proclamation on the door of Lloyd's. Certainly Boyle had chosen his target well. An insurance house. That would do it.

Beside the whiskery older man stood the captain of the ill-fated *Marquis of Cornwall*, who certainly had not expected this kind of notoriety to befall him. Together, harboring a maddening stew of emotions, they watched the crowd grow larger and larger around the document hanging from the single nail on Lloyd's. Men from inside Lloyd's, and even a few women, were beginning to slip out through that very door as word spread and they came to see the shocking announcement for themselves. No one tore it down. There was no point.

"Here come the press boys," the captain of *Marquis* said. A gaggle of somewhat younger men, many carrying notepaper and pencils, ran to the Lloyd's door and were already scribbling, trying to get close enough through the growing crowd to be able to read the notorious document. "That's the end of our chance to tear it to bits."

"I couldnae allow it," *Reindeer* reminded. "You know that." He chuckled then. "Cannae help but admire him. The man has a hundred sailors and one ship. He's an Agamemnon, that rascal, to conceive of this, never mind then to do it. With *one* ship!"

"Flirting with upheaval every day, the Yankees," the English captain said. "I had thought their reputation for caprice to be more or less folk legend."

The Scottish shipmaster chuckled again. "Well, if they're not legendary yet, they will be in a few minutes."

PROCLAMATION
issued by
THOMAS BOYLE, Esq.
COMMANDER of the CHASSEUR

WHEREAS It has become customary with the admirals of Great Britain, commanding small forces on the coast of the United States, particularly with Sir John Borlaise Warren and Sir Alexander Cochrane, to declare all the coast of the said

United States in a state of strict and rigorous blockade without possessing the power to justify such a declaration or stationing an adequate force to maintain said blockade; I do therefore, by virtue of the power and authority in me vested (possessing sufficient force), declare all the ports, harbors, bays, creeks, rivers, inlets, outlets, islands, and seacoast of the United Kingdom of Great Britain and Ireland in a state of strict and rigorous blockade. And I do further declare that I consider the force under my command adequate to maintain strictly, rigorously, and effectually the said blockade. And I do hereby require the respective officers, whether captains, commanders, or commanding officers, under my command, employed or to be employed, on the coasts of England, Ireland, and Scotland, to pay strict attention to the execution of this my proclamation. And I do hereby caution and forbid the ships and vessels of all and every nation in amity and peace with the United States from entering or attempting to enter, or from coming or attempting to come out of, any of the said ports, harbors, bays, creeks, rivers, inlets, outlets, islands, or seacoast under any pretense whatsoever. And that no person may plead ignorance of this, my proclamation, I have ordered the same to be made public in England. Given under my hand on board the Chasseur. THOMAS BOYLE By command of the commanding officer. J. J. STANBURY, Secretary.

Infested

THE CAPTAIN OF THE *Reindeer* drew up his horse-drawn cart in front of a dark fieldstone cottage set deeply within these rolling green Lowland hills, the lands of the ancient kings, with its old Roman roads cut into the landscape and its whispered memories of years counted in the thousands. His beard was wet from a passing rain, but like the old Scottish goat he was, he simply shook the droplets off and traveled on.

Giving the horse her good-girl pat on the shoulder, without which she would have followed him into the cabin, he left her to graze on the wildflowers and knocked the head of his cane on the door.

He was admitted by the captain of the *Marquis of Cornwallis*, whose trimmed English sideburns and curled mustache were so different from the free-roaming creature on *Reindeer*'s own face.

"Ah!" the Marquis exclaimed and snatched the other shipmaster by the arm to draw him inside. "I was afraid you didn't receive my note."

"Visiting my daughter in Linlithgow, bouncing her bairn on m'knee when your bosun tracked me down. What'n perdition's the crisis?"

"Have you been following the newspapers?"

"Not a bit." *Reindeer* sloughed off his coat and hung it on a kitchen chair, then took a seat where two rocking chairs were placed by the stone hearth. There was a fire going to offset the dampness, of which he was glad, and the heat felt good on his sore knees. "Is this the cottage of a friend?"

"It's my cottage. I fish."

"Oh, you fish."

"That's all right, isn't it?"

"Fine wi' me, aye."

"Whiskey?"

"Not before gloaming. What's all this about?"

"I've just returned from Glasgow," the English captain said. Holding some printed papers, he took the other rocker and sat forward on the edge of the seat. "There was an emergency gathering, if I may call it that, of ship owners and underwriters, as well as an army of Glaswegian merchants. They presented the Lord Provost with this and demanded it be presented to the king!"

He shook one of the papers.

"Cannae read it wid'out m'specs," *Reindeer* told him. "Read it to me, eh?"

"Why didn't you bring your spectacles?"

"Who expects to read in the countryside?"

Exasperated, *Marquis* straightened the paper and turned it so the firelight would help. "'Unanimously resolved that the number of American privateers with which our channels have been infested'—"

The elder man laughed. "Infested!"

"Listen!"

"Aye."

"—'the audacity with which they have approached our coasts, and the success with which their enterprise has been attended, have proved injurious to our commerce, humbling to our pride, and discreditable to the directors of the naval power of the British nation, whose flag till of late waved over every sea and triumphed over every rival. That there is a reason to—' No, never mind that part. Eh ... where is it? Oh— 'At a time when, in the plentitude of our power, we have declared the whole American coast under blockade, it is equally distressing and mortifying that our ships cannot with safety traverse our own channels, that insurance cannot be effected but at an excessive premium, and that a horde of American cruisers should be allowed, unheeded, unresisted, to take, burn or sink our own vessels in our own inlets, and almost in sight of our harbors. That the ports of the Clyde—'"

Again he was interrupted by the chortling of the older captain, who rocked happily and enjoyed the entertainment. "A horde ..."

"What's the matter with you?" *Marquis* demanded, apoplectic. "This is a petition that the Crown and the admiralty take action! Insurance rates have shot to the skies! The Admiralty is being pressured to recall ships from the American blockade to come back and guard our own ships in our waters! It's those American vipers! It's Boyle! We've lost fifty of our ships and more than one thousand crew this summer—in our own waters!"

"Yes ..."

"Are you drunk? You and I delivered his proclamation!"

"We did that, yes."

"We might as well have laid seventy-four guns to the Bank of England! What if someone saw us?"

The old man felt his eyes go wide. "*Saw* us? Who'd see us?"

"If it gets out that we're responsible, you and I could be shot as traitors!"

"For keeping our word of honor to another shipmaster? Neh."

"There's talk of torching that lawless den where these ships are built. Where Thomas Boyle's ship was built. That Fell's Peninsula!"

"Ah, yeh, worry not," *Reindeer* told him. "That place is so saturated with pubs, all they have to do is touch a whore's arse to it and it'll light. Read on."

Marquis blew out a funnel of breath on which his dram of whiskey traveled, and struggled for composure. "All right ... 'This meeting reluctantly feels it an imperious duty at once to address the throne, and therefore that a petition be forwarded to His Royal Highness the Prince Regent, acting in the name and on behalf of His Majesty, representing the above grievances and such measures to be adopted, as shall promptly and effectually protect the trade on the coasts of the kingdom, from the numerous insulting and destructive depredations of the enemy ...' I say, it's really not funny!"

"No," the Scottish captain agreed. "Not at all."

But he was laughing so hard that, outside, his horse answered.

Stragglers

GEORGETOWN
THURSDAY, SEPTEMBER 1

"IT'S YOUR BROTHER-IN-law, sir," Mildred announced after she had answered the frantic knock on the locked front door.

"Nicholson?" Frank Key asked, immediately thinking of Fort McHenry, where his wife's sister's husband was second-in-command.

"No, sir, the other one," the cook said. "Mr. West."

He was in his office in the house's wing, a comfortable and scholarly place of business, which the children were not allowed to invade, sitting in the green chair that had years ago accepted the shape of his personal rump in its leathered seat.

Now he missed his children ...

Key stood up abruptly at the appearance of Richard West, brother of Polly's other sister, a kind if bombastic man several inches shorter and much blonder than Key himself. West was in a dither, and wearing a cloak despite the summer heat, which was wet at the shoulders and hem. Rain.

"Richard!" Key exclaimed. "What's wrong?"

"Richard?" Polly appeared from the main hallway, confused at the sudden appearance of West. "What's happened? Is my sister all right?"

"She's anxious. As are we all."

"But Upper Marlboro's all right?"

"Yes, the British didn't burn us out, thanks largely to William Beanes. Which is why I'm here—Frank, I need your help. I need a lawyer."

"Oh? What've you done?" Half-joking, trying to assuage the grooves of concern in West's ruddy complexion, Key saw instantly that joviality would not work tonight.

"The Light Brigade was encamped not far from my house," West said. "When they arrived, William went out with a flag of truce and welcomed them, then dined the general—General Ross, Robert Ross—at Academy Hill. He invited them to make a headquarters of his mansion."

"Why would he do that?"

"Well, as he was known to be against the war anyway and as Upper Marlboro's most prominent citizen, he thought he could prevent the sacking of the town by putting up a conciliatory attitude. He even put on a Scottish accent and British'd up."

"Clever ..."

"It was, and they left the town intact. After they'd gone, William celebrated by inviting a gaggle of prominents to dinner on Saturday—his brother Bradley, Doctor Hill, and former-Governor Bowie, and a few others. During this dinner they got word that British stragglers were wandering through town, stealing food and horses from the farms. You know how Bowie is—veteran of the Revolution—"

"Oh, no," Key uttered, sensing what was coming.

West nodded. "Oh, yes! Off went William and the governor, marching around William's land, carrying a rifle! When they found a dragoon in the garden, eating the tomatoes, they seized custody of this man. It was a silly risk! The British had hardly left. Well, they got full of themselves and went out hunting for more stragglers and caught three or four and slapped a guard on them, but some others got away from them."

Key pressed his hand to his mouth and looked at his wife in horror.

West didn't stop. "The party ended and William and Sarah just went to bed, as if nothing had happened. Some of the stragglers found their way back to the main force and reported what William had done. You can imagine how the enemy reacted. They sent eighty-five cavalry men to capture him!"

"Eighty-five!" Polly clearly fought to keep her reaction down. She bit her lip as her face reddened and her eyes teared.

"That's how angry they were!" West erupted.

Key put a hand on West's arm. "Steady."

When he saw how he had upset his sister-in-law, West forced better self-control. "Sorry.

"Please go on," Key encouraged.

"They rousted William, Doctor Hill, and the boy right out of their beds. Those two were staying the night, sad for them. William was the main target. They dragged him out of his house, still in his nightshirt, strapped his hands, and slapped him on a barebacked horse, backward! With no britches! Bumping along on a horse's rump, barelegged!"

"Oh, God—" Key gasped, suddenly unable to catch his breath.

"An elderly man with weak knees!" West followed as Key tried to escape to the other side of the office. "They didn't even let him bring his spectacles! They rumbled him backward like that out of town and all the way to their fleet!"

"What's going to happen to him?" Polly asked.

"I went to Ross to plead for their release. I had a letter from the governor speaking of the 'great rudeness and indignity' with which William was bundled off, but Ross was possessed! Wouldn't even let me see him. Ross is ... he's bitterly insulted. Personally insulted. Furious!"

Though Key's throat was too tight for speaking, by now his mind was reeling with possibilities, angles of argument, points of order, legal machinations, and martial law.

"Ross allowed me to take Doctor Hill and the boy, but he was adamant to keep William in chains. He's being held in deplorable conditions aboard their flagship. They mean to put him on trial. If we can't free him before they leave our waters, he'll be sent to Halifax and dropped into a British prison. No one ever comes out of that pestilential hole, Frank. He won't survive."

West's steam seemed to abruptly play out. He moved from one foot to the other and back again.

"I've done all I can," he admitted. "I'm not tactful. And I don't have your influence in the government. I don't know what sanctions we need or anything. Frank, what do you think?"

The office fell suddenly silent, as if Key were here alone

again. He turned away, paced a few steps, paused, and fell into a motionless trance. Not even his brother-in-law dared break the soundless moment. They knew what was happening.

Slowly, he turned to face them. He felt as if something lost had been breathed back into his body.

"We need testimonials. If they want him on trial, then we need witnesses. Evidence. Mildred, my hat and cloak, please."

"But where do you think you're going?" Polly demanded.

Accepting his outerwear from Mildred, Key gestured toward the doorway. He gave his wife a little shrug and a wink.

"To be a lawyer," he said.

The Negotiator

THE HOME OF LUCY CUTTS
WASHINGTON, DC

FRANK KEY AND RICHARD West rode Key's two best saddle horses to F Street, with the smoldering air of the nation's burned federal buildings stinging their eyes and assaulting their nostrils. Key had been around the sacked city many times since the burning, but the sight of the sooty hulk of the president's skeletonized mansion never grew acceptable. He tried not to look, but the ghastly sight inevitably drew his gaze. The scale of the destruction crushed his heart every time.

The home of Lucy Cutts looked like a garrison camp, surrounded by American dragoons and militiamen determined to guard it against anyone who wished to do the president harm. Shamefully, after the humiliation of Bladensburg and the burning of the capitol, many of those vengeful persons were Americans themselves. With the formal mansion destroyed, nothing more than blackened walls, this was the new official residence, this house belonging to Dolley Madison's sister.

Key was waved through the guards, and two of them stood quickly to hold the reins of the horses.

"Stay here, Richard," he said to his brother-in-law.

"Gladly!" West exclaimed, and went with the horses.

Escorted by a militiaman, Key went wordlessly into the private home. Inside, he heard women talking in another room and deliberately did not follow the sound with either his ears or eyes. If Mrs. Madison were there, he did not wish to disturb her. The tale of her harrowing escape from the presidential mansion—just before General Ross entered, ate the dinner prepared for the president and her, then set fire to her home—turned his stomach. He had seen President Madison on the battlefield at Bladensburg and been amazed—a sitting president right there in battle—but now he knew to be glad of it, for otherwise the president might have been at his home here in Washington and might have been captured.

He shook the weight of that avoided tragedy from his shoulders and followed the militiaman through the house to a smoky retreat clearly occupied most often by men.

There, picking through a stack of papers and sitting on the edge of a desk loaded with newspapers both foreign and domestic, the slightly built President James Madison almost seemed like a child sitting on his father's desk. His emblematic black coat, white broom of hair, black shoes, and white stockings made this most scholarly and quick-minded gentleman look rather like a puppet seated on a shelf.

The president was alone, making Key sensitive to disturbing him. How often, in a time of war, could a president find a moment to be alone?

"Mr. President," the militiaman announced. "Mr. Key of Georgetown."

Madison's sharp eyes flipped from the papers in his hand to the visitor. "What a surprise," he said, and slipped down from his perch. "Pleasant to see you, Frank. Is it raining?"

"Hello, sir." Key extended his hand. "Sprinkling a bit."

The president shook the hand and closed the room's door after the militiaman left. "Do you have time for tea and sandwiches?"

"Actually, I must decline this time," Key began. "I need your help."

"Certainly. What about?"

"I'm going on an adventure, Jemmy. I'm going behind enemy lines."

—◊—

When Key left the Cutts residence, he was no longer in the company of his distraught brother-in-law, who was too close a friend to William Beanes to keep composure in negotiations. Now he was accompanied by the blessing of the American government from Madison himself, and a steady presence in the form of an American prisoner-of-war agent. John Stuart Skinner rode beside him, assigned by the president to accompany Key into the crucible of the enemy. Skinner seemed young and rash to Key, at first, only twenty-six years old with a puff of wavy black hair and shaded dark eyes, and was rather restless, a surprising characteristic for a negotiator. He had carefully sown amicable relations with the British, which he clearly did not want ruffled by the whims of a Georgetown civilian. Key knew the other man was doubtful of this mission's success. Skinner was not encouraging about Ross or Cockburn's giving way in a matter of honor. Key was doubtful himself, but other than Skinner there was no one more attuned to communing with the British, which Skinner had been doing for years as inspector of mail incoming from Europe and as an agent for prisoners of this war.

The two men chatted as young men do, but neither delved deeply into making plans for their mission. Almost as if they were simply travelers on a tour, they discussed ridiculous things—agriculture, music, satire, their law educations in Annapolis, differences in the law between Key's thirty-five years of age and Skinner's twenty-six.

Skinner let Key set the agenda, which helped get things done quickly, so quickly that Key nearly forgot in the whirlwind that he was on his way to meet face to face with the enemy—not just *the enemy,* but the highest commanders of the assault on the United States. How had this happened? How had he gone from a mediocre militia volunteer to an ambassador very nearly to the throne room itself? Even arguing before the Supreme Court had not been so shriveling. His innards twisted up and stayed that way. No less than William Beanes' very life was in his hands. If he failed, there would be no appeal. The revered surgeon would spend his last days languishing in a stone cell.

Prisoners

CHESAPEAKE BAY
MONDAY, SEPTEMBER 7

CHESAPEAKE BAY WAS THE way to the open ocean from the active harbor and ports of Baltimore and Washington. A wide and pleasant waterway, the river welcomed many fishing and boating enthusiasts in normal times. Banked by rich woodlands, the river was picturesque, yet also one of the most traveled catalysts of commerce in the world. Or at least it had been, before.

Frank Key was aware of the significance of this particular waterway as the packet sloop secured by John Skinner moved past Annapolis. This was not an American waterway today. It was in the charge of the king of England, blockaded and occupied by His Majesty's ships of war. He felt his knees quake a little as the packet bobbed under him and he tried to stay on his feet. Soon, though, he was forced to take an uncomfortable seat on a low-slung deckhouse, while Skinner had no trouble at all riding the rocking horse.

The closer they drew to the British armada, the more Skinner talked.

"We'll be appealing directly to General Ross, if he's there," the agent said. "I don't know him, so I won't recognize him to introduce you. We'll probably be presented to Admiral Cochrane.

Now, that's Alexander *Cochrane*, the supreme designer of the British military action on this continent. It's not Admiral George *Cockburn*. They are two different men. You must keep track of that, because they may both be present."

"Everyone on the coast knows about Cockburn," Key acknowledged. "The man with the torch. The '-burn' in his name is well fitted."

"Yes, that's him," Skinner said. "And be sure to pronounce his name *Co-burn*, and not *Cock*-burn. He'll throw us overboard if we say *Cock*-burn."

"Oh ..."

"I hope your famous silver tongue is well polished. This will be no courtroom."

At the mouth of the Potomac, he spotted the sails of the English flagship, and two hours later that British vessel was anchored and sending down a rope ladder for Key and Skinner. Key looked up from the rowboat they had sent for him, utterly intimidated by the tall black countenance of the ship-of-the-line, with its dooming gun-ports up and down the whole side. Skinner was up in three seconds, carrying the leather satchel with their papers inside. Key took somewhat longer, even with nothing to carry, his own weight pinning the rope-and-plank contraption to a concave posture fitting the side of the enormous ship. The planks didn't fit his shoes, forcing him to climb in an awkward side-on manner, and the prickly hemp rope made his hands raw. Rope ladders were the most unwelcoming devices ever invented.

Fortunately, two seamen were there to pluck him from his torment and roll him onto his feet on the ship's deck. Unlike the lightly rigged American schooners and packets, this ship was a puzzle of ropes, miles of it, webbed upward, across, diagonally, coiled and hanging from pins, running to and from huge wooden blocks up to wide yards holding bundles of sail canvas that looked nothing like the elegant square sails they were when working. Impossible to interpret, the rigging itself was intimidating. Add to that the huge guns sitting heavily on their trucks, waiting.

"Welcome back aboard the *Tonnant*, Mr. Skinner," a chubby midshipman said as he met them, in a crisp English accent with

impeccable enunciation, but a pronounced lisp he was working
to mitigate. "You and your companion are invited to take repast
with our officers. If you will follow me, and do take care where
you step."

"Thank you, Mr. Pelham," Skinner responded mechanically.
"Lead on."

Into the dark guts of the warship they climbed, and were led
toward the back of the ship where the officers lived, as foreign a
place as Key had ever imagined, and frightening in many char-
acteristics. The heavy scent of oil and hemp, of gunpowder and
fresh-sawn wood, told of the ship's recent battles and even of
her daily life. Everything around him spoke of assault, violence,
and martial purpose—to conquer. The dim surroundings were
lit only by light from portholes or open gun ports, or from glass
prisms ingeniously set in the deck to bring the light of day below. The populous English crewmen were everywhere, but, like
rats, managed to remain in the background, as if in a painting.

How disturbing to think that poor Beanes was imprisoned
somewhere in the dark decks even farther below. Key went cold
at the thought and tried to retain his presence of purpose.

In a cabin clearly for officers only, lit by a hanging lantern
and a bank of windows that made up the very back of the ship,
certainly the only glazed windows aboard. There was a table set
with pewter plates and cups, and laid out with a meal much more
sumptuous than men of the sea must normally have, even officers. Key knew he was looking at food plundered from burned
towns and ravaged farms, the primary means of provisioning
employed by the British during their occupation.

At the head of the table was a strong-jawed commanding
officer in his fifties, with hair graying just on the sides, holding
a nautical chart. Was this—

"Admiral Alexander Cochrane, allow me to present Mr. Francis Scott Key, emissary of the President of the United States."

Skinner motioned to Key, but did not make any gestures toward the admiral.

Key made a small bow. "Admiral."

"Mr. Key, welcome aboard the HMS *Tonnant*." The admiral
had a very soft voice, slightly high, offset by a firm sense of his
own authority. He nodded toward a younger commanding of-

ficer at the table, a man probably in his forties. "Please be presented to Rear Admiral Edward Codrington, in command of the Fleet."

Codrington, Cochrane, Cockburn—*Co-burn* ... Key felt himself start to sweat under his jacket.

"Please do be seated," Admiral Cochrane invited. "Midshipman, let's have some wine for these gentlemen."

Unsure of what to say or when to bring up the subject of Beanes, Key and Skinner simply took seats at the table, Skinner to Cochrane's right and Key beside Codrington. Surprisingly, the subject of an impending attack on Baltimore was not evaded as their meal was served, but was treated as if it were just an exercise of rhetoric. The Admiral and Codrington openly talked about a land assault at North Point, which would take the British troops overland to Baltimore, while ships of war made a simultaneous bombardment and invasion by water. They theorized about men and artillery, infantry movements, various targets from Chesapeake Bay to New Orleans. Wasn't it indiscreet to discuss the conquest of the nation right in front of that nation's emissaries? Key supposed such discussions were so natural to them, and they were so self-confident, that perhaps they were proud of their plans. They were courteous enough to refrain from asking the Americans what they thought or knew about Baltimore's defenses, luckily.

Perhaps they didn't need any information from their guests. They seemed to know quite a lot already—the lay of the land, the shape of the fork in the Patapso, and the two bodies of water formed by that fork. They spoke openly of their eight bomb ships with powerful thirteen-inch mortars, whose explosive shells could be flung from two miles out, and of hollow shells packed with the incendiary ingredients of powder, salt petre, pitch, and sulfur. They could set fire to Baltimore from a distance.

The macabre conversation was so interesting that when another officer entered, wearing a fairly plain uniform, nobody gave him much attention.

The handsome cinnamon-haired newcomer, carrying himself with a naturally graceful bearing, sat next to Key, greeted him only with a nod and accepted wine from the steward. Key looked at Skinner, but the agent paid no attention to the quiet officer, so Key gave him not a second thought. He would have to get accustomed to this, seeing British officers and sailors of war all around him, and knowing it was their obligation to destroy his nation, his home, and perhaps his life. He would be respectful, but there was a fine line to be crossed into fawning, which he knew must be avoided. Somehow he would have to be polite without being obsequious. They must see him in a certain respectful light if he were to be successful when his one chance came.

"I've found these eastern tracts to be quite similar to our midlands," Admiral Cochrane was going on, finishing a sentence Key hadn't heard as his mind wandered. "Before I came here, I was rather expecting deserts and jungles. Of course, your humidity here is brutal. I don't know how you breathe."

"It can be a struggle," Skinner said. "Of course, with exposure, it's possible to become acclimated. They say that in the South, natives hardly sweat at all."

"I can't imagine. Not quite as soggy here as Ireland, though. What do you think, Ross?"

Skinner snapped around like a weathervane and almost broke his neck. He gaped at the silent officer sitting next to Key.

Key took a few seconds longer to realize what had just been said.

Ross!

"I think," Ross began, trying to swallow, "that I'm too hungry to have an opinion."

His accent was clearly Irish, but not the guttural mumble of the lower class. This was a man who had always been privileged, supremely educated, and understood his obligations as an aristocrat. His reputation preceded him. Key knew he sat beside one of the most purely courageous military leaders of the age, a man not only willing but eager to lead his soldiers from the front of the brigade, who had many times proven his gallantry, so much so that even the American commanders admired him.

"Pardon me," Admiral Cochrane said. "I've been neglectful. Major General Robert Ross, please welcome Mr. John Skinner, prisoner exchange agent, and Mr. Scott Key, a barrister from— I'm sorry, where was it?"

"Georgetown," Key rasped.

"There you are."

"Exchanging prisoners?" Ross began. "Which ones?"

"One of yours," the Admiral told him.

His heavily shadowed eyes wide, Skinner now stared at Key and made a small nod.

Steeling himself as he did in those first few moments before standing to make his case in a courtroom, Key was careful not to clear his throat. He simply turned in his seat and placed his hands in his lap.

"Dr. William Beanes."

Ross made a sour growl, then opened his collar and pressed a folded cloth to what appeared to be a neck wound from some previous encounter. "Beanes! I've already dealt with this. Upon my arrival in Upper Marlboro, Dr. Beanes surrendered to me. He himself carried a white banner! By surrendering, he gave his pledge that he would not raise arms against us. He then went about an elaborate ruse of entertaining us, which I have since concluded was drummed up to stall our attack upon our next targets. And you think you can pacify me?"

"You released the other two prisoners to Richard West when he made his appeal."

"The other man had not made a pretense of surrendering. The boy carried no weapon. After his declaration of neutrality, Beanes betrayed his word and behaved in a hostile manner. The case against him is sealed. He is clearly Scottish by name and by his manner of speech, and as a citizen of Britain he owes fealty to the Crown."

Careful not to speak at this, to bring more attention to the fact that Beanes had been faking the Scottish identity and was in fact a third-generation American, Key let the detail pass, unable to calculate that the truth would help at all.

"This is a point of honor," Ross abruptly added.

Key remained silent, a skill of timing learned in the courtroom. Across the table, Skinner plainly wanted to say something and was watching him, egging him on with a glare. The agent received no satisfaction.

Ross picked up his wine, then instantly put it down again without drinking. "He betrayed my trust. It is an insult. A personal one."

Now that Ross had vented his anger, Key coolly began. "Dr. Beanes is a cherished friend of mine. He retains my friendship by his most constant devotion and purity of character. I have come not to make a legal appeal, but a moral one."

"Are you serious?"

Holding his hands still in his lap, Key raised one hand without lifting his arm, in a gesture that was, for him, almost wild. Pliantly he asked, "Would you compare the caprice of an elderly doctor to the rigorous scrutiny of martial obligation? Rather than conceiving of any deliberate insult, can we not agree that whimsy was more at work? That poor judgment and bad timing are often misinterpreted?"

Ross narrowed his eyes, but said nothing.

"Is it possible," Key went on, "that Dr. Beanes, lubricated by a good bottle, was simply overcome with bravado in front of his guests? This man is a surgeon, not a soldier. He is the quintessence of a non-combatant. His is a hand of healing, General. His talents show themselves in the aftermath of battle, not before, at a time when enmity is set aside and kindness rules if we are to remain above the savage. If we remove men of the gentle arts, like William Beanes, from the panorama of our disputes, all that remains is brutality."

With a tucked chin, Ross scowled. "I think you are not in a court, but on a pulpit, Mr. Key."

"It is a failing of mine. Please, let me present my evidence."

He reached for the leather satchel Skinner held on his lap, drew from it several papers of varying sizes, and directly handed them to Ross. "These letters are from British prisoners of war left wounded on the battlefield at Bladensburg. As we speak they are resting in field hospitals. They write of the gentle, dignified treatment, indeed lifesaving treatment, dispensed to them by Americans, and one American surgeon in particular. William Beanes."

Calculating the general's expression as he read the letters, Key had a theatrical sense of when to go silent and let other factors speak. At the head of the table, Admiral Cochrane was once again scanning the nautical chart that he had put aside before the meal, pointing something out to Codrington. Across the table, Skinner didn't look as if he were breathing at all.

Robert Ross flipped through the letters, then read two of them over again.

Key and Skinner waited.

The famous leader took his time reading. He then read over the letter from the fallen soldier yet again. At the table there was nothing but tension, except for Admiral Cochrane's taking a loud slurp of his wine.

Ross dug a little bit of dinner from between his teeth.

"The doctor deserves much more severe punishment than he has received," the general finally said. "Your representations of his character are strong, Mr. Key. I am bound to return kindnesses shown to our wounded." Dropping the letters on the table in front of Key, Ross bluntly told him, "On that premise, I shall parole him."

Skinner started breathing.

Holding back his shock, Key quietly said, "You're a man of integrity in a time of chaos, General."

"Integrity, integrity. That's the whole thing, isn't it?" The general's chair rasped as he stood up. "If you'll pardon me."

Had that happened?

Key was afraid to move as the irritated Ross exited the cabin. Key couldn't clap or even smile, shake hands with Skinner or in any way betray his composure. Years of courtroom practice served him now. Judges didn't care for gloating. Neither did admirals.

"Mr. Key," Admiral Cochrane began again, "you're a barrister, yes?"

"I am."

"In Baltimore?"

"Yes, sometimes."

"Do you happen to know anyone at this little Fort McHenry?"

Key paused, but could not divine any reason to keep secrets about that. "My brother-in-law is second-in-command."

"He is married to your sister?"

"One of my wife's sisters."

"Most opportune."

"I'm sorry?"

"Would you be considered, do you think, as an intermediary?"

"In what capacity?"

"To negotiate the fort's surrender. When the time comes, of course. Unless, of course, you'd like to do it early, before lives are lost."

Was this confidence or temerity?

Key fell back into his courtroom conditioning and thought he did a respectable job of not disclosing his true reaction. "I shall pray for divine guidance on the subject," he answered.

He was gratified when Skinner spoke up and rescued him from the moment. "I shall be honored to negotiate terms for an exchange of British prisoners for Dr. Beanes and—"

"No need for negotiation, Mr. Skinner," Admiral Cochrane spoke up. "There's nothing to negotiate."

Skinner blinked. "I'm sorry?"

"You and your party are not leaving. You can't stay aboard here, as the *Tonnant* will be active with many officers and such a presence would be indiscreet. You'll be put aboard the frigate *Surprise*, commanded by my son, Sir Thomas Cochrane, along with the crew of your truce vessel, which will be taken under tow. Under a guard of Royal Marines, you will be detained indefinitely."

"Admiral, I protest this," Skinner said, more loudly that he would've approved if Key had said it. "What is the precedent for detaining us?"

"You cannot expect us to free you in advance of our movement. The squadron is on its way to rendezvous with us. You've heard us discuss our land assault from North Point and the armaments of our ships. And Mr. Key's services may become helpful as events play out. It's time to put an end to the ant-like shipbuilding that goes on here. You and your party will remain with us while we put the torch to Baltimore. I'm sure you will come to appreciate your vantage point. It should be quite a show."

The Biggest Gamble

CHASSEUR

THE WEATHER DECK WAS crowded. Usually Tom Boyle and John Dieter wouldn't be awake at the same time, but neither wanted to miss the weekly wrestling match. A hundred men crowded the deck, laughing and shouting, betting and calling each other wicked.

Chasseur crashed along on a larboard tack, beating into in an east-northeast wind. She was easy on the roll, but not easy to handle. Dangerous as any low-railed privateer, with an enormous thunderhead of canvas towering over her, she rode the waves like a dolphin heedless of a rider.

"Sail!" Pierre Massu called from the bow where he was on lookout. "Forward of the larboard beam."

Letting the men go on with their wrestling match, Boyle pulled his spyglass from his belt and sighted down the new quarry.

Twisted into a leggy knot with John Thompson, the bosun, Dieter croaked, "What is it?"

"Schooner ... running ... pretty. I wonder why they're not wing-and-wing."

Pretty, but awkward for the other ship. Both ships as they approached each other were sailing in their respective worst courses for their rigs, with now-square-rigged *Chasseur* trying to beat into the wind and the schooner running from it.

Thompson took the opportunity of Dieter's distraction to break the mate's grip, get a knee under them, flip both their bodies completely over, and pin Dieter's head to the deck with a meaty forearm. Instantly the match was over. Half the crew cheered, the other half hooted the loss of their bets, and money began to fly back and forth with varying degrees of joy or annoyance. Third mate Paul Mooran held them apart while he tallied the bets. He was today's arbiter-in-chief.

Gasping for air, Dieter got to his feet and joined Boyle.

"The least you could've done was break his arm, you insect," Boyle complained.

"I sacrificed for the sake of my ship."

"Nobody likes you."

"Can't break our bosun's arm. What've you got there?"

"You cost me two hundred and ten pennies." Training the spyglass on the new sighting, Boyle worked to keep the target in sight while braced on the *Chasseur*'s bobbing deck. "Pilot schooner ... are the guns ready?"

"Gun crews, ready and stand by," Dieter called, not loudly since most of them were right here.

The crew wandered to their posts, so accustomed to this that they continued their banter and demands for a rematch.

"Should we load?" Gunner Edward Vernard asked.

"Load, but don't run out," Boyle answered. "I don't see a banner. No national colors. Let's close within long-run range. Hoist 'stop and wait for my orders.' Turn and head her off. Ready about."

"Ready about!" Dieter repeated.

As the signal flags skittered up their halyard, *Chasseur* quickly became a machine of a million parts, each cog working in coordination with all others, though it had taken a couple of weeks to get the crew at ease with the square rig. Most were sailors already and took to changes with the sixth sense of those raised at sea from boyhood, and Boyle's unremitting drilling had cemented their skills. Every movement of rig, tiller, and crew was well rehearsed over many aggressive conquests and several good runs for their lives. Many captures ago, Boyle and Dieter reached that magic moment at which they hardly had to deal with minute details of trimming in or slacking the sheets, of ad-

justing the topping lifts or fine-tuning the tiller heading, back-
ing the heads'ls or bracing the square tops'ls, as the crew had
become so familiar with *Chasseur*'s quirks and movements that
they were almost a part of her. The commanding officers had
only to give the helm a few little commands, and the changes
would be sensed by the sail-handlers, who would keenly adjust
the trim. They had grown a depth of confidence in themselves
and an intimacy with this madcap sea-monster beneath them.

The bow bobbed and swung around, the bowsprit drawing
circles on the sky. The sails pivoted, the wind struck and filled
them, and the ship leaned on her larboard shoulder, losing re-
markably little speed during the maneuver. *Chasseur* stretched
out on a beam reach. Her sharp hull cut through the flickering
water.

Their hair was blowing and they held on to the shrouds or
gun trucks or each other, and drove down on the schooner.

"He's not turning away," Deiter noticed, watching the other
ship. "Oh—there he goes."

As the other ship turned to her starboard, cooperating with
the signal flag order, the two vessels ran broadsides to each
other and the expanse of water between them shortened. Boyle
no longer needed the scope. "Fore-and-aft rigged ... fore square
tops'ls ... gray privateer hull with gunports. I recognize that ship,
don't I? ... That's ... isn't that the *Atlas*? Privateer out of Philadelphia?"

"Didn't *Atlas* get captured?"

"Did she?"

"Maybe I'm wrong."

"If the Brits got her, she wouldn't still be rigged that way.
They'd have messed her up. That's an American rig."

"Maybe somebody's using her as a packet. Can you count
the crew?"

Boyle used the scope again. "Emm ... one ... two, three ...
looks like maybe six on deck ... a man in the tops ... captain's aft
wearing a straw hat."

"Clothing?"

"Ordinary work clothes ... I like that hat. Run out two
twelves."

"Two twelves, aye."

"Fire a warning shot."

"Starboard battery, one warning shot!"

"Warning shot, aye," came Ed Vernard's response. He aimed the starboard gun that was already run out.

The starboard forward gun made a throaty *poom*, loaded not with a ball but with powder and wad, which reduced the sound but put the message across.

"Better to starboard. Prepare to close on her. Run up our colors."

The crew fell silent, anticipating another capture, letting the captain's orders be heard clearly. On the flag halyard running down from the spanker peak, the American flag climbed and unfurled itself behind them.

The unknown schooner turned more to its own starboard, slightly away as *Chasseur* closed the distance between them. Boyle met the eyes of Steven Sigsby and made a hand signal with his hands equally apart.

Chasseur changed course to keep parallel with the schooner and a boat-length behind. At every plunge of the bows a huge spray of foam rose in the shape of gulls' wings to erupt over the decks, drenching the men and rushing aft to the scuppers. The two ships pounded along in a duet of industrial pageantry with such flourish that Boyle, even after his entire life at sea, wished he could capture and save the moment, relive it a thousand times, show it to his children.

Dieter took the scope from Boyle and fixed it on the stern of the other ship. "Says ... *St. Lawrence*. Is that the name of the ship or her home port?"

"The *St. Lawrence* ..." Boyle tasted. "Never heard of it."

"Out of the Carolinas, maybe?"

"Trice the courses. Take some speed off this vixen before we overtake her."

"Trice the courses!" Dieter ordered, and the sail handlers called the order back.

Chasseur slowed as she came up on the schooner's larboard beam at cannon range. The expanse of water between them glittered a silvery blue, and there were dolphins jumping in child-like delight. They loved the company of ships, loved to run before them and teach their offspring to ride the bow waves. For a moment he let his mind drift, consumed by the spectacle of watching a gaff-rigged privateer sailing. Surely it was the most beautiful sight under heaven. Trimmed on a reach now, the *St. Lawrence*'s sails move like wings of a butterfly. He rarely got a look at his own ship from the water, and never underway. This was a treat.

A banner fluttered up a flag halyard leading from the main peak of the other ship. At first Boyle saw a muddled flash of blue and white. He waited for the red stripes and the blue star field. Instead, what unfolded and whipped before him was red, white, and blue in completely the wrong order. It flew from the ensign halyard of that other ship and slapped him in the face.

Dieter roared, "Union Jack! God damn it!"

Before Boyle could respond, flanks of red-jacketed Royal Marines popped up from behind the bulwarks of the *St. Lawrence* and drew rifles to their shoulders.

"Get down!" he cried and plunged for the deck.

Almost as one being his crew ducked. The eruption of enemy fire blew over their heads, engulfing *Chasseur* in rifle smoke. Only the few yards between the two ships prevented the volley from being devastating.

There was blood on the deck under Boyle's feet now. Someone was injured here, probably more than one. He followed the stream of blood and saw an unrecognizable corpse lying on the deck with its arms and face blown to gore. He had no idea who that was.

On the *St. Lawrence*, the captain threw his straw hat down and shed his jacket, revealing a blue-and-cream Royal Navy uniform. The gun ports opened and suddenly a half-dozen guns showed their maws at the *Chasseur*.

"Fire!" the other captain shrieked.

St. Lawrence's guns tore into *Chasseur*'s side, pummeling the chain-wales. Two of the fore shrouds snapped, and the main sheet, far back on the stern, was cut to pieces. The mast wobbled. *Chasseur* rocked bodily sideways and faltered as if she were stumbling down stairs.

Swinging free, the huge main boom swept across the deck as the ship rocked sideways.

"Heads down!" Thomas Coward shouted, just in time. Getting hit in the head by an uprooted tree could do as much damage as a cannon. "Get a preventer on that!"

He and three others raced to regain control over the boom.

"Chan'els are smashed!" Mooran yelled.

"Thank you," Boyle acknowledged.

"Reload!" the English captain shouted to his gun battery. His men were dangerously quick at it. Then he turned to his helm officers and made a hand signal.

"We should run!" Isaac Webb called to Boyle.

Boyle was uncharacteristically silent. Isaac was right.

"Tom!" Dieter demanded, stomping an imaginary foot.

That was all it took. Boyle had spent enough time to know that tone from a chief mate. Shaken from his astonishment, he made the biggest gamble of his life.

"Fight!" he answered.

"Fight, aye!" Dieter bellowed. "Battle-stations!"

A charge of energy ran through the shock-stricken crew. They were glad of it. Some shouted their energetic approval, and they changed from raiders to defenders of their nation.

Along the starboard length of *Chasseur*, gun ports scraped open. The tilted deck rattled as the men put their shoulders to the trucks and ran the guns out.

The other ship twisted sharply and came toward them, as if she meant to ram Boyle's ship. *Chasseur* shot past the schooner's bow. Instantly Boyle saw the new danger—the other captain was trained in war maneuvers and knew what he was doing. Ramming wasn't the plan.

Vernard warned, "Rake!"

St. Lawrence was moving in behind *Chasseur*, to a position from which she could slaughter whole flanks of *Chasseur*'s men by firing balls down the length of the deck—a devastating maneuver of war that terrified Boyle just to think of it, and here it was about to happen. If they succeeded, the damage would be irremediable.

"Helm up!" Boyle shouted. Desperately seeking eye contact with the two boys at the helm, he made a wild circle with his right arm and pointed to their larboard.

Wide-eyed, Sigsby and Low cast off the lazy tackle and leaned on the working one. Given the circumstances the boys moved with remarkable speed, faster than the sail handlers could possibly respond. *St. Lawrence* was crossing behind them, about to cross the T, with her starboard broadside positioned to rake Chasseur's deck. If she succeeded, the boys at the helm would be the first to die. Deadly fire would rush from the stern forward.

Chasseur began to turn upward into the wind. Would she be quick enough?

With a violent jump to her left, *Chasseur* dug her keel into the water and reared like a stallion. Her stern pressed downward and plumbed for the bottom. Into cold foam the amidships rail disappeared. Men stumbled and crashed into the bulwarks. Overton Addison almost went overboard, but caught himself on a kevel cleat. He hung there upside down with his legs in the sea. Boyle himself staggered headfirst into the mainmast pins. When he came up, his head was bloody. He felt the pounding of his heart in his ears.

Chasseur leaned hard and surged forward, her square sails catching the wind. Again the other ship was forced to run with the wind behind her, something the British crew managed poorly. They didn't understand schooners. Boyle called to Sigsby and Low. "Don't collide!"

Dieter shouted orders to the sail handlers to brace around and trim. The squares wheeled against the sky, fluttering madly. *Chasseur* lost its grip on the water and bobbled. Suddenly the two ships were broadside to broadside again, but they had switched sides. The gunners and men with small arms rushed from the starboard rail to the larboard rail, tripping over each other and spilling the coiled halyards all over the deck. Without being coached, the gun crews ran out the larboard twelves.

With *Chasseur*'s square rig suddenly her advantage, Boyle shouted, "Back the heads'ls!"

Deprived of their chance to rake *Chasseur*'s decks, *St. Lawrence* could do nothing as Boyle's ship dropped speed and kept side by side. Lacking the Americans' experience, the Englishmen had no idea how to regulate the speed of their captured schooner.

Boyle spun to the gun crews. "Tear the rigging apart! Forward guns, fore mast! Midship guns, main mast! Fire at will! Small arms, fire at will!"

Though the commands seemed general, he counted on his men. They knew how a schooner worked and how to disable one. Take out the sheet blocks, and the sails were useless. Punch holes in the heads'ls, put balls through the stays, crack the booms, destroy the bowsprit, shatter the deadeyes.

The other ship, though, was filled not with merchant sailors, but with trained seamen of the Royal Navy and armed Royal Marines. Those men had to be targeted, and that was the job of the small-arms men on *Chasseur*.

The twelve-pounder guns growled. Smoke and the stink of black powder suffocated the crew. Boyle jumped onto the main rail and strained to see. The smoke twisted away, revealing *St. Lawrence*. The single thunderstroke had demolished its rigging and pulverized the sails.

"Reload!" Dieter called angrily. He was red-faced with fury that they had been caught unprepared. Whether he was angry at his own crew or the other ship's crew for fooling them, Boyle couldn't tell.

They heard the cry, "Fire!" from the smoke-shrouded enemy. The bark of the British long guns carried the Royal Navy's mark of excellence and generations of practice. Men fell in torment from the brutal hammering. *Chasseur* rocked bodily.

"Fire!" Dieter shouted. His voice was reassuring—Boyle thought he had lost his mate to that blast.

All but one of the larboard guns were ready and blew their volcanic guts at almost the same time with ruinous accuracy. A God-shocking *whomp* rocked both ships. It was like being caught inside a flexing muscle.

The gray side of *St. Lawrence* exploded in three places. Flying wood took the bottom of the fores'l away. Severed lines danced in the air. British sailors and Marines flew backward from the concussion, dismembered by hot iron balls and fragments of the rail and bulwarks. Above the howling wounded, the tattered fores'l waved wildly, completely out of control. Blood spilled from the scuppers, draining down the outer hull in red stripes.

Above their heads a deep-throated cracking noise drew many terrified eyes. Boyle peered upward. The main topmast of *St. Lawrence* leaned far over, cracked at the doubling like a big fractured bone, and threatened to fall, held up now only by the stay, which wouldn't hold for long.

"Small arms, fire!" Paul Mooran's words were swallowed by the popping of discharging muskets, rifles, and pistols. Narrow funnels of gray smoke blew across the water to the other ship. On the schooner, a dozen red-jacketed Royal Marines crumpled.

A new volley blew toward them from the stumpy, powerful carronades along the length of the *St. Lawrence*. The coordinated hammering engulfed *Chasseur* in black clouds, pulverizing the ship's side. Wooden thorns, moving at the speed of bullets, tore into flesh. In the choking smoke, Boyle felt his body fold and fly backward and slam into the back of a starboard gun truck. When he felt for the decktop and crawled to his feet, his shirt was bloody across the chest and his left arm. Had somebody been bleeding on him?

Hoping the boys were still at the helm, he shouted, "Lay alongside!"

The ship wobbled beneath him.

Blinded by a veil of smoke, he called, "That's not your course! Boys!"

If they were dead—

As the following wind puffed the smoke away and his stinging eyes cleared, he realized that he was on his hands and knees, staring down at bloodied deck planks. The grain of the wood was etched in red, making a strange and distracting pattern.

No ... not the wood ... wood grain ... this would take some scrubbing ... the ships' boys with good knees ... *think*.

There was a loud bonk, but not a weapon. This was wood-to-wood—a heavy, hollow clunk, then another aft, then the first one again, midships. The vessels were grinding against each other. Their pocked hulls pounded hard once, twice, cracking the chain-wales. Hard bomping noises thrummed through the ships' bones.

He stumbled to his feet and dragged himself along the edge of the fore decktop. Snatching a pistol from one of his own wounded—was it loaded?—he called through a burning throat.

"Boarding party!"

—⚓—

An insane thought, a more insane command with the odds so much against them. Like it or not, the British had the best-trained military force since the Romans and only a fool would deny that.

Amidships, he stepped on a gun truck and up onto the ship's rail. Somehow the boys at the helm were still with him and kept pressing *Chasseur* up against *St. Lawrence*'s side, despite that the bouncing vessels had no fenders. Dizzy, he wobbled but managed to keep his footing on the rail. To his pride and gratitude, the rail was crowded now with his own crew, eager to follow him onto the other ship, in spite of everything.

Before him on the deck were dozens of dead and wounded Englishmen, piled together with arms and legs tangled and blood flowing as if from one giant creature. Groans of agony and senseless cries rose everywhere, some on *Chasseur*, many more here.

He waved away a cloud of smoke. Before him at eye level, the schooner's main mast held a gaping wound in the shape of a twelve-pound iron ball. The ball had struck a glancing blow, leaving an impression of itself notched into the mast just below the hoops. Structurally weakened, it could fall at any time. The strain of carrying the mainsail ... just a matter of minutes.

Automatically Boyle picked his way aft, raising an arm to block the shredded lines dangling in his way. Only then did he notice the blood on his sleeve, although he was unmoved by the sight of it. His head cleared as he tried to pick his way through the bodies to the one face he sought—the English captain who had caught him daydreaming. The diminutive young man was indeed still on his own command deck, sitting on an overturned gun truck. Beside him on the deck was the pulverized body of a man in a lieutenant's jacket, with no hat and no face.

Boyle cocked his pistol for better or worse and pointed it at the young captain's face.

"Stand down!"

The captain held up a defensive hand, and obviously had trouble moving just that little. His left leg displayed a ragged wound in the flesh of the thigh. He might have pulled out a large splinter, but was now pressing his other hand to the gory wound. If he stood up, he would probably bleed to death.

"They've struck!" Paul Mooran called. "Tom, they've struck!"

Dazed, Boyle blinked at the flag halyard behind the captain.

The Union Jack had been hauled down and was cradled in the arms of a very young boy with a wounded head. He couldn't have been more than seven.

"Your prisoner, sir," the captain of the *St. Lawrence* offered. "We can no longer maneuver." He made a sad motion toward the corpse at his side. "My lieutenant, Mr. Moycroft. He took the blow and saved my life. I think ... someone should know that."

"Loyal man." Boyle lowered his pistol. "You were out of uniform before. Doesn't that make you a spy or something?"

"Actually, it does. You can hang me on that basis. Or shoot me. If you don't mind, I'd rather be shot."

Was he joking?

"Tom!" Dieter appeared at his side. "The ship is ours. Are you all right?"

"What?" Boyle looked at him.

"You're wounded. Look at yourself."

Knowing an order when he heard one, Boyle looked down at his chest and left arm, where his shirt was streaked with blood. "Oh," he said, unimpressed. "I don't feel it."

"We don't have a surgeon aboard." With his usual resourcefulness, Dieter pressed a cloth to what looked like the worst wound, the one on Boyle's upper arm. Where had he acquired a cloth in this mess? Mates.

"Get some fenders between these ships."

"Fenders!" Dieter called, and left it to happen on its own. Somebody would do it.

Boyle looked at the *St. Lawrence*'s captain. "You duped me. A smart masquerade, Captain. I admire your ingenuity. You caught me naked as a belly dancer."

"I didn't know you could sail a square-rigger," the young captain said. "I thought you were a schooner man."

"I am. But sailing is sailing and the sea is its inconstant self. It pays to be diverse. Your name?"

"Gordon. James E. Gordon, lieutenant."

"James Gordon?" Dieter interrupted. "Isn't there a James Gordon in General Ross's assault fleet there on the Bay?"

"That's James A. Gordon. I'm James *E*. Gordon. It's a common enough name."

"John, let's have some bandages and clean cloths brought over here," Boyle ordered. "Collect the small arms and separate the wounded from the dead, then administer relief to the wounded."

"Will do."

But before Dieter could slip away, Boyle paused and gazed down at the smoke-stained face and tousled black hair of the English captain. "Don't I know you?"

"You do know him." But this was not Dieter's voice.

Boyle swung around. He knew the voice before he ever saw the familiar face. "Victor!"

"Tarkio!" Dieter exclaimed at the same time, and launched himself into a bear hug at this most unlikely moment, wringing Tarkio's blond head in his tattooed arms.

While Dieter still had their absent shipmate in a lock, Boyle found Tarkio's hand and held it as if to prove the other man was real and alive. "Yes, of course! That frigate! Victor! Where were you? Thank goodness our guns didn't strike you!"

"I was below."

"Bound?"

"Bound by my oath."

Dieter pulled back and held Tarkio by the shoulders. "Where's Bristow?"

"Oh ... Bristow died in the spring. Fell from the maintop. There was nothing to be done for him. Sorry, John."

"God rest him," Dieter uttered, clearly moved.

He and Tarkio and Boyle spent a silent moment in memory of their shipmate, during which Boyle remembered he would have many duties dealing with the dead and wounded of his crew just over the rail on *Chasseur*. Death was part of life at sea, part of life anywhere, really. Didn't make it any easier.

"Let's tend these men's wounds," Boyle said. "They're stalwart foes who deserve respect."

Reeling with delight at Tarkio's appearance, but still drawn away by his many immediate duties, Dieter slapped Tarkio on the back, smiled ridiculously for these circumstances, and bounded away.

Lieutenant Gordon winced in pain, then squeezed it down and conquered it, at least for the moment. He looked up at Boyle. "Why did you decide to fight us?"

"What did you expect?"

"Surrender. It's what a sane man would do when faced with a clearly superior armed force. Once again, Captain, you've shown yourself a provocateur."

"Or at least not a sane man."

"Once you saw that we were Royal Navy, I thought you would flee and I could run you down in one of your own privateer ships. I hoped to make a mockery of the spell-caster. Take away some of your hoodoo. You surprised me by facing us."

"I would not willingly have sought a contest with a king's vessel, but when I found myself deceived, the honor of the flag entrusted to my charge was not to be disgraced by flight."

He glanced casually at the U.S. standard still whipping from *Chasseur*'s main peak. When he turned again to the English captain, the younger man and Tarkio were both looking at the flag too.

There was something about that. Boyle let the silence speak for a few seconds.

Finally he interrupted his own poignant moment. "How did you get an American ship that hasn't been altered?"

"I stopped the alterations before they began."

Boyle smiled warmly. "You're a bulldog, aren't you?"

"Some kind of a dog, apparently." Gordon licked his dry lips and smiled, but weakly. "I have done my best, Captain Boyle. I know that. I had every advantage. You bested me anyway. You have my congratulations. You deserve your excellent reputation."

Boyle gazed at him with unshielded empathy. "You're too hard on yourself."

"He is," Tarkio confirmed.

"My crew followed me into this battle," the younger captain said. He looked at Tarkio as if in some kind of personal confirmation. "I have that."

Leaning back against the rail, Boyle felt suddenly at home about this enemy ship, and the hostility he had drummed up for the battle flowed away. "What do you think, Victor?"

After all, he had been their prisoner here for nearly three years. Who else would know?

Tarkio took a moment to consider the question, or pretended to. He folded his arms and made a conciliatory expression toward James Gordon.

"A light hand," he suggested.

"I agree," Boyle said. "Your ship is a wreck ... unlikely to make it to the States. I'll write a letter to *Chasseur*'s owners of our engagement, explaining that both your crew and mine fought meritoriously. We'll transfer clothing, food, and medical supplies to your ship for the comfort of your wounded. I will parole you and your officers and crew. After we affect repairs as well as may be done, you will conduct your ship to the nearest neutral port. You'll understand, certainly, if I pitch your heavy guns overboard. After all, we're still at war."

But he smiled as he said it.

Lieutenant Gordon nodded, and seemed content that he had put forth his best efforts.

Paul Mooran appeared with an armload of clean bandages, something *Chasseur* carried but fortunately rarely used because of the nature of privateering—a template well shattered today. "Can I bind you up, Tom? That arm—"

"I'm fine," Boyle told him, but took a rolled bandage from him and turned to Gordon. "Lieutenant, let me tend that leg."

"I'll do it, Tom." Victor Tarkio moved close and took the bandage from Boyle's hand. "He's my captain."

—⁓—

"To the captain or commander of any British ship of war who may capture the Chasseur, or whatever vessel Captain Boyle commands:

At sea, on board the United States privateer Chasseur: In the event of Captain Boyle's becoming a prisoner of war to any British cruiser I consider it a tribute justly due to his humane and generous treatment of myself, the surviving officers and crew of His Majesty's late schooner St. Lawrence, to state that his obliging attention and watchful solicitude to preserve our effects and render us more comfortable during the short time we were in his possession were such as justly entitle him to the indulgence and respect of every British subject. I also certify that his endeavours to render us comfortable and to secure our property were carefully seconded by all his officers, who did their utmost to that effect."

J. E. Gordon (lieut. and com. of late schr. St. Lawrence.)

Earthworks

HAMPSTEAD HILL, BALTIMORE
SEPTEMBER 11

STORM CLOUDS GATHERED OVER the city, darkening the afternoon. More than just portending rain, they seemed to suggest oncoming disaster. And that was more than just poetic symbolism.

Baltimore was less a city now than a military installation. They had expected to be attacked, and when the British paused rather than surging forward after the burning of Washington, Baltimoreans had awakened. A Committee of Vigilance and Safety had been elected, made up of merchants, craftsmen, a judge, and a sea captain, and they had put their strategic cleverness to work dividing the city into labor rotations to build earthworks running along the heights to the east. There, batteries of heavy guns were installed, and there they waited for the enemy.

The enemy had, perhaps unwittingly, unbuckled the vigor of individuals. From all over, Americans were rushing to volunteer. As the British rested or stalled or waited for more enforcements, or whatever they were doing, militia from western Maryland, Delaware, Pennsylvania, and Virginia flooded in, and of course had to be fed and quartered. Businesses stopped operating and began fortifying. Entrenchments stretched for miles around the city. Business owners, free blacks, and slaves began digging trenches and building earthworks, drilling artillery skills, and sinking vessels at the harbor mouth so deep-hulled British men-of-war could not ford in.

Mary had likewise virtually shut down her flag-making business and mustered with an energetic torrent of other Baltimore women. There was much to be done in the eddies of activity, trying to plan for something for which they had no design, no foreknowledge of how events would play out or where hostilities would even begin. Tonight she led a stout little donkey across the entrenchments on Hampstead Hill, northeast of the city, drawing a cart full of muslin bolts along the foot of the battery, bound for the hospital at Lazaretto Point, where a three-gun battery had been established to guard the waterway between there and Fort McHenry. There, she and two dozen other women of Baltimore would cut and roll all this muslin into bandages, to be ready to bind the men's wounds. This was her fourth donation of fabric for various purposes. She put her chin down and kept hiking forward, past a phalanx of men and boys digging trenches and building earthworks—three miles of earthworks. She avoided meeting their eyes, because chivalry was not dead and they would pause to nod a greeting to her or offer to help her, and she didn't want to interrupt their work that way.

Yesterday she had done the same at a field hospital set up near the earthworks on the west side of Fort McHenry, in preparation for wounded men there. She had visited her two important bundles: the two flags that had not yet been hoisted, that awaited the eyes of the enemy.

Major Armistead had not seemed at all well. He was exhausted, she knew, tireless in his quest to fortify the garrison. Seeing him that way gave her the pitapats. She had come to like him and his wife and to consider them her friends. Louisa Armistead was expecting their second child at virtually any minute, so had been sent to Gettysburg in Pennsylvania to keep her safe, which surely did not contribute well to the major's state of mind or body. No matter how Mary tried to steel her heart and remember that he was a soldier foremost, she did not prefer to see her friends under stress.

And his second in command at the garrison, Captain Nicholson—Judge Nicholson in another incarnation—had raised a volunteer artillery company at his own expense and named them

the Baltimore Fencibles, a unit of the city's most prominent
merchants whose interests involved protecting not only the city
buildings and homes, but the structure of commerce enjoyed by
the citizens. Mary had seen the energetic young judge mustering
his Fencibles in the city yesterday, and seen them marching in
town just minutes ago, rousted from their homes and hurrying
to the fort. Had she been a man, she would follow Nicholson too.
He possessed that special effervescence that steamed up other
people and got them moving.

They were wrapped up in a turmoil of pride that might see
them through, and the same for all the defenders here. These
were many of the same men who had been startled and had run
at Bladensburg. They had run because of inexperience and confusion. They had put their faith in their handsome uniforms and
hadn't realized there was more to war than a sparkling image.

That fantasy was gone. The men who would face the enemy in defense of Baltimore were awakened to the lessons of
Bladensburg and Washington. Their uniforms were scuffed and
filthy now, but they didn't care. Many had no uniforms at all
and also didn't care. Some estimates said there were as many as
ten thousand defenders gathered, and one hundred cannon. She
hoped that were true.

In the water between the star fort and Lazaretto Point,
across the north branch of the Patapsco, and from the fort to
Ferry Point across the west branch, twenty-four ships were being deliberately sunk to create obstacles against the British fleet.
The barriers were an attempt to block the two ways to Baltimore
by water, with Fort McHenry at the crux. Despite the ambitious
tactic of defense, she hadn't liked seeing those vessels deliberately scuttled. Baltimore's waterways were supposed to be free
for trade, for use by anyone, and Baltimore was a shipbuilding
center. To create something so precious as a sea-going craft,
then deliberately ...

But the one thing that had frightened her, had struck through
her inner fortifications and the shield of courage she put up before her daughter and nieces, was the sight of unshipped masts
being transported in wagon after wagon to Patapsco Neck. There
they were joined into a massive chain and strung out across the
river. That chain of giants now floated across the entire harbor

mouth, with a squadron of gunboats each carrying one gun ... the final line of defense if the British got through the sunken blockade.

"Seems I've caught the shakes, Tulip," she said aloud.

She shook herself and gripped the donkey's bridle so tightly that her hand hurt. She didn't have to do that. Tulip would follow her without being led, a sweet-tempered beast of burden who belonged to a neighbor's young son and was usually available for pick-ups or deliveries by the flag shop. Mary was hanging on more for herself than the donkey. Banishing her unhelpful reveries, she pulled her skirts up a little more and took longer steps across the rutted cart path.

All the fortifications in the world could not steady Mary Pickersgill's innards this night, or anyone's. Because she knew. They all knew. They had heard.

Fifty Royal Navy ships-of-the-line, frigates, and bomb boats were swiftly rolling north on Chesapeake Bay, carried by a dependable south wind. Some panicked messengers claimed the ships could now be seen from the mouth of the Patapsco.

The enemy was nearly here.

Bombardment Fleet

"I shall eat my supper in Baltimore or in hell."
General Robert Ross, September 12, 1814

PATAPSCO RIVER
EVENING, SEPTEMBER 12

THERE WAS NO MOON. No sky.

A guest of the enemy, Frank Key paced the deck of the cartel sloop aboard which he and Skinner had sought the English fleet. Now he was back aboard, with Skinner and William Beanes, the sloop's ten-man crew, and a muscular squad of Royal Marine guards to keep them here, anchored with the fleet of nineteen English warships. The water lapped and burbled constantly against the sides of the vessels anchored in a line stretching across the river from the cartel sloop. Tranquil clouds had hung above them for days, rendering the ripples a metallic gray with onion-colored crests.

His mood could not have been more accurately reflected.

"Would you care to take the next hand, Frank?" William Beanes asked. The doctor sat on the deck under a canvas canopy, dressed in a sailor's shirt and pantaloons, with John Skinner as the two of them played a game with a worn set of cards depicting English kings and queens of history.

"Thank you, no," Key said. For days he had declined. There was nothing in his brain but counting the bomb ships as they arrived to meet the ships-of-the-line and heavy frigates, reading the names on their sides, their horrific portending names—*Volcano, Terror, Aetna, Meteor, Devastation*, and the rocket ship *Erebus*.

"It'll make you sick to watch," John Skinner warned. "Sick in your soul."

"I am compelled."

He had been watching for two days as British boats came and went from North Point, landing armed English soldiers literally by the hundreds. Thousands. Hardened, experienced soldiers who would not shirk in the face of resistance. These were the warriors who would march with Ross and Cockburn overland to attack Baltimore, while Admiral Cochrane remained here to bombard by sea. One by land, one by sea—a two-pronged assault. For days those soldiers had slept on the decks of the ships that had brought them, evading the swelter of the lower decks, completely dressed and awaiting the order to begin the land siege. Now it was here.

Even as Ross and Cockburn themselves were rowed from the *Tonnant* to take command of the overland attack, Key had watched. He had shared one final gaze with Ross before the rowboat disappeared behind the fleet. Ross had given him a nod, but nothing more. Anything else might have seemed cavalier. Ross was not the kind of man to prance, one of the reasons he was so deeply loved and respected by his superiors and the men who were asked to follow him into battle. His reputation buzzed through the ships, making its way to Key's keen ears. To have such a commander at the fore of the enemy line was a reason for genuine concern.

All day the booming and cracking sounds of distant battle had rung across the water from somewhere on the North Point Road, in the direction of Bear Creek, which was halfway between the British landing point and the city. Maddening: there was no way to know what was happening. He would rather have plunged into that battle himself, clumsy and ineffective, than to stand here on this deck, useless, tormented by the distant thunder.

Then, the noise had gone silent as night fell. Why?

His heart pined for the serenity of Terra Rubra, to be in the crucible of his children and his parents, with Polly holding him through the night. How had he come to this?

He fought to keep his eyes open and did it. He drew another sustaining breath.

The sky held only a memory of light now. Clouds smoldered low, storm clouds that had not yet thrown a drop of rain. They, too, kept their secrets. Only a few lanterns on the anchored ships gave any sense of shape or presence on the dark river. He heard more than saw a rowboat sculling past him toward the *Tonnant*, but then he saw the oars, lit up with glowing yellow-green biological life clinging to them. He moved along the rail to a place where he could just make out the shape of the man doing the rowing and another one sitting in the bow.

"Hello!" he called. "Can you tell me what's happening?"

A shaky youthful voice responded. "Sir?"

"Can you say what happened today?"

"Engagement, sir," the oarsman called back.

"Where?"

"Seven miles from Baltimore."

"Has it ended?"

"For now, sir."

"Why has it stopped?"

The boatman rowed closer, seeming uneasy with shouting out. As the boat came into the pale haze of a lantern on the bow of the sloop, Key saw a bundle at the oarsman's feet, wrapped in something white or yellow that might have been a sail. Still, no sail was that shape.

"What is that?" he was compelled to ask. Some inner signal made him ask.

"A body, sir," called the other soldier in the boat.

Key stifled a chill. Why would a wartime corpse be given such treatment as to be rowed with an escort back to the fleet?

"Whose body?"

The two men did not answer.

"Speak up," Key urged. Clearly he wasn't going anywhere, and he might be somebody who could get them in trouble for not responding. That was the bet he made, anyway. "Who is it?"

Another moment or two passed before the boatmen found their nerve.

With a choked throat, the oarsman struggled, "This is General Ross, sir."

"General Ross?"

"Shot right off his 'orse, sir."

And the young man began to sob.

"Go on!" the other soldier snapped. "Row!"

A chill broke through Key's chest. Ross—the adored commander, the prince of martial courage so revered that even his enemies respected him. How would this news affect the assault? Would the British rise in fury, stoked by grief?

Thus, as the sounds of the oars pushing into the water grew small, a very long day faded into an even longer night of new fears.

The Red Glare

THE BOMBARDMENT FLEET
6:30 A.M., SEPTEMBER 13

Someone was singing. A bird. Its long, thin strain rippled across the early morning sky, under the clouds and above the water. A volcano exploded. The noise—

Francis Scott Key jolted awake, shocked by the gargantuan thunderclap. He felt the blood drain from his face. The concussion knocked him from his place sitting on the deck against a barrel, right over onto his back with his legs flailing. He rolled over onto his stomach and pushed to his feet, scrambling like a child.

"What in holy—" John Skinner stumbled out from under the canopy. His voice sounded thin and distant.

"Shells!" Terrorized, Key put his trembling hands on the rail and looked at the bombardment fleet. It really was a volcano—the bomb ship *Volcano* lobbing the first giant volley toward the fort.

"It's a ranging shot," Skinner guessed.

The *Volcano* launched another shell from with a force so ungodly that the entire bomb ship pressed into the water. The massive black ball soared into the air, arching beneath the low-hanging clouds, on a course for the fort more than three miles away. Against the dark clouds the fuse of the spinning shell could be seen flickering after the firing itself lit the fibers.

Beneath their feet, the sloop shuddered. Suddenly those miles seemed very small.

"What's happening?" Beanes called, still under the tarp. "Oh, God, what is it?"

"Stay there, William," Key responded. "It's begun."

Fort McHenry

"We were pigeons, tied by the legs, to be shot at."
Captain Joseph Nicholson

SUCKING SHALLOW BREATHS, TENSE and chafing, the Americans bore witness from their captured sloop a delivery of hell through the air.

The American crew of the sloop huddled either forward or aft, leaving the middle of the ship to the men who had hired them. It was Mr. Skinner's charter, after all.

And the British Marine guardsmen, they kept away also, creating the unreal spectacle of their red uniforms mixed up with the clothes of the American crew as they forgot who they were and stood dumbly watching the bombardment.

In the distance, Fort McHenry was little more than a scratch of brown on the green of Whetstone Point. Against the backdrop of gray sky, a smudge of color flipped lazily over the fort. The United States flag.

After the ranging shots, a pennant crawled up the line on the *Surprise*, the ship commanded by Admiral Cochrane's son. It was an order for the bomb fleet. *Move closer.*

The British fleet closed to within one and a half miles, and what a sight that had been. The process of moving several large vessels with any precision was on its own a spectacle, but one mankind had practiced for thousands of years and perfected. No one, of course, had practiced it to the extent of the Royal Navy. Select sails were set to use the little bit of wind, anchors were rowed out in boats, dropped, and then men lay onto the capstan bars and turned and sweated, chanting to coordinate their efforts, inexorably drawing the heavy vessels closer to the anchors. Then the anchors were raised—a grudging process in itself—and rowed out again. Kedging, they called it, a laborious project, which the British sailors seized with demonic energy.

All this way they towed the single-masted truce vessel with them until they thought the distance was right to demolish the fort. Anchors were dropped into the Patapsco mud, and immediately the bombardment began again. Deafening heavy weapons fired again and again, lobbing those powder-packed shells and shrieking skyrockets in such quick succession that a half dozen were in the air at the same time. The efficiency of the British volleys was humbling. After years of engagement with Napoleon, they knew what they were doing. Firing bombs was as ingrained in their reflexes as lobbing snowballs. The boom of one shot blended into the whine of the next, until there was no pause between them. Some shells exploded in the air, their fuses cut too short, while others reached the fort and disappeared, sometimes with terrible explosions on the horizon.

From this nearby, the masts of the USS *Java*, a new frigate lying nearly finished at Fell's Point, could be seen over the trees. Almost finished—not yet seaworthy—the new frigate was Oliver Hazard Perry's, the hero of Lake Erie, and he was there somewhere, with the ship. If only there had been time to complete it—such power, sitting there, useless. The British smacked their lips at the chance to capture her.

Frank Key watched every shot. His head whistled from the noise. His body was wracked by the vibrations that thrummed through the deck under his feet, and was never calm even for a moment. That city, that fort, had come to represent the whole nation, if only in symbol, and the British very well understood the powerful weapon of symbolism. If they could burn Baltimore, they would have accomplished a martial trifecta on the Chesapeake—Bladensburg, Washington, Baltimore. American morale would be smothered.

His whole body quaked. Those people were his friends, his associates, his family. Joseph, at the fort, right there, captain of the Fencibles. All at once he feared that he might never see his brother-in-law again, a true brother to whom he had grown close. To lose a vibrant, cherished relative like Joseph . . .his body shook so hard that he had to fold his arms around his chest to hold his heart in.

"Look!" he cried when Fort McHenry suddenly quickened and funnels of flame showed themselves along the shore. "They're shooting back!"

Holding a spyglass he had acquired from the captain of the truce sloop, Skinner came out of the tarped area where he had been huddling in desolation with Beanes. They had been drummed under what little cover they could find without actually going below, where somehow the reverberations and sounds were even worse. Together he and Key watched as cannon fire erupted along the parapets of Fort McHenry.

Balls soared, not with the same arch as the mortar shells, but on a flatter trajectory. Several struck the water, then after adjustment of the aim three balls smashed into British ships, including the ship towing the sloop. An explosion of wood and bits of everything a ship was made of came throttling at the sloop.

He and Skinner took a clumsy dive. A shower of wreckage struck the sloop's deck, sounding like a box of nails spilling across the deck.

They peeked up in time to see two more balls smash into one of the bomb ships.

The American crewmen cheered, and Key found himself caught up in the thrill. That joy was dashed immediately as the British ships returned fire with those giant mortars.

His anxiety piled onto itself until he could barely breathe. The British shells screamed through the air and easily reached the fort. Each time one fired, he waited with his pulse stopped and listened for the explosion.

"Abominable," he uttered.

"Sorry?" Skinner called over the booms of more shells and the whine of rockets.

"What's happening?" Beanes called from under the tarp. "Can you see the fort?"

Key forced himself to answer. "Yes, I can see it."

"Can you see the flag?"

"What?"

"Our flag! Can you still see the flag?"

"Oh. Yes, I see it."

Incendiary rockets from the ship *Erebus* made smoky trails across the blanketing clouds, wriggling wildly, landing who knew where. Those heavy mortar shells, packed with black powder, roared every few seconds from the bomb ships.

At Lazaretto Point across from the fort, cannons began to fire, taking their cue from Fort McHenry. The two batteries blazed away feverishly.

In the late afternoon rain began to fall, almost immediately changing from a sprinkle to a shower. Skinner went under the tarp, but Key refused. Skinner handed him his traveling cloak, which Key pulled over his shoulders, and a hat to banish the rain from his eyes. After an hour, the torrential showers cooled the air and pulled the sweat from his face. In ten minutes, it was downright cold.

The terror continued in the skies. On the sloop, the American crew and the Royal Marines fell into forebidding silence. Some disappeared below to hide from the rain and the hot sparks, hoping each in his heart that a cannon ball did not crash through the sloop's hull and take his head off. No one was chortling or cheering anymore. Everyone was half deaf by now anyway. The fort was under a jarring hail from the bombardment fleet, and responded with their own cannon fire that pummeled the British ships. When word came that the bomb fleet would be retreating, Key's mind was heartened to think that they might be giving up.

But no. The British were not so easily cowed. The ships hoisted their anchors and drifted back, but only about a half mile. There they dropped their anchors again, and continued shooting.

Still close enough to see the fort, even to see the flag with the spyglass. The flag now hung like a limp hanky in the rain. In the twilight, the red and blue colors were barely a mark against the white flagpole and gray sky. But at least it was still there. In fright's clutch, Key paced up and down the deck in the waist of the small ship.

Then, the cannon shots from the fort fell away. Two or three minutes later, the cannons at Lazaretto also went dark. The British kept firing, but the Americans had stopped.

He didn't say anything. Finally William Beanes' thready

voice came from under the tarp.

"Frank, what do you see? Why has the sound changed?"

"The fort has stopped returning fire. I don't know why."

"We're out of range," Skinner supplied. "Their guns can't reach us. They're saving ammunition."

"But the bomb ships are still firing."

"Their range is longer."

"A one-sided battle," Key mourned. He felt suddenly feverish inside his warm brown cloak. "Barbarism."

"Frank."

Beanes, from under the canopy.

"Come down here, Frank."

Under the canopy the deck was mostly dry, except for a trickle of water running from the exposed bow along the bulwark to the first scupper hole, and a mist being blown in. Beanes huddled in a dry spot, sitting on a folded blanket and wrapped in another, looking very worn and old.

Except for his eyes. Strange, his eyes were young today.

Key folded his lanky form into a crouch. "Something I can do for you, William?"

"No," the doctor said. "There's nothing you can do. Nothing at all. You're here. There is nothing you can do to affect anything."

Feeling a skittish tremble run across his shoulders, Key parted his lips to speak, but nothing came out.

Beanes lowered his chin and glowered from under his brows. "I know you want to influence events. You cannot. You are completely powerless. There is nothing you can do to change the fate of those men holding that fort or the women standing behind them to tie up their wounds. The people holding the line at Hampstead Hill. They dug the trenches. They set the battery guns. They will live or die in the mud and blood. Everything is up to them now. You are barren in all things today."

Stunned, the lawyer whispered, "Why are you saying this?"

"It is time for you to accept your own nature. You have set your own place in the world. The presidency has been offered to you. You declined. The Supreme Court has been dangled before you. You demurred. You took up the sword, but dropped it from your hand. Events moved forward while you remained bashful. You will have no validation in this war. You orbit the courageous. You are not one of them. Your only contribution will be to rescue a crippled old doctor who didn't know his own place. Know your place, Frank. Torture your tender heart no more. This is not the day of Francis Scott Key."

—⚌—

Cold rain rattled on the water just over the side. The mortars' boom hummed in one unending drone behind the doctor's cheerless words, but the words would not fade.

All through the night's malevolence, with rain slashing his body, thunder roaring in cadence with the hiss of rockets and the bedlam of mortars by the hundreds exploding in the air or slamming to earth, engulfed in suspense, Frank Key stood and watched. Time did not pass eternally here tonight, but halted its durable march. His feet were wet inside his boots and his body was wracked every few seconds with the wet night's chill. Impotent, appalled, consumed by dread, he watched the infernal fight between hellfire and the battle-born. This was his purgatory.

Even the skies were angry. Thunder, exploding shells, lightning illuminated the trails of red rockets and flares. Explosions in the sky whistled, flashed, and were snuffed under the storm clouds. All through the night, slapped by sheets of rain, deafened by mortar fire and thunder, watching bursts of lightning give otherworldly glimpses of the fort and the rain-drenched flag sticking to its mast, he waited in his personal hell.

There was no divine intervention. His terror went uneased. For eleven days he had been trapped here, given a platform from which he could stand in relative safety and do nothing more than observe history unfold before him. His reddened eyes watered. There was no way to know what was happening at the fort as it was pummeled. Now and then a defiant gun was fired from there, showing at least that they had not surrendered yet. There were sounds of guns, too, from Hampstead Hill and the land where the enemy had marched from North Point. Baltimore was making its scrappy stand.

His heart cried for those people and his arms ached to embrace them. His mind began to wander, to imagine what he might be doing if he were not here. Would he go to Hampstead

Hill and finally put to use some of the training he had taken last summer in the artillery? Would he kneel in the mud beside a gun or take up a rifle from a fallen defender? Leap upon a confused warhorse whose rider had been blown in half and make a charge against the enemy?

Would he?

At the stern of the sloop, a small group of Royal Marines stood in the rain, huddled with their weapons tucked against their bodies, guarding the world against the specters of a country lawyer, a prisoner negotiator, and an old doctor.

He prayed, but his prayers bumped against the clouds and fell into the river. Those people, those restless Americans, nimble-minded and living allegro lives, did what they did knowing they might die, actually die. Whether they agreed with the war or not, they were right over there fighting it, putting their shoulders against an invasion from a foreign power for the second time in a blink of years. It was they who deserved testimonial, honors, and song. Now that he was no longer thinking of himself, he thought of them, and he suddenly understood. They were fighting for their homes, their families, and even more, for their identities. Their right to *be* Americans.

A macabre quiet came over his mind. He let himself go into it. The boom of mortar fire drifted away until there was nothing left but the grim thump of his heart. Even that was slowing.

Sounds and movement drew his eyes. Rowboats were approaching, boats full of muddy and exhausted British soldiers, cradling many wounded comrades, unspeaking as they came twenty and thirty at a time and climbed onto the frigates and ships-of-the-line from whence they had debarked hours ago. Returning in triumph? Their job done?

John Skinner appeared at his side, but did not speak.

British Marines and American sailors crawled up from the sloop's hatches onto the soaked deck, looking at the sky. The rain was stopping. Clouds above grew pale and thin. Dawn.

Frank Key blinked as if he were coming out of a trance. After twenty-five hours of unremitting gunfire, the silence was terrifying.

"Why has the shooting stopped?" William Beanes asked from his hiding place. "Has the fort fallen?"

No one answered. They could not see. The fort was engulfed in mist clinging to the water. Slowly the mist began to rise and burn away. A sliver of sunlight broke as the clouds cracked open.

Key climbed to the top of the steps that would meet a gangway if they hadn't been anchored out here. He clutched one of the cables supporting the mast, and squinted into the dawn's early light.

"Can you see?" Beanes pleaded. "Is the flag still there?"

"Something's happening," Skinner murmured.

Key asked, "Do you still have the spyglass?"

Skinner handed it to him. Key put it to his eye and trained it on the fort.

The mist sparkled in its last throes before giving way to the morning sun. In the distance, the star-shaped brown ramparts of Fort McHenry were very still. The needle of the flag mast still stood, with some flicker of movement. Was the flag being lowered? Had it been torn away?

A sound, thin and small. Fife music. Snare drums. Whose?

More movement at the flagstaff; bits of color crawled up the white pole. The king's flag?

Then the fabric stirred in a soft morning breeze. No longer the cruel wind of the storm, this breeze was fresh and dry, carrying the scent of honeysuckle from the land. What a gracious morning this would be on any other day.

As the wing of an angel unfolds, so unfolded a sight of a lifetime. Key gasped as triumph burst through his melancholy. "Yes! I see it! It's still there!"

But he no longer needed the spyglass.

A flag, a huge American flag, a third as tall as the pole from which it flew, unbound itself and opened before the world. Upon the indigo field, fifteen giant stars flickered with light from behind. Enormous red and white stripes whipped happily as they stretched out on the breeze. After a day and night of noise, the ensign's mute proclamation reminded him of George Washington, standing on the portico with the diligence of a mute guardian. But more—the flag waved as a passive beacon, not to repel, but to invite. *You, too, come here.*

The fife and drum corps from the fort began to play "Yankee Doodle." The sound was small and distant, but the lilt of it carried over the water.

A few steps away from him, one of the British soldiers overcame the demoralization so evident in the faces of his fellows.

Right out in front of everybody, the Englishman exclaimed, "Splendid!"

A single cannon shot fired from Fort McHenry. *Poom*—a signal to salute the flag. What bravado!

The American crew of the sloop cheered. Even the British guards indulged in polite applause. Such a moment.

In the left pocket of his cloak, Key's hand closed into a fist as if in a small attempt to be big. It closed on stiff paper—one of the letters he had shown to General Ross.

As elation poured through his body, he drew the folded paper out. From his other pocket he drew the architect's pencil he always kept there. Doing what writers are compelled to do, he flattened the paper on his knee and scribbled a few words to remind him later of what he felt now.

O, say, can you see ... by the dawn's early light ...

Mary's Banner

As the last hints of rain evaporated in warm morning sunlight, Mary Pickersgill stood on the heights with her daughter, her nieces, and Grace Wisher. They had listened through the long day and night until morning again, counting fruitlessly the hundreds of explosions and rocket whistles, feeling the awful vibrations through the very earth beneath their feet. If anyone could sleep, it was only some accident of exhaustion.

Now the bombing had stopped. Never one to wait, Mary had struck out immediately to discover why the silence had fallen. She and many neighbors hurried to the rooftops and high ground, as word spread that the enemy was drawing back from both Hampstead Hill and the harbor. That might mean everything or nothing, for the British might always return, but messengers claimed the enemy army was getting in boats and rowing back to their fleet. They were not encamping or entrenching. They were leaving.

At her sides, Caroline and Grace took her hands, then the hands of the other girls. Together the women watched the raising of Mary's giant banner over the star fort. The flag was so big that it could not flap quickly, but instead waved this way and that way like the mane of a horse out of Viking mythology.

Her neighbors flocked around her, patting her shoulders and kissing her cheeks. More and more people crept up the hill to stand in the sunshine with the ladies of the flag.

For this morning at least, everybody knew the name of Mary Pickersgill.

Scribbles

BALTIMORE
SEPTEMBER 17

"JOSEPH! JOSEPH!"

The front door hung open as Joseph Nicholson rushed down the stairs and into the arms of his brother-in-law. "Frank! Thank God!"

Key clung to him, for neither had known the other's fate at a time when stinking, bloated corpses were being picked up in wagons and laid out for loved ones to identify.

"No one has heard from you in two weeks!" Nicholson exclaimed. "Polly contacted me, but I had no idea where you were!"

"I was imprisoned on a truce vessel, tied up to that fleet of British ships lobbing bombs at you. Eleven days they held us."

"Good Lord! What were you doing there?"

"Just a prisoner exchange. No matter. You're here alone?"

"I sent Rebecca away. Come in."

Still locked together, they moved into the parlor without even bothering to close the front door.

"What was it like?" Key asked. "I prayed for your deliverance every minute."

"Loud, is what it was. Nightmarish. The major believes the British fired as many as sixteen hundred shells at us, perhaps eight hundred rockets. We had only four men killed. Twenty-four were wounded. Some may yet die, but those are very light casualties considering the fury of that hell. Other than being muddy and cold, we held up all right. We did have a shell crash into the powder magazine, but thank providence it was a dud. It never exploded. Can you imagine if it had? I lost two of my

Fencibles and I'm inconsolable about them. It was I who talked them into volunteering."

"You're not responsible for their lives or their deaths, Joseph. They had the right to stand against the invaders."

"Well, I suppose. Thank you. Poor Armistead collapsed with exhaustion after it was over. He's still in a fever and half delirious. His wife sent a note that she had a healthy baby girl, so the news was a relief to him. What was it like on the truce ship?"

"Meretricious, compared to what you endured. The British were humiliated. They retired in great despair, quite mortified and demoralized."

"The rumor is that their commanders wanted to save them for future engagements. I'm proud that they were frustrated here. Did you hear that they were turned back from New York as they invaded from Quebec on the eleventh? And their fleet on Lake Champlain was defeated."

"We seem to have finally found our stride." Key disengaged his cloak from where it was slung over his arm. "I have something for you."

"For me?"

"Yes." He pulled a large rolled-up rag paper from the pocket of his cloak, where it had been protected from the elements by the shoulder cape.

Nicholson took the sheet and unrolled it, working to hold it open as he read the first lines of the rhyme scratched there in quill ink, with some words scribbled out here and there and a few smudges. He scanned the words, then paused and read the first stanza more carefully. "You wrote this for us?"

"It goes to the tune of 'To Anacreon in Heaven.' You know the melody."

"Everyone knows it ..."

"I worked on it while the truce ship sailed us to Baltimore, and finished it later that night at the Indian Queen Tavern. Do you know the place? Shameful food. Haggis and horse meat. I think the cook is new."

But Nicholson was engrossed in reading the lyrics again. He began to hum the tune, then to mutter the words along with it.

"John Skinner seemed to like the lyrics," Key mentioned. "He was the prisoner agent who accompanied me. I thought about making more changes, but he talked me out of it."

"Always second-guessing yourself." Nicholson hovered in the middle of the room, and read the four stanzas again, carefully, the way a lawyer reads a document, by taking his time.

Key gave up trying to chat and waited.

"Frank," Nicholson began finally, "I'm deeply moved by this. This is more than just a narration. You've done something profound here."

Key smiled shyly. "Hardly. I pilfered from some of my past work."

"I've read your past work. This is new. Major Armistead's banner. The Major and Mrs. Pickersgill ... "

"Where in the world did you get that tremendous flag?"

But the judge was reading again. "This is very ... American."

"Thank you. I did have a few epiphanies that night."

Nicholson looked up. "About yourself?"

"Oh, no," Key said. "About the nation. America is different from any nation before it. Being American is more than blood. More than nationality. We are an idea more than a place. Anyone, anywhere, can be an American. All a person must do is to embrace the idea that he owns his own life. Anyone who dares to climb out of a European slum or peek over the Urals. They are all Americans. We are a new race for the world. I want to appreciate you, Joseph, and those who inspired my writing of these lyrics. All of you who protected all of us. You have hammered home our right to be the American race."

Deeply moved, his brother-in-law smiled warmly. "Always the orator."

Key shrugged. "Just a humble preacher. Now that I know you're all right, I must go."

"So soon?"

"I'm leaving for Terra Rubra. My desire to join my family is no longer to be repressed. I wish to repose there and let the storms of life blow over before returning to Georgetown. I'm sure they've been fretting about my condition and yours."

"Give'm my affection."

"I promise."

Nicholson held the large paper between them. "May I keep this? May I have it published?"

"Published?" Key scooped up his cloak. "Where?"

"I know the editor of the *Baltimore American*. What's the title?"

"Oh, I don't know—whatever you think."

"'Defending of Fort McHenry'? 'The Defence of Fort McHenry'?"

"Whatever you think is acceptable."

"It would make a good handbill. To rouse public sentiment."

"I can't imagine anyone ... well, go ahead, if you must. Please don't put my name upon it."

Nicholson looked up. "Why ever not?"

"Because I am not the focus of it," Key said as he whirled out the door. "I'm not important."

*The Star Spangled Banner original manuscript, 1814,
written by Francis Scott Key. Used with permission of
The Maryland Historical Society.*

The Return of Pride

THE INNER HARBOR
BALTIMORE

"There he is. The *Pride of Baltimore*. How proudly they hail."

Along the shores, the docks, and in the trees, thousands of people cheered and waved little American flags or strips of red, white, or blue cloth. Children ran along the shoreline, trying to keep up with the schooner as she entered the Inner Harbor. Dozens of small craft sailed or waddled or paddled after the schooner in devoted escort. This had been the response ever since they had heard the ship's signal gun saluting Fort McHenry, and the fort's tribute cannon shot in response. They had been waiting for days, for they knew the *Chasseur*—that Tom Boyle—was coming home.

From a dockside park bench in a good place for viewing the whole harbor, the French Jew and Pdut sat in repose as the *Chasseur*, rigged in her perfect dress as a gaff-rigged schooner, the ideal rig for American's Atlantic shoreline, skimmed into the Inner Harbor all stretched out with her buttermilk sails in a cloud over her yellow-striped, shark-shaped black body. She was blazoned with her signal flags and pennants from the bowsprit up, along all the stays, across and between her mast tops, and down the peak flag halyard, a colorful madness that traced the silhouette of the schooner, all fluttering crazily. As she entered the harbor, the crew fired a single shot in tribute to her home port, and the people went wild with delight.

A make-shift orchestra of fiddlers, banjo players, fifers and drummers, and two buglers started up playing that song, the new song from that lawyer, and a chorus of four black entertainers in mismatched hats were singing it, actually quite well with their sonorous baritone voices, and one ambitious tenor who was very happy with himself. People around the dock dropped money into a bucket in front of the musical ensemble, and gleefully tried to sing along despite the octave-plus-half range.

"... *O'er the ra-a-mparts we watched, were so gallantly streaming ...*"

On the dock, displayed between two street lamps, was a huge banner painted with a salute from the adoring people of the city:

WELCOME HOME PRIDE OF BALTIMORE!

What grandstanding. Americans might claim nothing of royalty, but they certainly knew how to make pageantry. Today over Fort McHenry, that flag was waving for the return of *Chasseur*, the enormous flag that made the fort look like a toy. He saw the flag today just as the demoralized British had seen it from their squadron two miles away.

"... *gave proof through the night that our flag was still there ...*"

"The 'star-spangled banner,'" the French Jew uttered, tasting the words.

"*O'er the la-and of the fre-e-e, and the home of the brave!*"

The schooner then fired another salute shot and the crowd answered with more cheering.

"Too much people," Pdut observed.

"What did you expect? Boyle confirmed that American privateers will stand toe-to-toe with the Royal Navy. I don't think that's happened before."

In his hand he held the *Niles Weekly Register* edition, which he had kept for several weeks. He glanced down at the article now yellowed before him.

"*The action was very creditably fought on both sides, but to the American captain belongs the meed of having not only won success, but deserved it. His sole mistake was the over-confidence in what he could*

see, which made him victim to the very proper ruse practiced by his
antagonist in concealing his force. His maneuvering was prompt, ready,
and accurate; that of the British vessel was likewise good, but a greater
disproportion of injury should have resulted from her superior battery."

The French Jew let the newspaper fall to the street. "On top of all that, he was wounded too. How literary."

Now he could see the faces of the crew, and of Tom Boyle himself there on the afterdeck, waving at the crowd and directing the helm as his ship came into the harbor. *Chasseur* made a graceful loop, put her sails over to the other side, and circled as if she were a dancer on a stage. Well, she was, wasn't she?

Boyle wore a yellow shirt and black waistcoat, and the saucy blue neckerchief that by now was legendary. Clearly he knew the power of an image, and what the crowd expected to see.

"I thought I could trick him," the French Jew mused. "Employ him as a tool to break the Americans and deplete the British. But he would not be beguiled. He wouldn't even take my money. Instead, he went and blockaded Great Britain with one ship."

The first stanza of the new song was finished, but the quartet of male Negroes went on with the second stanza, though the crowd of people had not, apparently, memorized that part yet. The men's voices rose over the mumbling of the crowd, until the mumbling fell away and the people just listened and enjoyed.

> *"On the shore dimly seen ... through the mists of the deep, where*
> *the foe's haughty host in dread silence reposes ... What is that which*
> *the breeze, o'er the towering steep ... as it fitfully blows half conceals,*
> *half discloses..."*

"I never thought anyone could be bolder than Tom Boyle," the French Jew grumbled on. "I never counted on Tom Boyle himself. Because of him, the attack on Baltimore was rushed ... their silly little fort held against the bombardment ... the land assault was repelled ... now they're singing that lawyer's absurd song." He pursed his lips and blew a low sigh. "What do you do with a man who won't take money?"

"... Tis the star-spangled banner, O long may it wa-ave ..."

He looked around at the crowd, with its many disparate faces, its scatter of clothing styles and the many hats representing a hundred trades, as they sang and cheered together.

"They're infected with something, these people," he said. "I shall have to think more about these Americans."

"... And where is that band who so vauntingly swore that the havoc of war and the battle's confusion ..."

"But this war is not over," he droned on. "Other designs can be laid. Napoleon will rise again. I believe that. I will cling to it and make a new plan."

Beside him, Pdut abruptly stood up from the park bench, rearranged her skirts, and turned to face him with those silly-button eyes.

"I no like you anymore, Yakov," she said. "I leave you."

He burst to his feet and almost stumbled into the water. "What on earth!"

"I go from you. Make good life for Pdut. No you."

"But you're my wife!"

"I dibborce you."

She reached into her satin drawstring bag and rasped out an envelope, stuffed it into his hand, and nodded that the matter was done.

He stared at the yellow crumple, then blubbered, "How will you eat? How will you live? You don't even have any money!"

"No money prum you."

"But how will you survive?"

She put her stumpy chin up. "I American woman now. I work. I sew American flag."

"Flag!"

"Bye-good. No follow me."

While the bright sails and black hull of *Chasseur* made another elegant turn in the harbor and passed behind him, he stared with his mouth hanging open and watched Pdut lump away through the crowd, boldly shouldering people out of her way. She was so resolute that some of the men even doffed their hats to her as she passed. That had never happened before. And she never looked back at him.

He watched long after he could no longer see her. "Well, cock that ..."

"And the star-spangled banner in triumph shall wa-ave ... o'er the la-and of the free ... and the home of the brave!"

As the song of their own noble aspirations ended after four stanzas, the crowd of Americans—of a hundred languages and a thousand birthplaces—skylarked and reveled and cheered, watching the ship in the harbor turn again. The French Jew watched with solemnity, realizing how much he had learned, as the crew set the boom crutch in place, then tabled the main throat and the gaff jaws down to their seat at the foot of the mast, where the heavy sail and her yards were at perfect rest.

Now, together, her jibs were hauled down on the stays, making a ringing sound as they folded along the bowsprit and jib-boom. Rope fenders popped over the sides, held by four boys. Under only her staysail, the schooner floated toward her dock, where men waited to catch her four docklines and make her fast at home. There, the mayor, the city council, several leading clergymen, and the officers' families waited behind a red, white, and blue ribbon with a canopy overhead.

Yes, there was the Boyle family. His glowing wife, their thrilled children.

The spectators continued cheering, and hundreds flowed toward the schooner's dock to greet its crew personally.

With his mind a-jumble, the French Jew blinked as the crowd flowed past him and he was left standing alone.

He stood there quite a while, numb, and watched the dithering happiness on the wharf over there, while he was over here, without a compass.

After uncounted minutes, he felt his knee start to hurt and shook himself back to the moment. His mind began turning again. Plans. Opportunities.

"Perhaps I shall go west," he spoke aloud to nobody. "There must be someone in the wilderness who will take a bribe."

SPECIAL THANKS FROM THE AUTHOR

First and foremost to two captains of the Baltimore Clipper Schooner *Pride of Baltimore II*, with whom I have had the honor of serving on many voyages. Captain Jan Miles and Captain Robert Glover III, whose leadership on the sea and advice on this book I cherish sincerely. I'm proud to be able to call you "my captains."

To the ship *Pride of Baltimore II*, and all my captains and shipmates aboard, past and present.

To Ranger Scott Sheads of Fort McHenry National Park, for his assistance, information and advice, and for his stewardship over this important American monument. To the curators and volunteers at the Star-Spangled Banner Flag House, Baltimore, the home of Mary Pickersgill, and the adjoining museum, for much help and excellent information, and for preserving genuine treasures of American history. The photo of Mary Pickersgill's receipt for the Star-Spangled Banner and the storm flag is presented courtesy of the Star-Spangled Banner Flag House, Li1938.12.1

To the Maryland Historical Society for permitting publication in the book of a photo of the original manuscript of *The Defence of Fort McHenry*, later to be called *The Star-Spangled Banner*.

My gratitude to you all for your good advice and help.

HISTORICAL NOTES

The War of 1812 was not over until 1815. It ended technically in a draw, and relations between Britain and America returned generally to the same status as before the war. Britain had already decided to stop raiding American ships even before the war began, but the Orders of Council did not arrive until after war had been declared. The effects of this war are often downplayed, but in fact there were significant changes because of it: America decisively left its past behind and took its place as a burgeoning world power. The world discovered that Americans could and would fight, even against more powerful forces. The United States established its right to conduct free commerce on the open seas.

Similarly, the Americans learned that **Canadians** would also defend their right to exist, and would not be assimilated into the United States by conquest.

If the British had prevailed, there would be no United States. Every American, certainly every American teacher, should read at least one book about this war.

The parade of intrepid people involved in the war is worthy of our attention: **Joshua Barney, Robert Ross, President James and Mrs. Dolley Madison, George Cockburn, Joseph Nicholson, Oliver Hazard Perry, James Lawrence, Roger Brooke Taney**, and many other figures in the War of 1812 were larger-than-life personalities of great accomplishment and deserve to be household names. They should no longer go unknown in general knowledge of western civilization.

The United States, England and Canada are now bonded in amity, alliance and free trade. It is an irony that every Fourth of July, Americans celebrate the wrong war.

It is true that **Founding Fathers James Madison, John Adams and Thomas Jefferson** were still alive during the War of 1812. As much as possible, their own words have been featured or paraphrased in this novel. George Washington's speech at Terra Rubra is his own words.

Francis Scott Key and his wife Mary (Polly) would eventually have eleven children. Key rarely took accolades for the inspiring lyrics he wrote to fit the social-club song "To Anacreon in Heaven." He instead gave credit to the people who fought at Fort McHenry and those who fortified Baltimore and turned back the British land assault. He insisted that he, the lyricist, should not be lauded, but that those who inspired him to write those words deserved the appreciation of all Americans.

"The Star-Spangled Banner" was officially adopted by Congressional resolution as the United States' National Anthem on March 3, 1931.

Major George Armistead's giant banner, made by Mary Pickersgill and recognized as the original *Star-Spangled Banner,* is on display at the Smithsonian Institution in Washington, D.C. The term "Star-Spangled Banner" refers specifically to the United States' flag of 1814, with fifteen stars and fifteen stripes.

The myth that **Francis Scott Key** saw the big flag flying all night has been generally dismissed by historians and experts at Fort McHenry. During a thunderstorm, the big flag would have been impractical to fly. Key saw the smaller storm flag flying at night during the storm. When the storm ended, almost simultaneously to the time the British gave up the siege of Fort McHenry and the land assaults, the exultant soldiers at the fort fired a gun and raised the giant flag in the morning light, which Key and the British saw. At thirty feet on the hoist, the flag was one-third the height of the pole installed to fly it. That flag is the Star-Spangled Banner.

In 2013, the 200th anniversary of the making of the flag, the Maryland Historical Society sponsored the making of a **replica of Armistead's banner**, made of the same type of materials, sewn by expert quilters using Mary Pickersgill's methods, and in the same number of weeks (6) in which Mary made her flag. The replica flag was hoisted over Fort McHenry on Defenders' Day, September 14, 2013, two hundred years after Mary Pickersgill crafted it.

George Armistead lived only four years after the Battle of Baltimore, succumbing to a heart condition. **Fort McHenry**

is now an evocative national monument, well worth visits and appreciation.

Captain Tom Boyle is one of America's great unsung heroes. According to those who knew him and even those who fought him, such as Lieutenant Gordon, he was an affable, quick-minded, devoted friend, an entrepreneur of the first order, a superior captain who was both strong and flexible, a sailor of superior skills, a true community leader and neighbor, and a devoted family man. Everyone who knew him seems to have sincerely liked him, and he had the courtesy to like them back.

The names of **Boyle's crew** are for the most part taken from the real crew aboard *Comet* and *Chasseur*.

The battle between ***Chasseur*** and ***St. Lawrence*** did happen, but not until 1815, and is recognized as "one of the greatest battles ever fought by a privateer." (*Tom Boyle, Master Privateer*, Fred W. Hopkins, Jr., Tidewater Publishers, 1976)

As a merchant ship, ***Chasseur*** went on under a different captain to set a speed record of ninety-five days from Canton, China to the Virginia Capes, a record that stood for sixteen years.

After the war, **Tom Boyle** returned to merchant commerce. He died at sea in 1825 aboard a ship he had commissioned in Baltimore, with a copper bottom and a shallow draft for the coastal trade, which he named *Chasseur*. Upon notice of his passing, Boyle was lauded in the *United States Gazette* of Philadelphia as "the favourite of all who knew him."

Lieutenant James E. Gordon is a fictional construct, but is inspired by the real captain of the Schooner *St. Lawrence* (formerly the *Atlas*), which did surprise Tom Boyle and force him into a battle with a regular Royal Navy crew. Lt. Gordon as characterized in this book represents the attitude and fears of Britain during the first Napoleonic conquests. Gordon did indeed write the letter in advocacy of Captain Boyle's praiseworthy conduct during and after their broadsides battle at sea.

Mary Young Pickersgill was a vivacious and socially active lady who believed that women should learn skills and be able to support themselves. Earlier, in 1802, she established a retirement home, the Impartial Female Humane Society, and engaged in many community good works. The retirement home is still extant, now the Pickersgill Retirement Community in Towson, Maryland.

Her home on Pratt Street (formerly Albemarle St.) in Baltimore is now an inspiring museum called the **Star-Spangled Banner Flag House,** and should be visited by all Americans and citizens of the world, as a monument to free enterprise and individual human industry.

Caroline Pickersgill Purdy married and was widowed, and ended up living out her elderly years in the home for aged widows which had been founded by her mother.

Joseph Nicholson and **Richard West** were married to sisters of Mary (Polly) Key, Francis Scott Key's wife. He was very close to them, and to his sister Anne's husband, Roger Brooke Taney, who would later become the fifth chief justice of the Supreme Court. After Judge Nicholson passed away and his wife remarried, her family kept the original handwritten manuscript of "The Defence of Fort McHenry" for ninety-three years. Eventually the manuscript found its way to the Maryland Historical Society, where it resides today.

The French Jew is a dramatic construct whose role is to represent the attitudes of France, once again placed in the position of whether or not to involve itself in the American question. In this case he is a supporter of Napoleon, but also he is "above" national politics in his bigger motivations, which involve the furthering of power for the already powerful Rothschild Banking conglomerate, and its attempts to alter events to their advantage, which are also fictional speculation.

Fell's Point is still a gathering point for ships, mariners, and visitors, a lively place which I call "my second home," particularly the dock at the foot of Broadway, where I've spent many days and nights as a member of the crews of the Schooners *Alexandria* and *Lettie G. Howard,* and the Barkentine *Gazela of Philadelphia.* Of course, Baltimore's Inner Harbor is the home port of the Baltimore Clipper Schooner *Pride of Baltimore II,* a ship I'm privileged to have crewed many times as a deckhand, docent, and cook under four captains.